Work
Love
Balance

Sophie Loxton is the author of *Wild About You* and *Work Love Balance*. A former arts librarian and life-long romance fan, she began writing romance novels on her long commute. Sophie lives in Kent with her husband and rescue dog. You can find her on Instagram @sophieloxtonauthor.

Also by Sophie Loxton
Wild About You

SOPHIE LOXTON

Work
Love
Balance

**SIMON &
SCHUSTER**

London · New York · Amsterdam/Antwerp · Sydney/Melbourne · Toronto · New Delhi

First published in Great Britain by Simon & Schuster UK Ltd, 2026

Copyright © Sophie Loxton, 2026

The right of Sophie Loxton to be identified as author of this work has been asserted in accordance with the Copyright, Designs and Patents Act, 1988.

1 3 5 7 9 10 8 6 4 2

Simon & Schuster UK Ltd, 1st Floor
222 Gray's Inn Road, London WC1X 8HB

For more than 100 years, Simon & Schuster has championed authors and the stories they create. By respecting the copyright of an author's intellectual property, you enable Simon & Schuster and the author to continue publishing exceptional books for years to come. We thank you for supporting the author's copyright by purchasing an authorised edition of this book.

No amount of this book may be reproduced or stored in any format, nor may it be uploaded to any website, database, language-learning model, or other repository, retrieval, or artificial intelligence system without express permission. All rights reserved. Enquiries may be directed to Simon & Schuster, 222 Gray's Inn Road, London WC1X 8HB or RightsMailbox@simonandschuster.co.uk

Simon & Schuster Australia, Sydney
Simon & Schuster India, New Delhi

www.simonandschuster.co.uk
www.simonandschuster.com.au
www.simonandschuster.co.in

The authorised representative in the EEA is Simon & Schuster Netherlands BV, Herculesplein 96, 3584 AA Utrecht, Netherlands. info@simonandschuster.nl

Simon & Schuster strongly believes in freedom of expression and stands against censorship in all its forms. For more information, visit BooksBelong.com

A CIP catalogue record for this book is available from the British Library

Paperback ISBN: 978-1-3985-3671-5
eBook ISBN: 978-1-3985-3672-2
Audio ISBN: 978-1-3985-3673-9

This book is a work of fiction. Names, characters, places and incidents are either a product of the author's imagination or are used fictitiously. Any resemblance to actual people living or dead, events or locales is entirely coincidental.

Typeset in Bembo by M Rules
Printed and Bound in the UK using 100% Renewable Electricity at CPI Group (UK) Ltd

For Aelred, always.

CHAPTER ONE

I should have taken a Duvet Day.

I should have pulled the covers over my head and gone back to sleep when my dad texted me at 6am. He was letting me know the predicted blizzard hadn't materialised in Hertfordshire. A dedicated weather watcher, he monitors livestreams in various parts of the country, and his first message of the day is usually some kind of weather report.

When I finally emerged from my bed into rush hour, there were delays on the tube due to 'staff shortages' (Snow Day) and everyone was grumpy, tutting and shoving each other (Snow Day), and yet there was no snow, apart from a very light dampness in the air which felt more like mist. Everyone in London who wasn't already working from home had planned on taking a Snow Day, only to wake up and find it was a Grey Day.

It was a gritty journey, but by the time I sailed through

the door of EKArts, I looked appropriately zen. Serenity is my Unique Selling Point, my top attribute on my CV, my 'core value' – in Communications speak. Or, at least, *looking* serene is. I said a cheery hello to Security as I strode into The Hexagon, where I work. It's an ultra-modern building with a famous façade formed of hundreds of small hexagonal panes of glass, which means that even on the darkest of winter days, the light is optimised in the lobby. Unusually, I got the lift to myself and gazed at the mirrored wall as I mentally ran through my to-do list (vlog and socials content planning; reviewing a recent article focusing on the charitable arm of the organisation). So far, so normal.

I knew something was wrong the moment I stepped out of the lift and took off my hat. As I did so, I noticed the expectant hush of a roomful of people who had just stopped talking.

Normally on a Monday morning my team are dissecting their weekends and eating their breakfasts at the same time. Most of them are in their twenties, attracted by the creative glamour of working for EKArts and its founder, the famous artist Esme Kamińska. I'm a Senior Director of the company, with a seat on the leadership team, but I also like to think of myself as the kind of manager you could speak frankly to. In reality, the younger ones probably think me as old as their granny (thirty-three is the new seventy-two) only less trendy, because I permanently wear black apart from occasional instances when I wear white. But that morning I could practically smell the pensiveness in the air. Maintaining my sanguine expression, I strode through the open-plan area to my glass-walled office in the corner of the room. I figured whatever was happening, I'd soon know about it.

I was right. Sasha, my PA, reached me in approximately twenty seconds and flung the door to my office shut. Or, at least, she tried to, but it's a weighted slow-close door so despite the fact she piled most of her five-foot-two frame behind it, it continued to close at the same rate it always does, in its own sweet time.

Sasha's eyes were brimming with excitement. 'So, this is hectic! What's the backstory?'

My New Year's resolution not to check my mobile on the journey to work (in favour of reading a book) was clearly proving to be a mistake. I dug around in my bag and got my phone out. When I unlocked it, it lit up like a Christmas tree.

'Tell me everything you know,' I said, hoping she was being overly dramatic. Behind Sasha's head the door continued to close very slowly. Five ... four ... three ... two ... one.

'Esme is getting married to Ajax Banks!' cried Sasha.

I tilted my head.

'Ha!' I said. 'Good one.' Ours wasn't usually a team for practical jokes, but fair enough, Mondays made people do stupid things sometimes, and I guess everyone had been promised snow. But they'd overreached themselves, because the idea of our CEO and founder Esme marrying fitness influencer, entrepreneur and podcaster Ajax Banks was like suggesting Mickey Mouse was about to be crowned King of England. Impossible.

'What's wrong?' piped Sasha.

'I'm looking for the hidden camera,' I said, still holding my phone out, face up.

Sasha's face fell. 'I'm not joking,' she managed in a small voice, her expression earnest. 'Hasn't Esme told you? Look at the intranet.'

I was already typing my password in. Beneath my serene expression, my brain was assessing all of my recent conversations with Esme. As far as I was aware, she didn't even *know* Ajax Banks. Through the glass walls of the office, I became aware of the rest of the team arranged like meerkats. I lowered my eyes to the computer screen and kept my gaze fixed on it. Teams opened automatically first, and I saw an array of excited messages from colleagues. I minimised it and opened the intranet, buying some time by putting my lapis-blue glasses on.

It loaded slowly, because someone had headed the article with an enormous picture of Esme and Ajax Banks. They both looked slightly flushed and dishevelled in a very *particular* way. There was a headboard behind them. A postcoital selfie, *really*? And one loaded at such high resolution you could see the sprinkling of freckles across the bridge of Esme's nose which then crashed the web page.

I made an indiscriminate noise, which possibly sounded like 'no'.

'Dawson said Esme insisted on making the post,' Sasha said, in a faint voice, in defence of our web editor.

So it came straight from the horse's mouth. Esme had once

had a very famous song written about her: helpfully entitled 'Esme', it had referenced her red lips and smoky eyes. Those smoky eyes were now staring at me from the intranet and the expression in them meant trouble.

I blinked several times, trying to wake myself up from this ridiculous dream-slash-nightmare.

Eventually the page loaded, and I read the text below the photo with a sinking heart.

A confidential announcement from Esme & Ajax. Ajax & Esme.

> Sometimes life changes in the blink of an eye. Sometimes love hits like a lightning flash or a message from a higher plane. You know us both as discrete entities, but the one certainty we have is that we want to converge paths, to continue the journey of life together.

I sat up straight in my chair, correcting the slump that had crept into my posture as I stared at the screen. 'Sasha,' I said. 'Can you get me a coffee please?' I usually got my own drinks, but I handed her my refillable cup and she took it without protest.

'Are you angry?' she said quietly.

'No,' I said. (I was.)

'There's nothing on the external website or Esme's socials,' she said, almost in a whisper. 'I checked.'

'Good work,' I said. As she left, I messaged Esme a single question mark and continued reading.

> Together, we can breathe again. Prepare yourself for the wedding of the decade and the marrying of our plans, professional and personal, as Esme and Ajax, EKArts and Resilience Needs ... become one.

I'm sorry, what? They were planning to merge their companies? There were two parts of EKArts: the charity, which a separate team ran, with trustees in charge; and the business. The charity was protected and could not be touched. But my side of EKArts, the business side governing Esme's work as an influencer and her many collaborations in the design world, that was a different thing. Careful to keep my expression neutral, I picked up my phone and voice noted Esme: 'Please call me immediately.'

Sasha was returning at that moment, carefully carrying my cup while teetering on vertiginous high heels. She looked at the screen. 'She even spelt discreet wrong,' she said, supportively.

I glanced at her. I wasn't entirely *au fait* with the work of Ajax Banks, but the statement definitely had a joint feeling about it. As in, they jointly wrote it while smoking a joint. Something had gone awry for Esme to have been happy publishing such a 90s-pop-lyric imbued splurge which practically had two-become-one as its headline. Normally

I wrote her scripts, even her comments on socials; she had made faux pas in the past leading to near-cancellation, and was self-conscious about her dyslexia.

'It's not a mistake,' I said. 'She – or they – meant discrete as in a separate unit, not discreet as in quietly tactful.'

'Oh.' Sasha gazed at me as I sipped my coffee. When her phone chimed she glanced at it and tapped a reply with gel nails so long I was surprised she'd been able to do any basic tasks. One of my close friends had once had such a manicure and I'd had to button her coat for her. As she stood there, her ankles wobbled from the height of her shoes.

'What's with the stilettos, Sash?' I said, clocking the tightly fitted bodycon dress she was wearing. She normally wore some combination of t-shirt, trainers and jeans. So far, so parallel-universe.

'Ah,' she said, flipping a straightened strand of hair behind her ear then wincing as she accidentally scraped herself with one of her nails. 'I'm back on the dating apps. Thought I'd try a new approach, have a bit of a makeover.'

'As long as you're enjoying it,' I said. She was a decade younger than me, and new to London; as a result, I felt instinctively protective towards her. 'You're fantastic as you are, obviously.'

'Thanks, Lizzy.' She smiled perkily. 'Oh.' She glanced at her mobile. 'Esme would like to see you on the green floor. In ten minutes. And' – she cleared her throat, showed me the phone screen in a gesture of transparency – 'Ajax will be there.'

So Esme was going through Sasha rather than responding directly to me. At least I was dressed for battle. Along with my usual black tailored trousers and heeled boots, I was wearing a black Chloé silk-chiffon blouse trimmed with lace (Vinted), which made me look like a Victorian widow mourning her fifteenth husband, or a witch ready to do some magic, depending on your point of view – either worked for me.

'Right.' I took another sip of my coffee, took off my blue-framed glasses, and applied a top coat of Ruby Woo to my lips. Then I stood up, straightening my shoulders and rocking my head gently from side to side to relax my (already tense) shoulder muscles.

'Lizzy,' Sasha said, in a small voice, 'you look a bit scary.'

'Do I?' I said, smiling. 'Good.'

CHAPTER TWO

The green floor comprised all our meeting rooms and was on the fourth floor of The Hexagon. It was so named because it contained more plants than the Amazon rainforest: an enormous fern swiped me in the eye as I exited the lift, and I had to stop and double-check it hadn't taken out my eye makeup. Appearance as façade is very important to me, a hangover from my days in celebrity communications. I've always felt if you have a tiny chink in your armour, 'they' (journalists, your boss, your colleagues) will spot it at thirty paces.

Katrina, who staffed reception on the floor, gave a double-clap of excitement when she saw me. 'Isn't it romantic?' she said. 'I mean, so weird! But love conquers all!'

'Yes, indeed,' I said, giving her a hollow smile and thinking, *If that's the narrative you want to read into this.*

'BTW,' she said, her smile turning brittle, 'there won't be any redundancies, will there?'

'Not if I can help it,' I said. 'Where are they?'

'Succulent Room,' she said. I thanked her and went on, checking my clothes for signs of greenery. I saw the familiar silhouette of Esme, clasping hands with a long-legged man sitting beside her in the glass-walled meeting room. Yep, there were *Esme and Ajax, Ajax and Esme*: I tried not to look at them as I strode towards the door.

'Lizzy!' Esme came rushing out, embracing me in a cloud of Esme's Secrets – her bespoke perfume: a dense combination of rose and patchouli – which overtook me. She was dressed in a pleated shot-silk tunic over leather trousers, and she combined it with her trademark smudged eyeliner, 2am look, which somehow converted her from merely rich to hip.

'You're not answering your messages,' I said as I accepted the embrace mechanically.

'Don't be angry with me,' she whispered in my ear as she squeezed me in her pleated arms. Firmly, she steered me towards a large fern where we could talk out of earshot of the Succulent Room.

'What, exactly, is going on?' My voice was low but infused with steel.

'It's for real, Lizzy – he's amazing,' she whispered back urgently.

I needed cold, hard facts. 'How do you know him?'

She bit her lip. 'We met on Friday night,' she said softly, naming a club in Mayfair where she socialised. 'And we've been together ever since.'

She said 'ever since' as though it had been forty-eight

years rather than forty-eight hours. I waited for more words of explanation, but she already had her hand on my elbow and was steering me into the Succulent Room. A single, unimpressed looking cactus sat in the centre of the meeting table. I knew how it felt.

The rooms at EKArts were styled with a splash of eccentricity. Esme sat down on an Eames-style chair she'd selected for herself, upholstered in fake leather and with a laid-back slant to it. In a similar chair next to her sat Ajax, long legs stretched out, in a retro pin-stripe suit which he wore flawlessly, tailored to his muscled torso. My first thought was how large he looked, since I normally viewed him in a tiny square on my phone – either in the tabloids, with his latest model girlfriend, or on socials if he somehow sneaked into my feed. He didn't get up, possibly because he was modelling his handmade Italian leather shoes and they were at the perfect angle.

'Babe, this is my amazing Lizzy,' said Esme.

Ajax smiled serenely at me, looking so pristine it was as though he'd just stepped out of hair and make-up; with his perfectly symmetrical features, he could have been a model. *Yes, it is I,* his half-smile seemed to say. For a minute, I thought he was going to put out his hand for me to kiss it. Ajax was a fitness influencer and entrepreneur with a successful lifestyle app, as well as the host of *Resilience Needs* . . . a podcast which focused on various aspects of health, personal development and, er, resilience. I knew his figures were excellent, and he was royalty in the podcasting world, but I could not have him thinking that I would treat him as royalty.

I looked at him, unwilling to break the silence.

'Hey, Lizzy,' he murmured.

'Hi,' I said, infusing the word with as much coolness as I could without sounding rude.

I heard someone enter the room behind me, and turned just as he took a seat. *Goodness.* Who was he, my prize for turning up? This guy was much too handsome for his own good, but unlike Ajax, a small scar just above his lip gave his handsomeness enough grit to light up the attraction grid in my brain: dark eyes, strong brows, and brown hair thick on top with a fade cut, he wore his single-breasted navy suit with a relaxed panache.

'Hi, guys,' he said, in a soft Scottish accent.

As our eyes met, I felt an unexpected jolt of electricity which made me pause for a moment. One: I had definitely drunk too much coffee, and two: I needed to put my shields up with this man.

'Hi,' I said, keeping my expression neutral and sitting down on the office chair next to him.

Esme smiled a touch too widely. 'Lizzy, this is Oliver MacLeod, your opposite number.'

'Hi,' Oliver and I said again, in unison.

'Oliver is my right-hand man and Head of Vision,' said Ajax, ignoring the nose-wrinkle I made at the title Head of Vision, his expression indicating that I should be impressed. 'Ex-Army, Scots Guards. I'd trust him with my life.'

'Oh,' I said. 'Wow.' I glanced at Oliver, and decided sarcasm was my best defence. 'Are you also his . . . bodyguard?'

'Very much not,' Oliver said, mirroring my sarcasm with a curl of his lip. He was well-spoken, with the cultivated Edinburgh accent that so many people went gaga for, including me – *shields up*, my brain screamed, *shields up.*

'And this is Elizabeth Brinks, my Lizzy, Senior Director here at EKArts, who has an amazing reputation in the communications industry,' said Esme. 'I stole her away from it to make her the cornerstone of my company.'

'I have, in fact, heard of Ms Brinks,' said Oliver.

I looked at him properly then. He raised his eyebrows. 'By the way,' he said, 'please do call me Olly.'

'I can see this is going to be an amazing synergy,' said Esme, ignoring my narrowed eyes. When Esme was determined to be positive, she wore her smile like armour. Such intense, blinkered positivity set up a forcefield around her. You could have fired an arrow at her and it would have bounced off. Ditto for a cannonball.

'Guys.' Ajax leaned forward, his hands clasped together. 'We're so excited to share this news with you. Esme and I are getting married.'

'I know,' I said. 'The intranet told me. And this big decision is – the work of a few days, I gather?'

Esme's mouth quirked at the expression on my face. 'The thing is, Lizzy – when you know, you know.'

Any more clichés you want to roll out? I thought.

Ajax was nodding, smiling at his fiancée. 'One hundred

and ten percent.' *So there were!* 'And it's not just personal, it's professional. We're going to be creating a new product together which combines our skills. Taking things in a brand-new direction. Our baby.'

He looked between me and Oliver with a studied calmness, nodding gently, as though we were agreeing with every word he was saying, even though we were sitting there silently. This really didn't bode well. I'd been in the room with him for two minutes and I already wanted to kick him in the shins.

'A new dating app,' said Esme, ploughing on into the silence. 'Which will revolutionise the field. Called Chroma.'

'And it will do – what?' I said.

'People will be matched according to their artistic leanings,' she said, throatily. 'Via art choices, and a series of questions. No profile pictures until matches have already been narrowed down, no superficial flirting, just vibes. For people who want a deeper connection from the get-go; matched because of their souls, rather than their bodies.'

Olly and I glanced at each other, clocking each other's disquiet. Olly cleared his throat. 'I think attraction tends to be a combination,' he said, 'of both.'

I nodded, shamefully aware of the blush seeping across my face. When was the last fucking time I'd blushed? It had to be fifteen years ago. I really needed everyone not to notice this, but in my peripheral vision I saw Olly tilt his head and had a feeling he was looking at me.

'We'll discuss the specifics later.' Esme's glittering positivity flickered with steel.

'Chroma is going to be huge,' said Ajax, steamrolling on. 'But at the moment it's just a sketch on a cocktail bar napkin.' He glanced at Esme and she returned his look with hazy eyes. 'We're going to hit the ground running, start developing it, get investors on board. There'll be lots of promotional events, but the best event of all, after we're done, will be our wedding.' He reached out and took Esme's delicate, manicured hand in his bronzed, muscular one.

'So, as you're each other's opposite number, we thought we'd bring you together now, at the outset,' said Esme. 'We won't be merging our separate companies yet. But we'll need the expertise of both of you to help us tell the story of Chroma; to make this new' – she took a breath – '*adventure* sing, in all of its wild colours.'

Silence hung in the room. I wondered whether you could actually sing in colour. Olly cleared his throat. 'Well, that's excellent news,' he said, in a perfectly pleasant but expressionless voice. 'Congratulations. Perhaps Elizabeth and I can convene now, for an introductory chat. No need for the major players to be part of this.' He made a shooting gesture at them. Their faces broke into broad smiles. They were already stroking each other. If only there was a room that wasn't a glass box for them to use.

'If that's okay with you, Elizabeth?' Olly was already standing.

I nodded. 'Let's go.' I got my phone out and sent a message

to Sasha to cancel all of my meetings that day. I'd had a couple of journalists lined up to discuss the latest EKArts' initiatives. But Esme and Ajax's love match was going to blow what should have been a normal Monday out of the water.

CHAPTER THREE

Olly and I said nothing as we strode out of the Succulent Room. The Lily Room, positioned at the end of the hall, was empty. I entered the code into the keypad and turned the door handle, glancing at Olly as he held the door open from behind me.

'Happy Monday,' he said.

'Right back at ya,' I said, as the door closed behind us.

We both stood there for a moment, Olly taking in the room – a huge glass window overlooking the City, a table with an array of refreshments and a single, imperious-looking lily – while I gave a long, soft exhale in the hope of releasing some of my hidden tension.

'So,' I said, 'Head of Vision, eh?'

He pointed at me. 'Senior Director. What does that even mean?'

I conceded with a shrug. He was right. I'd gone from

being a communications professional to being someone who translated Esme's vision to the world, which had started off being just Comms but had ended up including strategy and ... pretty much anything she wanted me to do. 'Let's just say I'm a useful person.'

'I'll say.' He poured himself a black coffee, selected an apricot Danish from the covered dish of pastries and took a bite. 'Great building, by the way. I like the glittery glass. Apparently we'll be moving in.' Was he, in a weird, imperious kind of way, *attempting* to twinkle his brown eyes at me? Great: the man was good-looking, and he *knew* he was good-looking. This situation was doubly annoying and I was perfectly capable of transferring all of my annoyance onto him. I turned my back to Olly and made myself a coffee with cream. Green tea wasn't going to cut it this morning.

'So.' He sat down. 'What's the story? About them, and this app? I didn't have an inkling, and that's not something I say often.'

'I don't know the story other than what Esme just told me. They met on Friday, apparently.' I chose a *pain au raisin* and sat down opposite him tearing scraps off it.

'I had the impression you knew about things before they happened,' he said, and caught my eye. 'It's a *compliment*.'

I shook my head. 'Not this time. We'll have to do some reconnaissance.' I nibbled a tiny corner of pastry and assessed him as I did so. 'Ex-Army, eh?'

His gaze flicked back to mine. 'Since you're asking, yes,

I did notice the searing contempt with which you said the word *wow*. And you're—'

'Soft corporate world, all the way.'

'Not so soft though,' he said.

I raised an eyebrow. He named a few names and I waved my hand in the air to acknowledge them. In my last job I'd had the reputation for turning around the story about companies and individuals who weren't appearing as they wished, including for a famous footballer, which always gave me street cred. Coming to EKArts had been about doing something rewarding, not about money. Sure, Esme was a world-famous artist, regularly commanding six figures for her art, occasionally even seven, so she was technically a celebrity. But EKArts wasn't a rich person's plaything. Esme had established the charity – providing subsidised studios for young artists, and arts outreach for deprived communities and young people (the charity's employees, resident on the top floor of the Hexagon, would be sleeping soundly tonight, protected by their charitable status). Although I oversaw Comms for the charity, I was most involved in the other, legally separate, part of Esme's empire: the commercial side. Esme had expanded her fortune by branching out into commercial collaborations across the arts, from jewellery to textiles to hotel interiors; and all of this was bolstered by her social media following.

The kicker was, she'd long been underestimated because she was a woman, and because she was often photographed staggering out of a nightclub in the early hours. I'd met her at a party and it was the work equivalent of love at first sight (or at first conversation) – she was easily the most interesting person in the room as well as the most persuasive. By the end of that evening I'd agreed to work for her.

My job had involved getting people to take Esme seriously. Converting her reputation from art world wild child to respected businesswoman and philanthropist. It had been hard. Very hard.

I put down the section of *pain au raisin* I was holding and looked at it.

'I can't quite believe this is happening,' I said. I looked up and held his gaze. 'This stupid love affair could fuck up everything for EKArts, and for Esme. I've worked so hard for her brand to be taken seriously, and now she's back on the road to trivial.'

'You're not a great romantic then?' he said.

I shook my head. 'I could really do without Ajax Banks.' I said his name as though it was a swearword.

'Easy.' There was a firmness in Olly's tone. 'He didn't get them into this unilaterally, did he? And Esme isn't exactly an ideal influence on our brand either. Ajax is all about logic, science, physical fitness, finance, whereas your principal . . .'

'Yes?' I challenged him.

'I mean, no offence, but she does quite a lot of faffing around, doesn't she? All those melting ice sculptures and dried flowers.'

'Not a great authority on modern art, then?' I said, in

sarcastic echo of his romantic comment, which had somehow stung me.

He sat forward in his seat. 'All I'm saying is the potential for ruination goes both ways.' I could see the exasperation flickering in his eyes, but he was resolutely self-contained. 'So technically we agree.'

'Do we?' I said. 'Doesn't feel like it.'

He shrugged. 'It's just our bad luck that opposites attract.'

I sat back in my seat and we both fell silent. He got up briskly (he did everything briskly, it seemed) and selected another pastry with an easy grace that told of innate confidence.

I looked out of the floor-to-ceiling window, at the soft grey London skyline against the pale winter sky. 'I don't think I have the stomach for this,' I said.

Olly paused in the process of forking the pastry onto his plate. 'I mean, they're a bit sticky, but not too bad. Fresh this morning, I think.'

'*Not* the pastries,' I said.

He frowned.

'I've been in similar situations before,' I continued, not wanting to be disloyal to Esme, so framing things as vaguely as I could. 'Brilliant people – fragile people – prone to sudden enthusiasms, grand passions. Everything's wonderful, until it's not. Which is fine if you keep personal stuff personal, but they're mixing personal and professional together and as a cocktail, it's, what? Dynamite? Kryptonite?'

'Let's go with Kryptonite. You're not going to bail, are

you?' He looked at me steadily and I noticed amber flecks in his dark brown eyes.

His very compelling dark brown eyes.

I blinked, got a grip, and tried to logically assess him: Army posture, pristine Savile Row suit, Oxford shoes polished to a mirror shine. Hard, impermeable, but decent. In our world, façade is everything. You have to choose a statement and go for it. I'd gone for Black Widow, he'd gone for Decent Chap. An act, just like my appearance was, too.

'No,' I said. 'Not this week, anyway.' As I spoke, I wondered if he would tell his team what we'd talked about; use it to my disadvantage. I was normally a brick wall, a closed book. But the blab-monster had got into me today. I shut my mouth and pressed my lips together.

Oliver was assessing me, too, it seemed. 'For the record,' he said, reading my expression, 'for the duration of this – episode – what we discuss stays between us unless otherwise agreed.'

I held his gaze levelly. 'Agreed,' I said. Was he a friend or enemy? I couldn't decide. It was easy to talk to him, but that guaranteed nothing.

He grinned with unexpected brilliance. 'We're just two communications professionals, communicating. Finish that pastry, go on, lass.'

'Feeder.' I pushed the plate away. 'Let's go. I don't have the desire to talk strategy now, and I have a sense our role is largely going to be reactive.'

'We do need to have a plan though,' he said.

'I know. But let's talk about it later.'

He shrugged. 'You're the boss, Lizzy Brinks. But we're going to have to have a proper conversation eventually.'

'It's Elizabeth to you, and to anyone from Resilience Needs, dot, dot, dot,' I said.

He leaned back in his chair. 'You're the boss, Elizabeth,' he said, in a very different tone. He extracted a business card from his breast pocket and pushed it towards me. 'Can you ping me your number?'

My heart was surprisingly, but very definitely, racing. Caffeine overdose.

'I like your schtick,' I said, unlocking my phone and navigating to contacts, entering his number and then attaching my details and pressing Send. 'But I'm not fooled by it.'

He raised his eyebrows and bit into the pastry as his phone vibrated on the desk.

CHAPTER FOUR

By the time I got back to my office Sasha was dancing on the spot, like a puppy that needs to be let out for a pee.

'So glad you're back,' she squeaked, as I got my lipstick out and started to reapply it. 'Esme wants to see you in her office. She asked fifteen minutes ago.'

So the kingpin had finally disentangled herself from the arms of her lover. 'Relax,' I said. 'She can wait a bit longer.'

I thought Sasha was going to burst. Instead, she skittered out and across the office, leaving the door open.

I opened my email, put my noise-cancelling headphones on, and started to draft a resignation letter.

It's been a pleasure working with you ...
   I'm proud of everything we have achieved together ...

> Mopping up after two overgrown teenagers isn't my bag ...

Then, at the end, I pressed Ctrl+A and hit delete, my draft resignation and application for freedom disappearing forever, leaving me feeling very slightly better.

'Lizzy.'

I jumped and looked up. Esme was standing on the other side of my desk. I lifted my headphones off and hard rock blared out.

'You need to watch your hearing, babe,' she said. 'I've said your name three times.'

I smiled frostily. 'Thanks.'

'We need to talk,' she said. 'But not here.' I followed her gaze. Through the glass I could see the staff were desperate to make like meerkats but none of them dared. They were all working studiously, it seemed. The only giveaway was that nearly all of them were partially turned towards us, like sunflowers leaning towards the sun.

'Come on,' said Esme. 'Let's have a champagne brunch.'

I turned the music off. 'I'm not drinking,' I said.

'Of course,' she purred. 'Heavy weekend, was it?'

I liked being a mystery in the office. Therefore, Esme had no idea I'd actually spent the weekend lying on my sofa, contributing to WhatsApp conversations with friends and watching a documentary about cheerleaders with my cat.

I raised an eyebrow. 'Not particularly,' I said. 'But alcohol blurs my judgement, and I don't want to make any promises I can't keep. One of us has to have a clear head.'

We went to the place Esme always goes to when celebrating: the Teynham (pronounced Tennam), a plush, velvet-seated restaurant just off Piccadilly. It looked as though it had dropped out of the 1880s: all red velvet, ornate ironwork and poker-faced waiting staff dressed like penguins. Its champagne brunch was famous.

I let Esme order and as usual she chose a galaxy of things: fresh fruit, pancakes, cheese soufflé, figs and natural yoghurt. Meanwhile, I was mentally trying to construct an argument that would convince her not to go into business with a man she'd known for five minutes. Rather than looking at her face, I concentrated on unfolding the capacious white linen napkin, so starched that it was entirely self-supporting.

As usual she ignored my no-alcohol request, but when a waiter approached with champagne, I put my hand over the glass and gave him such a ferocious glance he withdrew bashfully. 'Sparkling water, please.'

'Play nice, Lizzy,' murmured Esme. I turned the same high beam on her and she sat back in her seat. 'And there I was thinking you might be happy for me.'

'It's ironic we're having this conversation here,' I said. 'Because it's where we had our first strategy meeting, three years ago. Do you remember?'

'Yes.' She turned her champagne glass by the stem with her elegant, manicured fingers. Like many artistic people, she was the picture of bohemian edginess, but with expensive accents. Her dyed burgundy hair looked as though it hadn't been brushed for days, but her nails had been expertly polished deep crimson with a gold lightning strike across each one.

We looked at each other. I didn't need to say anything else because we both remembered. It had been my first week working for her. We'd begun by speaking about EKArts and her goals for the company, but had slid into talk of her romantic difficulties within minutes. Beautifully made up, by the time we reached the second course there had been rivers of mascara running down her face. Her artistic career was going from strength to strength, but her image was a train wreck. When her love affair with a famous musician had hit the skids, he had overshared to his considerable audience on socials, his rants going viral.

'I just want to be known for my work,' she had said, at that lunch. Now, sipping my sparkling water, I wished I had written it down on a napkin and got her to sign it.

The Esme I worked for was the Esme I'd met at the party. The working-class kid, who'd started making art sitting cross-legged on the floor of her bedroom, charcoal stick on paper. The talent who had dazzled her art tutors and won a bursary place at the RCA. The woman who had ploughed some of her millions into subsidised art studios and charitable initiatives. The artist with a commercial eye for collaboration. But this side of Esme also co-existed with the other side of Esme: mercurial, impulsive, sometimes maddening.

My priority had been to repair her reputation. I'd done all the usual Comms stuff, working on Esme's story as an artist, getting to know her really well and identifying her core values and the messaging she wanted to put out. Subtly placing mentions of her in the press, and leveraging my contacts to get her a couple of interviews in premium publications where she could talk about the charity she was in the process of establishing. But I'd done a lot more than that. Before long, I was working on company strategy. Accompanying her to meetings with collaborators as she branched out. Coaching her on her communications style. The list went on, and on. I didn't even have words for the level of my involvement. Moreover, I'd given too much of myself to the process.

'I guess I did my job too well when the shit hit the fan last time,' I said. Esme was now operating from a place of security, provided by me. She was bored with it.

She stayed quiet as the fresh fruit arrived. When the waiter withdrew, she spoke. 'You don't get it,' she said, and put her hand on her heart while I speared a chunk of honeydew melon. 'When I started talking to Ajax, it was like the first time I met you.' I looked up at her face and she held my gaze. 'Like someone understood me, at last. The real me.'

High-gloss gym bro Ajax Banks had a soft, sensitive, artistic side? Somehow, my brain still couldn't fit those puzzle pieces together. 'I know you're in the midst of a whirlwind of very strong feelings,' I said. 'It's called infatuation.'

She raised an eyebrow, spoke firmly. 'This is golden, Lizzy. It won't tarnish. And remember, this is my *life*. It's not just business.'

'It's both,' I said. 'Your relationship, of course, is your own affair.' *Although I had to preside over the burning embers of the last one*, I thought. 'It's the business side that's worrying me. Bringing the two companies together – when they're so different? Art is your bag, and now you want to dilute that with a dating app? Esme, we've worked so hard to get your brand, your company, to this place. Do you really want to sacrifice it?'

'It's not a sacrifice,' she said. 'It's a marriage. The app is art-centric. Love and art. Can you think of a better combination?'

I could think of plenty of better combinations. Mournfully, I thought of my relaxed team in their jeans and smart trainers, their headphones and lunchtime yoga sessions. Then of the Resilience Needs staff, which if Olly and Ajax were anything to go by, was all sharp suits and step counts. 'The companies aren't a good combination.'

'We won't merge them yet,' she said. 'We'll do it after the wedding. Carefully. When things are established. For now, we'll be working on Chroma as a fifty-fifty collaboration. It's going to be huge. EKArts will benefit.'

I pressed my fingers to my temple. I didn't want to go too sledgehammer and tell her that it was trivialising her talent. At least the charitable side was safe, although I could imagine the gloomy faces of the trustees at the idea of

Esme going off on this tangent. 'Won't it require a restructuring of the business side?' I pushed back the thought of redundancies.

She shook her head and toyed with a freshly arrived cheese soufflé with her knife. 'No. We're doing it old school; Ajax says it will be like the early days of Silicon Valley. A small team. Exciting, fresh, no such thing as a mistake kind of feel. We'll handpick from both companies and bring some new people in, too. He already has a lifestyle app, so we can use his technical team.'

I suppressed a sigh, cutting into a pancake. 'This isn't Silicon Valley in 1990, Esme.'

'Come on, Lizzy,' she pleaded. 'This isn't like you.'

I thought of my deleted resignation email. The thought of leaving my job felt too exhausting to contemplate, my long list of financial obligations too pressing. I sliced the pancake into ribbons without eating anything, and this clearly disturbed Esme. She put her hand over mine. 'I know what we're asking of you will be a big change,' she said. 'But change is good. Give it six months. Promise me you won't go. I need you, Lizzy.'

There were tears in her eyes. Actual tears. Oh God. I felt the pull of guilt and obligation.

'I promise,' I mumbled.

'Excellent!' She clapped her hands and smiled through tear-spangled eyes, her distress evaporating. At once, I wanted to take my promise back.

My phone chimed.

> **DAD:** Where's the snow? That's what I want to know.

'I have to get back to the office, Esme,' I said.

I left Esme contentedly eating brunch and answering emails on her phone, and went out onto the buzzing pavements of Piccadilly, crammed with tourists, suited office workers and art dealers. I was wondering if a quick canter through Green Park might put me right – I might be an adopted Londoner, committed to urban life, but I'm devoted to its green bits – when I was stopped in my tracks by a message from Sasha.

> **SASHA:** I just saw we're going to do a dating app! So exciting!

So the word was out. I turned on my heel and headed for the underground.

CHAPTER FIVE

Oops, they'd done it again. Ajax and Esme, issuers of impromptu announcements, had put out a call for team members to work on Chroma. It was heavy on promises of excitement and on exclamation marks, and when I put in a call to Dawson and Rachel, the EKArts website team, they confessed Ajax had called them and insisted on having a username and password for the CMS.

'You gave a complete stranger access to our website?' I said loudly, standing outside a French pâtisserie as I took the call. I stared at the display in the window and wondered if eating an entire croquembouche would make me feel better.

'Esme cleared it,' said Rachel, who was clearly feeling Not So Brave from the tremble in her voice.

'But how did he get publishing rights?' I said. 'You have to approve everything before publication.'

Dawson mumbled into the speakerphone that Ajax had

insisted he clear it. 'On pain of death,' he said. Dawson was a frustrated medieval historian.

'Did he really say *pain of death*?' I asked.

'More like, publish it, or you're out,' he said. 'I still said no. Then a nice Scottish man came on the line and persuaded me to do it.'

I closed my eyes. There was a silence, followed by a whoomp-whoomp sound I couldn't identify.

'What's that noise?' I said, frowning.

Rachel again. 'He's eating marshmallows.'

Dawson only ate marshmallows when he was very, very stressed.

This was too much. I was going to set some boundaries, whether Esme wanted me to or not. I looked up a location on Maps and descended into the underground at a fast clip. I needed to look someone in the eye and get my point across.

Resilience Needs was based, surprisingly, in a mid-19th century building in Clerkenwell, a former workshop. The cheery security guard told me that 'Mr Banks has gone to the gym, but Mr MacLeod is available.'

'He'll do fine,' I said, removing my black leather gloves finger by finger.

I was directed up a concrete staircase, through a metal door into a room of bare bricks and white light; an open-plan office, smaller than EKArts, with barely a single interior wall in sight. Framed prints advertised Good Vibes Only;

Healthy Mind, Healthy Body; Only Begin. A cheery sign in mock-Victorian print pointed to a Refuelling Station which contained, from a quick glance, a variety of fruits, vegetables, protein bars and juices of many colours. Glancing to my left, I saw a young man in a suit who was trotting towards me. In one hand he was squeezing a grip trainer; yes, he was actually exercising on the move. 'Elizabeth?' he said.

'Yes.'

'I'm Carl, Olly's EA. He can see you straight away, if you'll follow me.'

I felt eyes on me as I strode across the open-plan office with my iciest expression on my face. Like me, Olly had his own glass-walled office; he appeared to be reading a document on his screen, sitting perfectly upright, jacket and scarf shed, shirt sleeves rolled up.

Very broad shoulders indeed.

Carl ushered me into the room without saying a word, and sped away, swapping the grip trainer to the other hand.

'Hey, Elizabeth,' Olly said, without looking at me.

'Hey, Oliver,' I said grimly.

He looked up and blinked; I saw him take in every detail of my appearance. Sniper gaze. 'Grab a seat. Nice march through the office, by the way.'

'Like Dante descending into the circles of hell,' I said, in as light a tone as possible. 'In the middle of my life, I have found myself in a dark forest.'

'I mean, great,' he said.

'By the way,' I said, giving him a chilly smile, 'no wonder

you hoovered up all of our pastries. Such an impressive array of healthy, *healthy* snacks.'

'Do I sense an air of criticism?' he said, his lips quirking up. 'We get gym memberships as part of our employment package. One of the cornerstones of Ajax's staff policy is his focus on wellness. Anyway, we need the *protein*. Otherwise we'd all be weak from working out so much.'

Completely involuntarily, my eyes flicked to his forearms, resting on the desk. God, they were big. Big and corded with muscle. Never mind the action which had to be going on under that shirt. Looking at him made me feel about as healthy as a Victorian consumptive booked on a last-ditch trip to Switzerland to see the mountains before I died.

Oliver cleared his throat. 'Something specific you wanted?' he said gently.

'Yes,' I said. 'I heard about the website announcement. Phoning my team and threatening them?'

'I threatened nobody,' he said, and I realised his soft, cultivated Scottish accent could also sound flinty and cold.

'Ajax did. You need to rein him in.'

He leaned back in his chair and steepled his fingers. 'Do I, though?' he said. 'I thought I'd let the puppy get his zoomies out of his system. Your puppy, too.'

'I think I understand the principle, but what are you even talking about?'

'Sorry. I bought my niece and nephew a puppy. He careers round and round the garden to get his energy out. Hang on, I've got a video from when they came over last weekend—'

'I don't care about puppies, *Oliver*,' I said, trying to ignore the vision of domestic bliss his words had conjured up.

He put his phone back down on the table. 'What would you prefer to do?' he said. 'Pull them into the office and give them a good dressing down? You and I know they wouldn't give a damn.' He gave an expansive *what gives?* gesture. 'So they've sent out some kooky internal comms. They're not stupid enough to make everything public without our guidance. Let them brandish Chroma, their new little toy, in front of the kids. Who have all signed confidentiality agreements on the day they joined us – ours have, at least.'

'Mine have, too.' I narrowed my eyes at him. This day was turning out to be one hundred percent more irritating than I had thought. *And* it was still only Monday.

Oliver's phone made the sound of a clown's nose squeaking (surprisingly whimsical), and he glanced at it. 'I've got to go in a minute. Meeting.' He looked at me again and frowned. 'Just chill out, Lizzy.' He put a hand up. 'Everyone else calls you Lizzy so I'm going to as well. Unless we fight.'

I shook my head in exasperation at his cheeriness.

'I don't understand why you're getting so stressed about this. Also' – he smiled – 'although it's great that you like quoting Dante, I think you might be overstating things.'

'*Great*,' I enthused sarcastically. 'Thanks so much for correcting my course. Please feel free to nominate yourself for most patronising man of the year.'

He got up, snapping his computer to sleep with a

combination of keys. 'Lizzy,' he said. 'I'm sorry to say this, but you're kind of being a dick.'

'You're the dick!' I snapped, outraged. I leaned forward. 'Rein Ajax *in*.'

'I have a meeting. This company doesn't run itself. Come back and talk to me when you're ready to be polite.'

'As opposed to calling someone a dick when they don't agree with you?' I said. 'Maybe I'll just give HR a call about that one. Your company or mine?'

We stood, glaring at each other. His gaze was blank and cool, and for a moment I glimpsed exactly why Ajax had hired him. Then he pulled his phone out of his pocket. 'Are you absolutely sure I can't show you a puppy video?' he said.

The mounting hysteria of the day overwhelmed me. A choked giggle burst out of my mouth. I slapped my hand over my lips, but there was no stopping the laughter, especially when he started laughing, too. I laughed until I couldn't breathe, spurred on by the suddenly hilarious sight of Olly's wide-eyed colleagues staring in at us. I only stopped laughing when my phone vibrated in my pocket and I pulled it out to see a message from a consultant about a meeting we'd been due to have.

'Oh,' gasped Olly. 'I really do have to go to a meeting now.'

'Puppies,' I said, a smile spreading across my face again. I frowned as I looked at my phone again. 'I really need to hop on a call with this person.' I checked my watch, trying to calculate how long it would take to get back to EKArts.

'So hop on a call with them.' Olly swung his jacket on. 'There's a hot-desking area just past the snacks. Make yourself at home.'

He walked past me without another glance and I suppressed the childish urge to prod him in the arm as he passed. The idea of fighting with a colleague – never mind physically prodding them – was so out of character, I started to wonder if I was having some kind of nervous episode.

Olly directed Carl to help me and I walked back across the office with him, feeling slightly mollified, and managing to slip a snack pack of almonds off the Refuelling Station as we passed it.

'May I get you a juice or smoothie, Lizzy?' said Carl, who had mercifully relinquished his grip trainer. He ushered me to a small circular table by a window, which had various sockets and an adjustable chair.

'Thank you, yes,' I said, gazing at the menu he handed me. Each smoothie seemed to contain more fruits and seeds than a health food shop and a farmer's market combined. I hadn't even heard of some of them.

I looked up at Carl's expectant face.

'Can I just have a purple one?' I said.

Not even a flicker crossed his face. 'Certainly.' He smiled and nodded, which reminded me of Ajax. 'Healthy body, healthy mind.'

'I prefer healthy disrespect for authority,' I said.

Poor Carl looked puzzled. 'I'll get you that drink straight away,' he said.

Work Love Balance

I glanced up to see Olly, about to disappear down the staircase, smiling and shaking his head. As he disappeared, my phone vibrated with a message from him.

> Don't toy with the children, Lizzy. They can't handle it.

CHAPTER SIX

I didn't stay long at Resilience Needs, despite the almonds and the glass of delicious purple goo Carl served me. It felt too much like setting up camp with the enemy. Instead, I took the meeting with the consultant, speaking much more softly than usual, then skedaddled back down the concrete staircase into the ice-grey light of the Non-Snow Day.

As I'd taken the call, sitting at the tiny desk in the adjustable chair, I'd glimpsed Olly, far below, hailing an electric taxi and jumping in, a bright, tweedy scarf doubled around his neck, off to his meeting.

I never took taxis – it felt decadent. It was engrained into me: public transport or walk. Just like the idea of a garden in London – the garden Olly had referenced a puppy racing around in – felt as remote to me as the idea of gold-leafing my living room.

That voice, those suits, that sense of controlled

self-containment. Either Olly came from money, or the not-so-equal pay gap was rearing its head and he was on a lot more than me. He was playing nice now, but I'd lay money on the idea that a man like that would want his way, and it was surely only a matter of time before he started speaking over me in meetings. I was sensitive to the idea; I'd spent my life battling to be heard in high-level meetings and was practised at fighting my corner, but I felt disappointment at the idea of going head-to-head with Olly.

He stayed at the back of my mind all afternoon as I answered emails. Popped back to the surface as I rattled home on the tube that evening. It was highly likely he was married, right? A garden was such a sweet, domestic thing to have, and he had that married air about him. He didn't wear a ring, but not everyone did.

Happy, coupled up, moneybags Olly.

I emerged from the tube into the winter darkness, checking my bank account on my phone in a sudden flutter of anxiety. I try not to think about money so much, I really do, but I've been the Responsible Adult in our family for more than a decade. Mum and Dad were chilled out, we-could-die-at-any-moment-so-let's-enjoy-life types who spent every penny they made and never really considered knotty, boring things like pensions and savings. Mum was our north star. After she died, Dad's happiness dissolved, and after limping on for a few years he sold the family home because he couldn't bear to live there anymore. He bought a nice retirement apartment that also has a not-so-nice service charge, which he had completely failed to take into account. After he'd spent the remainder of the house money, he soon learnt that his basic pension doesn't cover it – but my salary does. My brother, Alex, has a severe form of autism and other health complications which means living independently and working is out of the question. He's in an assisted living facility that he loves, paid for by a mixture of benefits and council funding, but I took on the bulk of the welfare admin and (how do I put this politely) the *fighting* I had to do to get him into The Cedars. I also pay for extra stuff, which he needs for his health and his happiness.

The saving grace is that Alex and Dad live near each other, so I can visit both of them together. It's not the life any of us envisaged. Dad is a good man, but his favourite state is denial. So apart from the occasional autonomous decision (like the, ahem, retirement flat) he relies on me. I go into battle for all of us, and I guess, if we're looking at silver linings, it meant I developed my hard façade early in my twenties. I toughened up fast, and it's hard to reverse that kind of thing or take it off for special occasions. I'd be lying if I said it hadn't affected my dating history; when people are ticking boxes on the kind of thing they want in a partner, they tend to leave out 'icy façade, often sarcastic and defensive' in favour of something sweeter and softer.

I keep most people at a distance. It's easier that way. My last boyfriend – who really seemed to enjoy my sarcasm, when we first met – ended up checking the electoral register to find my address because we spent all our time at his place. I came home one day to find him standing outside my block, a look of complete disgust on his face. That was a classic evening. *So* relaxing.

Pushing aside memories of my ex – and of my afternoon at Resilience Needs – I unlocked the door of my building and was assailed by the smell of mince and potatoes. The ground floor occupant seemed to specialise in school-dinner-type creations. Wrinkling my nose, I collected a chunk of official-looking letters, possibly related to Alex's care, and clomped up the stairs.

If you looked at me from the outside, you would wonder why, on such a very good salary, I still live in a grubby, tiny studio flat in in the rough part of Oval. Why I always order house white, never a more expensive bottle. I guess many people might chalk it up to a gambling or shopping addiction, or plain stinginess. I never disabused my last boyfriend of whatever notion he had formed; never told him what, financially, Dad and Alex need. I also didn't tell him my most expensive clothes are gleaned from daily monitoring of second-hand clothes apps, or that sometimes I've struggled to pay vet bills for Pebble, the world's most un-insurable cat, on the basis of her many pre-existing health conditions.

Talking of which, said cat was sitting on the doormat when I shouldered the front door open. She looked mightily peeved. This is not unusual. Despite being half ragdoll, supposedly making her affectionate and biddable, Pebble's default setting is annoyed. She used to belong to my neighbour Marge, but Marge went into a home and the next thing you know I had a harassed looking council official banging on my door asking whether I wanted 'it'. I had looked at Pebble, she had looked at me, and seemingly against my own free will I had opened my arms and taken receipt of her.

Pebble usually waits by the front door (from 7pm sharp, according to my internal security camera, a cheapo one I bought so I could keep an eye on her) and there she was, dodging my attempts to stroke her and mewing for her dinner. Which I gave her, before I busied myself making a cup of tea and checking my email while crossing my fingers to see whether Esme and Ajax had gone full circle and broken up. One could only hope. Instead, there was a flurry of messages from people asking if I minded if they applied to work on Chroma, and an annoyed email from Jacob, our Head of Finance, saying in tightly controlled prose whether I knew <u>what</u> was going on about the <u>budget</u> for this whole new <u>project</u>.

The joys of being on the leadership team for the business side of EKArts: Esme, me and Jacob, steering the ship. Esme full of inspiration, me and Jacob steadfastly practical. It had been a good balance until this week.

I started work on revising Esme's content plan for the next few months: the work I'd actually intended to do until my Monday was ruined. Unusually, I couldn't focus, and as the evening ticked on, I started investigating Ajax via the wonders of the internet, hoping that a bit of nuance might make me dislike him less. Like Esme, Ajax had come to the UK as a baby – his family hailed from Jamaica, while Esme's was Polish. Like her, he had fought his way up using his intelligence, force of will and charisma. For a moment, I glimpsed a seam of gold through the grey clouds: maybe this situation was workable. Then I stumbled across an announcement for Ajax's recent publishing deal. Six figures, for two books entitled respectively *Hacking Your Body: The Perfection Plan* and *A Millionaire in Moments*.

'And it's a no,' I said, out loud. Maybe Esme and Ajax had an emotional connection, yes, but they were so different on every other level.

'Why did she pick him?' I asked Pebble, eating my last mouthful of toast. Of course, in some ways the attraction was obvious: Ajax was ripped – having gazed at Olly's forearms for ten seconds too long, I could see the appeal of that – fitness focused, all regimented routine and tightly controlled, structured days. A touch of research showed me he hired from places like the Army and Oxbridge or Ivy League colleges, first-class graduates all the way. Staff with gym memberships, lots of goals and 'measurables'. He explored optimisation in his podcast, had a well-established lifestyle app and a coaching business which individuals could buy into. I watched a clip of him getting animated about marginal gains and turned it off.

Esme, meanwhile, was a YouTube and TikTok queen who filmed herself creating art and her vibe was the polar opposite. Her collaborations across the arts – including designing jewellery and homewares – focused on emotion and artistic merit. She was about luxury, rest and intuition: yoga and meditation, no gym visits; her skin was soft and perfumed, her hair left unbrushed, and she didn't care if you were late or early. She hired wild cards: Cambridge dropouts, artistic types, people like me (I'd studied for my degree at night while working my way up in the Comms industry). Even her employee benefits were different: we got five duvet days a year and free takeaway on our birthdays.

Both of them were famous for dating famous people. Models, musicians, actors.

They had one other thing in common: their charisma.

And now, Chroma. I opened a fresh message from Jacob.

> Somebody told me this dating app is about finding true love through artistic choices and WTAF THIS IS GOING TO BURN MONEY, THE QUESTION BEING WHOSE MONEY.
>
> **LIZZY:** Let's not panic yet, this is just Day One. Am sure things will settle.
>
> **JACOB:** I can smell it.
>
> **LIZZY:** ?
>
> **JACOB:** Burning money. It's an acrid smell. The kind of smell you can't get out of your clothes, like cigarette smoke back in the day. Only WORSE.

He really was on a roll.

> **LIZZY:** Breathe, take a dip in your cold plunge tub, we will confer tomorrow.

Jacob left me on read and, glad he had settled, I sat back and thought about how we would bring the two companies together. Esme's airy statement that everything could wait until after the wedding hadn't reassured me. The two leadership teams at least would have to meet and work out things together, surely? And had Olly said he would be moving into The Hexagon? It made my head ache. Even buttered toast, my drug of choice, couldn't fix it.

I FaceTimed my brother, Alex – or rather, I FaceTimed his carer, Jenna, who enables our calls because Alex is pretty much non-verbal. They showed me the painting Alex had been working on that day with his art therapist (an extra I pay for, which keeps him on an even keel): an impressionistic, naïve depiction of a bowl of roses. Alex loves arts and crafts with a kind of gleeful ferocity; there's something about the process which tunnels through the need for sensation in him, that quietens everything. When I had started working for Esme, I had brought with me that sense that art could truly change lives in the way it had changed Alex's. Esme had been passionate about the reach and impact of art; it was why she'd set up the charity.

I made lots of positive comments about the picture as Alex looked at me, then he disappeared abruptly and Jenna gently explained that his favourite TV programme was coming on.

After we'd said goodbye, I went to run a bath. The water never got properly hot, so I was just adding a boiling kettle of water to the tub when my phone vibrated. It was my newest colleague.

OLLY: I mean, just look at the wee thing.

Attached was a picture of a tiny, snub-nosed puppy, cinnamon coloured and fluffy. I smiled against my will.

LIZZY: I'm more of a cat person.

OLLY: But dogs are so charming.

LIZZY: What's his name?

OLLY: Pank.

LIZZY: ?

OLLY: My niece named him. The rescue charity told us he was found outside St Pancras station. Matilda shouted PANCRAS all the way home. Actually, she shouted PANCREAS all the way home. Shortened to Pank, which sounds better, right?

I felt a little stab of sadness in my chest. It was a sweet story; a story that said a lot about how happy Olly's family life must be.

I remembered the list I'd made about him: minted, married, mansplainy.

LIZZY: It's a great name. See you at work.

As I lay in the bath, inhaling the sweet fumes, I wondered what Olly's house was like. Looked around, at my turquoise bathroom suite I'd never got round to replacing. Most studio flats just have a shower, so my bath had seemed to be the epitome of luxury when I'd viewed the place, outweighing the fact that the living space was tiny and distinctly lacking in light. There was hardly room to swing a cat (as I said threateningly to Pebble, sometimes). As a result, I discouraged friends from visiting me. My social life was conducted in cafés, pubs and restaurants and – more recently – in the lovely homes my friends were setting up. But this place, which I'd always intended to be a stopgap, had become my permanent home.

I didn't think much about the dreams that were gradually fading away. I'd just been getting on with life: firefighting for Dad and Alex, progressing at work. Yes, I had quiet hopes of the life I might have – a partner, a couple of kids, a home and garden. In my twenties this had all seemed supremely doable, once I got other things off my to-do list. I'd dated here and there over the years but never found someone I'd really clicked with – and if I was honest, I hadn't put a lot of effort into it because I was so focused on work. One day, I thought, I'll find someone for me. Everything was fine.

But there were moments, places, people, that occasionally flipped that view on its head. And smart, good-looking, clean-cut Olly was one of them. With his happy life, probably a wife, house and garden and access to a puppy. He had those things in the bag. And I didn't know why, but somehow his example was bothering me. Like a magic eye picture, my life suddenly looked different. Could it be that I'd sleepwalked into a situation where the life I wanted was retreating from me, rather than getting closer? Receding, perhaps never to be reached, like the vision of an oasis in a desert? Because the firefighting never ended; and my to-do list never got shorter, magically regenerating itself as I ticked things off it.

Shivering, I climbed out of the now cool bath, wrapping myself in a towel and trying to push my sadness aside. I was still young, yes? There were lots of possibilities, personal and professional, yes?

Yes, I told myself. I travelled the few steps from bath to bed, where I lay, thinking about downloading some dating apps, inspired by Sasha's bravery, but somehow not doing it. Instead, I fell asleep and was woken by Pebble licking my eyelids at 2am. For a moment, on waking, I thought I heard a puppy bark.

Then I lay there, in the darkness. Took in the wail of a distant siren; the sound of the night bus passing at the end of the road; the column of light falling across the floor from the streetlamp outside. I listened to Pebble's soft breathing beside me, and drifted off into a patchy, broken sleep.

CHAPTER SEVEN

'Ready?' Oliver said.

I nodded. 'Ready.'

He clicked Send and sat back in his seat. The room was silent; the open-plan office was empty, all phones forwarded to voicemail. In the cacti-themed auditorium, where Esme and Ajax had briefed the company on developments over a breakfast buffet of fruit (selected by Ajax) and pastries (selected by Esme), I could only imagine what the noise was like. The excited babbling of over-hyped employees, tempered only by the glum faces of those in the Finance team.

'We should have done a drum roll or something,' said Oliver. I nodded. It seemed strange to be sitting there in the soft, lavender-scented silence while our press release winged its way to a variety of correspondents and news outlets, and mirrored statements appeared simultaneously across Esme and Ajax's socials.

Work Love Balance

It had been surprisingly fun to write their announcement. Olly and I had taken one look at the romantic gobbledegook produced by our respective bosses then each drafted our own versions before sharing and merging them: yes, we were announcing a romance, but we were also announcing a new dating app which Esme and Ajax, in their hyper-excited way, 'expected to revolutionise the way we form relationships, merging art and love for the first time'. Olly's version had been so resolutely formal, almost puritanical in its sparseness, I had felt obliged to add some warmth and sentiment.

I mentioned this to him now.

'I worked for the Royal Family for a while,' he said. 'Army followed by the royal household doesn't train you in expressing emotion.'

'I see,' I said, pressing my diffuser to release another burst of diluted essential oil. For the last week, my sleep had been patchy. Not least because eyelid licking seemed to be Pebble's new favourite hobby. If aromatherapy couldn't get me through this charade, I'd have to start chugging herbal sleep remedies. My make-up felt like the only thing holding me together. That, and the ribbed Versace shirt dress I was wearing with gold buttons down the front, which I'd got from Vinted for twenty quid because the owner may, or may not, have burned a cigarette through it (I'd neatly darned the hole).

'You tired?' Olly said.

'Fresh as a daisy,' I batted back serenely.

'So,' he said. 'You're a cat lady.'

I stuck my middle finger up at him.

'We're on those terms already, are we?' he murmured. 'You must tell me which finishing school you went to.'

'We are if you come out with many comments like that, mate,' I said, putting my glasses on. I liked calling him 'mate'; it made him wince.

'But you own a cat, right?'

'Accidentally, yes. I don't call you puppy man, do I, even though you bring Pank up at any given opportunity? I mean, I could start, if you wanted?'

'You'd only embarrass yourself.'

Elbow on the desk, I rested my chin in my hand. 'I'm immune to embarrassment, Olly.'

He laughed. 'That, I can believe.'

I had to give him that. He had a great laugh: open, generous. Every time he laughed, I found myself reconsidering the ways I'd pigeonholed him, and struggling not to laugh myself.

'So, what did you have to cancel today to staff the lurve hotline?' he said.

I sighed. 'I was due to have a lovely long content meeting with Esme and the creative team, talking about our strategy for the next six months. I'd been preparing it for weeks . . .'

'Nice,' he said. He'd been twirling backwards and forwards in his office chair in an unexpectedly playful way, smiling as we talked. But now his eyes focused over my shoulder and he sat up. 'Look,' he said.

I turned towards the empty office. One by one, the phones were lighting up; the touch screens, then the tiny LED lights that indicated voicemails were being activated. People were calling and leaving messages. We'd caught their attention.

At the same moment our mobiles, side by side on the desk, started vibrating. A friendly pool of journalists had our direct mobile numbers. We nodded at each other, almost imperceptibly.

'Good luck,' I said.

'Same to you, soldier,' Olly replied.

And we each picked our mobiles up, pressed answer, and started to speak.

I'll admit it, I slightly enjoyed the intensity of it. The quickfire questions of interested journalists, the 'no waaay' sentiment expressed by pretty much everyone I spoke to. If I hadn't felt so sure this whole venture would end in a bin fire, I would have fully embraced it. Although the fact remained, much as Olly and I tried to lever mention of Chroma into the conversation, people were interested for salacious reasons. One famous person had got it on with another famous person. Cue internet memes, opinions and press interest.

Olly and I had decided to stay in my office together in case we needed to consult each other on any difficult questions, but as my team started filtering back into the office after the announcement extravaganza, I went out to check on their mood. As Sasha passed me, she put her arm around my waist and dropped her cheek onto my shoulder. I patted her head. 'So much change,' she said. 'This week has been fun, but also ... strange.'

'Strange is one word for it,' I said, noticing as she walked back to her desk that she was carrying a new notebook with an E & A monogram embossed on it. I saw someone else twirling a monogrammed biro. I took another call which was easily dispatched, then went back into my office.

'What's with the merch?' I said, once Olly had signed off from the call he was on. 'Notebooks? Pens?'

'Nothing to do with me,' he said.

'They really don't care about wasting money, do they?' I opened my mouth to say I thought it was Ajax behind it, then bit my lip. I needed to keep Olly on side. 'Haven't they heard of the cost-of-living crisis?'

Jacob appeared in my doorway. His face was pale with fury. 'That's it,' he snapped. 'I'm done, Lizzy. They charged that whole charade to EKArts.'

I shot a look to my left, and Jacob followed my glance to glare at Olly. '*You*—' he started.

'Hold fire.' Olly stood up, drew himself to full height, and put his hands in his pockets. 'My colleague, Amber, is our Finance Director, Jacob. It is Jacob, isn't it? I'm not sure we've been formally introduced.'

Jacob folded his arms across his chest. 'Yes.'

'Look,' said Olly, 'I'm sorry this has happened, but things are in flux at the moment. I'm taking calls with Lizzy right now to deal with the media, but please call Amber, tell her what's happened, and say I've asked that the costs be moved so the split is fifty-fifty between our two companies. There won't be a problem.'

Jacob looked both relieved and deflated. 'Okay,' he said. 'Um ... well ... thank you. And sorry for, um ...'

I swear those words had never left Jacob's mouth in the whole time I'd known him. *Never apologise* was one of his mantras.

Olly sat down again. 'No problem.'

I watched Jacob go. As he passed me, he gave me a look of bewilderment.

'So you outrank your Finance Director?' I said.

Olly tilted his head and looked up at me. 'Of course. Don't you?'

'Yes.'

'Well.' He smiled expansively. 'We're equal then, aren't we, mate?'

Olly and I worked together seamlessly on the remaining enquiries, but then Olly had been calmed by a delivery of pastries. How the man managed to eat like that and look quite so buff, I had no idea. As he ate, he twirled a monogrammed biro in his hands, inspecting it. After everything had been dealt with, we reported back to Esme and Ajax. Esme looked flushed with excitement, glancing at Ajax's unreadable expression.

'So people really are interested?' she said. 'In the dating app?'

'A lot of the questions were about your relationship,' I said, but Ajax was already cutting me off, sweeping his hand across his beloved's face and tipping her chin up.

'I told you, Es,' he said. 'Chroma is a winner.' He turned back to me and Olly. 'We need a press conference.'

'Yes,' said Esme. 'A press conference. Definitely.'

'I don't think that's necessary,' I said. 'It's not as if we have the full details of the app to share yet – and the word is out about your relationship.'

'But a press conference nails everything down,' said Ajax. 'It makes it official – and if we invite TV, we might even get some airtime.'

'Exactly,' said Esme.

There was a moment of silence while I calculated whether this was the hill I was going to die on. Then, with one look at Olly, who was clearly doing the same thing, we silently reached mutual agreement.

'Fine,' I said. 'We can do it here.'

They glanced at each other, eyes in the shape of love hearts. 'I think there's only one place we want to hold it,' said Ajax, naming a very luxurious hotel in Central London.

'Why?' asked Olly.

'We' – they gazed at each other, Esme's voice soft – 'spent our first night there.'

'So you didn't just go to one of your apartments?' I said. 'No, wait.' I put my hand up. 'I don't want to know.'

Esme's eyes flashed. 'This hotel is the most romantic setting ever. We wanted to begin our love somewhere legendary.'

I managed an eye roll of such epic proportions that Olly choked on the piece of cinnamon whirl he was eating and called an early end to the meeting so arrangements could be made.

'We're going to have to work on your face,' he said, as we walked down the corridor. 'Seriously. You're dripping with contempt.'

I raised my eyebrows. 'I'd love to apologise for my Resting Bitch Face, but – oh no, hang on, I wouldn't.'

'Chill, armadillo,' he said. 'Remember you're the legendary Lizzy Brinks. Usually you're like a swan, a millpond, a bloody sheet of ice. I saw you give the press conference when you were representing that footballer.'

He was right. My tiredness had, unusually, upset my composure. 'I guess my game face has slipped,' I said. 'It won't happen again.'

His eyes twinkled with amusement. 'How on earth do you do it, by the way?'

I relaxed slightly. 'An excellent early boss. I've never forgotten her advice: be calm, and if you can't *be* calm, *look* calm.'

'Takes effort though, doesn't it?' he said, as the lift doors dinged open and we got in.

We stood there as the doors closed, opposite each other. His gaze was fixed on mine. It felt as though he was trying to read my thoughts.

'We don't need to talk about emotions,' I said, stiffly. I wasn't getting stuck in that trap: it was a classic manoeuvre which my ex had often made. He was an expert in locating a point of vulnerability and prodding it.

'Wow. I thought I was the uptight one. You just said "emotions" like it's a swear word,' he countered.

'Maybe it is,' I snipped. 'Look, I need a break. Let's go again in half an hour to write up the press conference speech, yes?'

He shrugged, held up his hands, and stepped out of the lift doors as they opened.

'And make sure you get yourself a healthy snack,' I said. 'Maybe a protein bar?'

As he walked away, he stuck his middle finger up, and I found myself smiling against my will as the lift doors closed in front of me. I carried on smiling all the way to my floor.

CHAPTER EIGHT

Thanks to my experience of working for rich people, I know money doesn't buy happiness. But it does hire a function room in the most exclusive hotel in town, with dusky pink silk wallpaper and vases of lilies so big they look as though they were grown in a fairytale kingdom peopled by giants. Against all the odds, we had pulled together a press conference in a week; both Olly and I had done a *lot* of sweet-talking (read, begging) to get a decent number of people in the room. And what a room it was.

'There's a wedding reception here this evening,' said Carl, Olly's assistant, blank-eyed with trauma, as we arrived. 'I had to promise we would not spill anything on the carpet or damage anything. *Anything.* Plus, they kept saying no so I ended up offering them double the normal rate to secure the room.'

I narrowed my eyes. This was getting more ridiculous by

the minute. Also, wedding? The lilies were giving me funeral parlour vibes. When Olly started sneezing, I gazed at the enormous orange stamens releasing their powdery pollen. 'Killer lilies,' I muttered to him. 'Don't get near them in your nice suit, you'll end up coated in orange like a cheese puff.'

'I think you're the one in danger, and ruining that outfit would be a crime,' he said, and I blinked at the idea he'd properly clocked what I was wearing when he seemed oblivious. I had changed into a white shirt dress with a wide white fabric belt, paired with nude high heels and (fake) moonstone earrings. White was the colour I went to when I wanted to feel strong and confident in front of cameras: out of the black trousers and the black blouse, into the white. I was also wearing red lipstick and just enough eye make-up to make it a disaster if I touched my face. I'd dressed up just before I'd left The Hexagon, mainly because the longer I was in the fancy get-up, the more chances there were it would be ruined by a bird shitting on me or by me forgetfully swiping a hand across my face.

'Let's both stay away from the lilies,' I said. We positioned ourselves at the back of the room as Carl hurried off to supervise the making of high-quality coffee. We'd written a dull, straightforward statement announcing the union of Ajax and Esme – or A&E as I now preferred to think of them, because their presence together in anything tended to set off blue emergency lights and sirens in my head.

Sasha was arranging monogrammed notebooks and pens on a table, her face the picture of excitement and anticipation.

She waved cheerily at me and mouthed 'so glamorous'. Once she had finished preparing the display, she stood there, taking in the scene as the journalists arrived.

This would mainly be a photo opportunity. Cameras were already set up at the front, focused on the raised dais which would later be hosting a bride and groom. Esme and Ajax were sufficiently famous that, if it was a quiet news day, they might get thirty seconds on the main news programmes. The room was filling up quickly. As the excited babble reached annoying levels, I sent the 'go' message to Esme. When she and Ajax emerged onto the dais, I found myself looking at the floor. It was the way she was clinging to him, her hands entwined around his arm as though she was surrendering all of her strength to him. Yes, he was clearly besotted, too, but he didn't look weak. And of course, it was him moving towards the front of the platform, ready to read the speech.

'God,' I muttered under my breath. When I looked up there was a man staring at me, his familiar bright blue eyes fixed on my face. I willed myself to keep my gaze steady even as my heart thudded with apprehension. Counted to three before I looked away.

'Who's that?' Olly whispered in my ear, having clocked him at the same time as me.

'Jack Dillane,' I whispered. 'He edits – and writes for – Skirmish.' It was a celeb gossip site. 'He wasn't invited but somehow he's found his way in. Typical of him.'

Olly turned his focus back to Ajax.

I kicked myself. If Jack had heard me voice my frustration,

he would make a drama out of it. A single word was enough for him to spin a whole story.

I forced myself to focus on Ajax. And to be fair to him, he pretty much stuck to the script, with the exception of adding 'my soulmate and I' to the last line. I cringed inwardly, trying to keep my poker face poker enough to avoid attention.

'When's the wedding, then?' called Jack Dillane.

There was a force field of tuts which prevented any need for an answer. Most of the journalists we'd purposely invited were polite, old-school ones. Shouting out was very bad form. But Ajax recovered, pinning a calm smile to his face.

'Soon,' said Ajax. 'But spiritually, we feel like we are already married.'

I braced myself not to show emotion, not to look at Olly, and definitely not to fake-gag as a ripple of laughter moved through the room.

Olly and I had instructed Ajax and Esme, and the journalists, that there wouldn't be any questions apart from a couple of pre-agreed ones, which now went ahead. But Jack's interjection had upset the balance and made the group restive. 'Just a couple more questions, Ajax?' called Phil from *The Times* in a hopeful way. I shook my head, half to myself, half in a reminder to Ajax not to allow it, although being at the back of the room it was unlikely he could see me.

'Yeah, why not?' said Ajax.

This was like herding cats. Before I could do anything, Phil fired the first salvo.

'Congrats and all, you guys. However, you'll have a lot

going on over the next few months, with the launch of Chroma and planning your wedding. Esme, will you still be pursuing B Corp status for the business side of EKArts, and Ajax, will your company be going for that, too?'

I could feel Olly freeze next to me even as I stiffened. EKArts had been working towards B Corp status for the last year, to prove the company was ethical, transparent and accountable. It was a huge plank in our company strategy, and we were almost there.

Ajax took a breath. 'I think I speak for both of us when I say that gaining B Corp status is important,' he said. 'But this' – he glanced back at Esme, who smiled encouragingly at him – 'is more important.'

I was up off the blocks like an Olympic sprinter. Without a glance at Olly, I hurled myself down the centre of the room, with complete tunnel vision, ignoring all obstacles, just as I heard Jack Dillane say, 'So your relationship is more important than the environment, than any ethical considerations, and even the planet?'

I skidded to a halt in front of Ajax. 'That's all for today, everyone. That last comment was off the record – so do not report it. Please help yourself to coffee, biscuits and monogrammed notebooks at the back.'

A hubbub broke out: slightly grumbly, but also accepting that everyone had been a bit naughty. Only Jack Dillane stayed motionless, his eyes fixed on me. 'Nice dress, Lizzy,' he called. 'What's the label? Symphony in orange and white? Or funereal florals?'

A couple of people sniggered, and I looked down. In running to get to Ajax I had inadvertently brushed against the gigantic lilies and was covered in a powdery streak of orange pollen.

'Thanks, Jack,' I said sharply. 'Off we go, everyone.'

'You look good in it, though,' Jack called. Then I saw Olly pass him and say something, and Jack's face shuttered. I watched him lazily walk over to the table and collect his merchandise from Sasha, smiling charmingly as he did so.

'Twat,' I murmured under my breath, fruitlessly attempting to brush pollen from my dress.

'I quite agree,' said Olly, arriving at my side. 'Let's go.'

CHAPTER NINE

'Why the hell did you do it, Lizzy?'

We were in a bulletproof BMW, crawling through central London, being driven by a scared looking man called Eric. Ajax's usual driver was stuck in Covent Garden where he'd been sent to pick up a 'roomful' of sustainably sourced wildflowers for Esme. The happy couple were cuddled up on the back seat, with Olly squashed into the corner, and I was in the front seat, glancing at Eric's frozen face as Ajax tried to carpet us.

'Because you were about to blow EKArts' strategy, and land us with one hundred unwanted headlines,' I said. 'Think: "Love is all that matters, screw the planet," says wellness guru.'

'Bullshit,' Ajax said, and I saw Esme's hand tighten on his arm.

'She was just doing her job.' Olly's voice cut through the

air. 'Lizzy did exactly what I would have done – the only difference being she got to you faster than I did. Next time, you should consider sticking to the plan, unless you want the same thing to happen again.'

I glanced at my phone: a message from Sasha.

> Everyone loves the merch! ☺. It's nearly all gone. Should we re-order for future events? X

I tapped 'No' and looked back up. Olly was staring coolly out of the window at the traffic. Esme was grappling with Ajax's arm like it was a king cobra she was trying to tame. 'Lizzy,' she said, her voice wavering. 'Let's put this to bed. Apologise to Ajax.'

I turned away and stared straight ahead at the road. I felt so angry I didn't trust myself to speak. I saw Eric glance at me. He was sucked into the soap opera now, waiting with bated breath for things to kick off.

Luckily Ajax decided to speak again before I could formulate an outburst. 'I've got two degrees, Lizzy. I can handle a few questions.'

'No one disputes that. But you pay us for honesty, Ajax.' Olly's voice was hard. This was an Olly I'd only seen glimpses of: tough, clinical, his brown eyes drilling into his employer's face, his voice as cold as an ice floe. 'Unless you don't want us here, giving you world-class advice? I can imagine Lizzy's got piles of offers and I've got one or two myself. Can't move for LinkedIn headhunters these days.'

Man, he really was going for it. I kept my face still and impassive. To add extra coldness to my expression I thought of Jack Dillane. Esme shifted in her seat, her hand locked on Ajax's arm.

'Okay, okay.' Ajax finally gave a little ground. 'Let's not get too worked up, Ols.' He thumped Olly on the knee, a gesture of apology. 'You did tell me Lizzy would be a firecracker.'

I craned my neck back and looked at them, gimlet-eyed. Olly had the decency to appear embarrassed and turned to look out of the window. Ajax gave me a wink and kissed Esme's hand.

We passed the rest of the journey in silence, watching the lights of London emerging out of the failing light.

The car sped off, taking Esme and Ajax to their current love nest – puzzlingly, an apartment in Canary Wharf, which didn't sound like the most romantic place in the world – leaving me and Olly on the grey pavement outside The Hexagon with a keenly sharp wind in the air. Olly had elected to get out with me, as he wasn't intending on returning to his own office and he clearly didn't want to spend another minute in Ajax and Esme's company.

'So,' I said, as the car disappeared around a corner. 'I'm a firecracker, am I?'

'I don't think that was quite the wording I used,' he said, concentrating studiously on adjusting the knot of his silk tie.

'Mmm, I probably don't want to know the language you

used,' I said. 'And I guess you told Ajax you could disarm me with your olde worlde Scottish charm?'

He looked intensely uncomfortable. *Jackpot*.

'Just for the record, Olly, I'm not easily charmed. I appreciate you holding the door for me and all, but it doesn't make me go all gooey inside.'

He cleared his throat. 'Noted,' he said.

'Also, did I imagine it, or did you pretty much offer my resignation as well as your own?'

He mock-saluted. 'Certainly did. If it helps, I knew he would back down. Ajax's bark is worse than his bite.'

'Is he a good person?' The question came out before I could help it. I saw his gaze flicker, but he didn't take his eyes off my face.

'Aye.' A quick answer, without thought or invention. 'I think he is.'

'Good to know.' I nodded at him. 'Are you coming in?' I glanced at my phone; it was half four. There was another cheery message from Sasha. 'Going to measure up your new office?' An area on the floor above mine, previously used for hotdesking, had been allocated to 'key members of the Resilience Needs staff', and they were due to move in in ten days' time. 'Just to get things off the ground,' Esme had said, deliberately vaguely.

'Er, no – I'm heading off.' He put his hand out and a taxi appeared, seemingly from nowhere, something which has never happened to me in my entire life.

I blinked at my Insta notifications then back up at his face to see him grimacing.

'I've got a date,' he said, looking as though he'd rather have a dentist appointment.

'A date?' The image I had of Olly's home life crumbled. 'Oh.'

'Yes.' He looked vaguely wounded. 'Don't look so surprised. I'm thirty-four, not ninety-four.'

'An excellent age,' I said, thinking *mine, next birthday*. 'And I'm not, I just thought—' My phone pinged again as he leaned into the window and named a private members' club in Soho.

'Also' – he emerged from the cab window – 'what *was* the deal with Jack Dillane? Is he an old acquaintance from footballer days?'

I compressed my lips. Calculated whether I could lie, and decided it wasn't worth the bother.

'He used to be my boyfriend,' I said.

Olly's jaw literally fell open and looked as if it was going to stay that way, until the taxi driver asked him whether he was getting in, mate. He yanked open the door and climbed in, then popped his head out of the window at me. 'I have supplementary questions,' he said.

'I think we've had enough of those for today, don't you?' I said. 'Have a good evening.'

He sat back hard in the seat as the taxi took off, a strange look on his face. Feeling slightly dizzy, I watched it spin off towards the West End. *Blood sugar dip*, I thought, blinking. I obviously needed to eat something. Not almonds or purple gloop. And it was probably best if I didn't think about Olly going on a date because it was making me feel ... weird.

I looked at the message on Instagram.

Hey flower girl. What gives? JD.

I deleted it, blocked Jack Dillane's latest incarnation on Instagram, and began mentally planning what I was going to have for dinner.

That evening, eating cheese on toast with a packet of mixed-leaf salad (so glamorous), I raked out a heap of gardening magazines from under my bed and started going through them, the radio playing in the background. For the sake of my stress levels I put Classic FM on, and Pebble was uncharacteristically mellow, watching me as I wielded my scissors, cutting out images of plants and flowers I liked, to paste into my garden inspiration scrapbook.

'Shall we do the road garden again?' I asked Pebble. 'Or is this just for the scrapbook?'

Pebble showed zero interest in what I was saying, but I liked to think she was gazing at me in solidarity rather than with the eyes of a hunter. The year before, in a burst of inspiration and community spirit, I'd planted up a tiny scrap of land to the right of the entry to the flats. It was basically a triangle measuring three cats by three cats, but I planted some African daisies, lavender, and verbena. My mum had been an amazing gardener; my happiest memories were of being with her in the garden, surrounded by swathes of white and purple flowers, the sounds of bees buzzing and birds singing. I often visualised the garden I wanted one day, but the road garden had been a physical thing: doing something with my hands, and the earth.

The other residents had thanked me and it had flourished pretty well, until someone mounted the kerb and drove over it one evening. By the next morning a group of kids had decided to finish the destruction, pulling up a few squashed flowers to take elsewhere (hopefully to their beleaguered mums). I hadn't touched it since, occasionally wondering whether I should start it again. Someone else had taken to hanging tin cans planted up with violets to lampposts the summer after, with the words 'water me' perkily written on the side. I'd noted this cheeriness, and wondered how people kept it up.

I sat still, cross-legged on the floor in my pyjamas, magazines spread around me, wondering what Jack would say if he could see me now. Something scathing, something dismissive. He'd tell me I was boring, burnt-out, beyond help. 'I just always thought you had more of a spark to you than that, Lizzy-Lou.' He was a master at conveying his disappointment that I wasn't what he thought I was. Never quite enough. It had come as quite a shock, after the first three months of our relationship, when he'd love-bombed me relentlessly.

No. I was not letting him back in my head.

'Maybe just for the scrapbook,' I said to Pebble, taking her unblinking gaze as agreement.

CHAPTER TEN

'We've got great news,' said Ajax proudly. It was the day after the press conference and we were sitting in a meeting room, one of Esme's meditation tracks playing in the background. 'EKArts and Resilience Needs are going on a working holiday! A quick trip away from the office, to brainstorm Chroma, followed by a meeting for possible investors riding on the crest of that wave of enthusiasm. And it's going to be in . . .'

I glanced at Olly. Every day really was like Christmas Day here – you couldn't move for surprises.

'Drum roll,' murmured Olly under his breath. He had shadows under his eyes. I did, too, but they were from lying awake having imaginary arguments with Jack Dillane, followed by me being annoyed with myself for wasting any of my bandwidth on that horrible man.

Whereas Olly . . . Olly had been on a *date*.

Ajax was sipping a sports drink rather than finishing his sentence. I gazed at Esme's smiling, unlined face. She looked happy, yes. But also slightly ... absent. Like she'd taken an accidental blow to the head or had a little too much Botox.

'Venice!' Ajax cried, and I couldn't help but jump. He was never one to hit a beat, that man. He'd clearly taken the framed admonition to 'Expect the Unexpected' on the wall of his office to heart.

'Great.' Olly sounded tired. 'Also, why?'

'It's the city of romance,' said Esme softly. Her eyes met mine. She'd told me Venice hadn't exactly been a happy experience for her when she'd travelled there with her musician lover, who'd written the song 'Esme'. It had just come out, so they'd been papped relentlessly, and despite Esme's status as a body-positive icon now, things had been different then, and she had been mercilessly critiqued over her appearance in the tabloid press. Maybe she fancied a do-over now that she was more confident and established.

'We'll be announcing the date of the wedding then, too,' said Ajax.

'Before the investors' meeting or afterwards?' asked Olly.

'Details TBC,' said Ajax, and I saw Olly's shoulders sag momentarily. 'Our main focus on the trip will be Chroma.'

Chroma: the dating app which would connect people through art, because people wanted to be connected on a deeper level. *Not my experience*, I thought, then had to mentally correct myself from being bitter and twisted. 'Remember, Lizzy,' Dad had said over the phone the evening before, when I'd made the mistake of briefly mentioning my irritation with the lovebirds, 'women can either age like a fine wine, or like vinegar.'

Later on, feeling vinegary, I'd googled Olly, just after midnight when I couldn't sleep. Flash-bang-wallop, there'd been images of him stumbling out of a nightclub with a model the year before. I'd felt a mixture of glee tinged with an unsettling sadness. 'Ah, the beautiful people,' I'd said to Pebble, whose look suggested she *was* a beautiful person, thank you very much.

I hadn't felt insecure about my looks in a long time. I'm plain, I know I am. Hence the bright glasses, the rich red lipstick. I know how to make a statement and I'm comfortable being *jolie laide*. But someone like Olly could pull an all-nighter and, like Esme and Ajax, still look like he was destined for stardom the following day.

I felt the merest twitch of Olly's elbow against mine, and was back in the room.

'My EA, Tara, is across the arrangements for the week,' said Ajax. 'We want every detail to be right.'

'Right down to the colour of the towels,' said Esme airily.

'Which will be white,' I said. Everyone looked at me. 'What?' I said. 'Rich people's towels are always white.'

Ajax grinned, showing perfect, pearly veneers. 'What we need from you both,' he said, 'is a fire speech for us for the potential investors.' And with that, he began to reel off a list of topics he wanted covered, which 'Tara will email over to you.'

'But none of this is about the detail behind Chroma,' I objected.

'We can fill in the detail when we've worked it out,' said Esme throatily. 'Just cover the things Ajax mentions for now. And brainstorm some related content? Do you think you could have something for us by tomorrow? I know, I know, it will mean working late. But you can use my office, it's more comfortable than yours, Lizzy. Just dial up for food. We want a draft as early as possible so we can let it percolate for a couple of weeks, and we can add to the content in the run-up to Venice.'

She didn't say the words which I knew were hanging in the air. *We pay you enough to work late and the deadline isn't optional.*

'Right,' I said.

'I guess I'll cancel my plans,' said Olly, tapping away on his phone. It looked like it was his turn to be the grumpy one.

'Meanwhile, we'll be selecting the Venice Chroma team,' said Ajax. 'We leave in three weeks. And you'll both be coming, of course.'

'What?' Olly and I said in unison.

'Business class, of course.' Esme twinkled.

'Of course,' we chimed, as though we'd rehearsed it.

Ajax frowned slightly. 'Good to see you two are so . . . in synch,' he said. 'But don't get too cosy. We need you to bring your different skills to the table, to spark off each other.'

'Sure,' I muttered.

'Absolutely,' said Olly, absentmindedly jabbing at his phone screen.

I spent an hour with Sasha, tying up some loose ends on press enquiries and freezing other projects. I hated the process. And clicking some of my current projects into archiving felt horrible, like I'd run out of time or failed in some way. Last week, I'd been spinning lots of plates, sure, but it was my normal, everything running as usual plate-spinning, and I felt nostalgic thinking about it.

'Anything else you need from me?' asked Sasha, after I'd given her a list of holding messages to send out.

'I think that's it for now.' I smiled at her. She looked different again: her hair pulled into a high, glossy ponytail, her skin powdered and her lips blood red, like a 50s starlet. But more than that, it was her expression. She looked less sunny than usual, and slightly buzzed, like she'd drunk one too many espressos.

'What's with the new, new look?' I said, updating one of my contact sheets. 'Another makeover? You don't need it.'

She touched her face. 'Oh, this – do you like it? I bought the lipstick on the way in today.' She took a breath. 'I might have met someone. *Very* early days. He mentioned how he's into this burlesque performer, Dita von Teese. I looked her up and – ta dah!'

'Well, that's great,' I said. 'Do remember, though, Dita von Teese looks the way she does for herself, not for a man. Plus' – I hesitated, wondering how to put into words the harshness of my own experience without revealing too much – 'the best people fully accept you for yourself. He's not been telling you to change, has he?'

'Oh no,' she said, 'he's great.' She tilted her head. 'Don't you worry about me.'

'Good.' I smiled and turned back to my work, wondering if I'd said too much.

'And,' she said. I looked back at her. 'If I'm going to get anywhere in the corporate world, I'm going to have to develop a bit of rizz, aren't I?' She gave me her usual sunny smile, and sailed out of the room without waiting for a reply.

As she went to her desk and settled down, I puzzled over her words, which had sounded very un-Sasha-like. Then I looked at my screen and saw another ten emails had arrived in the last two minutes. I didn't have time to worry about it.

CHAPTER ELEVEN

'Good afternoon, my lady.' Olly's sarcastic tone rang out as he came in step alongside me, heading for Esme's office. I carried my work backpack, complete with snacks, make-up bag, essential oils spritzer and insulated cup for coffee. If I was heading into a late-night speechwriting session, I would need all these things. And Olly had ... nothing at all, apart from his laptop tucked under his arm. Walking in a smooth glide, tweed scarf doubled up around his neck, he looked positively bouncy.

'You look more perky than you did earlier,' I said. I didn't add that the twelve o'clock shadow he'd sported earlier had very much suited him, roughening his smooth good looks in a way which had literally made me catch my breath. Now, he was converted back to his clean-cut self.

'You have the best espresso machine in your breakout area,' he said. 'Juice wasn't going to cut it today. Although we could work out together later, if we hit a lag? The gym's not far and I could sign you in.' There was a definite competitive glitter to his eyes.

'Sadly, I don't have my workout gear with me,' I said. In fact, I didn't even know where my workout gear *was*. I did Pilates routines gleaned from YouTube, in a pair of old leggings and a Race for Life t-shirt. Not quite Resilience Needs standard.

He shrugged. 'Takeaway and caffeine it is,' he said.

Olly and I settled into Esme's office. I'd forgotten how *luxe* it was. So luxe, in fact, that I found it difficult to relax; I deliberately kept my own office austere and professional. In Esme's office there was an abundance of soft fabrics, from the deep buttoned armchair in teal to the mustard yellow chaise longue to the piles of cashmere throws. Olly enjoyed it at first, posing like a Roman emperor on the chaise longue with a bunch of grapes (there was a vast fruit bowl) but after five minutes he got tired of it and laughed at me, perched on the edge of one of the armchairs. 'Shall we just sit at the meeting table?' I said, and he agreed.

We set up our laptops on the small dark circle of wood and Olly wheeled a flipchart over. I felt a lot better: it was still cosy, but more formal. This, I could deal with. We began brainstorming the points for the speech Ajax had emailed over, jotted down possible content ideas for discussion, then moved onto Chroma, the dating app which was currently just a beautiful dream in the mind of its creators.

'What do we say about this?' said Olly. He had finally taken off his scarf and was eating the grapes in earnest, two at a time.

'Make shit up, I guess,' I said. 'Do you ever stop eating, by the way?'

'You have raised this point before,' he said, giving me a picture-perfect smile. 'And it's how I keep my metabolism high. Plus, once you've lived off army rations you learn to appreciate real food.'

I looked up from my screen, but for once he didn't catch my eye, concentrating on his grape selection a little too hard. 'Where did you serve?' I asked.

He paused. 'A number of places.' When he finally looked up, his eyes had lost their twinkle. 'My first posting out of training was in Afghanistan. I served in other locations, too, but it's fair to say that stayed with me.' I felt a shift in the air. A tightness in my chest which surprised me.

'Anyway,' he said, cracking a smile, visibly trying to push away what he'd just said. 'The important thing is, we're here now, with this excellent fruit selection and – excuse *me* . . .' He had opened the bar to the side of him, and its marquetry door revealed Esme's whisky collection in all its splendour.

He turned to me and raised an eyebrow. 'I had no idea you soft southerners would have such a fine collection. Fancy a drink?'

'Nope,' I said. 'Not now, anyway. I need to think. Let's order food and get some text on the page.'

Around us, the rest of the office shut down. Beyond the

smoked glass walls of Esme's office lights were turned off and groups drifted out into the twinkling London night. Sasha was the last to go, fixing Olly with a saucer-eyed gaze as she forced her feet into mint-coloured stilettos. 'Is there anything I can get you before I go?' she said, waving in a courier who delivered us our noodles and steaming bao buns. 'I'd stay later, but I have a date.'

'Even if you didn't, you wouldn't have to stay late,' I said. 'Go and have a life.'

She smiled. 'I'll be in late tomorrow, if that's all right? There's that acrylic still life workshop I've been wanting to try.'

'Sure.' I nodded. 'See you.'

As Olly tucked into the food, my fingers drummed on the keyboard. 'How about this?' I turned the laptop to show him the finely tuned paragraph I'd just typed.

He scanned it with his dark, unblinking eyes. 'Looks great. You're giving me an easy ride here. I'd take out the "however", though.'

I hummed in agreement and deleted it as he gave a groan of ecstasy. 'You have to try one of these buns.' He leaned over the table, one balanced in his chopsticks. My mouth watered, but the gesture felt too intimate. So intimate that – good God, was I blushing again? I snatched it prissily with my fingers and took a tiny bite, giving him a thumbs up as I chewed.

'You're not one of those dreadful people who still use the thumbs up emoji, are you?' he said.

'So what if I am?'

'Dear, dear, dear. So modern looking, and yet so stuck in the past.'

My heart sank. 'Is this another thing I'm missing now that I'm not twenty-one years old?'

'The very same, my dearest passive aggressive colleague.'

I pointed a biro at him. 'I'm not passive aggressive, I'm aggressive.'

A slow smile dawned across his face, and I turned back to my keyboard, somehow unable to meet his eyes.

'So,' he said as Sasha turned the last light out in the wider office and disappeared, leaving it lit by safety lights in blue-tinged darkness. 'You're mother, then?'

'Hmm?' I frowned at him as I finished the bun.

'There's a maternal air to your relationship with your team,' he said, those eyes fixing on my face.

'I like a happy team,' I said, with a shrug. 'That's all.'

'You see' – he gracefully waved another bun in the air – 'I like a team that's professional and turns up on time.' He frowned as he took a bite and chewed. 'I'm polite, don't get me wrong, but we're not here to make friends.'

'I like to mentor younger people who might not have a chance in this industry ordinarily.'

'There's mentoring, and being an invested mentee,' he said. 'And then there's "sure, hon, take the morning off any time you want".'

'She's going to an art workshop,' I said.

He raised his eyebrows. 'Is she, though?'

'Now who's the one being old-fashioned?' I said. 'EKArts employees are encouraged to explore the arts during working hours, within reason. Now, if you've finished criticising my management style, let's brainstorm what we're going to say about B Corp status.'

Olly nodded his assent, offering me another bao bun.

It was 11pm before I let Olly loose on the whisky; charmingly, he seemed to be waiting for my permission. The bulk of the speech was there, we were just finessing details, and we had a couple of pages' worth of content ideas. I gave him the nod and he strode over to the drinks cabinet at speed.

'Easy,' I said, as he sloshed Laphroaig into a crystal tumbler.

'Easy?' he said. 'I don't think so. We deserve as much as we want, or need, to get this thing finished.' He slid the glass across the table and watched me take my first sip.

God, it was good. Fiery and peaty. Within a couple of minutes, the room felt a lot more comfortable. We sampled a tiny bit of one of the other whiskies. Then we had a third, yelling 'chin chin' at each other as we knocked it back, more like tequila than Scotland's finest. 'I need a break,' I said, kicking my shoes off. Olly was still laughing at an impression I'd done of Phil from *The Times* at the press conference. Again, it was his laugh which threw me off balance. I enjoyed our banter, but I still felt he was hiding behind the barrier of his manners, every word considered, every gesture intentional. Then he would laugh, and it was as though I'd unlocked an entirely different Olly.

'Sooo,' I said, warmed by the whisky and abandoning any attempt at hiding my nosiness. 'Are you from Edinburgh?'

He nodded. 'Originally, although we moved around a lot with my father's job.'

'What brings you to bad old London?' I sipped the liquid fire. It stung in a very good way.

'My brother married a Londoner,' he said, pulling a sad face. 'I wanted to be near him and his family. If you ever meet him, do not tell him that. His head is already the size of Edinburgh Castle.'

I laughed a bit too loudly, adding a measure of water to my whisky to slow me down. When I looked up, he was watching me with his warm, rich dark eyes.

'What was the name of your date last night?' I asked abruptly. Just to be clear: I never would have asked this if I wasn't three sheets to the wind. And also just to be clear: the question had been nagging at the back of my mind all day.

'Ah,' said Olly, slumping back in his seat, the first time I'd seen him relax his spine. 'Jemima.'

I snorted, then nodded an apology at his narrowed eyes. 'Sorry, it's just your names go so well together. They sound so posh. I can see the wedding invitation already. What's she like?'

He made the 'perfect' sign with his right hand, then adjusted his cuff. 'Cut glass accent, blonde, nice figure, intelligent conversation, loves dogs and horses.'

'That's quite a tick list,' I said. For some reason all the mirth had left me, but I kept the smile on my face. Men like him were so predictable. *The army officer wants a wife: pearls, polo, extreme poshness.*

Olly was inspecting the whisky in his glass. 'I've been aiming for someone I'd be expected to be with; someone with their own life who wants a person like me. Who wouldn't mind the long hours, the fact I'm not there half the time. Someone self-sufficient, who could plan the parties they want, play tennis at the weekend, do fine without me. God, this sounds weird, doesn't it?'

'Certainly does, Brideshead,' I said. 'All very cucumber sandwiches and croquet on the lawn. You seem to want someone who doesn't really care about you. So yes, weird. Marriages of convenience aren't so common these days, I believe.'

'A marriage of convenience with some dirty sex thrown in sounds pretty good to me,' he said, and knocked back his whisky. 'Fancy another?'

'Tiny bit,' I said, really wishing he hadn't said the words 'dirty sex' while he had his rich brown eyes fixed on me. But, if challenged, I could say the blush was from the alcohol. The way things were going I'd have to stop wearing blusher in the office.

Olly sloshed three fingers' worth of gold liquid into my glass.

'I don't know what you mean when you say "expected to be with",' I prodded, after another fiery mouthful. I was clearly plastered but this observation pinged only distantly in my mind and was easily ignored.

Olly looked at his glass and sat back in his chair. 'My mother said she always saw me with a practical, no-nonsense country lass, preferably from a monied background. She thinks that would suit me.' He barked into his drink. 'What she really means is someone like her. She came from money and always said she married down. My father struggled to live up to her expectations – he was a workaholic, too; is, I should say, since he's transferred all of his zest for employment into the game of golf. My mother holds everything together, keeps the home fires burning, organises dinner parties etc etc. I thought I was different. But maybe I was wrong.'

I said nothing. This was beyond my experience. Over the past few days, a camaraderie had built up between me and Olly, but now I felt it fading. We were not alike. As he toyed with his glass, I noticed his cufflinks: gold, set with blue stones, probably sapphires. The faint hit of his musky aftershave suddenly smelt ridiculously expensive. One bottle was probably worth a month's grocery bill to me. I twitched my hand to my mobile, and checked Dad hadn't called me.

'But enough about me.'

I glanced to see Olly's eyes had settled on me. I raised my eyebrows questioningly.

'What's the deal with Jack Dillane?' he said lightly. 'He was clearly punching. What was the attraction?'

I swallowed hard. Tried to think of a witty deflection and came up blank. 'He was charming, I guess.' The question turned me inwards. Yeah, he was charming. Handsome. Irreverent. Sexy. Good at love-bombing, great at romantic gestures. Until the compliments turned to criticisms; until the teasing turned sour.

'Lizzy.' Olly's voice broke into my thoughts and I flinched. 'Sorry. Are you okay? I didn't mean to upset you.'

'I'm fine,' I said, pushing back thoughts of Jack and smiling. 'So, how come you're only aiming for a girl in pearls *now*?'

It was a clumsy change of subject, but he gallantly accepted the baton. 'Rebellion, I guess,' he said, trying, and failing, to suppress an embarrassed smile. 'And let's just say, before I joined the Army I wasn't exactly fighting women off.' He leaned forward and whispered, 'I was a bit nerdy. Book smart but not streetwise.'

'Shut up!' I cried. 'Spare me the mock humility.'

He laughed properly then. 'Aye, it's true. Then the Army happened. I was focused on my career – still am. And, oh God, this makes me sound really sad.'

'I won't tell anyone.'

'Okay. I wasn't used to having offers, I guess. The idea of a woman being interested in me was novel and enjoyable. Possibly, gratitude isn't the best basis to start a relationship on. And once people see past the whole gym-body thing, maybe I'm not as fun as they think. My last girlfriend thought I'd spend the whole time taking her to parties and exciting jaunts. Confession. I hate parties.'

'Me too,' I murmured, regrettably out loud.

'And I can be intense. Focused on work.' He gave me a glance. 'Apparently that's really boring.'

'Tricky,' I said, attempting to sound detached.

'The woman I met last night' – his voice was soft, and he was looking into the middle distance – 'covered all the criteria. She also seemed to like the idea that I'm very work focused.'

I put my glass on the table, and it landed more heavily than I'd intended. The soft light in the room played over Esme's whisky selection. 'So, what's the problem?'

He glanced at me. 'There was no' – he clicked his fingers – 'spark.'

I exhaled more noisily than I'd intended. 'The spark thing, it's overrated. And how can you tell, really? On a first date?'

'Come on,' he said. 'You can tell immediately.'

'Nope,' I snapped. *Why so frazzled, Lizzy?* 'There are a hundred different factors that might affect the outcome of a date. Nerves. The kind of day you've had. Whether it's raining. The reverse-halo effect – a cognitive bias—'

'Thank you, professor,' he said grittily. 'I gave it a chance. I even went for a kiss.'

I found myself unexpectedly breathless. 'And how was that?' I managed.

He made a slow thumbs down gesture, the ends of his mouth turning down, emoticon style. I choked my laugh into my drink. When I'd recovered, I was annoyed to see the enjoyment glittering in his eyes.

'Poor Jemima,' I announced to the room. 'Are you sure the problem wasn't you?'

It was his turn to choke into his drink. 'Are you implying I'm a bad kisser?'

'No, no, no.' I was. 'It's just, as a technical exercise, a good kiss is fairly straightforward. And it might be you. I don't want you blaming Jemima for something that's not her fault.'

'Thanks,' he said. 'Also, I didn't say it was her fault. A bad kiss is blameless, most of the time.' He put his glass down and leaned forward. 'Go on, then,' he said. 'Hit me with it. What makes the perfect kiss?'

I felt perfectly, drunkenly, in control. 'It has to be gentle, but firm, hen,' I said, doing an approximation of his Scottish accent. 'No tonguing straight away.'

He laughed: that magical sound, again.

'I mean,' I continued, 'you're asking a question really, aren't you? And you just have to listen to the other person's answer.'

He held up a hand. 'I don't need a diagram or an essay paper on this. You do it, if it's so easy. Come on, Brinks. Put your money where your' – he took a breath – 'mouth is.'

It seemed like a reasonable idea at that moment. Perfectly logical. Even if my thoughts were spinning. Any warning indicators were dulled by the way the whisky had warmed my blood, the general feeling of relaxed (drunken) goodwill in the room. I drifted forward, glimpsed his (perfectly fine, actually quite nice) mouth. Then looked up.

We locked eyes. Neither of us looked away – or, it seemed, *could* look away. We were inches from each other. His eyes were that dark, unknowable brown, flecked with the colour of the whisky – a burnished gold-citrine – but they were growing darker by the moment as his pupils expanded. *Oh,*

I thought, *Olly's eyes are drinking me in.* But I didn't move. Couldn't move.

'Your eyes,' he said, softly, 'are the colour of—'

'Pond water?' I said, and sat back so hard in my seat I almost whiplashed myself. He stayed where he was, leaning forward, his forearms on his knees, looking faintly dazed.

'Sea glass,' he said. 'I was going to say sea glass. I found a beautiful piece on Jura.'

'Enough of the charming anecdotes,' I said, slipping my shoes back on and getting up to briskly shut Esme's whisky collection behind its marquetry doors. 'We're drunk.' I turned back to the laptop and clicked Ctrl+P. 'I'll send this to print. Then in the morning we can look at it with fresh eyes. I know it's old-fashioned, but I always think it helps to read it on the physical page, don't you agree?' I was babbling, and I didn't wait for his reply, sweeping out of the room and across the darkened office, into the corridor that housed the printer. I needed air.

CHAPTER TWELVE

There was no denying it as I strode towards the reassuringly solid printer, its screen glowing blue in the low light. I was feeling a bit – *wobbly*. Almost panting. The drink. Definitely the drink. Ignoring the very low, perilously low, dip my stomach had taken as I stared into Olly's infuriatingly gorgeous eyes. *Don't fall for a charmer, Lizzy,* I thought. *Not again.* Also, *you're at work. You're at bloody work.*

I collected the printouts and stomped back to Esme's office. Olly had completely regained his composure and he looked as though he'd been drinking mineral water all night. Hands in pockets, he was taking in the room, and arched an amused eyebrow at me when I threw a copy of the document down in front of him and scrabbled mine away in my backpack.

'Here she is,' he drawled. 'I admit it, you almost had me there.'

'Hmm?' He didn't deserve a coherent sentence. Entirely

coincidentally, I was incapable of forming one. In that precise moment.

'Sketching an image of yourself as a goddess of the romantic arts, when we all know' – he gave a smirk, an actual *smirk* – 'that's not where your talents lie, my beloved ice queen. Come on, you got me.' He looked around, exaggeratedly. 'Were you recording that? It was a prank, right?'

I recovered my voice. 'Get stuffed, Olly.'

'Nope, I've got your number. You won't fool me again. The day I'm surprised by something you do, is the day I buy pizza and chocolate muffins for our whole health-conscious company.'

The thought of the look of distaste on Ajax's face at the arrival of two dozen Four Seasons pizzas was enough to make me laugh out loud. But more than that, I was rankled by the look on Olly's face, the I've-got-your-measure, I've-seen-everything smugness that made me want to prove him wrong.

'Deal,' I said. And before he could move or say anything, I took his face in my hands and kissed him.

It was the first kiss I had promised: firm, tender, a light tug on his lower lip. Practically in slow motion. And I thought that would be that, I really did – but he didn't move away, and when I inhaled, I caught the heady scent of him, a sweet, expensive muskiness that smelt too expensive for me.

Oh, you want the full works, do you? I thought. And, because my blood was currently forty-five percent proof, and his mouth was surprisingly delicious, I gave it to him.

Like I said, a first kiss is about asking a question, and waiting for the answer. And if there's anything I'm good at, it's listening.

So when his mouth answered mine with a tug, when he pulled away for a breath, then kissed me again, then another breath. When his lips parted, and mine parted and I felt the whisky sweet touch of his tongue. Another question.

The sweep of our mouths as our tongues met.

Another question.

His hands closed over my waist and my skin lit up with electricity at the precise moment I heard him murmur my name and he ran one hand through my hair.

I pulled myself away – tore myself as though I was, in fact, being electrocuted. Stood, staring at his dazed face.

I was only glad I hadn't fallen over backwards in my leap away from him. I tucked a spare strand of curly hair behind my ear and turned away, zipping up my backpack. 'So!' I semi-shouted, shrilly. 'We'll reconvene tomorrow morning, at eight?'

There was silence. I whipped round. Olly was leaning on Esme's desk, his hands gripping it. He looked as though someone had walloped him in the face with a custard pie, minus the custard: blindsided and confused.

'What the—' He cleared his throat. 'What the hell just happened?'

I compressed my lips. 'My thoughts exactly. Although, admit it – it's fairly straightforward. The technique, that is.'

'Technique?' His eyes shot to my face, rather than the

space in thin air he'd been focusing on. 'I guess I've been doing it wrong.'

I clapped my hands together. 'My work here is done. See you tomorrow.'

I admit, it was slightly cowardly to sprint away as fast as I did (so fast, the soles of my trainers were practically smoking), but by the time I got down the corridor – dimly and sustainably lit – to the lift doors, I was starting to recover my wits.

As I mashed the lift call button, I was already getting the emotional hangover – the faint tinge of a warning that I was going to be *very* embarrassed the following day, once the whisky had worn off.

The lift ticked its way slowly up the floors as I rocked on my trainered feet like a runner preparing for a race.

'Lizzy.'

I turned. It was Olly. I hadn't heard him approach on the carpeted floor.

I was trying to formulate something to say when he got to me in one step, pressed me back against the wall, and kissed me again.

This time, I wasn't prepared. This time I was not trying to prove some ridiculous point, whatever the point was, because I had totally forgotten it in the avalanche of sensations as his mouth swept over mine. Dear lord, this man could kiss as well, *better*, than anyone I'd ever kissed. And this kiss wasn't slow or questioning. It was passionate, definite, what was the word – I gasped as he softly bit my lower lip – I always had the right word for everything, but I was losing it in the scramble of each of us trying to get closer.

Then his hands slipped to my waist and he pulled my hips against his and I felt the pulse of our bodies against each other, the very definite proof that he *liked* me *a lot* – just as the lift went ding and the doors opened.

And the word popped into my head, the word that described our kiss perfectly: *hungry.*

The chime of the lift had broken the spell, because suddenly he stepped back from me, looking as startled as if I was a hypnotist and had just clicked my fingers in his face.

'Back in the room,' I piped, trying to push down the hysterical laugh that was rising in my throat.

'Lizzy, I—' He'd stepped away from me and seemed to be catching his breath. I could see his face was flaming with embarrassment. Yes, Olly had just pretty much pinned me against the wall, kissed the hell out of me and produced incontrovertible proof that he was physically attracted to me in a move that was nowhere near the cool, charming, in control person he presented to the world. I felt a twinge of pity for him: in the last few days we'd both been thrown off course by Ajax and Esme. Like rubberneckers at the scene of an accident we were veering across lanes and pumping our own brakes.

Steer into the skid, I thought. 'You're very draining, MacLeod,' I said sarcastically, cutting off his stutterings, which were definitely heading in the direction of an apology. 'Why is it you always have to have the last word?'

I stepped into the lift, pushed a button, and glimpsed his stunned face as the doors closed.

Then I leaned against the wall of the lift as it descended, trying to suppress the feeling of being a champagne bottle whose cork was about to pop.

CHAPTER THIRTEEN

The clock showed 2am.

I was sitting on the sofa in my studio flat, my head in my hands, a hangover-headache already beginning its tell-tale throbbing. A large glass of water sat untouched in front of me – that was the thing, I knew what I was supposed to do, I'd just failed at the final hurdle: drinking the water. At my feet, my laptop backpack lay, forlorn. I hadn't even managed to take my coat off. When I looked up at the window (I had failed to draw the blinds), I saw a woman with a desperate expression on her face, lipstick kissed away leaving a soft stain of cherry-red. My body was like a loaded gun, and there was no way I was sleeping anytime soon, my blood shot through with adrenaline and lust. Finishing off this excellent combination was embarrassment.

I got up and drew the blinds. Then watched Pebble stuff her face with luxury cat food. I'd set up her little machine to feed her (a new purchase which I'd hoped she'd love), but the bloody thing had malfunctioned and she'd been so angry at the sight of me, when I'd leaned down to say hello she'd tried to swipe a claw across my face.

When my phone vibrated on the coffee table I had to count to ten, steadying myself before I picked it up.

> **OLLY:** Lizzy, I apologise.

This was so toe-curling. Was it possible to die of embarrassment?

I sat, staring at the screen as the words 'typing' appeared by his name.

> **OLLY:** Things went too far. I respect you as a colleague and I hope you can forgive me.

I made a tortured 'squee' noise. Pebble, replete, landed in my lap like an asteroid. The thump pushed the rest of the breath out of me. I put my phone down on the coffee table, and gently wrapped my arms around her, submerging my face in her smoke-grey fur. I know you're not supposed to hug cats. However, Pebble submits to these gentle semi-hugs, it's a deal we've made. She sat in my arms, an unimpressed look on her face, but making no move to leave me.

Finally, I released her from purgatory and picked up my phone.

LIZZY: I'm sorry, do I know you? Just kidding. Please don't worry about it, we were both drunk, it's been a stressful week, etc etc. Let's agree never to speak of it again.

OLLY: So you regret it then?

I bit my lip. Hard. My breathing doubled. Thank God we were doing this by text.

LIZZY: Yes, of course, don't you? Mixing work and romance leads to disaster.

OLLY: Yes. So glad we feel the same about this. Thanks for being so understanding.

LIZZY: It's fine, we're both adults. Good night.

I put the phone on silent.

Of course, he considered this all a terrible mistake and if he thought I was going to say otherwise, he was out of his mind. I was not going to be a trophy on his mantelpiece, or a notch on his (breathe) bedpost. Olly was one of the beautiful people, and he dated beautiful people. Sure, he got on well with someone like me; could like me, respect me. And it would work well for him if I was fully charmed by him. But I was in no doubt that my place was in the work-friend zone, and in all honesty, this was the zone I was most comfortable with. Swapping sarcastic quips, raising eyebrows, occasionally receiving confidences (although frankly, if Olly ever wanted to confide in me about his romantic life, I would have to stop him right there). I'd created my persona, my barriers, for a reason. When I ventured out of the friend zone (hey Jack!) things got messy. I didn't like messy.

That kiss was something else though. It was absolutely fucking something else.

New tortures occurred to me. Had I lost his respect by snogging him into the middle of next week? Only time would tell.

There was no way I could sleep. I wandered in circles then went and put the kettle on. I just needed to sleep. Sleep, and wake up with all of this in proportion.

There was a reason why I always pretended to be calm, why I kept myself detached. Olly was a complication, an entanglement, in a life that had no room for either. And I'd fixed it, so I could ... relax.

Although I was definitely not feeling relaxed.

Pebble had wandered off, so I went to the niche that housed my bed, and which was half-heartedly screened by a curtain. The grey drape, in a shade called 'Stormcloud', had been smart when I bought it, but it had unhooked itself from some of its rings and now looked forlorn, a bit tatty and saggy. 'I should definitely fix that,' I said to myself, for the hundredth time, then thought how lucky it was I wouldn't be bringing Olly back here.

To see my bed.

Unimaginable. And yet, for a moment, our bodies pressed together, our mouths rough against each other, totally imaginable, in technicolour. A high-definition vision that every single part of my body took interest in.

I took a deep breath and groaned in disappointment, then glanced to see that my phone's message light was flashing. My heart rate spiked as I picked it up and pressed to open it.

Voice note from Esme.

Voice note from Esme.

I pressed to play them, listening to her talk about a love-themed exhibition she was planning, textile designs for an upcoming project, and whether I thought she should branch out into a ceramics collaboration. She often sent messages late at night, and I got my laptop out to take down her thoughts and make notes on how workable her ideas were. I could have left it until the morning, but I liked to get ahead of things and frankly, I knew I wasn't going to be sleeping any time soon.

And in a strange way it was soothing, to do this. To switch on my working brain, to concentrate on something other than my embarrassment.

This, I could do. But handling what had happened with Olly? That might take a day or two.

CHAPTER FOURTEEN

I woke to a host of work-related messages, none of which were from Olly. Pebble's feline mind had clearly calculated that her endurance of my late arrival home deserved a full day in the flat with her – fair swap. As I drank my morning coffee, replied to Esme's stream-of-consciousness voice note about her latest reel, sent at 6am, and sketched out some thoughts on how we could progress towards B Corp status in the face of Love's Young Dream, Pebble lay on my lap, radiating warmth and emitting the low purr of a cat who thinks it's Saturday. It was almost physically painful to lift her out of my lap, made worse by the look of pure outrage on her face.

> **SARA:** Zoom later? Breakfast meeting for me, dinner meeting for you? Message me when you can talk.

I smiled at the message and replied with a thumbs up which – despite Olly's chiding – I knew she wouldn't be offended by. Sara is my best friend, and also my most distant friend in terms of miles, since she moved to Australia five years ago. In our younger years in London we'd shared a rented house, part of a much wider circle of friends and acquaintances who'd nearly all scattered to the winds since. Me and Drew (another housemate) were the only ones left in London, although Drew's home was much nicer than mine, and peopled with many pets and small people along with his delightful wife, Charlotte. I loved them, but I found the cosy glow of their domesticity occasionally unbearable, and would suggest meeting for a drink in town rather than a trip to their gorgeous home where I would eat their homemade sourdough and question my life choices.

It was the same faint twinge I'd had when I'd imagined Olly in cosy domesticity. *Not for you, Lizzy.* Why did life seem so effortless for some people?

On other days I was quite sane and understood that everyone had their own issues, even if they were out of sight, hidden behind a glowing, filtered Insta account or cheery voice notes.

Also, it wasn't as if I'd been all-in on building a personal life. At the roulette wheel of life, I'd very much piled my chips on the work number.

My phone summoned me.

> **DAD:** Too cold for snow. Issues with Alex's benefits. Can we speak later? I'm worried.

In a fantasy moment of shared responsibility, I'd given Dad access to Alex's Universal Credit account. I checked the Journal section every week, where issues or updates were recorded, but recently Dad had taken to looking at it every couple of days, even though any 'actionables' were delegated to me. I suppressed a wave of nausea at the idea of sitting on the phone for hours waiting for a harassed employee of the Department of Work and Pensions to pick up.

> **LIZZY:** I'll sort it at the weekend xx
>
> **DAD:** You won't be able to ring them at the weekend, love. So sorry but if you could call this morning or log on and look at the Journal.

I put on my thickest winter coat (vintage Jaeger, nabbed amid fierce flames of competition on Depop) and a fake fur snood, which objectively should have looked ridiculous but weirdly suited me. Leant to kiss Pebble, who ducked. And on the way out, dialled my father.

By the time I arrived at the office I felt as though I'd been awake for twelve hours. Part of that was discussing with Dad the labyrinthine possible reasons why the DWP was asking to re-assess Alex in case he was 'fit to work'. Clearly whoever had flagged him had never witnessed one of my brother's meltdowns, a fury so intense and elemental that it usually involved smashed furniture or, at best, a glass or plate. He could occasionally say a word but often didn't; and the fact that he wasn't officially classed as non-verbal – an oversight I'd never been able to have corrected – had made a civil service employee tip their head to one side and wonder out loud if we were lying shirkers.

My brother was not a shirker. Ordinary life was intolerable and incomprehensible to him. He *could not* work. At the thought of the many hoops we would have to jump through to prove that, I had to swallow back barely suppressed fury.

The seething expression must have still been on my face when I walked into the lobby of The Hexagon and saw Olly, Jacob and Amber – the Finance Director of Resilience Needs – laughing at something.

'Good morning,' said Olly, nodding at me briskly, hands clasped behind his back.

'Hey, Lizzy,' said Jacob.

'Morning, all.' I gave the group a brief smile, adjusting my expression to my usual serene blankness, looking everywhere but at Olly's face as I swept past.

Jacob fell into step beside me as I walked towards the lift. 'Everything okay, Brinks? You had a face like thunder when you walked in.'

'I'm fine.' I managed another smile, while pushing the lift button. *Do not think about last night*, I thought, thinking about last night.

Jacob lowered his head towards me. 'I have to say, I do envy you getting to work with the lovely Oliver so closely.

That man is hot with a capital H. It's lucky I'm married otherwise I'd be giving you girls a run for your money.'

'Girls, Jacob?' I said. 'I'm a fully grown woman, thanks very much.'

'I never doubted it, darling,' he said.

A peal of laughter made us both turn back. Amber was laughing at something Olly had said and was clutching his arm as she did so.

Jacob patted his heart. 'So sweet. Giving it her best shot.'

'This is the slowest lift in the world,' I hissed.

Of course he would be making Amber laugh, I thought as I finally got into the lift. Because the camaraderie we have is nothing special. The man is charming. Not only has he spent the last few years working in Communications and schmoozing everyone, he's been in the Army, so he knows the importance of building team spirit and cementing alliances. All of our backchat is part of a strategy to create a professional bond between us, and therefore meaningless to him.

Good to get that sorted, then.

The lift opened. Head back, and grateful I'd managed to apply a full face of make-up while kicking a toy mouse around for Pebble, I finally exited the lift and strode into my office.

On the centre of my desk sat a silver-coloured gift bag. Inside, peering up at me like beautiful harbingers of trouble, were a dozen red roses. Plush, deep crimson, and trembling as though they were scared of my laser-like gaze.

I sat down at my desk and, as though ripping a plaster off, pulled out the tiny envelope with my name written on it.

I meant it when I said you looked good. JD.

First feeling out the gate: disappointment. A weird dip in my stomach. *Right*, I thought, *they're not from Olly*. So I was relieved, yes? Why on earth would Olly send me flowers when I'd told him we were a definite no-go? Not disappointed. Relieved. Disappointed. Some kind of cocktail of both.

Second feeling: twenty-four carat gold rage. This, I could handle. Jack Dillane, toying with me again like a cat playing with a mouse. Or rather, attempting to toy with me. *Thinking* he was toying with me when actually I didn't give a rat's arse because his spell had been broken long ago.

'You absolute fucking arsehole,' I muttered to myself, completely silently as far as I was aware.

'Nice flowers. And even better expletives.'

My second worst nightmare after the flowers. Olly was standing in my office, clearly having jogged up several flights of stairs. As straight backed and perfectly groomed as ever.

'Still sneaking up on people, then,' I said, trying to sound cheery but landing on snarky.

I saw from his face that the jab had landed and I automatically regretted it. 'Everything okay?' he said. When I looked back at him, his expression was unreadable, his gaze dark and steady. I started moving papers on my desk and jabbed at my keyboard. Because I was very important and I didn't have any time to look at him. Important and keyed up. Perhaps it was me who needed the gym membership.

'Fine,' I said. 'Aren't you meant to be moving in on Thursday?'

'That's the date the boxes arrive,' he said. 'But since all of my meetings are here, I've already co-opted a desk upstairs. Hope that's acceptable?'

I looked at his set expression, which indicated he wasn't really asking.

'Of course. I hope you've done your officially mandated workout this morning.' More snarkiness – snarkiness beyond my control.

'6am. I needed to clear my head.' There were undercurrents in his voice, but I refused to be pulled under: I smiled blandly and finally managed to raise my eyes to his face again. But he wasn't looking at me. He was staring at the flowers.

'They're from Jack effing Dillane,' I said. Somehow, I needed Olly to know they were about as welcome as a swan attack at a wedding. 'He's having a dig.' I handed him the card in a gesture that I hoped conveyed full disclosure.

'Or trying to get back with you,' said Olly, reading it and handing it back. His eyes had iced over.

I gave a hollow laugh. 'Believe me, not on the cards. Do you want them? Maybe for one of your dates?'

The silence felt beyond awkward. We looked at each other for a long moment, both of us expressionless. 'It's just that I want rid of them,' I said, lamely.

'Allow me,' said Olly brusquely, picking them up. 'I've sent you a calendar invite for 11am. A potential interview for Ajax and Esme. See you then.' He strode out of the office. As he headed for the floor exit – presumably to jog up approximately fifty steps to his new office – he lobbed the flowers into the bin.

'Tell me, then. What's so interesting about them?'

The face of Cali George, celebrity interviewer par excellence, loomed as wide as the moon on Olly's computer screen. That is, if the moon had access to the best skincare and beauty treatments available to mankind. Cali had to be well past sixty and she looked like a daisy freshly picked on the first day of spring. I considered asking her what shade of eyeshadow she was wearing.

'Come on, Cali. Five-point-two million Instagram followers combined, that kind of interesting.' Olly was throwing a small, leather covered blue ball from hand to hand, with no thought of usual Zoom etiquette. This soldier was off duty, and I could see from Cali's expression she was intrigued by him. I sat forward in my chair, still and attentive, trying to capture the mood and assess what Cali needed from us. I also raised my eyebrows when he quoted the figures: Esme had one million followers, Ajax four-point-two million. I guessed people cared more about working out and life hacks than they did about art. The kind of newsflash I didn't need.

I had to admit it was a real coup of Olly's to have got ten minutes with Cali, having heard on the grapevine she had a gap in her interviewee schedule because a well-known film director had dropped out. In an age of clickbait, Cali's interviews, released each Sunday, were appointment-to-read whether digital or printed in the Sunday supplement of the broadsheet newspaper she worked for: funny, insightful, occasionally snarky. Defying whatever any algorithm would predict, her no-bullshit style attracted devoted younger readers as well as the older demographic. Cali was such a celebrity she even went on chat shows as an interviewee. Above all, her words brought attention, and that was what Ajax and Esme wanted, although I couldn't quite fathom why that was such a focus for them. It made some sense – they'd attract more attention for the app, perhaps more investment – but why did *they* want to be the story?

Olly was quoting some epic figures to Cali about Ajax and Esme's appearances in the media. Reach of articles. Percentage of clickthroughs. All of them apparently committed to memory, because he had no notes, speaking serenely to Cali's impassive, ring-lit face.

'You know me,' she said, when he'd finished. 'Figures are great, but I need to be intrigued. As in, *I* need to be interested.'

'It'll be no holds barred,' said Olly. 'And no copy approval. Ask them whatever you want.'

I gave him a flinty glance. He shrugged in reply and focused on the screen. 'They're on board, Cali. Go wherever you want to on this. Whoever else tells you that? And you've got to admit' – he leaned forward – 'it's all a bit weird, no?

Who would have put them together? It's like they come from different universes.'

Cali bit her lip and I knew the deal was done. 'You might have convinced me,' she said. She was playing it cool, but I could see the excitement glittering in her eyes.

'They'll get the cover, of course?' I chimed in, naming a celebrity photographer who could be guaranteed to produce a flattering image (and who, conveniently, owed me a favour).

'Bloody hell,' huffed Cali theatrically, unable to hide a smile. 'It speaks. Yes, darling, there'll be lovely pictures.'

I smiled at her. We knew each other of old. 'Thank you.'

'I consider this a favour though,' she said. 'I don't normally do *couples*.' She said couples in the way you would say *deplorables*.

'Two for the price of one,' said Olly. 'We won't charge you this time.'

'Cute,' she said, and ended the call without saying goodbye. A signature Cali move.

CHAPTER FIFTEEN

The interview was set for early evening in one of The Hexagon's higher-end meeting rooms on the green floor. Alongside a multitude of ferns, the room contained sofas with canapés laid out on a mid-century table. The presentation screen had been discreetly stowed away. Cali had asked to interview Ajax and Esme at home, but they'd demurred: their 'coupling' was so recent, Esme said, they were still looking at properties to buy together.

Earlier that afternoon Sasha had told me a large number of pizzas had been delivered to the Resilience Needs office and Ajax's ultra-healthy workforce had descended upon them like jackals, tearing off slices dripping with cheese as though it was the first food they'd seen in months. I'd won my bet with Olly, and he'd ordered up the unhealthy food that was his punishment.

'I heard you bought pizzas for your team,' I said, as we

strode towards the interview room. 'Didn't you fancy the choccy muffins?'

'The pizza place didn't have any. Also, I have no idea what you're talking about,' he said, without looking at me. He held the door open to the meeting room, where Esme was already sitting in Ajax's arms, and Cali was unpacking her notebook, recording device and gold-plated pens. As I passed him, I caught the scent of his expensive aftershave and tensed involuntarily, an instinctive reflex of attraction that I couldn't quite get on top of.

Olly and I attempted to fade into the background, but I saw Cali's eyes narrow slightly when she looked in our direction, an indication that she definitely did not want us to interfere in her interview.

With excessive lavishness, Ajax had ordered two bottles of champagne in a silver wine cooler and I saw Esme gulp a huge mouthful from a flute as Cali settled down. I noticed Cali accepted a glass, but didn't sip it.

'So,' Cali said, once her recording equipment was set up, opening her hands in an expansive gesture, 'guys!' She gestured to them and the room.

The three of them laughed. I fake-laughed. Olly just watched.

'How did all of this come about?' Cali took a sip of champagne. A fake sip, to my eye.

Ajax went misty-eyed. 'True love, I guess.'

He began a forensic examination of the ways in which he and Esme were compatible. Number one was their intense *sexual* connection. As he said the word sexual, he brought his hands together, miming a spark exploding.

Olly started coughing and gave Ajax a *tone it down* look.

Cali turned glittering blue eyes upon us, swivelling in her chair. 'I can take it from here, my loves. I'm not used to having my interviews managed.' She glanced back at Ajax and Esme. 'That's fine with you, yes?' Her tone was non-negotiable.

'Sure.' Ajax looked relaxed. Esme sucked an olive off a cocktail stick, her smudged, kohl-rimmed eyes wide and innocent. I opened my mouth to protest but thought better of it, at the precise moment Olly's elbow nudged mine.

'Have a great time!' I said, and we glided out of the room as though we were on wheels.

'Pub?' Olly said to me as the slow-close door finally shut behind us, but I noticed he couldn't seem to look at me.

'Bad idea,' I said, thinking there was no way I would ever combine his presence with alcohol again.

'Sure,' he said flatly. 'So come upstairs to my so-called office and at least have a coffee.' His mouth tightened, his tone was imperious. 'There are other people around, we won't be alone.'

'Fine,' I said, my voice sounding ridiculously cold, my body as stiff as a board.

Olly was as good as his word. His assistant Carl was busy creating a collage of positive slogans on one side of the office floor, and although he was at a distance, his presence defused things. A small table had been set up with drinks and snacks for the Resilience Needs employees, and I watched as Olly poured me a coffee and – straight-faced – offered me a banana, before waving me towards his desk.

'Clearly this interview is going to be a car crash, with Ajax and the sex talk, so maybe we can brainstorm a recovery plan,' I said, sounding falsely perky.

'I've got to recover from seeing it first,' he said, making Ajax's 'spark' gesture. 'So maybe tomorrow. Perhaps a night of sleep can cleanse my mind.' He looked at me. 'He wasn't like this before they got together, you know.'

'Are you blaming Esme for him being cringe?'

'Not Esme, per se. It's safe to say the whole situation is making *everyone* a little crazy.'

'Agreed.' I felt a blush rising in my face. An actual, real-life blush, which in my previous life I had been entirely immune to, and yet which now happened regularly, always in Olly's presence.

'Lizzy?'

'Yes?'

'About what happened between us.'

I glanced up to see that Carl was a safe distance from us. 'It's absolutely fine,' I said sharply.

He swallowed, I saw a muscle in his jaw flex. 'I just wanted to check everything is okay.' Our eyes met, and there it was, the thing I hoped had been caused by the whisky: some kind of spark, some kind of connection, which – I was pretty sure – I was imagining into life. An echo of that heady, crackling way we'd looked at each other just before we'd kissed. He wasn't smiling now, but even so he had the kind of dark brown eyes you could look at, and look at, and look at. He was too handsome for his own good. I dragged my gaze into the middle distance.

'As I said, everything's fine,' I managed. 'And as we agreed, it's best if we never speak of it ever again.' I tried for a smile.

'Great,' he said, seeming insultingly relieved. 'I'll bury it five fathoms deep.'

'Me too.'

'Great.'

'Great. Also, your team must be thrilled, you allowing them to have pizza.'

'Oh, that. Yes. Well, a gentleman keeps his word.'

'Ha!' I segued into an awkward laugh. 'Can you imagine how ridiculous it would have been if we actually got together? As well as a nightmare, professionally.'

He folded his arms, looked down. 'Sure, yeah.'

'I mean, also, my life is so complicated, you wouldn't believe it.'

He tilted his head, frowning. 'You're not – in a ... situationship?'

'No! God, no!' I caught the hesitation in his expression. 'I have a father.'

'Aye, most people do ...'

I held up a finger. 'And a brother, Alex. Who has severe autism.' I paused, saw he was listening intently. 'He has other health complications, too. But he's doing well at the moment. My mum died thirteen years ago.'

His expression softened. 'I'm sorry.'

'It's okay. But what I'm trying to say is, I have to look after them both – not physically, but you know, as the responsible adult.'

'I think I understand,' he said softly. But of course, he didn't. He had no idea.

I looked down at my hands. Somehow this felt real, too real. Talking to my polite, guarded colleague about Dad.

'You've finished your coffee,' he said, noticing my discomfort. 'Let me get you another one.'

I was grateful to him for giving me a moment of space. As he walked away, Olly's phone lit up on the table, white letters on a black background.

ISOBEL (TINDER)

I released a lungful of breath. Another babe for the babe magnet. How did he have the energy to be on Tinder?

He returned to the desk and put a coffee down in front of me, along with a protein bar. 'Dinner,' he said. 'Don't say I never get you anything.'

'Thanks.' I straightened my shoulders, smiled, and nodded towards the vibrating phone. 'Someone wants you,' I said, trying to insert some arch cheeriness into my tone and (yay me!) succeeding.

His eyes flicked to the screen. 'Right,' he said.

ISOBEL (TINDER) rang off, then immediately rang again, the phone purring on the pale wood of the desk. Olly stayed on his feet.

'She's a persistent lady,' I said, taking a sip of my drink. 'Mmm, great coffee, thanks, mate.' Okay, so the 'mate' sounded super awkward, but it did the job of persuading him our conversation was over; I saw all softness fade from his face and he snatched the phone up.

'Excuse me.' Turning away, he said 'hello', and walked towards the stairway.

I watched him walk away, noting his super-confident glide, the fist bump he gave Carl as he passed him. And he claimed he was a geek who previously had no appeal to women? Come on, the man was born a gym bro, surely. So I'd been sensible to shut down our connection. Really sensible. Almost painfully so. There wasn't actually a non-fraternisation clause in my contract (I definitely hadn't checked this the night before) but all in all, us being together would be a really bad idea. The kind of thing that could explode and leave shrapnel embedded in my career for years to come.

I opened the protein bar, which looked reassuringly like chocolate. The first mouthful was fine, the second not so good, the third like a mouthful of soil. I closed the packet and unobtrusively posted it into the bin.

'Hi.' Blank-faced, Olly had returned, and sat down.

'Hi!' I was trying too hard to be relaxed.

'You've got a bit of . . .' He gestured to my face.

'What?' I put my hands to my face.

He leaned forward and brushed his thumb against the corner of my mouth. It was an innocuous enough gesture, but the brush sparked a shiver which moved through me and seemingly into him; for a moment we stared at each other, still, breathless.

He pushed his chair back, hard. 'Look, it's been a long day for both of us. Let's go.'

'Sure.' I stood up, brushed myself down. Was he going to meet a date now? I wanted to ask him so much. Of course he was . . . I needed to seal this thing off. I held out a hand in a weirdly formal way. 'Shall we start again? Friends? As in, work friends. Not proper friends.'

He half-smiled, half-frowned. 'Sure,' he said, and shook my hand. 'Let's start again. Hi, I'm Olly, I'm thirty-four and I'm from Edinburgh, now Finchley. I live alone, I work too hard, and I like good whisky.'

'Cheeky.' I rolled my eyes at the twinkle in his, but couldn't help smiling. 'Hi, I'm Lizzy. I live in Oval, with a psychopathic cat called Pebble, who I inherited from a neighbour. You could say my life is work-centric. Pleased to meet you.'

He still had hold of my hand.

'Agree to reset?' I said, while my brain screamed *his eyes are so amazing.*

He hesitated, gave a little sigh. 'Agree to reset.'

We shook briskly, then let go.

CHAPTER SIXTEEN

My evening ended, as many evenings did, with a call from Esme. As I walked towards the tube, having parted awkwardly from Olly in the lobby, she called me to give an impressionistic account of the interview. By the end of our conversation, I had no idea whether Cali George was going to be my best professional friend ever or whether she'd done a number on us. It sounded as though both Ajax and Esme had been irritatingly open with her.

'It's just . . .' Esme was talking, talking, not missing a beat. 'I think he got more words out there than me. And I keep trying to impress him, which is weird, no? I'm feeling a bit needy.'

I know the feeling, I thought, trying to recover my own equilibrium. But another, more snarky part of my brain thought: *no shit, Sherlock*. It had taken Esme's therapist years to iron out some of that edge in her, the sense that there was something missing, that she wasn't enough. It wasn't Ajax's fault that it was creeping back – I'd heard her say similar things in the past – and hearing them again raised a familiar dread in me, a sense that we were heading into troubled times for her and for EKArts.

After I'd tried to reassure her, I hung up and messaged Chiara, Esme's art dealer. She sold Esme's work internationally and had emailed me about the slowdown in Esme's content over the last few days. Esme would normally be creating shorts of artwork for YouTube and TikTok, but her love affair had put a halt to that. It was starting to rain, the dark London streets reflecting car and streetlamp lights from their wet surfaces. I walked with the phone to my ear, pulling up the collar of my wool coat. When she answered, I took shelter under a shop awning.

'Are you working out of hours now?' I asked her.

'Always on call,' she said. 'Not all superheroes wear capes.'

'I thought work-life balance was your thing.'

'Anything for you, though.' She paused. 'I saw a snippet of the press conference on TV. That was quite a spectacle, girl. Good news, though: we had an uptick in enquiries about Esme's work the day after it aired. So no need to worry yet about her socials slowdown.'

I gave a 'hah'. 'Great. Have you spoken to Esme about it? This whole situation is having a major impact on her. I'm worried that if things go wrong, it will affect the business. I keep trying to find the right words to speak to her about it.'

'Lizzy.'

I stopped at the note of firmness in her voice.

'Yes?'

'You can't protect her from making mistakes in her personal life.'

She'd slipped out of her jovial tone into full seriousness, her change in tone alarming.

'I know you steer the ship for Esme – Lord knows what she'd have done without you. But there is such a thing as caring too much, especially where work is involved. If EKArts goes to hell because she's fallen for the most good-looking man on the internet, that's her lookout, and it's her business.'

'No, it's not, not really,' I said. 'You've seen the effort it's taken for me to get the company on track. What if she jeopardises it? I'm just grateful the charity is separate and safe.' I thought of Esme's slightly stunned look over the past few days. 'I'm worried about her.'

'And I'm worried about you,' she said. 'It's almost nine at night and you're still focused on work. How are things?'

'I'm fine!' I insisted. 'Have I not sent you enough memes recently?' Memes were mainly what our relationship consisted of. The last one I'd sent was of a dog lying in a hammock questioning the meaning of life. I'd read somewhere that sending memes to people was the equivalent of a penguin giving a pebble to someone the penguin loved, so the process of sending memes had become known as 'pebbling'. So cute. I should definitely stick to pebbling and not conversations In Real Life. I should also tell Pebble she needed to do the cat equivalent of pebbling and start giving me bite-size pieces of affection.

'How's your brother and your dad?' Chiara said.

'They're fine. I'm fine.'

'Good. Now, Lizzy. If Esme wants to fuck up, you have to let her. You're not her mother, her sister, or even her friend. I understand why you are protective, but now you just need to let her do her thing. And if I'm honest . . .'

'Please, do be honest,' I quipped.

She paused. 'I'd say cut your losses now. You're an intelligent woman and maybe you need to be doing interesting work rather than managing someone else's personal drama.' There was a brief silence. 'I deal with a lot of artists, Lizzy. They're dramatic people. The truth is, some people just live the same story – again and again, wearing out everyone around them. Do *not* tell Esme I said this to you. She'd have my guts for garters.'

A taxi ripped through a flooded gutter, and I pressed myself against the shop front to avoid being drenched. 'Are you telling me I should leave my job?' I said.

'I don't tell people to do things,' she said.

'No,' I said. 'You're just a world class persuader.'

She laughed. 'Only when it comes to getting them to spend money.'

'I'll take it under advisement,' I said. 'Thanks for the free therapy.'

'Who said it was free? I'll email my invoice, headed consulting fees,' she said, the smile re-entering her voice. 'But just think about it.' Her tone was firm, serene.

As I hung up, the rain started to pour harder, and I waited beneath the shop awning for a moment's grace to sprint into the tube station. Chiara's words repeated themselves in my mind like a song lyric stuck on repeat, sending my thoughts into uncertain places. I'd always respected her straight talking, her clarity. And yet ... the idea of leaving EK Arts. My resignation emails, drafted but never sent, acted as a pressure valve of sorts. And I'd had plenty of professional offers. But something was stopping me from doing it. The money? Or Esme? Or the sense that somehow, I had to stay there or everything would go wrong for the business?

I shook off the thoughts running through my head as the rainfall softened and stopped, then dashed across the waterlogged pavement and down into the humidity of the tube.

CHAPTER SEVENTEEN

'What I don't understand,' I said, bleary-eyed, 'is why you keep trying to set me up with a man from Finance.'

It was 4am, otherwise known as 2pm in Sara's part of the world. Clear-eyed and stunning, my friend was sitting casually by the garden doors of her home in Queensland, and the backdrop looked so lush and tropical it was like one of those fantasy made-up backdrops that everyone experimented with in the early days of Zoom.

4am in London, and I had changed out of corporate-Lizzy clothes, shedding my work persona with relief. I was in my pyjamas and a sweatshirt that said I'm Only Speaking To My Cat Today, last year's Christmas present from my dad. Pebble had not yet appeared, and was probably coughing up a furball in some inaccessible corner of the room, like behind the washing machine or under my bed.

I'd fallen asleep on the sofa when I got home,

sledgehammered by my tussles with thoughts of resignation intercut with visions of kissing Olly. Why was it, the moment you decided you couldn't have something, you really wanted it? Waking early, I'd messaged Sara for our chat at 3.45am. *Don't-mention-Olly*, I thought, as I clicked on the Zoom. *No-need-to-mention-him-at-all.*

Sara's face appeared in front of me, beloved and beaming. We waved and howled hello at each other in our usual fashion.

'So, what's happening?' she said.

'I kissed someone at work,' I blurted out. 'An unsuitable person. In my defence, he has a lovely Scottish accent, so I can't be held accountable.'

'That's not like you.' Across thousands of miles, I could see doubts ticking across her brain. It was Sara who had nursed me through my break-up with Jack, listening to my doubts, my self-questioning as our relationship turned sour and my confidence faltered. 'How unsuitable?'

'Relax. He's a nice man, if a slightly annoying one.'

I gave her the goss. She didn't like the sound of him, but that might have been my fault. Making out he was arrogant but missing out funny, mentioning he was ripped but not that he was steaming hot in more idiosyncratic ways. I was unfair, because I wanted to reassure myself I'd made the right decision; convincing her was part of convincing myself that my commitment to work wasn't cheating me out of the best kisses of my life. And, unlike me, Sara was a clear-cut person; she dealt with absolutes, not nuance. It was something I had always enjoyed about our friendship: the glorious certainty she had when she said things as opposed to my let's-look-at-every-angle approach.

'It was a great kiss,' I said to her. 'But, you know, unsuitable.'

'Good practice though, for when the right one comes along,' she said, sipping a spinach smoothie I immediately segued into taking the piss out of. We moved on to other topics, hoovering up the everyday details of each other's lives. After a few minutes, she looked serious again.

'Are you absolutely sure you're okay about this bloke? After Jack ...'

'I'm fine, don't worry. We've agreed to reset. I'm only telling you because it's the juiciest news I have. Stop press: two colleagues get drunk and kiss inappropriately. And stop frowning,' I said. 'You'll ruin the Botox.' Sara had told me she had just come back from the 'aesthetic pharmacist' and her face was box fresh. She gave me her middle finger.

'Can we just consider, for a moment, any men in your Finance department?' she said.

I questioned her overly enthusiastic emphasis on men from Finance.

'I like them, for you,' she said. 'They have to be relatively honest. Clever. Dependable. Sensible. Excellent qualities in a partner. Also, most are minted.'

'You know that *men from Finance* don't necessarily *come with finance*?' I tilted my head at her.

'Your Finance Director will be on six figures,' she said, raising an eyebrow. 'What's he like? First of all, is he a he?'

'Yes,' I said. 'Although his opposite number is a woman.'

'Picture Finance guy.'

I did. Lovely Jacob. Smooth-skinned, uptight, immaculately styled and living happily with his husband in Kensington.

'He wouldn't be interested in me,' I said.

Sara was momentarily distracted by her husband, who walked past the camera, topless, drinking a sports drink.

'Dex!' I shouted. 'Put some bloody clothes on!'

He waved and blew a kiss.

'He's eating me out of house and home,' said Sara. 'Honey? How many eggs was it this morning? The full dozen?'

'Nine,' he said.

'Impressive,' I said, wincing.

'And how is work?' Sara switched her attention back to me. 'As the main achiever in our friendship group, please tell me tales of your kickass life. Not just about your hot colleague.'

'I guess I'm just . . . kicking ass,' I said. Then, after a pause. 'Sara?'

'Yes, love?'

'Sometimes, when I'm having a hard day, I write a resignation email. I always delete it. Is that . . . normal?'

Her face told me nothing. 'How often are you doing it?'

'Once a week.'

'Bloody hell. Maybe start looking for another job, then. Didn't you say last time people keep trying to headhunt you?'

I nodded. 'Yes – but. Thinking of leaving versus actually doing it. When I try to imagine the future, I run into a brick wall. It doesn't feel possible.'

'Love.' Over the connection, I could hear her voice softening. 'Of course it's possible. You're anything-is-possible Lizzy.'

I looked at her beloved face. Wondered how I didn't have the faith she had. I'd been more confident in the past, hadn't I?

'Lizzy? Are you okay?'

'Yes, of course! I should probably go to sleep for a bit,' I said. 'Now, go and eat some protein, or put some bee-flavoured serum on your face, or whatever it is you healthy people do.'

'When are you coming to see us?' she said. 'You look as though you need some sunshine.'

'My pallor is intentional. I don't know, sorry. Things are pretty intense here.'

'Don't let them get too intense,' she said, blowing kisses as we waved each other goodbye.

I shut my laptop and padded across the room, lukewarm cup of tea in hand. Pebble had emerged from the shadows and was lying in the middle of my bed, watching me with her hunter eyes. I got out my clothes for the approaching day: my uniform. Black jeans, blouse, designer blazer. Other variations on that theme hung in my wardrobe. Pristine shoes, some trainers, some high heels. I selected a pair of large, geometric green earrings and a chic glass necklace. Every day I did enough to keep the show on the road, to give an impression that I was high-gloss, impermeable, ready to go into battle – just like Olly, in my own way. Mercifully, no one ever saw my place. It was shabby, borderline chaotic in a way that my work life and appearance never was. The idea of a new boyfriend seeing it (not Olly, definitely not Olly) made me want to curl up with shame.

I'd kept Jack away from my flat until the disastrous day when he'd found his way here. We'd always met at his place; we'd gone on minibreaks. He'd only ever seen capable, smooth, polished Lizzy: neatly packed luggage, blow-dried hair, lip gloss and perfume. As we'd got closer, he'd started identifying the chinks in my armour: asking searching questions, testing my responses, making covert criticisms which gradually sharpened over time into real malice. Luckily, although our relationship had been intense at the beginning, some intuition had stopped me from fully letting him into my life. Sex was okay, but my flat, my family? That was real intimacy. The relationship had limped on, me feeling stuck but disorientated by the way he switched between adoring me and disliking me. When he'd turned up at the flat, we had the argument which was the beginning of the end. Our tickets had already been booked for a minibreak, so we went, but it was on that break that we eventually called it quits, and I emerged from what felt like cold fog into warm sunshine again.

I flipped open my laptop again and checked my calendar. My previous schedule had been cancelled, meetings put on hold, projects stalled. All I could see were finance discussions (without the romantic connotations Sara had hoped for), Chroma strategy meetings, an entire half day allocated to beginning 'target audience' discussions for the new platform, and the frustrating need to repackage old content because Esme had slowed down producing anything new. With their love and enthusiasm, Esme and Ajax had relentlessly cleared the decks of any meaningful work.

There was nothing I couldn't dial into. I decided to work from home.

CHAPTER EIGHTEEN

'I'm so grateful, Liz. I don't know what I'd do without you.'

'No problem!' I cried, hoping my voice sounded more cheery than fraught, or at least fifty-fifty. I was on my knees in the beige-coloured bathroom belonging to Bill, my neighbour. He lived directly above me, having taken over Marge's old flat (Marge being Pebble's previous 'mother'). I'd corrected his use of the name 'Liz' three times before just accepting he was never going to call me anything else. He was a genteel, delicately mannered man of eighty-two, whose late partner had taken the lead in what he referred to as 'maintenance issues'. His flat leaked water like a sieve.

He'd called me in a quavery voice that morning to let me know that the 'er, lavatory' was leaking and I was now attempting to stem the (mercifully slow) seep of water, which I was relieved to see was clean, with a mop, while speed dialling our usual plumber who was entered in my phone as 'Sweary Jim'.

'Hello?' Jim said, in a deceptively cheery voice.

I attempted to explain the problem while Bill flapped his hands in the air by way of assistance.

'All right – *fuck!* – sorry about that, just dealing with a faulty ballcock – you *motherfucker* – I'll be there in about half an hour,' he said.

I thanked him and rang off, calculating what that meant in Sweary Jim language. 'He'll be here in an hour or two,' I told Bill. I piled another loose mop pad on top of the small pool. 'Just keep wringing these out, it will be fine.'

'Thank you so much, Liz,' he said. 'Is there any way you could just stay here until he arrives?'

Back downstairs, quite a while later, I had a missed Teams call from Sasha. I explained I'd been helping a neighbour with a leaky toilet, and she said 'Why?' in a voice that indicated I had lost my mind.

'Let's call it my good deed for the day,' I said.

'Okaaay. Anyway, the photos are through,' she said.

It was the photo shoot for the Cali George interview, and the moment I opened the pictures I couldn't suppress a groan. Ajax and Esme were soft focus, bathed in gold light, both dressed in white. They were draped over each other like footballer and WAG in the early 2000s. The good thing was, it could now be read as ironic and retro rather than braggy. As I looked at them, I received an email from Olly.

Dear Lizzy,
What do you think of the images?
Best, Olly.

So, it might have been me who had introduced a cooler tone to our frequent email exchanges, but it still looked odd to me.

Dear Olly,
A bit rich for my taste, but I am assuming the subjects are happy, in which case, I am.
Best wishes, Lizzy.

That was the current state of affairs with me and Olly. Nicely distant, nicely professional. Deeply unsatisfying.

As I started replying to my other emails, I heard the reassuring sound of Sweary Jim screaming obscenities at Bill's toilet cistern.

Returning to work after two days at home, I felt surprisingly relaxed. Bill's toilet was no longer leaking, the Cali George interview was home and dry (even if we awaited publication), and I'd received a blue jar full of expensive, sweetly scented bath salts which were meant to 'rebalance' me, overnighted care of an online order by Sara. I'd had long, hot baths on each evening working from home, and lying totally still, emptying my mind, had done wonders for my soul and my sleep. And, most importantly, I had started to restore some of my own crumbling facade: I'd even managed to give myself a pedicure and a manicure and deep condition my curly (by which I mean frizzy) hair.

The space from being at work meant I could breathe a little. When I left the flat, my brain had even slowed enough for me to be a tiny bit in the moment. I noticed the glittering pavements spangled in frost, and the sight of a very perky robin who I saw as I walked across the churchyard on the way to the tube.

Although my commute had slightly put paid to my freshness (there's nothing quite like sitting in a packed tube carriage in a winter coat), I arrived at The Hexagon feeling quite chilled, all things considered, head held high, immaculate, cheerful smile on my face. That was, until I got to my desk, and stood, gazing at the many heart-shaped, foil-wrapped chocolates scattered across it, remembering the roses, feeling my heart sink.

'Surprise!'

Sasha had temporarily marred her high-gloss, film star look by donning a pair of antennae on a headband, topped with hearts.

'Not bloody Jack Dillane again,' I said, carefully hanging up my (Nicole Farhi, care of Oxfam) coat. 'First roses, now chocolates.'

'What do you mean?' She stood opposite me, looking bewildered, and I realised she hadn't been in the office to witness Olly hurling Jack's bouquet into a bin.

'Just a ridiculous ex of mine.' I sipped my coffee. 'Sent me a shedload of roses not long ago, out of the blue.'

'I know who Jack Dillane is,' she said. 'But that's ancient history, isn't it? Why would he send you flowers? These chocolates aren't from him, by the way.'

I frowned. Had I really told Sasha about my relationship with Jack? Then it clicked. When I'd first come to EKArts we'd been at the tail end of our relationship, and he was always big on grand gestures, so she'd likely taken delivery of an elaborate bouquet or a bottle of champagne at some point.

'No reason,' I said. 'Where did the chocolates come from?'

'We all got them. They're from Ajax and Esme.'

I raked them into my desk drawer, leaving one, which I picked up, peeling off its red foil. Not exactly sustainable. B Corp status was feeling further away every minute. The heart-shaped chocolate had an A&E imprinted on it in white chocolate. I bit into it. It was top quality shizzle: chocolate truffle infused with champagne, probably ordered from a Bond Street chocolatier. As it melted on my tongue, I thought sadly of Jacob's fury. 'I need to speak to Esme about all of this unnecessary expenditure,' I said, 'before she bankrupts the company.'

'And there's a note,' said Sasha, looking fretful. 'They've arranged a team-building event. Fun, after work.'

'Compulsory fun,' I said. 'My least favourite type.' I smiled at her, but she just looked preoccupied. 'You okay?'

'Yes.' She did not look okay.

'Are you going this evening?'

'Might do,' she said, 'for five minutes. But I have plans.'

This was unexpected; she was usually at the head of any conga line. I watched her traipse back to her desk as I ate another chocolate, examining the stiff piece of card upon which the chocolates had been scattered.

Ajax & Esme, Esme & Ajax
invite you to

The Silent Disco

5pm in the covered courtyard
Relax, kick back, bond.
#lovealwayswins

I typed a message to Olly.

> **LIZZY:** Did you know about the Silent Disco? #lovealwayswins #bleurgh

It blue ticked immediately.

> Olly is typing
>
> … typing
>
> … typing
>
> **OLLY:** No.

For a moment I wondered whether he might pop down from the upper floor, so we could joke about it. A little light mockery to ease the grey mood I'd started the day with. But, as hinted by his monosyllabic reply, it was to be an Olly-free day in my office. Which was great, right? Good. Not dull at all.

CHAPTER NINETEEN

I had feared the Silent Disco would be another high-budget fiasco and that Ajax and Esme had helicoptered someone like Calvin Harris in, to bang out their favourite hits in funky celebration of their endless love. Imagine my delight, then, when I turned up in the covered courtyard and caught a school disco vibe. Hallelujah, it was distinctly lacklustre. Ajax and Esme had apparently ditched it last minute in favour of a spontaneous minibreak in the Cotswolds, and (dear, beloved, sensible) Finance had put the brakes on spending.

A gnomic member of Ajax's team was handing out the wireless headphones. 'One charge lasts ten hours,' he told me flatly.

'Thanks,' I said, popping them round my neck and thinking *definitely won't be here for ten hours.*

Hospitality had been wheeled out to provide basic catering, but I was glad to see all the drinks were non-alcoholic, if garishly coloured, and the snacks were budget: cheese straws, jellybeans and some bizarrely flavoured tortilla chips which were definitely going to taste like battery acid. I sighed contentedly.

Jacob strode in, hands in pockets, scanned the room and the arrangements, nodded at me in satisfaction and departed. I read his expression: just for once, the budget had not been blown, and he was off home to relax for the first time in a while.

In the time I'd taken to look around, younger members of the team had trickled in, coltish and bright-eyed. I watched them whooping, laughing, and beginning to dance, most of them completely unselfconscious. Within five minutes, half were drinking mocktails and throwing chocolate hearts at each other, the other half were doing some hardcore dancing. I had a feeling this party might get messy later, but I found myself smiling. At least someone was having fun with the A&E lovefest.

Cautiously, I put the headphones to one ear. They were playing Dua Lipa, *Don't Start Now*. God, I loved this song.

Someone tapped me on the shoulder and I whirled round.

It was Olly. Dressed in his navy suit, not a hair out of place, but his tie off, a slight concession to informality. As I spun around, his hands flashed to my waist for a moment as though to steady me. Then, disconcertingly, he took a step back, looking at me as though I was an unexploded bomb.

'Can I have a word?' he said. He was not smiling.

I put my headphones back round my neck and followed him to a quiet spot behind a monster potted palm. 'It's not the interview, is it?' I said. 'Have you seen advance copy? Because if Cali's shafted us—'

'It's not that.' His voice was low, level, his eyes unblinking. There was something else: his voice caught on the words, a hesitation, barely perceptible, but at odds with the confident image he usually portrayed.

He held his phone out towards me, waited for me to read it.

MODERN ART ROTTEN TO THE CORE, SAYS AJAX BANKS.

Beneath it was a quote from Ajax on the subject. The gist of the article was that under Ajax's influence, Esme would be taking EKArts in a new direction. I gasped. At the bottom was a quote from Esme herself, saying that Ajax was 'helping me look at things with new eyes.'

Said the woman who was an international artist; whose charity, business and whole life was based on the power of art.

Shock and anger blazed through me; I looked up at Olly.

'Yep, it's a zinger,' he said. 'If it makes you feel any better, Ajax said that thing a while ago on the podcast. It's been blown out of all proportion. He had a celeb guest in' – he named a hot stuff actor – 'and they were joking about, showboating.' He named the art exhibition they'd been discussing. 'There was rotten fruit in the exhibition, they started making silly remarks.'

'The fruit was a comment on the impermanence of human life,' I said.

He cleared his throat. 'Whatever you say.'

I shook my head. 'I can't believe Esme gave a quote on this. Someone must have called her directly and caught her on the hop. We'll need to draft a response, quickly. I'm amazed I haven't had people on the phone already.'

'It was published two minutes ago.'

'Right,' I said, clicking into efficiency mode. I hit 'Call' against Esme's name in my phone. She did not pick up. I looked back at Olly. 'Do you want to pop up to my office with me? Get it sorted?'

He took a step back, looking anywhere but at my face. 'If you don't mind making a start, then sharing the document. I'd prefer to do things remotely, if possible,' he said. 'The last couple of days have worked well, yes? We can figure things out by email and hop on a call if needed.' His eyes flicked back to my face.

'Of course,' I said, handing his phone back. 'Is anything wrong?'

He frowned. 'No. Everything is fine. It's just ...' He glanced in the direction of the dance floor, where hands had been raised, trance-style. Looked down at his feet. 'I think we should minimise the time we spend in a room together, don't you? As you said, EKArts and Resilience Needs aren't a natural fit. As this latest debacle proves.'

His words, and the cold tone in which he said them, stole the breath from my lungs. 'Right,' I said. 'I guess the work friendship's off, then? No problem.'

I turned on my heel and walked away, removing the headphones in one smooth movement and putting them back on the table from where they'd been distributed, before heading for the staircase. As I crossed the room, I was aware that Olly was following me, and picked up the pace, but he caught up with me as I reached the stairs.

'Lizzy.'

'What?' I put venom into the way I said it. Not wanting to admit how hurt I was. If he wanted cold and remote, he was going to get it.

'Will you let me explain?' he said, softly, his expression grim.

I gave my best fake smile. 'No need. Everything's crystal clear.' I turned and climbed the steps two at a time, with a toss of the head that said, *take that, gym bro.*

'*Wait*,' he said. But I ignored him. He was so close behind that when I reached the top of the stairs I broke into a run, sprinted across the landing, flew through the door and across the empty open-plan office to my own, where I piled my full weight behind the slow close door, then locked it.

Olly arrived at the door just as I locked it and batted his hands against the glass. 'Lizzy!' I could barely hear him, and made a heroic attempt to ignore him, starting to shut down my computer as he pressed his hands against the door.

When he spoke again, his voice was deeper, louder. 'Don't make me force this door open. You know I could do it.'

I strode across the room and stood facing him through the door. 'Are you threatening me?' I bellowed.

Something changed in his face. He stepped away. 'Of course not.'

Play fair, Lizzy, my inner voice chimed in, inconveniently, combining with the kicked puppy expression on his face to defuse the sharp edge of my anger. Huffing, I unlocked the door and turned my back to him as he came in.

'Hey.' He stood on the opposite side of the desk as I kicked off my heels and put my trainers on.

'Well,' I said tightly, '*this* isn't very remote.'

'Do you have a problem with me keeping my distance?' he said. I glanced at his face; expressionless, like mine, apart from his eyes. 'You seem to.'

'I thought we reset everything.' I double-tied my left trainer and tried not to look at him. Because he looked smoking hot and I very much needed him not to.

'We did,' he said. His dark eyes were blazing and searching my face in a way that sent a little flutter from my stomach up my ribcage and into my chest.

Breathe, Lizzy. I stood up, hands on hips. 'So, if we reset, there's no need to go full Greta Garbo on me,' I chimed, finally managing to hold his gaze. 'I think I can just about keep my hands off you, okay?'

I made to move past him, but something stopped me. The absolute tension between us, like its own separate force in the room, drew me up short. I remembered the taste of his lips, the way he had pulled me towards him. I had been merry then, and I wasn't now, but I certainly wasn't clear-headed either; I was possessed with a heightened feeling that was completely beyond my control. My eyes focused on his collarbone; his shirt was unbuttoned at the top and that tiny patch of skin became my sudden obsession. My brain-slash-hormones were rolling around like a monkey in a sack. We stared at each other, both of us breathing hard, the silence fizzing until he finally broke my gaze and turned away. When he turned back, his voice was clear, businesslike, as though he was at a meeting.

'You're the one who's gone Greta Garbo, Lizzy.'

'I—' I struggled to put words together. 'I don't understand.'

'You disappear from the office and start sending robotic messages. "Best wishes"? Shit.' He shook his head. I sensed hesitation, which was so rare in him. 'Must, must swear less. Anyway. I was trying to keep things uncomplicated.'

'Uncomplicated is good,' I said softly.

'Unless the complication involves Jack Dillane, I guess?' he bit back.

'Olly!' I stepped back, and, deflated, sat down in my chair.

'Sorry.' He flattened his hands, a gesture that said *I surrender*. Shook his head again, in exasperation. 'That was not okay. I apologise.'

'Damn right. And it was a great example of why work relationships aren't *workable*.' I stared miserably at my desk. Feeling right didn't mean feeling good. 'Apology accepted, by the way.'

'Thank you. Ping me the document link once you've started it,' he said.

I nodded to indicate I would, and just like that, the atmosphere lost its charge, its high-definition colour.

He flashed a smile; that hard, shiny, PR smile. It was like the first day I'd met him, and I felt despair uncurl itself in the depths of my stomach. We had dismantled our defences, but he was building them high again – I needed to do the same.

'So glad we survived our first proper fight,' I said, in a tone that sounded airy but was also one hundred percent forced.

He laughed; not his wonderful, rich laugh, just an exasperated *ha*. 'See you later,' he said, his hand brushing my office door as he walked away and left the floor.

Buzzed, and unsettled, I put my computer back on and started the statement to defuse the latest A&E situation. Typing, typing, typing; forcing all of my pent-up energy into action, striking the keys hard. Left Esme a voice note explaining. Forwarded the link to her and to Olly. Then I jumped as my phone buzzed.

> **DAD:** Thanks for dealing with the benefits query, Lizzy. Alex has had a good week so far.

It was nice that he thought it was dealt with, but I'd just started the process; requesting a time to speak to the person who'd been allocated as Alex's so-called 'work coach' from the job centre. Still, I highlighted Dad's message, gave it an (old school) thumbs up, put on a coat of lipstick and shut the computer down. It had been one of my mum's cardinal rules: always put your lippy on, even if you're just nipping to the shops. You never know who you might see, friend or enemy, either way you could meet them with your defences intact and your armour on. Or maybe I'd added that last bit myself.

Mum's lipstick colour: a soft, barely there rose pink. Mine: a hard, bold, sock-it-to-them red.

As I passed over the bridge on my way out, I glimpsed Olly on the dancefloor with his team below.

Worst news ever: he could really move, and the hummingbird was fluttering in my ribcage again.

Second worst news ever: Amber had temporarily shed her work persona and was bumping and grinding next to him. I felt a whiplash of jealousy so cutting that I had to do a minute of deep breathing to calm it, and somehow my eyes found their way back to them. They looked amazing together and I had to stifle – honestly – a bark of anguish that rose in my throat. As if to taunt me, Amber moved closer to him, and with a toss of her perfectly coiffured caramel locks, she executed a near-perfect slutdrop. There was a slight recklessness in her movements which indicated she must have had a hip flask alongside all those mocktails. I saw him smile and applaud her and she shrieked with laughter.

Excellent: he'd found a woman with the upper thigh strength to match his own, and I wanted to literally kick myself. Olly had found himself a *woman from Finance*.

At least I had been sensible, quashing a potentially damaging work love affair. Because sensible was such an enjoyable thing to be.

Home time, Lizzy, I thought, as I stomped angrily off towards the exit. *Your furious cat needs you, you sensible woman.*

CHAPTER TWENTY

The sound of a text alert in the form of windchimes broke the incense-heavy silence.

I ignored the tuts of my fellow yogis as I fell out of an attempt to do a shoulder stand and reached for my phone.

> **ESME:** I'm sooooo nervous about tomorrow. Did you really like the photos?

I typed as unobtrusively as I could.

> **LIZZY:** Photos were gorgeous.

'Please,' the yoga teacher said, a serene smile not quite hiding her irritation. 'I do ask everyone to digitally disconnect during these sessions.' In the background, soft music played, the same three strings on repeat.

'Sorry,' I whispered, putting the phone to silent and lying back down on my mat. 8am on Saturday in a south London community hall, and every time I stretched my arms out, they swept through a scattering of crumbs from a kid's birthday party the day before.

'Connect the core,' intoned the teacher. 'And breathe. One, two, three.'

The joss sticks she had lit were potent. There was smoke at the back of my throat.

'Focus on the word I asked you to choose at the beginning of the session.'

I blinked. What was the word I'd chosen at the beginning of the session? And was it wrong to get stressed about the fact I'd forgotten the word I had promised to remember? On silent, my phone's message light flashed. I gritted my teeth.

'Now, let's all gently gather ourselves into corpse pose,' the teacher said.

The latest Esme/Ajax story about their appreciation for art (or lack of) had been easily dealt with: a few phone calls, a smoothing-over statement. The surprise element of Communications was you never knew when a mountain was actually going to be a molehill, or vice versa.

Freed from any obligation to untangle Esme and Ajax from their most recent faux pas, that afternoon I ignored catching up on work in favour of visiting Dad and Alex. As ever, it felt quite fun catching a non-rush hour train, even if I was dressed in the clothes I usually wore to work. 'Are you going to a funeral?' a man on the train said, recklessly ignoring my Resting Bitch Face. He was drinking lager with his mates and had his shirt off, thus emboldening him.

I smiled blandly, wondering if I should say 'yes, hopefully yours.' But I didn't fancy my chances of coming out unscathed, so I put my sunglasses on and got a book out.

My work phone and personal phone had fallen silent, but I found myself checking them repeatedly, failing to jerk myself out of my hyper in-touch, vigilant work mindset. Luckily, we were soon through the London suburbs and into the countryside proper, hurtling towards the village where Dad and Alex lived: Dad in a block of retirement flats, where he had a better social life than I did, and Alex in a nearby assisted-living facility.

As always, I collected Dad and we walked the short distance down a narrow, tree-lined road, to Alex's, to drink tea in one of the communal areas with Alex and his carer, Jenna. It could be hard to get a response from my brother sometimes, but as we walked in, his eyes met mine, and his smile flashed bright, momentarily, warming my heart like a shaft of sunshine. I sat beside him, put out my hand, and for a moment his fingers brushed my palm.

'Izz,' he said.

'Hi, Alex,' I said.

He was gone then, focusing back on the tablet which was a permanent feature, removing his hand, turning away. He pressed to play a piece of music which he had on repeat, as we arranged the drinks and I produced a pack of jammy dodgers.

Dad, Jenna and I made small talk until Alex indicated that he wanted to get back to his painting, which our appearance had interrupted. He said an approximation of the word 'bye' five times in quick succession.

'Okay, I love you,' I said. He waved jazz hands in my face and exited at speed.

'Thanks again for sorting the benefits, love,' said Dad, as we wandered back to his block, his hand looped in my arm as we negotiated the slippery pavement. 'Did I tell you about the argument Ros had with Pat over the hash browns?'

He enjoyed explaining the minutiae of his retirement complex to me, and I enjoyed seeing him engage with life. Mum's death had frozen him; fastened him shut like a treasure chest whose lock I could never unpick. He'd never recovered from it, despite my every effort. I'd lived with him long after I started working, cooking healthy meals in the evening, trying to interest him in activities and hobbies, trying to entertain him with anecdotes and funny stories about my day. I don't think he wanted any of it.

Mum had been everything to all of us. There wasn't a single problem she didn't have a solution for; often the solution involved having a cup of tea and a biscuit. When I thought of her, it was in the garden or our house, carefully tying her sweet pea plants to canes; making an apple crumble; sitting with Alex and humming to him when he couldn't sleep. She had been so proud of me, but in a hundred different ways I felt I hadn't lived up to her standards. She had an open heart, and her calmness, unlike mine, had been a real, warm, authentic thing, not cold and forced.

I had, eventually, moved out, and Dad had sold the house. Around the time Dad had realised he was running out of money, I'd noticed he'd got quieter. He hadn't shared the problem with me. Then, one afternoon, he'd called me, saying he had chest pains. He hadn't wanted to call an ambulance. As I sat there, waiting for a doctor with him in a crowded Accident and Emergency waiting room, the pains gone for now, he'd murmured to me that he was in a 'spot of bother' with money. That was the day I realised how, silently, he turned his stress inwards. How corrosive his apparent calm was.

The doctor came. As Dad described his symptoms as 'probably nothing' to the puzzled medic ('it's all gone now, maybe I just ate something'), I was gripped with the icy realisation that he was, effectively, defenceless; that I would have to be the hard, strong voice of reason.

'He was in so much pain he could hardly speak,' I'd said to the doctor. My voice firm, implacable. The same voice I would use to sort out his financial affairs, or to deal with the council when they queried Alex's level of care. I could cry later, be emotional later, but not here, and not now.

With my acceptance of that role, Dad's silence had dissolved. He now saw himself as the helpful person who could remind me of what needed to be done, who could flag up worries before they even broke cover. It wasn't always easy. I accepted now that I would never fix his sadness, never mend what was broken. But I could defend him. Do my best to keep him safe. When I visited him, I tried to please him, to soothe him. And every time I heard him describe 'breakfast wars' (apparently it wasn't the done thing to pile eight hash browns on your plate when everyone else wanted one), or smile at something, I felt as though I'd won a kind of victory, however small.

After describing the hot breakfast tussle, he asked me how work was.

'Busy,' I said. 'I have to go to Venice the week after next.'

'Venice?' he said, looking incredulous. 'In winter? It's sinking, isn't it?'

I shrugged. Esme and Ajax were fixated on it as the epitome of romance, even in February, notorious for being extremely floodable. Not that they cared about the potential problems this might throw up. 'Venice is Venice,' Esme had said, when I pointed out the timing. I had repressed the urge to say, 'And stupid is stupid.'

'Pack your wellies,' said Dad.

'And—' I paused. 'Next week, there's an Architectural Open Day at work,' I said. 'Part of East London Architecture Festival? There are tours of the building, it's quite a structure. Would you like to come, Dad? I could see if it could be arranged for Alex to come, too?'

Mum wouldn't have hesitated. And I wondered – had I been keeping my family at a distance? Had I been wrong to keep my work and my life so separate?

'Oh.' He thought about it, a slightly awkward expression

on his face. 'Don't worry, love. London's a bit fast-paced for me. And you know how Alex likes his routine. I don't think he cares too much about seeing the sights, do you?'

'He might like the change,' I said, but I saw the look on his face: pained, worried. 'It's okay, I'm sure you're right. And there's always another time.' I felt a strange cocktail of disappointment and relief.

He nodded. 'I hope the day goes well. Did I tell you Janine has invited me to join the walking football club?'

CHAPTER TWENTY-ONE

I logged on at 7am the following morning and speed-read Cali George's article on Ajax and Esme.

At the end, I released a lungful of breath I hadn't realised I'd been holding. Clicked on Esme's EKArts Instagram profile and saw the numbers had increased. Ordered a bottle of champagne to be sent to Cali. Then Pebble stuck her claws in my arm and I tried to interest her in a fake mouse on a stick.

I left her toying with it and sent a message to Esme.

> **LIZZY:** The article's great. I particularly liked her ref to you as having a lightning quick mind in a pre-Raphaelite body.

> **ESME:** thanks babe. I accept I look fire in the pictures too. Next stop Venice!!!

She added enough heart emojis to sink a gondola.
My phone buzzed.

OLLY: Are you happy with it?

I stared at the words on the screen. I should have been relieved that our messages were now free of banter, slightly stilted and wholly professional. And yet, I felt unsettled; maybe even faintly disappointed.

LIZZY: Yes, happy. You?

OLLY: Fair to moderate.

LIZZY: No chance of rain.

OLLY: There'll be water enough in Venice.

LIZZY: Have you been before?

OLLY: No. You?

LIZZY: Yes.

OLLY: The unsinkable Lizzy Brinks. Are you going to the Architectural Open Day?

The Architectural Open Day had been scheduled a year in advance as part of a local festival. There would be tours for members of the public, with some extra perks for friends and family of staff – a buffet lunch in the covered courtyard. Resilience Needs staff had been invited, at the insistence of Esme who was, worryingly, starting to describe the two companies as 'a family'.

This was a very big red flag for me. The moment a manager started describing their team as a family you knew some toxic shit was about to go down.

> **LIZZY:** Yes, I'm going. Are you?

> **OLLY:** Yes. Got to go now. Have a good Sunday.

I lobbed a string ball at Pebble and she dived on it triumphantly. Outside the window it was a reasonably bright day for February. I could go out for a walk. Do some shopping. Read a book in the bath. Instead, I sat, in itchy indecision, wanting very much to message Olly again. It was like trying to resist dessert when you were really, really hungry.

Things had changed in the last few weeks. Before, I'd been a model of efficiency, even if my serene appearance was skin deep. I'd been even. So why did I now feel so ... empty? So bored? So antsy? Why, even now, was my hand hovering over the phone, threatening to type a sarky quip in an attempt to draw Olly in, seemingly against my own free will?

Pebble had returned to me, bored of her toys. I picked her

up and put her in my lap. She gazed up at me, a low purr emanating from her depths.

'You're very affectionate today,' I said. 'What should I do about Olly?'

She looked at me and I read no Olly-related insights there. Instead, she was definitely saying 'set up my indoor water fountain for further playing'. So I did.

I abandoned the idea of going out, putting a 'luxury' ready meal in the microwave (roast dinner for one), then steamed some broccoli, and settled down to work on one of my inspiration scrapbooks.

The scrapbooks were stuffed full, now: one for the house, one for the garden. By which I mean, of course, my imaginary house and garden. In truth, the garden one had taken over a bit in the last year. If I saw something I liked online, or in the monthly gardening magazine I subscribed to, I cut it out and pasted it in. I also had an online vision board on the go. I dreamed, really dreamed, of having an outside space one day: even if it was a tiny courtyard. I imagined somewhere where I could grow flowers for the house and herbs for the kitchen. It would be a kind of paradise, after years of living in a studio which mainly smelt of plug-in air freshener (currently on the go: Sea Minerals). I noted how I could make a herb shelf using a discarded pallet, or create my own bee hotel. By now I had enough scraps of inspiration to furnish a garden the size of a National Trust property.

Meanwhile, on my city windowsill, a pot of basil wilted and an African violet screamed *please God, not more fumes*.

The magazine also came with a free pack of seeds each month, and I popped the seeds into a shoebox under my bed. Each January I would discard the ones that had passed their 'plant by' date, bidding farewell to California poppies, Nigella, and Foxgloves. I'd always look through the ones left behind: the ones which I might plant, if something amazing happened. Like if that premium bond my godmother had bought me came up trumps, or my occasional lottery ticket purchase delivered the goods.

I busied myself cutting out an image of a border peopled with Baby's Breath and Alliums while Pebble splashed cheerfully in her water fountain. The microwave pinged, and I dished out the food and settled down on the sofa. When my phone buzzed, I paused, a forkful of broccoli mid-air. It was Elena, another friend who I'd been close to in our twenties, and who was now happily coupled up with three kids.

> **ELENA:** It's Sunday and the kids are screaming and Derry has gone to play football and I am cleaning, actually cleaning, can you believe this is my life? Please tell me you are doing something exciting, L. I miss miss miss my single days. Tell me you are drinking champagne.

I put my fork down and approved her message with a heart.

> **LIZZY:** That's absolutely what I'm doing.

ELENA: Thank God, please drink more for me.
Hang on, the chicken is burning.

I carried on eating, messaging app open beside me as I flicked through the magazines. She didn't return to the phone.

I made a cup of coffee then opened a document I was working on, thoughts on how the policies of EKArts and Resilience Needs could interconnect. I had shared it with Olly and, as I started to type, I saw his initials appear on the screen. He was working on it, too.

I sat there, adding a sentence here and there, watching as our initials danced around each other, every small change, every new sentence, heartening me. The document was like an embroidery we were each adding colours to. I found myself wondering what he thought when I added a bullet point; smiled when he mistyped a word and deleted it. Teams was open but we didn't message each other. We just kept working, quietly, in parallel. Until finally, there was nothing to add. I sat there for a minute or two, reading it all through. Saw Olly's initials disappear as he closed the document. Then I closed it, too. My cup of coffee sat cold, on the table beside me. It was the calmest I'd felt all weekend.

CHAPTER TWENTY-TWO

Venice loomed on the horizon. Depending on who you were, it was either looming like Christmas (exciting, fun, most people) or looming like an iceberg (ready to sink everything, me). Around meetings and sending briefings and strategy documents between the two Leadership teams, I started packing for the trip, figuring if I started with a week to go, I wouldn't end up in some kind of frenzy with a need for last-minute panic purchases. I made a list, then another one, and started reading up on Venice, very much focusing on the gelato and the art and not on the fact that 'Venetians are sophisticated, put-together people, and they expect visitors to be sophisticated and stylish, too', a slightly terrifying warning which I came across when trawling the internet for tips. A quickfire Zoom conference with Sara confirmed that my grooming immediately needed to be prioritised. I chose a sultry dark red nail varnish which I applied myself, booked a hair appointment, dug out my most expensive bottle of perfume (which was approved of by Sara with the words *you go, girl*). However, I fell at the final hurdle.

'Do it.' Sara was firm.

'I'll look stupid,' I wailed.

'Winter or no winter, you will have to show some flesh!' she shrieked. 'Go *on*! Dex, tell her!'

Dex's face loomed into view, tanned against the minimalist white surfaces of their beautiful house. 'It's a no-brainer, Liz.'

Sara shoved him out of the way. 'She hates being called Liz. You're not helping.'

I put my head in my hands. When I looked up, Sara was pointing down the camera. 'Do it.'

'Okay, okay,' I said. 'But if I go to the Open Day and people laugh at me, I'm reversing it.'

'If people laugh at you,' she said, 'I'll fly over and help scrub it off. But for God's sake exfoliate before you go.'

I saluted her wearily and googled the number of the nearest tanning salon.

My friends Drew and Charlotte were due to come to the Open Day as my significant others, along with their children, Haley and Blake. We were going to make a day of it, and I'd even arranged for my neighbour, Myra, to feed Pebble, seeing that the automatic food dispenser had died a death.

I'd been looking forward to seeing my friends. Also, I was hoping for some moral support, not least because I'd been working from home and was going to be trialling my new look before we took off to Venice on Monday. I'd taken Sara's advice and booked in for a spray tan, opting for an extremely light honey colour which had transformed me from Victorian invalid to looking vaguely like I might belong in the real world, where people were healthy and did outdoor sports or drank wine on Venetian terraces. It was, though, a departure from my usual deathly pale look, which I liked to think of as 'classical' rather than 'anaemic'. I attempted to stylishly muss up my newly highlighted hair (couldn't be seen to be trying too hard) and put on indigo jeans and a cream cashmere jumper, a last-minute purchase which – shocker – was not second-hand.

Otherwise, it was business as usual. Everything totally fine. I was certainly not nervous about seeing Olly. Not at all. Not even a tiny bit.

I was just about to leave when my phone rang.

'Lizzy? It's Drew. So sorry. Haley has got some kind of lurgy and now Blake is saying he's got a headache. We were just about to set off.'

I felt a lurch in my stomach. Going in alone. It was fine. Totally fine, I told myself.

'Don't worry,' I said. 'I'll come and see you guys soon.'

'I can still come?' he said.

'Doesn't Char need you to help?' I said, hearing Haley wail in the background.

'Lizzy?' Charlotte came on the line. 'Take him with you. He's no use to me here.'

Drew again. 'Thanks, my sweetest darling. Is that all right, Lizzy?'

I exhaled in relief. 'That would be great, actually.'

I'd decided today was officially a day of treats, and on the way to the tube I picked up a coffee. A latte with a dash of almond syrup, to be exact, a treat I limited myself to once a week (normally on a Sunday morning, but what the hell). I headed for my favourite coffee shop, an independent which stocked an obscenely delicious range of Italian chocolates and biscotti.

I was served by the proprietor's son, a good-looking young man who was always polite and chatty. As he rang up my items, he smiled. 'I like your hair,' he said.

I almost dropped the pack of chocolate truffles I was adding to my order. 'Oh!' I said. 'Thank you.' Out of work, my façade was down, and an icy deflection felt inappropriate. As a result, I did not know what to do.

'You look very beautiful today.'

'Hah!' I exclaimed, suddenly, biting back the sarcastic comeback I would have been tempted to give if I was at work.

He gently pushed my coffee and chocolates towards me, because I'd become unexpectedly dithery all of a sudden, then I bid him a loud and cheerful farewell before leaving, almost tripping up as I opened the door. Sara and Dex really had been right about the tan.

As I walked away, I tried to calculate how long I would have to wait before I could go into that shop again. I'd have to wait for the tan to fade, clearly. Buy a hat, dark sunglasses, possibly a wig.

I met Drew at the tube station nearest to The Hexagon, and despite my self-consciousness, absolutely nothing on his face betrayed the fact that I looked any different from usual Lizzy. But then that was what I had always liked about Drew: his dreamy, up-in-the-clouds approach to life meant he never judged anyone according to their appearance. He was the ultimate creative – he worked for an uber trendy graphic design company – and was prone to passionate enthusiasms. He was also one of the kindest people I'd ever met. Today, post toddler meltdown, he wore a look of relief to be out. His hair was sticking up, he was wearing his usual selection of silver earrings, a pair of green cords and a rainbow striped jumper.

'Wow.' Drew looked at the front of The Hexagon. Its glass and steel frontage stretched up into the pale London sky, the canopy – faceted with hexagonal panes of glass – glinting in the winter sunlight. 'This place is epic, Lizzy.'

'Thanks,' I said. 'I can't take credit for the architecture, but I'm glad you like it.' Seeing it through his eyes reminded me of the optimism and excitement I'd felt when I started working for EKArts. Funny how I never looked at this extraordinary building anymore, just rocketed through the door each morning and up to my minimal office to work. As a newbie, I'd been fully convinced that it was a modern, forward-focused company, interested in innovation but also in a sustainable, ethical approach.

I had no idea, that first day, how personal it would become. That I'd wear my work now like a backpack filled with stones. The thought stopped me in my tracks for a moment, before I gathered myself and went on, trying to look relaxed.

We bypassed the public queue waiting for a tour of the building and went through the staff lane. I introduced Drew to Alix and Ashley, our sustainability and EDI reps, who were at the entrance to the covered courtyard.

'Do you know why Sasha bailed on today?' Alix asked me, frowning. 'She was meant to be giving tours – she's left the team short.'

'No.' I glanced at my phone, in case Sasha had messaged. 'That's not like her.'

Alix shrugged and turned to talk to a new arrival. I put my phone away. It wasn't just not like Sasha, it was the antithesis of how she had been since I'd known her: conscientious, sunny, always willing to take part in things.

'Maybe she's rebelling against the tyranny of work,' suggested Drew cheerfully.

I rolled my eyes at him. 'Maybe. I guess I'll find out next week.'

The covered courtyard looked serene. Its solar-powered water feature trickled clear water over white stones in the borders. As Drew enthusiastically commented on the planting (including the monster palm tree Olly and I had argued behind at the Silent Disco), I started to relax. My colleagues were arriving with partners and children, flatmates and friends, and the noise level started to rise, a buzz of talking and laughter. There was a buffet of salads, breads, cheeses and fruit laid out on white cloths, and waiting staff handed out sparkling wine or elderflower cordial.

'I feel like I'm on holiday,' said Drew, attempting to balance his glass and plate, as he enthusiastically ate a piece of Brie with a slice of baguette and a handful of red grapes. Meanwhile I attempted to gracefully nosh on a folded lettuce leaf filled with Baba ghanoush.

'I was talking about you to my colleagues the other day,' he said, sipping his elderflower.

I made a questioning noise through the Baba ghanoush.

'Just saying to them, what a big deal you are. When we moved to London, you were our north star, but always so quiet. Always going to your room when things got raucous, or making us big breakfasts to nurse our hangovers. Always the sensible one. Then you turned into someone who could take on the press and be part of the change for companies like this. You're such a leader now, Lizzy. To see you do what you've done – you're amazing.'

'Oh, stop it.' I swatted him on the arm and took a glass of sparkling elderflower from a waiter, waving at a member of my team who was chasing her toddler. 'It's just a job, like any other job.'

'Please stop downplaying yourself.' His blue eyes were suddenly serious. When dreamy Drew focused, it could be disconcerting. 'Look, she'll kill me for saying so, but Charlotte said to me when she first met you, she was seriously intimidated.'

'What?' I shook my head. Tried to equate what he was saying, and failed. I could project confidence when it mattered: bargaining with journalists, or on a podium at a press conference, but this kind of one-to-one, up close and personal compliment made me as uncomfortable as all get-out.

'You really don't see it, do you?' Drew disconsolately bit into a grape. 'Note to self: must instil sense of self-worth in Haley. It's too late for you.'

'It certainly is.' I smiled at him, and he pulled me into his side for a quick hug, sloshing his elderflower drink.

'Hi.'

I whipped round. Olly. It was the first time I'd seen him in over a week and I gave myself a mental high five for not gasping out loud at how good he looked, even as I tried not to stare. This was not navy suited, on-duty Olly. He was wearing a boxy apple-green shirt and black jeans with brown suede Chelsea boots. He looked so different that I actually did a double-take. Seeing him not-so-pressed gave me that vaguely unsettled, surprised, oh-dear-you're-hotter-than-I-thought feeling. I'd thought he was hottest in his work suits and polished Oxfords, but it turned out that was what was reining his hotness *in*.

Most startling were the little boy perched on his shoulders carrying a stuffed dragon toy and the little girl clutching his hand, wearing a unicorn t-shirt and a ballet tutu. Olly was followed by a man who I assumed to be his brother – he resembled Olly but was shorter and stockier – holding hands with a petite woman with sleek cornrows and a sweet smile. They were both looking around with intense interest, pointing things out to each other, and had that relieved, released-from-school look about them that parents have when they're allowed out with someone else in charge of the kids.

The look in Olly's dark eyes temporarily silenced me. He was frowning, looking surprised with a side helping of smouldering.

''Lo,' said the tiny child standing next to him.

'Hello,' I said, smiling. 'You must be Matilda?'

Her eyes widened at the breadth of my spooky knowledge and she took hold of Olly's leg.

'Well remembered,' Olly said. 'Tilda, George, this is Lizzy. She works with me.'

They gazed at me with saucer eyes. 'And,' he said, looking round, 'this is Stephen, my brother – don't listen to a word he says – and Tash, my sister-in-law.'

We all traded hellos and handshakes, Olly's family looking at me interestedly.

'Hi, I'm Drew!' said Drew, smiling seraphically as he shook Olly's hand. I saw Olly's jaw flex for a brief moment before he smiled politely. 'Do you and Lizzy work closely together?'

'Kind of,' said Olly. 'You could say I'm good cop.'

'Hey!' I said, as Drew gave a shout of laughter. 'Not fair.'

'I concede.' I saw the glitter of amusement in Olly's eyes. 'It's not fair that I have to be good cop all the time.'

'Well,' I said, ignoring the buzz his look was giving me,

'thanks so much for the constructive criticism, etc, shall we all move on?'

'I didn't mean it,' Olly mouthed, and there I was, blushing like a teenager.

'Can I just ask,' said Stephen suddenly (and mercifully) zoning in on Drew's plate, 'is there Stilton on the buffet? It's all I've been thinking about since we arrived.'

'He's such a cheesehound,' said Tash.

'Yes! They have a great Comté too,' said Drew, 'and Manchego. Although it seems to have run out – that's Lizzy's favourite, isn't it, hon?' I nodded and smiled, letting them embark upon an enthusiastic cheese-related conversation. Meanwhile, Olly and I stood, silently, facing each other, as George chewed on his dragon and Matilda started to sing a song, none of the lyrics of which were comprehensible. Olly glanced around the room, as though looking for someone else.

'Weather's not too bad, is it?' I said, because my mind was blank as I took him in. Well, not blank exactly ...

'I guess,' he said, giving me a strange half-smile.

Drew, Stephen and Tash concluded their conversation, and our respective groups headed in separate directions. I fought every instinct I had to follow Olly with my eyes as he and his family left the covered courtyard to go on a brief tour of the building. I told myself I could definitely wipe the memory of the curve of his bicep in that shirt, and suppress the purely physical desire I'd had to stand very, very close to him and inhale his scent.

This crush was getting out of hand. I just needed a man,

that was all. A man for my minibreak, like hiring skis for a holiday. Perhaps I would get to Venice and find a lover. That would definitely sort out some of my problems.

Drew was finishing his fourth slice of Brie when he nodded at me. 'Your colleague's coming over,' he said.

'Which one?' I said, not wanting to turn and look.

He grinned. 'The Scottish guy who looks at you like he wants to tear your clothes off.'

'*Drew!*' I hissed.

He shrugged. 'It's true. Excuse me, let me just send a pic of the spread to Char.'

I turned to see Olly standing there, looking at a loss. In the far corner of the room, Stephen, Tash, George and Matilda were inspecting some of the foliage and it seemed Tash was explaining something.

'Hey,' I said, as casually as I could.

'Can I have a quick word?' He looked extra serious.

'Sure,' I said, attempting a smile. 'At the potted palm, as before?'

He exhaled, looked regretful. 'Why not?'

We went over, a little way from the rest of the crowd.

'Have you, er—' He made a vague gesture in the direction of my face.

'What?' I said.

He smiled grimly. 'Had what beauty influencers would refer to as a Glow Up,' he said. 'As in, you look – amazing. Scrub that, inappropriate.'

I tried to ignore the lurch my heart gave at the intensity

of his gaze. 'Just made a tiny bit of effort. Thought I should spruce up for Italy. You know what people say. When in Venice, do as the Venetians do.'

He gave a micro-nod and didn't take his eyes off my face.

'What is it you need?'

He cleared his throat. 'Did you have a look at the branding briefing document?' he said.

I frowned. 'Yes, of course, but that's not urgent. We don't need to talk about it now.'

'Right,' he said.

We stared at each other.

'Are you ... okay?' I said. I tried to guess what the intensity was about. 'You're not resigning, are you? Working remotely forever? Planning an art heist in Venice?'

'No. I ...' This man was never short of words. What on earth was he failing to say? 'Have you sensed any ... fallout from the Cali interview? Hearing any criticism of the lovebirds through back channels?'

'No.' It was my turn to frown. Back channels? Were we working for MI5? 'Have you?'

He cleared his throat again. 'No. Great. Well.' He opened his hands out in a distinctly awkward gesture. 'I got you this.' He handed me a folded napkin.

I opened it: two substantial chunks of Manchego cheese.

'Your ... friend, Drew, said it was your favourite. Problem is, everyone else likes it, too – so I got a couple of pieces for you when a ... fresh plate came out. I mean, it was nothing – I got Matilda some cherry tomatoes, too.'

Cherry tomatoes? I was blushing, and so was he. 'Thank you.' I looked at the cheese, then back at his face.

'So,' he said. 'Friends again? Work friends, that is?'

'Yes,' I said. 'Of course.'

He smiled. 'Good. I'd better get back to the bairns. They have lots of questions. As you say, we can discuss the branding on the plane.'

'I never discuss anything on a plane,' I said, as he turned away. 'I'll have my headphones and eye mask on from take-off to landing.' *I may also be heavily sedated*, I didn't add. Being out of control was a difficult experience for me. 'Also, I think we're on different flights. I'm sure we can manage a chat when we get there.'

'Fine,' he said. 'Bye.'

'See you,' I said, as he turned and paced away, looking at the ground as he did so. Drew was busy re-raiding the buffet table, so I watched as Olly spoke to his family, then waved in the direction of Carl.

'I am off the charts impressed with this place,' said Drew, returning with a heaped plate. 'This Stilton is lush.'

'Okay, last orders,' I said, looking at my Manchego package and swallowing down a hard marble of delight which had suddenly appeared in my throat. 'Once you've finished that, we're going on a tour.'

Cheese meant nothing, I told myself. I would get to Venice and find myself a gondolier.

Drew embraced the tour of the building with the enthusiasm I knew he would. In between exclamations of delight, he asked so many questions that, by the end, the tour guide – a chipper graduate from EKArts – looked exhausted, and I had to lead Drew away.

'This has been so amazing, Lizzy,' he said, as we went down the stairs. 'I really wish Char, Haley and Blake could have come. They would have loved it so much.'

I glanced over into the covered courtyard and saw that tea and cake was being loaded onto the tables. 'More refreshments?'

He followed my gaze. 'I thought you'd never ask. Can I take some for the fam?'

'Of course!'

Smiling, I watched him carefully choose cake for Char and the little ones, before he selected his own piece – a slice of chocolate cake topped with crushed pistachios.

I was laughing and tucking into a piece of red velvet cake when Carl appeared at my elbow. His relaxed outfit (lumberjack shirt, baggy jeans, New Balance trainers) was in contrast to the furrow on his brow. 'Sorry, Lizzy, a quick question?' he said.

I put my fork down. 'Yep?'

He did a double blink which seemed to indicate unease. 'I've just been finalising some of the travel arrangements for Venice. Can I just check, are you bringing your' – he glanced at Drew – 'boyfriend with you?'

'My what?' I started coughing.

'He means me, hon.' Drew was camping it up. I'd seen that expression on his face before – he was about to do something outrageous. I held up a hand to stop him.

'No, Carl, I am not bringing Drew with me and he's not my boyfriend. Where did you get that idea from?'

'Nowhere,' said Carl in a slightly strained voice. 'I'm just tying things up. I was told that it wouldn't be wise for us to bring plus ones?' His questioning intonation was reaching a higher and higher pitch. 'And I wondered if anyone had told you? It just occurred to me?'

'Well, that's very efficient of you,' I said. 'But no need to worry.'

'Hey, I'd love to come to Venice, Lizzy,' said Drew. 'I'm sure Charlotte won't mind if we have to share a bed.'

'Do not listen to my maddening friend,' I instructed Carl, who was looking confused. 'I am going to Venice on my own. Now go and enjoy your day.'

Carl nodded and went off.

'Lizzy.' Drew was speaking through a mouthful of cake. 'Can I work for your company?'

'No,' I said, smiling. 'Come on, let's go. I have to finish packing for Venice.'

CHAPTER TWENTY-THREE

On my way home from the Open Day, I treated myself to some window shopping as I answered messages from Jacob. He had ruined his enjoyment of the weekend by worrying whether Esme and Ajax had overspent on the Open Day.

> **LIZZY:** It's fine. No champagne, and they weren't even in attendance. Why weren't you there?

> **JACOB:** I'd rather tap dance naked down Oxford Street than spend a day staring at that building, darling.

I put my phone away. I really needed a digital detox, but the idea of being disconnected brought me out in hives. What if I *missed* something? I decided to try and meditate on my journey home. Ha. Double ha.

When I came out of the tube, I pulled my phone out of my bag, on autopilot, and checked it.

Ten missed calls from my neighbour Myra within the last twenty minutes.

I stopped dead in the street, earning a muttered rebuke from a pedestrian behind me as they swerved dramatically. I hit Call. Myra picked up on the second ring. 'Ohmigod, Lizzy, I'm so sorry, I'm so sorry.' She sounded on the verge of tears.

'What's happened?' I heard my voice. It sounded eerily calm.

'I went to give Pebble her tea, and she just' – she caught her breath – 'she just ran out. Honestly, I don't know how she got past me, she was like lightning. And some idiot had left the front door to the block open.'

As always, my mind zeroed in on the worst-case scenario. 'Is she . . . dead?'

'No! That is, I don't think so. But she's gone, Lizzy. I've been out looking for her. I took some of her kibble, rattled it, called for her. I've been all around.' She named three of the parallel streets and a local park. Kudos to her for venturing there on an already dark winter's afternoon.

The idea of my aggy house cat facing down cars on the main road brought tears sharply to my eyes. 'Myra, it's okay. I'm five minutes away. I'll deal with this when I get back.'

'I'm so sorry, honestly, I don't know how she did it.'

I choked back a sob, thinking, *don't cry, don't cry, don't cry.* 'She did it because she's an evil mastermind.' I started to jog. 'I'll be there any minute. Don't worry, okay? Bye.'

As I turned into my road I slowed down, scanning every front garden, every space between cars, glancing behind every rubbish bin. Myra was in the entrance hall when I let myself in, arms folded across her chest, looking tearful. I tried to reassure her as much as I could, my eyes ranging over the entrance hall as I spoke, looking for any sign of Pebble. It would be just like the ragdoll Goldfinger to be hiding in a corner of the actual building she lived in. But I didn't see her.

After I'd released Myra from her purgatory and she'd gone back to her flat, I sprinted up the stairs to the flat two at a time. Someone was cooking what smelt like a field full of cabbage, but I left the front door to my studio open just in case Pebble returned. My hands trembling, I logged on to my laptop while using my phone to email one of my (many hundreds) of Pebble photos to myself. I had done an Instagram post and was typing out a poster text at splintering speed when my phone started ringing.

Olly.

I answered on speakerphone. 'Yes?'

'Hi, Lizzy. Sorry to bother you, but I think we really should discuss this branding briefing before Venice. I just looked at the first page and I'm feeling underwhelmed. Can we have a quick chat now?'

I snatched up the phone and put it to my ear. 'It's not a good time,' I said. I heard the waver in my voice and bit my lip. *Do not cry, Lizzy Brinks*.

'What's wrong?' His voice had changed.

I got up and went to the window, suddenly unable to

speak. I needed to be out there, looking for her. Never mind the bloody posters. As I stood at the window, scanning the pools of light cast by streetlamps, I heard the screech of car tyres and couldn't help the strangled squeal that came from my mouth. I looked down. It was two cars having a standoff over a parking space.

'Lizzy?' Olly's voice cut through my panicked thoughts. 'Speak to me. Are you all right?'

I swallowed hard. 'It's Pebble.'

'Your cat?'

He remembered my cat's name? 'Yes. She's escaped. I don't know where she is. She's a house cat, she can't fend for herself—' Here it came. A wave of emotion took my voice. I held myself still, my body braced against the feelings drowning me, willing myself not to cry. Silence would have to be good enough. I couldn't get the words out.

'Lizzy. Where are you? Send me a pin drop.'

'No,' I squeaked.

'Please? Just do it now.'

I shook my head to the room, the chaotic, shabby room.

'Please, Lizzy. Let me help you. Look, I know you live in Oval – if you don't tell me, I'm just going to get in a cab and drive around and around until . . .'

'Okay, okay,' I snapped; the only way of fending off my sobs was to be angry. 'I'll do it.'

'I'll be there as soon as I can. Have you posted anything on social media?'

'Just Insta.'

'Send me a picture of Pebble. I'll be there soon.'

Shaking my head, I sent him the location and the picture. Then I put a handful of treats into Pebble's bowl and went back outside, rattling the bowl and not caring whether I looked deranged as I squawked my cat's name at regular intervals, in a wheedling voice she definitely would have rolled her eyes at. I wanted her back, and I wanted her back right now, so I could message Olly and call off the dogs.

When I saw him – his upright, soldier-straight stance; his long double-breasted charcoal wool coat; his quick, urgent walk – I felt a wave of shame. In my burst of emotion I'd pin-dropped him into the heart of my shitty life, the part I kept hidden from everyone I'd ever worked with. All that admiration in his gaze? All that sense that I was a high-achieving colleague, forever viewed from a distance? I could see it dissolving as he walked down my street. For a moment, I considered letting him pass me – it was dark, after all.

'Lizzy?'

'Olly.' I remembered the look on his face earlier, and ran my hands through my now tangled hair, free of any Glow Up. Thank God it was dark. I felt hopeless.

'Any sign?'

'No. Look, thanks for coming, but I shouldn't have involved you in this. Please go home.' I tried to avoid his gaze.

He gently took my arm. 'You need a strong cup of tea and four spoons of sugar,' he said.

'I need to find Pebble,' I said, stubbornly.

'I've put the picture of her on four local 'lost pet' sites on

Facebook,' he said. 'Give yourself half an hour.' He glanced around. 'Where's your place?'

I swallowed hard. The moment of truth. I led him across the road to my block, opening the front door so he could be sledgehammered by the smell of cooking cabbage. I bet he'd thought I lived somewhere that had Jo Malone room scent misted out by an infuser, not in a yellow brick late-20th century block smelling of school dinners. 'You're on Facebook?' I said, trying to distract him from the grimy entrance hall carpet as I stomped up the stairs ahead of him.

'I am now,' he said. 'Joined in the taxi on the way over.'

I dismissed whatever this information meant and tried to stop myself from starting to cry. 'I hate this bloody cat,' I said, opening my front door.

'Lizzy,' he said softly. 'I think you love this cat.'

As we walked into my flat he paused, and I went ahead to the tiny kitchen area, putting on the kettle, and not wanting to observe him as he looked at its small proportions, the patch of damp where Bill's radiator had leaked last year, my line of ten-year-old budget IKEA bookcases bowing under the weight of too many books, and the cheap laminate on the floor. Never mind the baggy curtain pulled across the niche where the bed lived. After I'd got the mugs out and put the kettle on, he took over the tea-making, spooning sugar into the cups. He looked so out of place there, in his dramatically sexy coat, his artfully dishevelled weekend clothes, the signet ring glinting on his little finger. But then I suppose I looked out of place to him, too. With the eyes of a bemused stranger,

I looked around my tiny studio, at the details I so often shied away from. This room was part living room, part kitchen, part bedroom, and I could cover it in ten paces. Him in five. I glanced up to see him watching me. He looked away, poured hot water into the mugs, and stirred.

'You can say it,' I said.

'Say what?'

'That you didn't see me living somewhere like this.'

He handed me my mug. 'I wouldn't be so ill mannered. Take the weight off your feet. Do you have any biscuits?'

I shook my head, folding my arms across my chest. His voice softened. 'Come on, Lizzy. Take a minute.'

I sat down on the sofa and immediately noticed an area that Pebble had been scratching at, which made me miss her like crazy and also feel weird that Olly was here looking at it.

'What's this?' Olly had picked up my gardening scrapbook, which I'd left on the table.

I snatched it from him. 'Nothing. Just – you know, I might have a garden. One day. Even though I'm not sure I have the gift for it.' I waved in the direction of the fading plants on the windowsill.

He smiled, nodded, but I could see the cogs turning in his brain. He picked up his tea.

'Please,' I said. 'Don't – I don't know – *look around*. Don't' – I was rigid with stress – 'please, don't tell anyone at work.' *That I live like this*, I wanted to say. 'About this place.'

He put his mug down, swallowing hard and sitting back on my lumpy sofa. 'Of course. So, what gives?' He gestured to the room. 'I'm pretty sure you earn what I do. You don't seem like a cocaine fiend to me, so is it the bingo?'

It was a good line, but I was far from laughing. 'Do you even know what property prices are like in London for normal people?'

'Yes,' he said quietly. 'I know. But still.'

Still.

I thought about Dad and Alex. What they needed, and how I needed to be prepared for the future, if things got even more expensive. How I was too risk averse to try to get a bigger mortgage, to take on the financial burden of a larger place.

'I told you before, I have obligations.' The silence lasted several seconds. I didn't want to say more.

He frowned at me.

'What?' I said.

He raised his hands in an 'I surrender' gesture. 'Sorry for prying. None of my business.'

'No,' I said. 'It's just – it's complicated. Thank you for coming. You're a good' – I paused – 'friend.'

He swallowed, his expression unreadable. 'You don't always have to be strong, you know,' he said, watching me. 'I know your whole vibe is strong and steely, but emotion is allowed.'

'Au contraire, mon frère,' I managed to say. 'I actually do have to be strong. It's required of me. And I am. Also, I don't notice you scoring high on the emotionality scale.'

'Perhaps we're the same kind of creature, then.' He stared

at me, those dark eyes suddenly looking intense. I could feel pressure building in my chest. God, I wasn't going to cry *now*, was I? Have some kind of weird meltdown? It was then that I realised I wasn't just rigid because of stress: it was the sheer effort of preventing myself from catapulting into his arms, because the man was like a complete and utter magnet. I looked at him, and I felt to my bones how amazing it would feel to be enfolded in those strong, nicely scented arms. How safe. How delicious. And as I thought it, I noticed that he, too, looked as though he was braced, his hand clenched tight over the arm of the sofa. He took a breath, as though to say something, at the precise moment his phone pinged.

He picked it up, stared at the notification, then hit call, walking over to the window. Had I wiped the dust off the blinds recently? I thought. Probably not. A minute later he said, 'Hi, where are you?' and strode out.

I sipped my scalding tea, wondering if Olly had deserted me for a Tinder date. I glanced at my phone, seeing that Myra had forlornly messaged to ask for an update.

I was thinking of what to say to her when I heard a noise, and turned to see a complete stranger standing in the doorway to my flat, holding a cat carrier, Olly standing behind him. 'Wha . . . ?' I squeaked. Yes, I wasn't even speaking in complete words at that moment, never mind sentences.

'This your cat?' the man said flatly. 'My wife let it in our flat. It ate my yoghurt off the kitchen counter.'

I tried to take a breath and instead a weird squawk came out. A furious Pebble stared out through the grille.

'Sorry,' I said, finally managing to say actual words. 'She can be a bit food orientated.'

'Almost took my eye out when I tried to move her,' he said, in the same tone.

'Sorry,' I said again.

'We're very grateful, Terry,' said Olly. 'Let's get her out.'

'Good. I need to get this carrier thing back to my neighbour,' Terry said.

We shut the front door and released Pebble. She skidded across the floor and skedaddled in the direction of my bedroom 'niche', where I was pretty sure she would wedge herself in the gap between the headboard and the wall, which was one of her safe places.

'Is there a reward,' asked Terry flatly. There was, in fact, no question mark at all at the end of the sentence. He evidently expected one.

'Um.' I started to look for my purse; my belongings were scattered around, and I couldn't remember what I'd done with anything.

'I'll take care of this,' said Olly. He nodded at me. 'See you at work.' He ushered Terry out and I heard them speaking as they descended the stairs, then the bang of the front door as it shut.

After Olly had gone, I messaged Myra to give her the good news, then sat on the floor and peered under my bed, head against the laminate, looking at Pebble. I caught sight of one blue eye. We blinked slowly at each other.

Apart from the mug left on the coffee table, there was no sign that Olly had been there. No trace of his expensive aftershave in the air. I busied myself, washing up the mugs, and chopping some veg for dinner. But there came a moment when I couldn't do anything other than pick up my phone.

> **LIZZY:** Thank you for coming today. It was really kind of you.
>
> **OLLY:** No problem, what are *work friends* for.
>
> **LIZZY:** Pretty sure there should be a question mark at the end of that sentence.
>
> **OLLY:** Thanks for the copy edit, hen.

I smiled in spite of myself.

> **LIZZY:** No problem, hen. Did you have to give Terry some money? Please let me know, so I can reimburse you.
>
> **OLLY:** I didn't give him money. He was fine. Have a good evening.

I looked back at the messages more than once, that evening, every time I forgot then remembered he had been there. Had to admit to myself that, for all of my 'must stay professional' resolutions, a very big *What If* had still hung in the air. What if one day – we kissed again? What if we gave into what we both wanted to do? Without even knowing it, I'd treasured that thought – that sense of promise and possibility. I was pretty sure he'd felt the same.

Of course that was over now. His venture into my life, into my flat, had put paid to everything. He didn't want a budget queen of his heart, professionally or personally. I'd revealed another dimension of myself to him: cat lady from the wrong side of the tracks. And now he wanted out.

I couldn't blame him.

CHAPTER TWENTY-FOUR

Tanned, manicured and exquisitely dressed (even though I do say so myself), I flew into Marco Polo airport alone. First of all, because I didn't want anyone to see me if I had some kind of panic attack during the flight (I didn't, as it happens, and I kindly request ten out of ten for not screaming during a short bout of savage turbulence). Secondly, because Esme and Ajax had decreed that Olly and I should travel separately, as they did, in case one of the planes crashed. 'Apparently,' I said to Sasha, as she gave me the travel documents the day before, 'we are the royal family of the business world.'

'I'm so excited!' she shrieked, and did a little bounce up and down on the spot. Which was touching, but made me glad that I wasn't travelling with her, either. At least she had returned to her normal cheerful self. I'd spoken to her about her no-show at the Open Day and received a tearful apology. She'd said she had a migraine and, in her agony, forgotten to text an apology. It didn't quite add up to me, but with everything else that was going on, I was prepared to let it go.

The airport was busy, but not as busy as I'd thought, and I found my way to the Alilaguna readily enough. As the boat ploughed its way through the greeny-blue water of the Grand Canal, I put aside my thoughts of work and let myself take a deep breath. As a whole, I was suspicious when people talked in hyperbole about places they'd been on holiday, but Venice did something to my heart that no other place had ever done. I was glad to be alone for the first few hours that I returned to it. Arriving at San Marco, I stepped up onto the cobbles and took a deep breath of the sharp, canal-scented air.

I'd spent two days in Venice at the end of my liaison with Jack, utterly miserable, but insulated from that misery by the beauty of the place. It was where everything with him had ended, so in a way, it was the place I'd got my freedom. Somehow, despite the pain, happiness had found me, and it was all because of this ancient city and its mysterious, heart-swelling beauty.

There was the complete absence of traffic, other than on the water. Walking along the cobbled streets there was no chance of being mown down by a speeding van. Turning into a deserted courtyard or an alleyway lit by historic lamps, you might think you had gone back in time several centuries. There was the city's extraordinary beauty; the pastel colours of the palazzos, the glass glittering in shop windows, the lines of black gondolas with their lapis-blue covers, bobbing in the water. And the light, of course there was the light. Limpid, crystalline, art-inspiring. Even in the cold of late winter the reflection of sky on water took my breath away. The sweet sharpness of the air made me huddle into my coat.

As I walked down the narrow streets, I felt glad that I'd turned down the opportunity to stay at the same hotel as Esme and Ajax, opting instead to stay in one of the more reasonable hotels. Their choice was world famous and eye-wateringly expensive (of course), but I didn't feel comfortable in its baroque, perfumed atmosphere. It wasn't the hotel's fault, I just wasn't the kind of person who enjoyed seven-star comfort – I didn't want someone else placing my napkin on my lap for me – and I also felt as though their love affair had cost the company enough. Jacob's increasing pallor in meetings made me wary. I was shaving several thousand off the bill for the trip by choosing to stay somewhere else. He could thank me later. The truth was, my unease at the whole situation had increased, not least because of Olly's foray into my bubble.

My hotel was a long, thin building, 15th century, overlooking the Grand Canal. It looked like a warm column of light with its weathered pale yellow stucco, its long, arched windows accented by dark wooden shutters. It may have been the light, but there seemed to be no sharpness in its outline, and it was softly age-worn like so many buildings in Venice. As I walked into the reception and up to the polished wood reception desk, the scent of jasmine hit me and sent me back in time three years. I'd asked for somewhere central but reasonable in price, and I couldn't fault Sasha's choice. But she had also, inadvertently, picked the hotel where Jack and I had taken that minibreak, and where our tattered relationship had finally dissolved like mist over the lagoon. Coincidences happened, but I could have done without this one.

When she'd handed me the documents and I'd realised, my paranoia had kicked in for a moment. Did she know what she had done? Then I thought about just how crazy that sounded. Nor was there any sign on her face that the hotel choice was loaded: she wore her same open, innocent expression.

So here I was again, in this wonderful place, swallowing back some difficult memories. Of course, there was no sense of recognition on the receptionist's face – I was just another tourist, offering up my work credit card and thanking her in hesitant Italian. There was no need to worry that the past was going to intrude on the present, other than in my own mind.

Once I got to my room, and looked out of the tall windows onto the water, I started to relax. I had a small sitting room and a bedroom, both decorated with ornate damask wallpaper, with large Venetian mirrors, marble side tables and a draped bed. A neat pile of fluffy white towels lay on the bed, embossed with the hotel's coat of arms. I ran myself a bath, relaxed, and didn't even look at the branding briefing I'd been planning to refresh my knowledge on or the strategy document I'd been sent. But I knew, in the pit of my stomach, that I had to earn this trip. Show my worth, again and again, as Ajax and Esme hurled themselves at investors with a breathless account of their love story.

After my bath, I went down for a quiet dinner, alone in the corner of the dining room, which was lit by candles. The food was simple but extraordinary, like the best Italian fare. I ate *cacio e pepe*, which was so good I was pretty sure I was going to dream about it that night, and a scoop of gelato (I knew from previous experience to ease myself into my ice cream diet gradually). As I drank an espresso from a white and gold cup, and padded up to bed, I could have fooled myself that I was on holiday. Getting here early had been an excellent idea.

Being quiet and calm was good for another reason as well. Sitting in my robe, looking out over the water, my usual mental armour set aside, I opened my phone and looked at a picture I kept in the album. A picture of a photo: me, Dad, Mum and Alex, twenty years ago. I felt tenderised, allowing emotion in in a way that was rare and unexpected. I could feel the warmth of my little brother, leaning against me; the touch of my dad's hand on my shoulder as he drew us all together, Mum laughing as my aunt took the photo.

'Happy birthday, Mum,' I said softly.

I slept deeply and only woke at 9am the following day when my phone vibrated on the bedside table. I picked it up.

JACOB: There's trouble in paradise.

CHAPTER TWENTY-FIVE

The argument had started in the water taxi. Ajax had taken an earlier plane than Esme and, like the lovelorn suitor he was, had spent some time in the business class lounge at Marco Polo airport, kicking his heels waiting for her, filming some content, and buying her gifts.

When Esme arrived, she had taken her time finding her way to him. She had stopped, inexplicably, for a coffee, and to call a friend. By the time she found Ajax, her suitor was annoyed, to say the least. Fuming, the couple boarded the water taxi with Jacob and Olly, who had rebelliously taken the same flight. Ajax wondered aloud at Esme's ingratitude. Esme wondered aloud at his attitude. And the rest was, apparently, a mixture of shouting, sarcasm and expletives.

I'd agreed to meet Jacob at La Cantina so he could have lunch and decompress, but when I got there – early, obviously, because it is physically impossible for me to be late – I found Olly, who looked about as happy to see me as a man who'd ordered roses and received a manure delivery instead.

'Hi there!' I gave him my perkiest smile.

'Hi. Shall we go in?' he said gruffly. 'I'm sure Jacob and Amber will be here in a minute.'

Amber, I thought. Obviously Olly's invite – Jacob hadn't mentioned she was coming. *Ouch*.

'Jacob said there was an issue between Ajax and Esme,' I said.

'Yes,' he said, holding the door open for me. 'I hopped on Esme's flight. One of my less stellar decisions. You had the right idea travelling alone. When they started on each other, if there'd been any possibility of me not being run over by a vaporetto, I would have jumped into the canal.'

I gave a cry of laughter, and saw his eyes unexpectedly shine in response, giving me a feeling of happiness so sharp it made me catch my breath. 'Also, you would have died of hypothermia in approximately ninety seconds,' I said. 'Maybe it's just a lover's tiff, a bit of drama for the sake of it.'

'Grand passion on the Grand Canal?' said Olly briskly. 'It didn't seem like it. They were bickering like children. Like they'd been married twenty years, and they were sick of the sight of each other.'

In that case, shouldn't we all go home? I thought. I remembered Chiara's advice. I should have bailed before it got to this.

'What are they doing now?' I said.

'Don't worry. I put them down for their naps,' he said,

rolling his eyes. 'Oh, hey.' He waved in the direction of the entrance. 'Here's the gang.'

I watched the two Finance Directors picking their way awkwardly through the tables. I couldn't help a slight feeling of sadness that I wasn't going to get to have lunch alone with Olly. Which made no sense.

'Hey!' Olly said. Amber was smiling a little too brightly for my liking, and flicked a gimlet-eyed glance at me before homing in on Olly. Jacob, as ever, looked glum, but managed a smile for me as he dropped a comradely kiss on my cheek. 'It's like I envision pound signs leaving the EKArts account all the time,' he said. 'It's on a loop, even in my dreams.'

Olly clapped him on the back. 'Try to relax. Let's sit down.' He herded us towards one of the small high tables.

'I thought the Venetian way was to eat standing at the counter?' I said. It was probably a good idea if we got lunch over with, sharpish. Amber was looking at Olly as though he was a Venetian small plate that she very much wanted to consume. And I did not like the way that was making me feel.

Moreover, I knew why she was looking at him like that. He was out of his suit and looked ridiculously good in a black denim shirt with snap fittings and black jeans. Double denim. Which he made look double good. Never mind the fact he hadn't shaved and his dark hair was ruffled.

'I'm a lazy tourist,' he said, sitting at one of the small high tables. 'Humour me. Do you like my shoes, by the way? I just bought them as a present for myself for enduring the journey.' He swung a foot to reveal glossed leather loafers.

'Very Resilience Needs,' I said, and we held each other's gaze for a moment.

'They look fucking *gorgeous*,' said Amber, so intensely that even Jacob looked up from his phone.

Olly didn't seem to notice the intensity. 'Thank you,' he said, and started talking to the waiter.

'You'll all be delighted to know there will an *acqua alta* today,' said Jacob. He showed us his phone screen, and the alert that had popped up. High water.

I looked down, straightening my dress self-consciously. It was a recent charity shop purchase which I'd saved for Venice: a short sleeveless knit dress, stretchy but suitably demure (and black, of course) with a rounded neckline, white trim and metal buttons. I'd also brought the big guns out in terms of footwear: my blue velvet Maysale Manolo Blahniks. I was approximately their third owner, but they worked very well indeed, if viewed from a reasonable distance. I caught Olly looking at me for a moment too long and felt a curl of satisfaction deep in my stomach.

'It's great that we're in Venice and everything,' said Amber. 'But what is this app even about? Apart from art and love? Does anyone have the foggiest?'

'Lizzy knows,' said Jacob, glancing up from his phone then looking back at it.

It was true. I'd dedicated a truly tragic amount of time to working out what, concretely, Chroma was all about. Sighing, I pulled out my notebook and pen.

'Aye aye,' said Olly. 'Work in progress.'

'So,' I said. 'Here you are, the user. When you set up your profile, you swipe right or left on a series of works of art.' I drew a box around 'art', then an arrow. 'Then you answer questions on your preferences, hobbies, etc.' I wrote 'questions'. 'Then, an AI component or some kind of algorithm . . .'

Jacob rolled his eyes. I glared at him.

'. . . creates a brief paragraph on you,' I continued. 'Sums you up on the basis of the choices you've made. And produces your matches, which you then select from. Oh, and your profile picture can be styled according to your preferred type of art – so, you can look like you're sitting in Renaissance Italy, for example. Finally, we're going to try and broker partnerships with some galleries, for reduced price access to exhibitions – so you can have a discounted arty first date.'

'So you don't see pictures of people, until you're matched, at stage three?' said Olly.

I nodded.

Jacob put his phone on the table. 'Huh.'

Olly nodded. 'It's . . . what's the word?'

'Weird?' I said. 'Yes. But it will be a novelty – surely there's always space for a new app? And both Esme and Ajax have big audiences.'

'Listen to Pollyanna over here,' said Jacob.

'I suppose it's kind of nice,' Amber said, 'trying to connect people through something intellectual.'

I swallowed hard. I'd been on dating apps, even though ice ringed my heart at the thought of trying them again. And the point was ... people wanted to see each other. Sometimes attraction really was that immediate, that visceral.

Like the first time I saw Olly. I looked up and our eyes met, and for the briefest moment, I felt as though he could read my thoughts.

The food started arriving. Amber began an animated conversation with Olly, twirling her fingers in her hair. Jacob offered me some aubergine swimming in olive oil, and I refused it with a sad shake of the head. Seeing Olly and Amber side by side, conversing cheerfully, robbed me of hunger. I felt hollow and full at the same time; restless, glitchy.

I was attempting to eat a piece of bread when my phone rang and Dad's name popped up on the home screen. I snatched it up; he never called me unless it was urgent, preferring to message. Frantically, I looked around for somewhere I could dart to, to take the call, but we were surrounded by people in the small cantina. I hit answer. 'Hang on a minute, Dad,' I said, as softly as I could, putting him on hold mid-sentence.

Beneath the table, I felt Olly's hand on mine, the briefest brush which sensitised my skin. 'You can take it back here,' he said quietly, not looking at me. 'Behind me in the corner. Might be quieter.' He nodded at something Amber said. A plate of oysters arrived.

I hopped off the stool but, in my haste, turned my heel. Olly's hand caught my elbow, to steady me. His eyes met mine and just for a moment I flashed back to the night we had kissed; finishing each other's sentences, laughing together.

The tiniest glimpse of a familiarity, a connection that hadn't gone. I nodded at him in thanks as I scooted around the table into the corner, turning away from the group and hit the button to unhold. 'Dad? Is everything okay?'

He was talking so quickly I could hardly keep up, especially with the noise of the cantina around me. After a moment I realised it wasn't a medical emergency – both he and Alex were fine – and I put my hand to my chest as I caught my breath.

'Dad, slow down. What exactly is the issue?'

It was money. Alex had had some extra physio sessions and somehow, I'd missed the notification for it; as a result, I hadn't put the money to cover it in Alex's account and the payment had bounced. Normally the physio's office would have called me, but I'd been travelling, and Rebecca, the office manager, hadn't thought to leave a message. Dad was panicking.

'Dad, it's fine. I just have to move some money. Their call didn't get through to me because I was on a plane, okay? I told you, I'm in Venice. I'll sort it when I get back to the hotel. Yes, I will call Rebecca about it. She won't think it's your fault. She won't.' On I went, soothing like a mother hen, trying to keep my voice low so my colleagues didn't hear me.

Eventually I was able to end the call, and took a breath to process the dissonance I was feeling. It was as though I wasn't in Venice: I was in my flat, in my pyjamas, several spreadsheets open at once, trying to work out how to keep my family safe, and everything paid for, without drilling into the nest egg I'd been saving as 'plan C'. Thank God I had my back turned to the group, so they couldn't see my face.

'Sorry.' I went back to the table and took a sip of my white wine. Two minutes before I had tasted every note in it, now it tasted like ditchwater. 'I've got some stuff to sort out. I need to get back to my hotel. I'll see you all this afternoon for the first brainstorming session.' I looked at them, all in jeans, and decided I'd get changed, too. Going glam for brainstorming was clearly overkill.

Olly nodded, raised his hand and turned back to Amber, who didn't even manage a 'bye'.

'See you later, Lizzy,' said Jacob, tearing off a piece of bread.

I waved to nobody in particular and weaved my way through the other diners, pulling my coat on. *Venice, Venice, beautiful Venice*. I said the words to myself like a meditation, clattering down the narrow streets and small squares that I loved so much, the *calli* and *campielli*. Time seemed to slow, noise seemed to soften. Down a short flight of time-hollowed steps and onwards.

I shook off the thought of Olly. Olly laughing with Amber, smiling at something she said. She was the perfect match for him, objectively speaking. Amber definitely had her shit together. She always looked great, she always spoke precisely and assertively at meetings. She was chill. I would lay money on the idea that she lived in an elegant flat with cashmere throws on her sofa and an entire room which was an actual bedroom.

Don't think about the bedroom, Lizzy.

Don't think about how Olly's lips felt. How he tasted.

But somehow it was impossible to forget the sensuality of that kiss. I had the sense it was going to be scored into my memory for all time.

I gave a little squawk of frustration, startling a passerby. 'Sorry,' I said. I was turning to walk on, when I saw a figure ahead. A man dressed in a cream linen suit, walking with a certain gait that was so familiar, I stopped dead in my tracks.

Was my mind playing tricks on me?

The man looked around and I turned away, instinctively hiding, staring into the window of a bakery and putting my hand up to shade my face. When I looked back, he was gone. It had been a few seconds that I'd looked at him, a snatched glance; I told myself I must have imagined him.

My phone buzzed. A message from Dad asking if I was dealing with things. I swore under my breath and picked up my pace, still wary. Was I hallucinating? Being haunted by past memories in the midst of intense stress?

One minute I was imagining myself in the arms of Olly. The next minute I was being haunted by visions of my ex walking down the street in Venice. Both of these things were clearly impossible.

This afternoon we were going to be brainstorming Chroma, so I needed to get my game face on. Never mind Venetian fantasies, called up by the echoing streets and the reflections on water.

I needed to get a grip. Fast.

CHAPTER TWENTY-SIX

We might have been in the poshest hotel in Venice, but in the end, a work meeting is a work meeting. Which was why, at the sight of EKArts and Resilience Needs colleagues gathered together, clutching cups of coffee and tiny biscuits, I had to fight the instinct to turn on my heel. After lunch I'd flipped to casual and dressed in a cropped grey cardigan with large buttons and acid-wash wide-leg jeans, along with my deeply unstylish fake fur-lined boots. Meanwhile, Jacob had changed back to formal. I considered how long it would take me to get back to the hotel and put on a safe version of my usual black outfit, then discounted it.

The chatty, happy staff members included Sasha, wide-eyed with delight at being in the room. At the last minute, several other members of staff who'd previously been uninterested in Chroma had signed up to come along, too. Funny how a trip to Venice got everybody on board with the new dating app that was apparently being invented out of nowhere.

Sasha threaded her way through the group and arrived at my side. 'I've had enquiries on B Corp status from the *Financial Times* and *Communicate Magazine*,' she said to me.

'Did you send them the standard press release?' I asked.

'No, er, I'll do that this evening,' she said. 'Also, there's a bunch of meeting requests for the week you get back. I'll forward you details. I can't quite work out which ones you'd want to go to. And did you see I emailed Dawson about the website issue he asked about?' Sasha had access to my email inbox for urgent matters, i.e. when the number of unread emails went over two hundred. I winced to myself. My lovely day, travelling, eating pasta and sleeping, had led to a build-up of messages. There was also the matter of a strategy document I'd been sent but hadn't seen fit to comment on. I'd put it off till today then got caught up with fixing the payment problem for Alex's physio. This wasn't what I was normally like; things were starting to get on top of me.

'I didn't see you'd responded to Dawson,' I said to Sasha, 'but thank you. I'll catch up with things this evening. I really need to nail down the specifics of the happy couple's announcement.' They had vetoed our early draft – the draft Olly and I had written before that smokin' kiss – having let it 'percolate' until this point. They wanted something that gave more details on the new app (when we'd first written the statement, we'd had no idea what those details were); something which 'delineated their joint philosophy', which was, precisely, what? And although I'd said 'yes, of course, no problem,' to their instructions, as I always did, I now found myself without any idea of what we were supposed to write. We were back to square one and due to present to potential investors in four days' time.

Sasha went to get another cup of coffee. I glanced across the room to see Olly standing there, his laptop tucked under his arm. He'd put on a dark green jumper over his denim shirt and his eyes popped as though a filter had been applied to the scene. No matter where I looked, our gazes kept snagging. I didn't need this.

Jacob, who was dressed in a bespoke tweed suit and looked as though he was very tired of everyone milling around, called for people to take a seat at the large U-shaped table that had been set out. As the room settled, Esme and Ajax entered, their argument seemingly forgotten. Just this once, they were dressed similarly: Esme in a cream boiler suit with a long magenta scarf wrapped around her neck; Ajax in white trousers and shirt, with a chunky, ink-blue cardigan, his usual suit left in his suitcase.

Esme went straight to the live whiteboard and switched it on, beaming the phrase ART IS LOVE / LOVE IS ART into the middle of it, a love-buzzy smile on her face. It was definitely time for me to exit. All of my tolerance had been used up by apologising to Rebecca as I transferred a chunk of money from my account, and soothing Dad. ('You know it was your mum's birthday yesterday,' he'd said, as though I wouldn't remember. 'I know, Dad,' I'd muttered.)

I stood against the back wall as Esme began to speak in her husky voice.

'Esteemed colleagues, I am so pleased, *so* pleased to welcome you here to work on our baby project, Chroma. Chroma will use art to match would-be lovers, ensuring people are matched on a far deeper level than dating apps normally manage.'

There was a random scattering of applause.

'I want you to bring your whole selves to this process. We want this app to reflect life in its beauty and complexity, darkness and light. To unlock the secrets of attraction.'

Ajax was nodding.

I glanced up, and my eyes met Olly's. He pointed questioningly towards the exit. I nodded and followed him.

'So,' said Olly gloomily. 'As you said, people will be matched according to their responses to specific artworks, and a series of questions. Then they will be shown their matches. The Resilience Needs technical team have put together a very rough idea of what some of the screens might include, or look like, as a jumping off point. Lots of the discussions over the next few days will be about look and feel, as well as what kind of art and questions will be included.'

We were in the room next door to the brainstorming session, and we had the better deal than the group. It overlooked the lagoon, with floor-to-ceiling windows, a mahogany table and velvet upholstered Rococo chairs which made our flipchart look very out of place.

'I know there are plans to talk about colour palettes, and

trying to vision board ideas for the aesthetic,' I said. 'Our people will take the lead on that – obviously to be refined by a design agency later.'

'And today they're brainstorming the questions that people answer when they sign up.' Olly put a printed list of bullet points on the table. 'These are A&E's first thoughts, which they'll be talking about now.'

We looked at them in silence. 'It's quite a mix,' I said. The questions involved everything from logic puzzles to favourite colours. 'They'll need to consult a psychologist, or similar, to firm these up?'

'High likely,' said Olly, his tone brusque.

'Do we need to cover all of this in the speech for potential investors?' I said. 'We don't have much that's concrete to work with. We can keep things fairly conceptual.'

'I think Deliberately Vague is the phrase you're looking for,' he said sharply. 'But, in my experience, potential investors will ask detailed questions.'

'But if we don't have the answers . . .' I said.

His mouth remained in a grim line. 'I guess in the art world, you're used to winging it like this,' he said.

I was opening my mouth to ask him what he meant by that, when the door swung open and Jacob stomped in. 'Fuck my old boots,' he said in a murderous whisper. 'Esme's issued a directive. We have to go to a masked ball. One of her millionaire patrons is in town, and she's scored an invite for some of us to one of his epic parties. Apparently EKArts will foot the bill for the costumes.'

'Oh, Jacob,' I said. 'I'm so sorry.'

'Esme's friend owns a *Renaissance villa*,' Jacob said. 'I thought she was taking the piss when she said it to me, but they definitely do. I just checked.' He named an art connoisseur and private collector who had more money than God. I pulled my saddest face in an attempt to calm him.

'Very sorry to hear you're being forced to attend a party. Shouldn't you be in the other room keeping tabs on the Chroma budget?' said Olly, checking his phone.

I put my hand on Jacob's arm. 'We'll sort it later,' I said, as calmly as I could possibly manage considering I'd just drunk my fifth coffee of the day.

Jacob made an indiscriminate noise that sounded a bit like 'gah!' and stomped out to cast a shadow over the freestyle buzz-creating session in the next room.

'Esme's disrupting everything again,' said Olly. 'That woman's like a hand grenade.'

I met his gaze with my own. 'I'm sorry, what?' I said.

'Ajax is behind on his podcasting schedule. He's missed a week of recording. We're getting questions from sponsors as well as listeners.'

'And you're telling me this why?'

'Well, sorry, Lizzy, but I thought you might be able to do something about it. I didn't want it to come to this but speaking plainly – Esme's bad for business. I didn't realise how bad, until now. We're losing engagement, and engagement is everything for Ajax. She's a distraction the company can't afford.'

'A distraction?' I said. 'What do you think he is? She's behind on her content, too. She's not creating anything. Whose idea was it to go to the Cotswolds? Who told her to bin off the interview I got for her on Radio 4 talking about women in art? Go for it, though, Olly – blame the woman!'

'Nope.' He shook his head. 'Don't say that about me. I'm blaming the person who told him to take a break from his recording schedule. I don't care if she's a woman or a cocker spaniel. I heard her say the words "Fuck the Sponsors".'

'You're missing the point,' I said. 'Ajax is *your guy*. Speak to him. Unless you're saying it's my responsibility to sort everything on your behalf – do you want me to make you a cup of tea as well?'

Olly's phone buzzed on the table. He looked, then glanced away.

'Please don't let me stop you from taking that,' I said sarcastically, wondering where my inner bitchery was coming from. 'Tinder never sleeps, after all.'

I saw the anger flare in his eyes. He spoke through gritted teeth. 'Let's just get on with what we're paid to do. It's hard enough dealing with this shitstorm without your sniping.'

'Sniping?' I jumped to my feet. 'You're the one who started the *sniping*. Who do you think you're talking to?'

'I know who I'm talking to and that's what's so disappointing,' he said, holding my gaze with his dark, fiery eyes. 'You're the fucking bee's knees, and you're phoning it in. Zero comments on that last strategy document.' He waved his phone in the air. 'When did Lizzy Brinks last have nothing to say? Where's your head at?'

'Thanks for highlighting my inadequacies, Olly,' I said, far louder than I had intended, and ignoring the guilt I felt at dropping the ball on the strategy document in favour of getting annoyed. 'And accusing me of phoning it in is pretty rich coming from you, a man who – as far as I can see – devotes most of his strategic skills to finding a tradwife.'

'For your information,' he said, in a hoarse voice, 'I haven't been on a single date since *that* night. Not that that should bother you.'

'It doesn't,' I shouted, lamely.

'When are you *ever* going to understand?' he said hoarsely. 'I'm not your enemy! Can't you see that I—'

'*Guys*.' Carl had come in and was waving his hands, pulling a face. We both swung round. 'Lower your voices. Esme is about to do a guided meditation with the group.'

I gave a laugh of desperation and put my hands up to my face. 'Of course she is! A guided meditation is the answer to everything!' I said. I turned back towards Olly, saw hurt mixed with anger in his face. Somehow, the hurt was worse. 'I'm through with this charade,' I said, half to myself.

I turned and started to walk towards the door.

'Elizabeth,' I heard Olly say. '*Lizzy!*'

I slammed the door shut.

CHAPTER TWENTY-SEVEN

I wasn't stopping for anyone. I walked briskly across the entrance hall, nodded to the smiling porter and slipped through the spinning entrance door. Once outside, I broke into a jog and headed down the narrowest street I could see, pounding along the slick cobbles.

Olly's words pounded in my head like the throb of a headache.

Sniping.

Disappointing.

Nothing to say.

They stung. I'd always considered myself to be tough as old leather professionally, but this was beyond the professional. This was personal. And even worse, he was right. My enthusiasm for work had been fading but I thought I'd kept that hidden. Kept the show on the road. How come he'd seen through that?

I came out of the alley into the middle of St Mark's Square, suddenly feeling a sharp coldness seeping into my boots. I looked down. Water was seeping up through the paving stones at a rate of knots.

Acqua alta. High water.

A cold wind whipped across the square. I'd left my coat behind; I felt the chill pierce through my clothes. I stood there, numbly, watching the water rise. A small group of women in yellow gum boots were laughing and kicking questionable water at each other. But I wasn't laughing. I felt an unfamiliar, frightening feeling: a bone-deep exhaustion. When a spray of water flew over me, soaking me, I ignored their apologies and turned away.

I was sinking. Just like Venice. Emotions stacking on top of each other, pushing me down.

As I stared at the water, and it rose to ankle depth, my phone chimed. Dad's chime. I pulled it out and looked at it.

> **DAD:** Love, maybe we should pay for Alex's stuff in advance, so there aren't any mix-ups. Also, I checked the Journal – there's a message from his 'work coach' – is this the reassessment thing?

I closed my eyes, trying to hold my emotion in.

Remembered Dad saying *it's your mum's birthday*, as though I wouldn't remember.

Remembered Jack looking at me as though he could see

every single fault in me. Saying 'great façade, Brinks, but not much behind it, is there?'

Sniping. Disappointing. Nothing to say. And this was the career I'd spent my life energy on.

As I stared at my phone, I saw the number of emails in my inbox ticking up by the moment.

Knew that in ten years' time, I would still be sitting on the floor of my shitty flat, cutting out pictures of gardens I could never have. Wondering what the fuck had happened to my life.

The feeling started in my torso, as though it was rising up from the depths of me. I heard myself sob; felt warm tears running down my face as I shoved the phone back in my jeans pocket. I knew, instinctively, these were *old tears*. Tears I'd held back from shedding; griefs I hadn't wanted to face. I thought of Chiara's warning voice, at the other end of the phone, in the rain; I thought of Pebble, and how her disappearance had drilled down into an unsettling knowledge – the realisation that my cat had become one of the only sources of joy in my life. The feeling as friends left London, or began new lives; my decision to keep the world out of my life, of my home, dating men like Jack Dillane, who didn't have a scrap of tenderness in him. I had cultivated hardness in myself. But it wasn't really me.

Even now, I had to protect myself: I didn't want the women dancing in the water to see me crying, so I put my hands over my face. When would all of this stop? A tiny voice in my head started suggesting outlandish things. Maybe I could just stay here, maybe I could just disappear. Disappear into Venice. Start a new life. That was possible, right?

I could just pretend I had died. Perfectly rational, totally straightforward.

Of course it wasn't. I was never going to escape my life.

When I felt two hands grab my shoulders from behind and turn me, I put up my hands in fight or flight. The tiny thought at the back of my mind was: *what a weird way to start a mugging*. When I caught sight of Olly's face, his expression full of concern, I pushed at him, but he pulled me towards him with such strength I didn't even try to resist, splashing against him, and dealing him a half-hearted thump on the shoulder which, of course, the man mountain didn't even feel. Our bodies met with a jolt.

'What the hell were you doing, running out here like this in the middle of a flood?' he said hoarsely. 'Something could have happened to you.' I saw him take in the expression on my face, my dissolving make-up. He took hold of my shoulders. 'What's wrong?'

I was shaking my head, the tears falling, trying like a sensible woman not to dissolve entirely at the look of desperate concern on his face. I needed space. I needed not to feel like this. I wanted to feel nothing.

'Why are you crying?' he said, holding me close. Somehow the full deliciousness of his touch made me want to weep even more. 'Please, speak to me.'

I tried to say something smart in response but couldn't get the words out. Instead, I shook my head, gave up the fight and buried my face in his chest. He held me as I sobbed, one arm around my waist, the other hand curled around my neck.

I finally emerged from the sanctuary of his hug, gulping in breaths. 'There's stuff going on,' I said. 'My dad.'

He nodded, trying to read my gaze. 'We'll sort it,' he said. 'But you're shivering. We need to get you somewhere dry.'

A wavering Venetian bell sounded the hour. This place was so ridiculously picturesque. Yet again my life was falling apart in Venice. I remembered Jack chiding me after our disastrous minibreak: *at least the shit went down somewhere pretty*. The man knew how to reduce everything to its cynical essentials, to make everything beautiful sound seedy. I started crying again.

'I'm sorry,' he said. 'I'm so sorry.' He dropped his face to the side of mine, inhaled. 'I was being a dick. I just' – he took a breath – 'I feel like you're disappearing in front of me.'

I felt the words in the depths of me.

I didn't want to tell him that part of the reason I'd felt so lost since Pebble's disappearing act was because I was haunted by our what-might-have-been. That kiss. That I'd been turned from what I considered to be a perfectly self-sufficient, relatively unemotional person into someone who was feeling things too much.

'I thought you liked the sniping,' I said, as he took my face in his hands and gazed at me.

Something gave way in his face. 'Are you kidding? I fucking *love* the sniping,' he said.

'I thought we were friends.'

He gave a hollow laugh. 'Fat chance, with the crush I've got on you. I'm glad you can't see half the things that go through my head,' he said. 'By the way, that dress, this morning. Were you actually trying to kill me?'

I felt jittery with the joy rising in me. 'Not trying,' I said, managing a teary smile, 'but if you were an incidental casualty . . .'

I was silenced by him kissing me.

He kissed me as though he was trying to wake me from a nightmare. He kissed me as though he had found the secret of eternal life on my lips. Basically, he kissed me like we were in a fairytale, rather than two harassed colleagues trying to keep our bosses' shows on the road.

The women in gumboots cheered. We broke apart. 'You should give out those kisses as rewards,' I said, trying not to hyperventilate. 'People could buy an experience voucher or something.' God, I was talking gibberish, trying to gather myself.

'There's a problem with that,' he said. I looked up at him. 'I only want to kiss you. It's all I've been able to think about.'

I felt something give way inside me, some kind of barrier being breached by a wave of feeling. But I couldn't. No, I thought. No. *Not. More. Feelings.* But something else was saying an even bigger Yes.

'Lizzy,' he said. 'This water is bloody freezing.'

I looked down. 'Oh no! Your new shoes.'

He gave a rueful smile and shrugged. 'I guess I'll never

have to make the effort to live up to them. Not sure they're really me anyway. Please, can we go on the *passarelle*.'

'If you put it like that,' I said, and gave a practically girly scream as he picked me up in his ridiculously strong arms and started to wade through the water to find one of the raised walkways.

'Bellisimo,' one of the women called, her face shining with the brightest of smiles.

CHAPTER TWENTY-EIGHT

Olly's hotel was the closest place to get dry. Like me, he'd turned down the chance to stay somewhere ultra-posh and was staying in a 15th century brick-built palazzo which was even more genteelly ancient than mine; it was beautifully old-fashioned, with pointed windows, beams, and terracotta and white chequerboard floor. We slipped past the mahogany reception desk with its wall of keys hanging behind, and went up a winding staircase to the first floor. He opened the door and let me pass. 'I'll behave honourably,' he said. 'I promise.'

I went to the window, arms folded across my chest, watching him as he walked to the wardrobe and grabbed a towelling robe. 'If you need to get changed,' he said, handing it to me.

'I'm fine,' I said. I'd stopped crying and I felt a mixture of relief and shyness. I stood awkwardly in the corner of the room, not sure what to do. 'It's mainly my feet.'

He got a jumper out of the drawer – so neatly folded, I remembered his army background. He rolled it up and put it over my head; the sleeves came way past my hands. But it was soft, and warm, and it smelt deliciously of him. 'I'm getting changed,' he said. 'I got splashed by those women, the ones re-enacting *Singin' in the Rain* in front of San Marco. Do you want a cuppa? There's water in the kettle.'

I shook my head, watching him as he extracted more perfectly neat clothes and went into the bathroom. I inspected the refreshments tray, trying to alleviate the buzzing tension I felt. 'Ooh, fancy biscuits. But shortbread? Not very Venetian?'

'What's that?'

He stepped back into the room, completely shirtless, and my mouth dropped open. His torso was smooth, taut and so immaculately muscled, so perfectly symmetrical that an art student would have grabbed their sketchpad and charcoal there and then. Its smoothness was interrupted by a faint scar on his lower chest which somehow made him even more perfect. I considered the ethics of taking a picture so that I could look at it in my loneliest times. I took in the double arrow tattooed on his right arm, all the while thinking *wow, those gym trips really are working*. In short, I stared at him for about fifteen seconds too long. 'Sorry,' I said. 'I didn't realise you were . . .' So fucking fit. A work of art. Possibly a Greek god. 'Tattooed.'

He gave me a hooded look. 'Like you, I don't give up my secrets all at once.'

I swallowed, wondering, if we ever got naked (because getting naked, I now realised, was definitely on my agenda), whether my fanciest underwear would make up for the fact that I wasn't honed like an athlete. I started to edge towards the door. 'I should probably go.'

'What's up, Lizzy?' he said. 'Hang on, are you – you're not scared? Of me?'

'No,' I said, thinking, *oh yes, I am*. 'Not of you.' Of *us*, of *this*. 'This is just – getting complicated.'

He walked over to me, gently took me by the arms, and kissed me, lightly, on the lips. 'Is that okay?'

It was more than okay. It was lovely. Delicious, like champagne; comforting, like honey in tea. I could feel myself melting. I gazed at him, hazy-eyed.

'Come on, sit down.'

I perched on the edge of the bed, hearing him pad across the floor. When he returned, he sat behind me, and gently wrapped a blanket around me. I felt some of the tension in my shoulders unlock; I leaned back, against him, felt his sigh as he leant his head against mine, dropping a kiss on my shoulder.

'You know,' he said, 'I'm so sorry I upset you earlier.'

'It's okay.' I glanced over my shoulder, hazarded a look at him. 'This job's been going south for a while.' I turned to face him. He didn't need to pull me towards him. I put my arms around him, my hands flat against his muscular back, revelling in at last being able to touch him. Then he dipped his head and gave me one of those kisses that made me entirely forget where I was, *who* I was, even. And it was so unfair. After all, I had started it. The kissing. And now it was completely outside my control.

He was intoxicating. So, so intoxicating. And he was looking into my eyes as though he adored me. But I still felt as though I didn't know what was happening inside, not really: Olly existed for me in fragments, his cool expression, the way he stood, perfectly upright, hands in pockets, defences in place. Invulnerable, charming. All things to all people. But this was also the man who had waded through canal water to get to me, who had whispered apologies into my hair and kissed me as though we were in a black-and-white film. And now, my brain and my body converged in agreement.

Stop fighting this.

I leaned into his kiss and deepened it, my whole body against his. His hands at my waist, I felt his thumbs move over my hip bones and I almost broke in two out of sheer desire.

How did *hip bones* get to be erogenous?

We kissed, and kissed, and kissed some more; and I suddenly felt no nerves, no nerves at all that his hands were all over me. Carried along on a tide of desire, I no longer felt that I had to hide anything, that it was anything but natural when his fingers played over the front of my underwear, landing on that place. That tiny touch sent a bolt of sensation so electric through me that I jolted back.

'Interesting,' he said, breaking from me, our faces close. 'I mean, I knew you were sensitive, but—'

'Say another smart remark and I'll slap you,' I said, trying to catch my breath.

'Don't make promises you can't keep.'

He moved his fingers again, this time more searchingly, and my breath hitched, my voice murmuring his name.

'More?' he said. 'Do you want to ...'

'I think,' I said, 'I think, I do.'

He looked me in the eyes, saw something that troubled him. 'I'm going to need a definite yes. I don't want this to be something you regret, and we don't have to do anything now. We can take it slow.'

Olly being restrained was more of a turn on than I could have imagined.

I shook my head. I did not want to take it slow. I knew if I took it slow, my logical brain would kick in again. And right now, sensible Lizzy could exit stage left, thank you very much. This man made me feel safe and warm through to my bones. But he also made me feel desire, and the tension that had been between us for the last few weeks was pushing me on, a hard-edged, hungry certainty of what I wanted. 'Yes,' I managed to say.

His eyes darkened. 'Are you absolutely sure?' His hands were on my waist and this single touch alone was driving me insane.

'Yes, Olly. I'm sure. For God's sake! Please.'

He laughed and we kissed again, pulling off the last of our clothes, until we were both entwined feverishly on the bed.

His gaze snagged on mine. 'Pretty please,' I said, smiling. A real smile.

'You are unbelievably beautiful,' he said.

He kissed deeper, closer, our hands searching, finding. It might have been minutes or hours before I heard the rip of the foil as he opened the condom; I was suspended in bliss and warmth.

I felt the smooth, assertive push of him, my own voice echoing his as he entered me in one seamless, exquisite movement. I felt my body flicker into the beginnings of ecstasy, a tide of pleasure rising in me ridiculously quickly. It had only been moments and I was already on the edge, trying to hold it back, and failing. I said his name, gasping with it.

'Keep saying my name,' he said.

I banished questions from my thoughts. I banished thoughts from my mind. Let him take control. He sensed my desire to yield; the way we touched each other was like a conversation in itself. To not be in control, to not be responsible, was blissful. Physical shivers, in response to his every touch, his every movement. He slowed the process, exercising the kind of restraint I felt incapable off, until I could not stave it off anymore.

I was a mess. Nothing coherent came out of my mouth, apart from a moan of protest when he changed the angle. His smile as I dragged my nails down his back almost undid me.

'I can feel you,' he said, his body rocking in that beautiful, endless, movement. Weak with desire, pretty much just holding on to my sanity, his superior strength did not bother me. Maybe it never had. 'I can feel you.'

'Please,' I begged him. 'Don't stop.' And then I was lost.

I was aware of Olly crying out, burying himself deep in me in one last thrust as I came, my body ecstatically tightening and releasing in a lengthy cascade of pleasure. I cried out, hardly knowing whether to laugh or cry, and settling on both. I couldn't remember ever feeling like that before. A pleasure so deep. That sense of complete, totally spent, satisfaction.

I lay back on the bed, swiping a hand across my face to brush away a tear.

'Did you just lose your mind, Brinks?' Olly said, against my skin.

'Cheeky,' I managed, breathlessly. 'What about you?'

He looked deeply into my eyes. 'I lost my mind about six weeks ago, Lizzy. I've been waiting for you to catch up.'

My stomach flipped with joy and lust. 'Six weeks ago, as in . . .'

He nodded. 'That. Fucking. Kiss. You've got no idea how many sleepless nights that gave me. In good ways and bad.' I laughed, swiped at him, and he caught my hand and kissed it.

'You okay, though?' His voice was soft, his eyes questioning.

I stretched, laughed. 'Okay is nowhere near how good I feel.'

'Good.' He wrapped his arms around me, and I clung to him unashamedly, burying my head in his neck. 'Good.'

CHAPTER TWENTY-NINE

My phone started ringing and I sat up in bed, catapulted out of a deep, dreamless sleep.

Blinked.

It took five seconds for my brain to catch up, to remember.

I was in Olly's room. I was alone in his bed. I could hear the shower running.

The phone screen told me it was Esme, video call.

I jumped out of bed and started to collect my clothes, my hands fumbling as I tried to put on my bra. I was just pulling on my jeans when Olly appeared, wrapped in a towel.

'Uh-uh,' he said, shaking his head as I reached for the phone. Gestured towards my hair.

Cursing, I ran to the mirror. The last traces of my red lipstick were smeared; my curly hair stood wild, to attention, like I'd been pulled through a hedge backwards – or, you know, had the best sex of my life.

'Lizzy, breathe,' said Olly, looking amused. Esme rang off. 'You can call her back. Just ... compose yourself, then take the call over there.' He gestured to a pair of armchairs in the corner of the room. 'When you call back, say you're having a drink with me here.' He was drying himself, pulling on a shirt and buttoning it swiftly, efficiently.

I stood at the mirror, running my fingers through my hair, adjusting my necklace, wiping off my lipstick. But there was no erasing the glow I had about me. My eyes were bright, my skin suddenly dewy. One nicely fraught hour with Olly and I looked like I'd spent a weekend at a health spa.

We were both ready in a couple of minutes and sat down in the armchairs.

'Lights, camera, action,' murmured Olly.

I whacked him on the knee and hit Call.

Esme and Ajax's faces swum before me, an enormous headboard behind them.

'Is that a bed?' I said, my voice sounding ever so slightly high-pitched.

'The most enormous bed,' said Esme. 'And relax, no one's naked. We're just staying cosy here in light of the *acqua alta*. Ended the brainstorming session ten minutes ago.'

'Oh, right,' I said, carefully not looking to my left. 'I just got caught in the water. Am drying off and having a cup of tea with Olly.'

'Hi, guys.' Olly smiled, looking relaxed.

'I'm glad we've got you both here,' said Ajax. Even to me, who was permanently annoyed by him, his tone sounded clipped. 'So we got some great thoughts down on paper, the team are real livewires. We're so proud of them.'

Yada, yada, yada, I thought, trying to keep the thought from my face.

'The thing is, when Ez and I went to find you guys and see how you were getting on with your speech for the investors, we found nothing but an empty flipchart. So, what's happening? Do you have a fresh draft for us yet?'

'Olly and I had a very constructive conversation,' I said, trying to ignore the fact that, out of sight, Olly had just put his hand on my knee. 'But the thing is, we need more material from you. A little detail, at least. Like, say, the works of art users will view at the beginning of building their profile.'

'My paintings,' Esme answered without hesitation. 'And possibly an installation or two, if the tech team give us the okay on that.'

'Wait a sec, my honey.' Ajax was rubbing her back.

'What?' Esme seemed slightly irritated. 'I'll develop work especially for the project. We talked about this.'

'I mean, yeah, we chatted, but not in any depth. To be honest, I thought you were joking about that. We're going to need big hitters – Van Gogh, Dali, Picasso, Emin, Hirst.'

I found myself in the unusual position of agreeing with Ajax. 'A range of works would be helpful to give people a choice. But we'll need to factor in image licensing . . .'

They weren't looking at me or hearing me. Esme's gaze was fixed on Ajax. 'You're saying I'm not a big hitter?' she said piercingly.

'Of course you're a big hitter. But we need a range of work for people to connect over.'

'Maybe you can hash this out between yourselves,' said Olly. 'Then let us know. And any detail that you have. Send us some voice notes and we'll get that statement done.'

'We need this to be wow,' said Ajax. 'We need the world's attention to be captured.'

Like when there's a disaster of some kind, I thought.

'We really don't have the details, though, do we?' said Olly. 'Chroma is still an idea, not fully fleshed out.'

'Include more personal stuff,' piped up Esme. 'More on our love affair.'

'What happened to, when others go low, we go high?' said Olly. Miraculously, there was something about his intonation which meant the question sounded pleasant rather than negative.

'We all know the way this works,' said Ajax. 'Sex sells. You're not working for the Royal Family now, Olly.'

'So I gather,' said Olly.

'And a wedding date?' I said. 'We were going to announce that, weren't we?'

Esme gazed down the lens. 'Oh,' she said. 'Yes.'

'And, re: going personal, anything specific you want us to include?' I said. 'Perhaps something you talked about at your first meeting? You need to give us something to work with, something you're comfortable sharing.'

'I'm sure you have quite enough to get started,' said Esme. 'We'll send you voice notes to help.' She pressed the end call button and their faces vanished.

Olly's hand was still on my knee, and I slotted my fingers over his. It felt perilously, dangerously good. Like I was in safe harbour in the middle of the most crazy storm, but also on the verge of creating our very own storm. A good one. I gave him a bemused look. 'Why are they being so shady?'

He raised his eyebrows. 'Search me. This has all gone a bit too off piste for me.'

'Do you mean everything?'

'Not this,' he said softly, a smile tugging at his lips, warmth filtering into his dark eyes. He licked his finger and prodded my arm. 'Is there any chance I can persuade you to take off those wet clothes?'

I elbowed him hard, and he gave a shout of laughter, pulling me against him. We were just about to kiss when a ping indicated the first of Ajax and Esme's voice notes landing in our phones. We sighed in tandem, and, groaning, I looked at my phone and noted the ever-climbing number of emails. 'I've got to go,' I said, resting my forehead against his and making a sad face. 'I've got to go back to my hotel. Maybe something miraculous will occur to me about the speech.'

'Are you settled there all right?' he said playfully. 'I mean, there might be a spare room here. Just saying.'

I shoved him cheerfully as my heart rate quickened. 'It's a very nice hotel, thanks. I've stayed there before. Came here on a minibreak with bloody Jack Dillane, would you believe?'

His expression darkened, but he just nodded. 'Right.'

'Sorry,' I said clumsily. Why had I said that? Was I trying

to prove something to him? That someone else had wanted me? I put my hand on his arm. 'Jack wasn't anything special. We weren't even that close. He was actually ... not very nice.'

There must have been something about the way I said it, a touch of the pain Jack had caused me, because Olly gently pulled me towards him and held me close. 'I'm sorry to hear that,' he said, so softly it was almost a whisper. Then he held me back, looking at my face. 'Can I walk you back to your hotel?'

'No. Thank you. Honestly. You just stay here, in the dry, coming up with genius words for our crazy bosses.' I brushed his collarbone with my fingers, mainly because I couldn't help it. 'I'll stick to the *passarelle*, I promise.'

He kissed me. And I knew I was in deep trouble. Because if anything, his kisses got better: setting up a deep ache inside me that was very quickly proving to be addictive. I could talk smart, but I was falling like a stone. And if I forgot to be sensible, work was going to get even more complicated.

I took a deep breath. 'Can we agree to keep this between us?' I said lamely, feeling as though strong magnets were pulling my body towards his. 'I think we need to have a discussion when we get home. About what this is, what we both want.'

'Will the discussion involve large amounts of physical touching?' said Olly.

I couldn't help my cry of laughter. 'If you like.'

'I like,' he said.

'It's a promise,' I said. 'But I think, for now, we just need to be calm and sensible and concentrate on getting through this business trip.'

'No distractions,' he said.

I nodded. 'No distractions.'

'Agreed.' His expression was military-grade unreadable.

I got up, picked up my bag. Looked at him. He was sitting on the bed. Shirt unbuttoned at the neck, jeans on, hair wet from the shower. His dark brown, amber-flecked eyes fixed serenely on my face, as though he was taking every detail in.

I didn't want to leave him. I didn't want to leave this room.

'I'll see you later,' I said, and went quickly, before I could change my mind.

CHAPTER THIRTY

The next two days passed in a blur, and I was grateful that years of dealing with things on behalf of my family meant that I had excellent compartmentalisation skills, so was able to banish thoughts of Olly in the bedroom from my head. Most of the time, at least.

Esme decided, in her wisdom, that she wanted me to be part of the Chroma team sessions, to lead breakout groups. This took me away from working on their statement, and away from working with Olly. And in the sessions, they were asking questions that I thought should have been answered by wider focus groups, gathering people's subjective thoughts on art, and on what was important when dating. Esme and Ajax were excellent at flourishes, at injecting positivity into the room, but their charisma – so powerful when they were acting together – started to look like empty performance to me.

'We need to do proper market research,' I said to Esme.

'All in good time,' she murmured.

'Has a decision been made on which images to use?'

'For the beta version they're using pieces from my last exhibition,' she said, not looking at me as she spoke. 'But we will want a range of artists, so we can be in contact with public collections when we get back to the UK.'

In the past she had communicated, if anything, too openly. Voice notes, emails, stream-of-consciousness chats which it had been my role to turn into concrete actions. But now she seemed shut off, and when I queried what the technical team thought about timelines, she shut me down.

'Why don't you concentrate on finding yourself a beautiful costume for Anderson's masked ball?' she said. Anderson was the collector and party thrower who adored Esme.

'Because that's not my job,' I insisted. 'And I'm not even sure I'll be going.'

Olly had stayed out of the way, carefully crafting the speech based on gushy voice notes from the happy couple and the vague technical details I picked up at the sessions. He sent me drafts of the speech, his emails brief and light.

> Have a liqueur before you read this version. O.

A couple of times during the day sessions I caught sight of him, his eyes on me, but he was always being diverted away by another member of his team, by Ajax, or even by Esme.

Every so often a message would arrive from him on my personal mobile rather than the work one.

>**OLLY:** Are you okay?

>**LIZZY:** I'm fine. Are you okay?

>**OLLY:** Always.

I concentrated on documenting the group sessions on Chroma. If my experience had taught me anything it was the importance of writing stuff down to protect yourself when the shit started getting thrown later. You never knew what was going to happen: someone who'd agreed to do something might renege on it, or an intern might claim in three years' time they'd come up with the Chroma logo. Well-written minutes were the stuff of accountability and protection.

I was in the business centre, attempting to upload my latest notes after a morning of bumpy internet connection, when Sasha came in. She didn't see me at first and set up her laptop, chewing her lip as she typed. I tapped her on the shoulder, and she swung round. 'Oh! Hey!' She minimised her screen. There was something about the way she did it which sent a barely heeded flicker of unease across my consciousness. I took a breath. I was getting paranoid.

'Hey, Sash, working on your lunch hour?' I said.

'Same to you,' she said, with a bright smile. 'I guess I'm a chip off the old block.'

'Don't work too hard,' I said. 'I'm just writing up some of the points from this morning's meeting.'

'Wow, you really are writing everything down. Isn't there someone else who can do that?'

The truth was, if I'd entirely trusted her to capture everything, I could have asked her. But over the weeks my relationship with Sasha had changed, slowly, almost imperceptibly. As I looked at her now, I sensed, with a jolt, something like hostility behind her smile.

'It's good for me to make sure everything's being noted,' I said. 'Once I'm done, I might send the notes to you to format, if that's okay.' We had an office template for minutes, a dark art for most people. Usually once a week, someone in the office exploded in the face of its minutiae (it had about five different margin settings and eight types of bullet point).

'Or you could just do it yourself?' she said.

For a moment, I thought I'd misheard her, and my shock was echoed in her own face. She converted her expression into a fake smile. 'Guess I said that out loud,' she said.

'You did, yes,' I said. 'Is there a problem with you doing admin?' Doing admin was approximately ninety percent of her job description.

She ran her fingers through her ponytail. 'No, of course not, it's just – well, I thought you said there'd be scope for development in this role?'

I suppose travelling to Venice and being part of the team brainstorming Chroma isn't enough development, I thought. I could feel my expression tightening. 'There's fifteen minutes of the lunch break left, Sasha. Perhaps we can talk about this at your next appraisal? Make sure the job is developing?'

'That would be good,' she said, turning back to her computer.

After the afternoon discussions, I arrived back at the hotel, exhausted. It was the masked ball that night, followed by a final day of brainstorming, then a meeting for potential investors the following afternoon. The conversation Olly and I had had with Esme and Ajax was stuck in my brain, on repeat. Something was rotten in the state of A&E, I just couldn't work out what it was.

As I closed my hotel room door, I took my shoes off and gave a groan of relief. I wouldn't be remotely missed at the ball – I mean, everyone would be wearing masks, for God's sake. I envisaged a long evening of lounging around, perhaps ordering up a *cacio e pepe* for extra comfort. Now what was the Italian for *supersize portion of pasta, please*?

Draped across my bed was a long pale blue dress decorated with cream lace, and a Venetian mask. Beside it, a stiff piece of cream card with Esme's monogram on. I groaned out loud, but not with relief this time.

Dearest Darling Lizzy,

Don't even attempt to duck out of this. You are Colombina, my sweet girl. The water taxi will collect you at 9.

E xx

I sighed and let my laptop bag drop to the floor. The mask was beautiful, if you wanted to attract attention. Pale gold, with almond-shaped cutouts for the eyes, it was elegantly decorated with glass jewels and had a plume of feathers dyed blue to match the gown. And I mean an *enormous* plume of feathers. The dress flowed to my ankles, in 18th century style. Esme had even chosen a pair of glittering shoes to go with the mask and dress: strappy sandals with applied crystals. I checked the label but decided not to google the cost.

Honestly, what was wrong with me? I was going to a masked ball in Venice wearing beautiful clothes, and I was being severely ungrateful. This was an opportunity most people would dream of, but I just wanted to put my pyjamas on and dial up the pasta.

There was one other thing I had to do before deciding about the evening: I checked Alex's Journal on his Universal Credit account. In a corner of the breakout room the previous day I'd managed to answer a call from his 'work coach' and discuss Alex's case, having sent them copious paperwork before I'd left for Venice. To my intense relief, they had ruled that Alex was not capable of working, and the official notification was now recorded on the Journal. I felt my shoulders sag with relief; I sent a soothing text to Dad, then messaged the person I wanted to be with, right now.

LIZZY: Are you going to the ball?

OLLY: Er, yes, I'm Cinderella, don't you know? If you mean the ball of nightmares, yes, I am. Unless you want to bunk off and eat gondolier cake with me on the side of the canal.

I was smiling.

LIZZY: Normally the answer would be yes, please, let's bunk off, but Esme has sent me a costume that looks like it costs four figures.

OLLY: Who are you going as?

LIZZY: Colombina, apparently.

OLLY: What a coincidence, I happen to have a massive crush on Colombina.

LIZZY: Ha! How do you even know who Colombina is?

OLLY: I'm a cultured man. Also power googling like a pro.

I snorted.

LIZZY: Just to clarify: Colombina isn't that supermodel who was so trendy a few years ago. I know models are your type.

OLLY: I have no idea what you're talking about.

I frowned, remembering the picture of him stumbling out of a nightclub with a model. Why was he playing dumb?

OLLY: Lizzy?

LIZZY: Still here.

OLLY: Let's come back to Venice one day. Let's come back when we don't have to act professional.

LIZZY: I'm struggling to 'act professional' now.

OLLY: You have no idea.

I stared at the screen.

OLLY: And … you don't answer.

I looked at his messages, the flicker of suspicion I'd felt cancelled out by the feeling of warmth blooming in my chest like roses opening in spring sunshine. Olly felt like a secret that I wanted to keep; a source of happiness that I wanted to hide from the world, just in case outside influences tarnished *us* – whatever we were to each other. This was a beautiful, dangerous feeling.

LIZZY: Yes. Let's come back, one day.

OLLY: Said with minimal enthusiasm. But I like it.

LIZZY: Minimal enthusiasm is my MO.

OLLY: Maybe we'll test that at some point.

LIZZY: It's just, I'm not sure I really know you, Olly. As in, you're lovely, but you're lovely with everyone. You know how to make everyone laugh, when to be nice, when to be cool. You're a social chameleon. You're great at communicating.

OLLY: Communicating is my thing . . .

LIZZY: But who is the real you? I'm not sure I know you, really. Is this too deep for messaging?

OLLY: Damn right. The next time we have a conversation like this I want you to be in my arms.

I bit my lip.

LIZZY: See you later.

OLLY: Buh-bye.

I put my phone on the bedside table and stared at my costume, glittering at me in the gloom.

CHAPTER THIRTY-ONE

By the time the water taxi had transported me gently through the blue-black, lights-on-water, Venetian night, my teeth were chattering.

Before coming out I'd had the hottest shower imaginable, the water violently rattling through the length of the hotel's pipes as though it was fighting its way out. I'd lotioned and potioned myself to the max (my expensive perfume definitely counted as a potion) and spent a long time on my eye make-up and my lipstick, as that was all that was designed to be seen behind my mask. On the surface, I told myself I was doing this for my own sake, and perhaps I was, but I would have been lying to myself if I didn't admit that I also wondered what Olly would think of my appearance. He was used to tired Lizzy, competent, presentable but corporate Lizzy. I had to admit it to myself now: I wanted to dazzle him. I wanted him to want me.

The gown fitted perfectly. As I had buckled my sparkling shoes, I chided myself, told myself to enjoy the evening. Not to be a spoiled brat longing for PJs and a bowl of pasta, when I was going to a *Ball* in *Venice*. But somehow every signpost in my mind was pointing to the exit. In the past I'd learned not to ignore those signposts. And yet, here I was.

Disembarking, I followed the directions on the back of the invitation, walking away from the shimmering, oil-black water down a narrow street, its stones smooth with age, then through an archway, into a dramatic torchlit courtyard where there was a firebreather and a fire juggler, the flames brilliant and hypnotic in the night. There was already a scattering of people, dressed in brightly coloured costumes. I felt a twinge of irritation that I wasn't able to identify who everyone was. There was no chance of me controlling this situation.

'Sweet, sweet Lizzy.' It was Esme, masked herself, but her low, carefully modulated voice was totally recognisable. Her tone was as rich as any actress set to recite Shakespearean sonnets – she had had voice training when she first ventured on to YouTube – and I had the sense that every inflection, every catch in her voice, which always gave the sense that she was full of feeling, was somehow deliberate. Had she always sounded like that? I wondered now. Or had she carefully calibrated herself over the years as she grew ever richer, ever more remote from normal life? She was wearing a corseted silk red gown, high to the throat but almost entirely backless, and my eyes darted over her, trying to catch an impression of her shimmering silhouette, the smooth gold of her mask, decorated with red gems. As I approached her, she raised her mask, but I did not raise mine.

'Good evening,' I said, executing a mock curtsey.

She air-kissed my mask. 'Colombina really suits you.'

'And this' – I gestured to her outfit – 'really suits you. Have you greeted the host?'

'Of course,' she said throatily. 'It was the first thing I did. He's delighted to have us here. Wants us to kick back, all of us.'

'How many of us are here?' I felt weird about it; surely Anderson's invitation had been meant for Esme and Ajax alone. Another reason why I would have been happier in my hotel room.

'Eight, or thereabouts,' said Esme, hazily. 'You know what it's like. I don't like leaving people out.'

I nodded, my gaze raking across the courtyard, steeling myself against her lack of accountability.

'I feel like I disappoint you, Lizzy,' she said, trying to hold my gaze. Typical Esme, to dive right into this at the most inopportune moment. The firebreather let out a billow of flames and some bedazzled partygoers shrieked with delight.

'Sorry you feel that way,' I said briskly. 'My bad.' I needed to wrap this up: a freezing, flame-filled Renaissance courtyard wasn't the place to have a work autopsy. 'Let's just get the app done, and you and Ajax wed.'

I saw a slight flicker in her expression, but couldn't read it. She reached forward and squeezed my arm, engulfing me in her perfume. 'I have to get back to my king,' she said.

'Enjoy the party, my Lizzy. Canapés and amusements now, hard partying from eleven.'

I nodded and watched her float away across the courtyard. When she'd disappeared inside, I pulled my mask back and took some deep breaths of the Venetian air, shot through with smoke. The moment I did, some of the other revellers joined me, identifying themselves and sounding frankly relieved that they had worked out who I was.

'Guess who!' squealed one voice, and when I looked around, I saw Sasha. She was wearing a purple mask, richly decorated in gold filigree patterns and with a plume of what looked like peacock feathers. She put her arms around me and squeezed me, and I had to resist the impulse to step away. 'What do you think?' she said, and I could smell the alcohol on her breath. 'Am I the belle of the ball?'

'Very likely,' I said, somehow managing to usher her away from me. Luckily, at this point we started moving as a group into the main building, more revellers arriving behind us. I put my mask back on.

Inside, the main room was dramatically lit with pools of darkness and light: chiaroscuro, like a Caravaggio painting. The walls were decorated with astonishingly elaborate wooden marquetry depicting flowers and birds; the ceiling was gilded. The room was perfumed with dense, incense-like scent, but nothing could quite block out the smell of alcohol, emanating from the vast silver punch bowls dotted around the room, full to the brim.

'I'm as drunk as a skunk,' muttered Georgia from Finance,

leaning against me as she passed. 'I only had one tiny glass of the stuff. Don't get any on your hands, it'll take your nail varnish off.'

Masked waiters were handing out tiny blinis dotted with caviar and bruschetta topped with aubergine. I declined them and went in search of a non-alcoholic drink. Instead, I found some champagne, and allowed myself a glass, which I sipped in the darkest corner I could find.

As I stood there, I watched as a figure entered the room and looked around. They were wearing a costume covered in multi-coloured diamond shapes, a black mask and a tricorn hat. It was a ridiculous costume, the tight trousers too short. And yet, there was a familiar broadness to the shoulders, a certain uprightness to the walk, which made my heart beat faster in recognition. I watched in something like a daze as Georgia pointed in my direction and he strode across the room, stopping a foot away from me.

'Hello.'

I felt relief uncurl in my stomach at the sound of Olly's voice. Until that moment I hadn't realised how tense I was. I had to hold myself back from reaching out and touching him, grounding myself against him. *Easy*, I thought. *We might be in masks, but you're still working.* I looked up at him; beneath the mask, those brown, glittering eyes were unmistakable.

'Hey!' It was Amber, arriving at Olly's side in a gust of intense and fruitily sweet perfume. I recognised her from her hair. She looked so well-groomed, it was almost as though she was lacquered. 'Lizzy,' she said, 'are you Colombina?'

'Er, yes, you?'

'Same.' She didn't sound entirely pleased about it. 'Are we all Colombina?'

'I'm not,' said Olly.

Amber erupted into laughter.

'On the sauce already?' Olly said to me, nodding towards my champagne glass.

'I was going to stick to water, but Esme referred to Ajax as her king, so there we go.'

He snorted. 'I understand perfectly.'

'Eeek.' Amber frowned, then tapped Olly's arm. 'I think there may be cocktails in the other room. Come with?'

'Sure.'

I had no way of gauging his expression, what he was thinking. I couldn't see his face, but there was that stand-back, military-straight rigidity about the way he was standing; maybe my questions by text had put him off. My heart sank; modern relationships felt so much like a game of chess, with their don't-blink-first subtleties. I just had to brazen it out.

'See you,' I said, in a sing-song voice, trying to sound playful.

As Amber started to drag him away, he touched my hand. 'I will see you later, yes?' There was a sudden seriousness to his voice, the slightest hint of insecurity, that turned a key inside me. This wasn't a game. And I was mad for him.

'You will,' I said softly. He nodded and followed her.

CHAPTER THIRTY-TWO

Just as they had across the centuries, the masks worn at this particular masked ball provided cover for bad behaviour. I don't know if it was the setting, the anonymity, or the spectacular punch which melted everyone's inhibitions so effectively, but before long unidentifiable incarnations of various characters were snogging in dark corners and (so I heard later) doing far more than that outside in whatever nearby atmospheric alleyway people could find. Venice was built for romance but, above all, it was built for intrigue, fantasy and deception.

'This party is plain seedy,' said Jacob to me, his eyes icy behind his harlequin mask, when the clock hit eleven. 'I am out of here.'

I blew a kiss and watch him stomp out through the crowd to get a water taxi, removing his mask as he did so and texting his husband with stabby digits. A moment later I heard the DJ begin his set, the bass thudding through the historic building. A drunken cheer went up, and people started making their way through to the ballroom, snatching at each other's hands, laughing and already dancing.

I downed my last mouthful of champagne, put the glass carefully on a marble side table, and traipsed after them. I vowed to myself I would have one look around, show my face (or mask), then say goodnight to Olly and go.

I pinpointed the host: a diamond-studded *medico della peste* or plague doctor, sinister but pleasingly dramatic, dancing with a stunning woman who I was pretty sure was a world famous model and who saw no need for a mask. People were keeping a deferential margin of space around them on the dance floor. Esme and Ajax were dancing, too, intimately entwined. Esme whirled expansively in her red splendour, diamond necklace and earrings glittering in the gloom; I don't know which masquerade character Ajax was trying to be, but he was definitely dressed as a king, an actual gilt metal crown perched on his head above a gold mask. I was pretty sure there wasn't such a thing as a king in the *Commedia dell'arte*, possibly he'd just gone ahead and made the character up.

I hadn't been consciously keeping track of Olly – that's what I told myself – but I saw him now, at the side of the dance floor, arms folded across his chest, looking on as Amber whispered into his ear. The stab of jealousy I felt proved to me that one, I was possibly losing my mind, and two, two glasses of champagne were two glasses too many.

But rather than departing as I'd intended, I allowed myself to move onto the dancefloor with the others, not wanting to leave Olly quite yet, even if he was on the other side of the room. Meanwhile, the enormous punchbowls were being carried into the ballroom, their contents newly refreshed.

Somehow the DJ had managed to combine elements of Renaissance music with dance tracks, and the effect was both disorientating and heady. Caught in the crowd, I found myself dancing enthusiastically, wondering whether there was something else in that champagne.

As I whirled and twirled, I was joined by a man in a black cloak, wearing the beaked mask of the plague doctor: a more muted version of the costume worn by the host. Whoever this person was, they were out of breath and were trying to echo my movements with their own. At a slight slowing of the beat, they leaned sweatily close and said, in an approximation of an Italian accent, 'You are really moving like a goddess on the dancefloor, beautiful lady.'

I leaned back, frowning behind my mask as my mind tried to identify the voice. 'Neil?' I shouted incredulously above the newly resurgent beat. 'Is that you?'

The way he reared back told me that yes, quiet Neil from IT was having the time of his life. He did a few half-hearted hip bumps.

'I'm almost old enough to be your *mamma*, Neil,' I said in his ear. He'd just joined fresh from uni.

'But age is just a—'

I danced away from him, holding my hands in a thumbs

up, then a thumbs down. He shrugged, spun dramatically around and focused on a different person.

As I danced on, I caught sight of Olly. He was dancing, too, and Amber was going nowhere, her body swaying suggestively near his. Amber, the excellent dancer with the strong thighs that allowed her to ace slutdrops. Amber, who looked ridiculously good next to Olly. As I looked, watching her move around him, my reaction was bone deep, visceral. *He's not yours, he's mine.* At the exact moment I thought it, I saw him glance over her head and at me.

We locked eyes, the music fading even as I felt the vibration of it in my body. We were both just about still dancing; our gentle movements echoing each other in the perfumed room; glittering colours in the darkness as everyone else moved around us, Amber dancing seductively, the people around me frenetic, their hands in the air.

Full volume was restored when a body slammed against me from behind. It was Neil again, punch-drunk (although not in the traditional way) and ready for a second try. I simultaneously tossed my head with annoyance and saw Olly carving his way across the dancefloor, a certain grim determination in his eyes that made me slightly fear for Neil's safety and my heartbeat rise to triple time.

'Leave it, Neil,' I said sharply in his ear, and physically shoved him in the opposite direction. Before Olly could reach me, I tipped my head in the direction of the door. He nodded, and we made our way in parallel across the polished wood floor, already sticky with spilt drinks, far enough apart not to cause comment. But as we entered the dark doorway, we were beside each other, and he reached out and slipped a piece of paper into my hand. I looked at him questioningly.

'For you,' he said. 'I'll see you in the courtyard in five minutes, by the second doorway to the left'.

And he was gone, arcing off to another corner of the room.

I walked into the darkness of the cold Venetian night, taking shelter in the doorway he'd mentioned. The firebreather and juggler were gone, the only light from the flaming torches set at various points around the courtyard. The quietness was a relief. I opened the piece of paper Olly had pressed into my hands. I was shaking, but it was the cold; yes, it was definitely that.

```
Lizzy,
    You say you don't know me. So I thought I'd
tell you ten things you don't know about me.
    I'm the original bookish guy who stammered
and no one wanted. You didn't believe me
when I told you (yes, I saw the look on your
face) but it's true.
    Yes, I work hard to fit in around people,
but I refer you to the above.
    You make me laugh more than any person
I've ever met.
    My tour of Afghanistan was a brutal ex-
perience, and my nightmares are so bad
```

it takes me a long time to let people in. Including people who want me to go to parties all the time (did you google me?! Is that how you know I went out with a model?).

I went out with a model. She was also a person. And we weren't compatible.

I typed this love letter because my handwriting is so bad, I don't want you to be put off by it.

The first time you kissed me, you ruined me for anyone else. I want you so badly I can hardly breathe.

I'm crap at talking about myself which is how I only got to seven things (eight if you count this).

So,

let me show you who I am.

Olly.

'Still reading?'

I spun round to find Olly standing there, mask still on.

'Hey,' I managed. I took a deep breath of his scent: musky, slightly spicy. Ridiculously expensive. I had tasted that scent on his skin. It made my mouth water.

He gestured to his outfit. 'I didn't get the chance to ask, what d'you think?'

I tilted my head, looked at the too-short trousers. 'I mean, I wish I could say you look good.'

His laugh was low, honey-sweet. 'What can I say? It was the last Arlecchino in the shop. Good news: Arlecchino is Colombina's sweetheart. Bad news: almost every man here dressed as him, and every woman dressed as Colombina, so it doesn't have quite the romantic impact I'd hoped.'

I laughed, too. 'Not quite.' I waved the piece of paper at him. 'This did, though.'

The amusement faded from his eyes. 'When I try to explain things to you, I get tongue-tied, sometimes. Thought it was safer to write things down.'

I shook my head in disbelief. 'But you always seem so confident.'

'We aren't always exactly what we seem, though, are we?' he said, looking at me knowingly. 'I was pretty sure you'd clocked the hesitation in my speech sometimes. It can be quite obvious, but I always act as if it's fine, keep ploughing on. That's the trick, I've found. If you believe you're confident, other people will believe it, too.'

I nodded, fighting the urge to press myself against his torso and wrap my arms around him. I had noticed it: the occasional falter, or repetition. But I'd also noticed how he'd never displayed any reaction to it, never stopped, never lowered his voice.

'Did I tell you that you look fucking amazing?' There was no hesitation when he said that.

My breath caught in my throat. I shook my head.

'Eighteenth century you is just as hot as twenty-first century you.' He put his hand in his pocket, produced a small diamante keyring in the shape of a heart. 'They're handing these out. They're not tacky at all.'

'*Grazie, bello,*' I said.

'Lizzy Brinks,' he teased, 'did you just speak Italian to me?'

'*Sì.*'

'Please, *please* do not do that to anyone else. I'll have to fight a hundred men to keep you. And I'm a lover, not a fighter.' He dropped a light kiss on my lips, and I felt a tingle run straight down my spine.

'How did you shake off Amber?' I said.

He held me back from him; I had the delicious sensation of his strong hands holding my arms, gently but firmly. His eyes were bright, curious. 'You're not . . . jealous? Are you?'

'No,' I said.

He dropped his lips to mine, firmly this time. As we kissed, I caught the scent of the Venetian breeze, knife sharp, the goose pimples running across my skin. We broke apart. 'Okay, so what if I am jealous?'

His eyes kindled. 'Then that would be very, very sexy,' he said.

'Hmmmph,' I snipped, wriggling as a token of protest but definitely not protesting when he kissed me again, deeply, hungrily, and my knees threatened to give way as I gripped onto him. When we broke apart his eyes were serious.

'And what if I said to you that the sight of whoever that beaky guy was making a move, made *me* want to remove him permanently from this occasion,' he said in my ear.

'I mean, that's a little heavy,' I murmured.

'Consider it unsaid,' he said grittily, 'but also, not.'

'Olly?' I fitted my head into the crook of his neck, kissed his throat, felt him swallow.

'Mmm?'

I felt no need to lie; no need to be anything other than honest. 'Can we go somewhere else?'

'I thought you'd never ask.' He silently watched as I put the mask over my face, standing close to me. We each put our hoods up, and feeling safely anonymous, held hands, walking together over the cobbles in the direction of the water.

CHAPTER THIRTY-THREE

'I don't want to assume anything,' said Olly, his hand in mine, mask finally off. 'But are we going somewhere *together*?' His expression was pure poker face. I would have thought there was no hint of uncertainty there, but I appreciated the question.

'Yes,' I said. 'Together is good.' *More than good*, my champagne infused mind trilled.

'Your place or mine?'

'Yours,' I said. I didn't want to go back to my hotel room, to see my corporate clothes, my work laptop, the notebook where I'd been making notes for Esme and Ajax's speech. I didn't want to see the traces of work Lizzy there. I just wanted to be me. Create our own little bubble, just like we had a few days before. Then, I hadn't known just how incredible that would feel; now, the anticipation made me feel dizzy with excitement.

He nodded and led me onwards, through the softly lit alleys and streets. As we walked, I folded myself against him, my head on his shoulder; felt his hand stroke my hair. I wanted to give up the fight in that moment, even though I didn't really know what I was fighting. Olly's confession glowed in my mind – it had an openness I'd been unprepared for. I could feel the tension seeping out of me, a relief from something I hadn't even known was hurting. Had I ever really relaxed with anyone like this? The feeling was new, or at the very least, long lost. With my exes I'd always been on guard, just a little, holding something back. I'd stayed composed, self-contained.

'Tough day?' Olly murmured, into my hair, as I swayed against him.

'The toughest.' I looked up at him, saw the soft flame of a lantern reflected in his eyes. If I shook myself, surely this wasn't real? Surely this handsome – no, beautiful – man would disappear in front of my eyes; surely he was magical, like Venice? Then I remembered him in The Hexagon: his laugh, his ability to eat pastries like they were going out of fashion, his steely-edged sarcasm.

'What are you thinking about?' he said, an intrigued smile on his face.

'Can't really say,' I said.

'Funny that,' he said. 'Me neither.'

We kissed, and picked up our pace to the hotel.

The night receptionist's expression was a picture of seen-it-all neutrality as we passed the desk, masked, hand in hand.

We were barely inside the door of his hotel room when we started kissing, and he just about managed to slam it shut before gently pushing me against it. Our kiss was X-rated, impolite, nought to sixty in mere seconds.

'Let me,' I said breathlessly, suddenly very much *feeling* the tightness of my clothes, watching as he tugged at the tie to his cape. 'Let me take this dress off. It costs a bomb.'

'And it looks very rippable,' he said.

I laughed. 'Just, let me.' I fiddled with the buttons, the ties, the zip. 'Your room is so—'

'Sexy?'

'Tidy.' I finally managed to tug the dress over my head and saw him take a breath at the sight of me in my poshest underwear. I offered a hymn of praise to myself for bringing my good underwear to Venice. I mean, what were the odds?

'We wouldn't get on,' I warned, kicking my shoes off, reaching for the buttons of his shirt. 'I'm too—'

'Sexy?' he said, and pulled me on top of him as I started laughing again. Oh, the glory of that feeling: landing on that hard, muscular body and the fact that it was *his* body, his hands at my waist, his touch so gentle that I wanted to yield, to cling to him. There was only one thing wrong with this picture: some of his clothes were still on, but that was easily remedied.

He looked like he was carved from marble, but that was incidental: I just wanted *him*. We lay there, mouths clashing, hands exploring. When he put his hand into my underwear

I saw his eyes spark. 'Ready,' he whispered into my neck. It wasn't a question.

'You wouldn't believe,' I said, as he leaned to get a condom from the table by the bed.

He lay down on his back, took my hands in his, raised them over his head. 'On top,' he said.

He released one hand, flipped the bedside lamp on.

'Noo.' I reached to turn it off, he gently caught at my wrist.

'I need some lights on. I want to watch you.'

My breath caught, a mixture of hunger and apprehension. I let my fingers glide over his hip bones; he groaned. 'When's the first time you wanted to do this?' I said. 'Was it when we kissed?'

He smiled, putting his hand up and brushing my hair away from my face. 'The kiss did drive me wild. But let's just say you had me at hello. The first time I met you, and you ... blushed.'

I leaned over him and kissed him deeply. 'I think it's my turn to say please,' he said grittily.

I sank onto him, sighing with sheer relief at the feeling. All words left me as I closed my eyes – all words, and pretty much every thought other than what was happening in that precise moment. I heard him struggle to slow his breathing, felt each of us holding back, trying to delay the pressure of release, which was building so quickly as our bodies moved naturally in exquisite rhythm. As I quickened, he took my hips and slowed me down. 'Slow and steady wins the race.' We both started laughing, breathlessly.

'I want to know what you want,' he said.

'You.'

'Say my name.'

'Oliver.'

He touched me; I trembled, trying to contain the feeling, trying to hold back.

'Elizabeth,' he said, 'I like the way you say my name. I want you to feel so much pleasure you never say anyone else's name in that way.'

I almost lost my mind at the sound of his voice. I put my hand to his chest, felt the tension he was holding in his body, an echo of mine.

I looked deep into his eyes, and I knew my expression told him everything he needed to know. Our second time together, and we were already learning what the other wanted. We were a little rougher with each other, playful, but our touches bolder, exorcising the frustration between us, my nails hard in his back as he flipped me over, and we began again. I was out of my body, my rational self obliterated. Peaking together, our voices were raised in such a crescendo I wouldn't have been surprised if the night receptionist had heard us.

Lying back on the bed, I was breathing as though I'd run a four-minute mile, and I didn't know whether to laugh or cry; put my hands to my flushed face, my tangled hair. I glanced at Olly and saw he was similarly dishevelled but definitely less out of breath than I was. 'Bastard,' I said. 'I need to get to the gym more.'

He gave a shout of laughter. 'You can always exercise at home. With me. Like this.'

Slowly, I turned on my side and wrapped my arms around him. He felt like a new and exciting place, and simultaneously like home. Fireworks, and Sunday afternoon, combined. He held me tight as I nuzzled into him, catching my breath. 'Are you angry with me for dragging you away from the party?' I said, playfully, into his chest.

He laughed, a sound that made my heart warm. 'Lizzy, I don't think I can ever be angry again. You might just have cured me of all negative emotions.'

'Me too,' I said. And the way he smiled at me made me feel as though I had discovered the secret to happiness. That everything would be all right. I hadn't felt that way in a long time.

CHAPTER THIRTY-FOUR

We woke early and made love, sleepy and gentle with each other in the pale winter light. The taste of his skin was familiar to me now; already, there was an intimacy that lay between us, as though this wasn't all new, as though we had just been waiting to discover it. Afterwards we lay still, moulded together on the bed, unwilling to face the day.

'What time is it?' I said, basking in his warmth, my head on his chest.

He reached for his phone. 'Just after six,' he said, putting it down and wrapping that arm back around me.

'Early riser.'

He gave a throaty laugh. 'Did you sleep well?'

We had gone to sleep *very* late. 'Very, very, very well.'

'Me too.' He sighed. 'Like I said, I get ... nightmares sometimes. But not last night.' He kissed my hair. 'That would have been a rude awakening for you. Me yelling the place down.'

I touched the small scar above his lip, then kissed it; thought of how he had held me at my most vulnerable; how he'd seen the most chaotic part of my life and not turned away. 'It wouldn't have been a problem.'

He looked into my eyes: questioning, uncertain, faintly defensive. It felt unbearable and beautiful all at the same time. I kissed him to stop him from having to say more and to show him his vulnerability didn't faze me.

'This is a stand-out morning,' he said, when we parted.

I sighed, settling into him. 'Meetings begin at ten. I guess we should check emails before, in case any new crises are developing.'

'I always hope there's an email from you,' he said, then groaned. 'Not cool, MacLeod. Should definitely have kept that to myself.'

I laughed. 'Definitely.'

'As I'm confessing things,' he said, running his fingers over my collarbone. 'Do you remember Carl quizzing you about whether you had a boyfriend, just before Venice?'

'When I brought Drew to the Open Day?' I said, glancing up at his face.

He nodded, looking rueful. 'That was me, I'm afraid. I couldn't find a way to ask you, so I got him to.'

'As in, my friend wants to know if your friend fancies that guy,' I said, laughing.

'Yeah, yeah, yeah, I know, it's juvenile.'

I kissed him on the cheek. 'It's sweet.'

'Fuck off.' We both started laughing and he pulled me to him again.

I traced my fingers over his chest, then onto his upper arm, over the tattoo on his bicep, a simple black line with two arrow heads. 'What's this?'

His jaw tightened. 'It's a reminder. It's from a Buddhist saying. Basically: if you're hurt by something, then you've been shot by an arrow. But if you choose to dwell on the pain in a way that's unhealthy, then you shoot yourself a second time, with suffering. I'm reminding myself not to dwell on suffering. I had it done after I lost one of my friends in Afghanistan.'

I nodded, tightened my arms around him and felt his answering squeeze. I had a hundred questions I was dying to ask. It was as though I could never know too much about him now. I also felt, *ugh*, needy. It reminded me of Esme's vulnerability over Ajax. The kind of vulnerability I had been fleeing from for a long time. It was terrifying.

'Now would be a great time to admit you've been secretly in love with me since the moment you saw me, by the way,' said Olly. 'I've got to make *some* ground up here.'

'I admit nothing,' I said tartly, still stroking him. 'You were simply an esteemed colleague when we first met.'

Except the first time I saw you I thought you were the hottest man I'd ever seen or heard, I thought, but didn't say, because I already felt raw, open.

I thought of the things to be dealt with today. My unread

emails. It was like being drenched in cold water after sitting in warm sunlight. Automatically, I sat up and perched on the edge of the bed, reaching for the dress I'd worn the night before, trying to mentally prepare myself for the walk of shame, Venice style.

'Hey.' Olly sat up behind me and curled his arm around my waist. 'No need to get up just yet.'

I lay back down, my body flush against his, but it was too late to stop my mind from racing towards work. How were we supposed to work today? How were we supposed to nail Esme and Ajax's speech when everything was still so up in the air? And I needed to call Dad, to check he was okay after everything that had happened in the last few days. The blissful quiet of my mind was already dissolving under the pressure of a hundred bullet points. I sighed, trying not to tense, and failing.

'What's up?'

I shifted in his arms. 'Just. Got a couple of things to sort out at home.'

'Anything I can help with?'

I shook my head. 'Nothing worth talking about. Today is going to be challenging, isn't it? They'll want to know the script. The final version.' I sat up again and reached for his shirt from the floor. It was deliciously infused with the scent of him. Far nicer than the crumpled dress on the floor.

'We'll get some coffee, hammer it out. It's pretty much there, anyway. And I can sit and watch you working away while wearing my shirt which is, frankly, quite the turn on.'

I laughed. 'No. That's not going to work. I need to go back to my hotel and transform myself into corporate Lizzy again.'

'Do you?' He sounded unconvinced.

'Yes!' My voice was brittle, fake-cheerful. I stood up, wondering if I could take the water taxi home in his shirt alone, deciding against it, and picking up the dress. It offered full body coverage, at least. 'This has been so wonderful,' I said, removing the shirt and pulling the dress over my head, my hands unsteady. 'But I can't give myself the luxury of pretending it's real life. Real life means grey-skied London, financial obligations, family worries, and our bosses having a car crash of a love affair. All of this ... was magical, but it's not the real world.'

He watched me adjust my dress, propped up on one elbow, taking in my expression. 'Are you ... running away?'

'No!' I squeaked. Even to me, my voice sounded comically high pitched.

'I'm sorry, what?' He cupped a hand to his ear. 'I think there was a bat in outer Mongolia that didn't hear you.'

I picked up a pillow and threw it at him.

'Come here.' The tone of his voice changed. Firm, unyielding, slightly rough and – I had to admit it – very sexy. Obediently, I walked back to him and knelt on the bed.

'You used the past tense, just then,' he said. 'Was last night – and the other day – a casual thing for you?' He held my gaze. *I can take it*, his expression said.

Here's your out, Lizzy, I thought. If I wanted to step away from the abyss of intimacy, he was giving me the chance to exit gracefully, despite everything we'd shared. But every instinct, every *cell* of my body rebelled against the idea of that. Against the idea of lying to him. 'No,' I said. 'Not casual.' It wasn't exactly a declaration of affection, but it was all I could manage.

He exhaled. 'Thank fuck for that. Get out of here, then.' A slight smile twitched on his lips. I was starting to depend on that smile.

I leaned forward, kissed him. 'Thank you. Let's take care of business then take care of this.'

He rolled over, got up. 'Agreed.' Then he went to his wardrobe and got out the sweater I'd borrowed from him after the *acqua alta*. 'For the trip back,' he said. 'It's cold out there. I'll see you later. Don't lose it, it's one of my best ones and I'd have to invoice you.'

'Such a smartarse.' I pulled it over my head.

'Takes one to know one.' He pulled me close, inhaled, groaned. 'Go on, go. Or I'm not going to let you go at all.'

CHAPTER THIRTY-FIVE

Back at my hotel, I'd just stepped out of the shower and was wrapped in a fluffy hotel bathrobe when my phone, charging by the bed, started ringing. Sighing, and raking wet hair out of my eyes, I answered. It was a video call.

Esme's face swam before me: evidently hungover, pale-skinned, bedhead hair, smudged eye make-up, but somehow looking gloriously romantic. I glimpsed sketches all around her, and my heart gave a little leap of hope: she was creating again. Ajax was not next to her, but that enormous elaborate headboard was behind her.

'Morning,' I said.

'Hey, babe,' she said, sipping a drink. 'I'm kinda 'disappointed you're alone, if I'm honest. I heard you and Olly are getting friendly.'

Fuck. My stomach pitched as though I was in a boat and had hit a wave. I snatched the phone up from the bed where it had been resting and eyeballed her. 'Where did you get that from?'

She gave a shrug and a little snicker. 'I don't reveal my sources unless you're in the room with me.'

'Right,' I said tightly. 'What can I help you with?'

'I was thinking, about the speech, one extra dimension to bring up might be ... hang on.' She glanced at another phone, read a message, tilting her head. 'I've got to go.' She abruptly ended the call.

I swallowed down my annoyance, feeling vulnerable. Over a decade in the industry and I'd always been calm, a brick wall, professional and nothing else. There had been something gleeful about the way Esme had looked at me, a how-the-mighty-have-fallen cheekiness on her face. I did not want my personal life to become a subject for discussion.

I walked back into the bathroom and pinched my cheeks, staring at my tired but animated face. It had been a long night, and my body ached pleasurably. The memory of being with Olly literally made me roll my head backwards and have to take a breath. But I couldn't ignore the fact that my heart was aching, too, and a vague, unresolved dread was haunting me. How could we possibly make this work?

I went back out and messaged Olly, wishing I'd never left his hotel room.

LIZZY: Esme just called. There are rumours about you and me.

I stared at the screen, waiting for him to read it, but he didn't. Went to the wardrobe, dragged out black jeans, a white outsized shirt and some pointy boots. Selected (fake but impressive looking) cream-coloured pearls for my ears and neck, then checked my phone again. Nothing.

I'd just finished applying my eyeliner while listening to a weather-related voice note from Dad (a new development: one of the ladies at his retirement complex had taught him how to record one) when I heard my phone go off again.

I walked over to it and opened the message. It was from Esme, and it was written in block capitals.

ESME: COME TO THE HOTEL NOW. URGENT.

No kisses, no 'babe'. I rang the number, but she didn't pick up. Then I rang Olly.

'Hi, Lizzy.' His voice was all business.

'Hi,' I said. 'Have you heard from Ajax?'

'Yes, he said something's just happened and we need to come to them right now.'

'Esme, too. Do you have any idea—'

'Nope, sorry. We should have stayed in bed, you know.'

I couldn't help the smile that was stretching its way across my face. 'I wouldn't have wanted to tire you out.'

He gave a low laugh. 'That's fighting talk. I'll meet you at the hotel and attempt not to look at you lustfully.'

I remembered Esme's words, a flicker of alarm in my chest. 'People are gossiping about us.'

'I don't care.'

'I do. Maybe we should cool it?' It was just a suggestion. But also a test. Because he should just say 'no', right? He should push me into us carrying on, because then it wouldn't be my responsibility when my career crashed and burned because of a work affair.

There was a silence.

'I'll see you at their hotel in half an hour,' he said.

'Okay,' I said. 'See you.'

It was half past eight when I made it to Esme's hotel, and Venice was bright and cold, the sky and the lagoon pale, heart-scouring blue, dotted with boats. On my way I'd encountered a logjam of gondolas on one of the narrow canals, a sign of Venice's reawakening out of winter. On arrival I was directed to Esme and Ajax's suite, and was shown in by a man in a maroon uniform. They had their own butler, of course they did. Their suite had a drawing room which would have suited an eighteenth century noble, all gold framed mirrors, glittering glass and velvety, jewel-coloured furnishings. A show-cone of macaroons in various pastel shades greeted me when I went in, and I suppressed the urge to pick a couple off and devour them — I still hadn't had breakfast. Impassively, the butler poured me a tiny cup of coffee in a white and gold porcelain cup.

'Babe.' Esme entered the room and held her arms out to me in a way that brooked no avoidance. As I embraced her as briefly as I could, she was followed by a grim-faced Ajax.

A minute or two later there was a knock at the door and the butler showed Olly in.

My heart stopped clean in my chest at the sight of him. Back in his navy suit, but with rifled hair, he looked worried in a way I'd never seen before. Was it us, or Ajax, who had put that look on his face? I swallowed down my concern, went over to the cone, picked a pistachio green macaroon off it and ate it in two bites.

Ajax cleared his throat, looking uncharacteristically uncomfortable. 'Hey, I appreciate you guys getting here so quickly, especially after such a heavy night, we all really tied one on.' He tried to smile. *Tried to smile? Ever-cheerful Ajax?*

'No problem.' Olly had sat back in his chair, looking superficially relaxed. Somehow, though, I noticed the line of tension in his posture. After our night together I felt like my experience of his body had crystallised and I could read his body language to second-sight level.

I said nothing, but stayed perched on the edge of my seat.

The key thing I noticed was, Esme and Ajax were no longer holding hands. Gone was the love-bunny, hearts-for-eyes vibe that had permeated all of their interactions since that first announcement. They sat next to each other in separate chairs, both looking a little dishevelled but clear-eyed, purposeful. Zero sentiment. Neither of them was smiling. Esme looked as though she was waiting for Ajax to speak, but when he didn't, she did.

'There's been a development,' she said. 'In the last hour.'

Olly and I waited, silently. Ajax had started to flick through his phone, his expression bleak. Then he held out the phone.

'We need to make this go away,' he said.

Both Olly and I got up and went to it, looking at it together, breathtakingly close, but I had no chance to focus on that.

The image was a grainy shot. A paparazzi shot. But perfectly legible.

It was of Ajax. Unmistakably Ajax. And he was kissing a young man, against a Venetian streetscape. I gave my head a little shake, blinked several times. I thought I'd never be surprised by anything, after my years in the business. The affairs, the scandals I'd seen at one remove. And yet, in this moment, I felt shock at the idea of this particular chessboard dissolving and rearranging itself. Shock, tiredness, and disbelief.

'What is this?' I looked up at Ajax's awkward expression, at Esme's impassive face. 'You're *cheating* on her?'

'Lizzy.' Esme's voice was perfectly calm. 'It's not quite the whole story.'

I fixed my eyes on her face, and I saw her flinch at the gaze I turned on her. I forced myself to sit back down in the chair, straight backed. Glanced over to see Olly doing the same.

'I suggest you give us the whole story right now, then,' I said. 'Everything.'

'I agree.' Olly sounded tired.

Esme rang the tiny, ornate jade table bell on the coffee table. 'Of course. But first, more coffee? Or something stronger? Babe' – she brushed Ajax's knee with her hand – 'I've ordered you a serenity smoothie.'

I took another cup of coffee, as did Olly; Ajax had a green-coloured liquid which had obviously been custom-made for him, and Esme had a glass of champagne, ironically. I noticed that she seemed dominant now, rather than Ajax; he kept his head down as he sipped his smoothie, dejected, and she patted his hand. What the hell was going on?

'Right,' she said, once the butler had slipped discreetly away. 'Here's all the news that's fit to print. And some that isn't.' She tried to smile.

I kept my eyes fixed on her face.

'The thing is' – she took a breath – 'our relationship. It wasn't entirely what it seemed. Not to start with.'

I narrowed my eyes and tilted my head.

'Lizzy, Jesus, less of the evils please,' she breathed. 'Look. I'll level with you both. Chroma has been floating in the air for a while. Ajax and I came up with the concept a few months ago. We met at a charity event last November and ... spent the night together. Had a long breakfast. Talked about collabs.'

My astonishment must have shown on my face because Esme looked faintly embarrassed. 'We've met over the years here and there ... occasionally spent time together.'

'On the down-low,' blurted Ajax, then returned to his smoothie.

'Anyway. When we met again, on that Friday, we thought, let's make a splash.' She swallowed. 'Admittedly, a few class A substances may have been taken – in moderation. But we thought: let's go for it, and why not do it together? We would be an amazing combination, and launching an app while being a couple would give us lots of juicy extra publicity. I know this sounds mercenary, I really do. But the world is so competitive now. We aren't the new kids on the block anymore. And hype is everything.'

Olly cleared his throat. 'So the whole big romance is entirely fake?'

'Yes and no.' Esme looked regretful.

'We have a spark in the bedroom.' Another stellar input from Ajax.

I picked a blackberry macaroon from the cone and crunched it savagely. 'And yet,' I said to Esme, 'you don't seem worried that Ajax has been with someone else? When you said to me you were feeling vulnerable.'

Esme looked slightly shamefaced. 'It's true, I've had a lot of *feelings* recently. But the guy in this shot—'

'It was just a casual hook-up,' said Ajax, to me rather than Esme.

'He's easily bored,' Esme said. She looked stone cold chilled about all of it. 'And, honestly? I'd feel worse about it if it was a woman. I knew Ajax was bi. And we both need excitement from . . . various sources, every so often. But the bond between us' – she patted his hand again – 'I feel like, genuinely, that's on, like, a soulmate level?'

Ajax nodded.

Silence fell. I made a note to put the word 'soulmate' on my list of banned terms.

Olly was the first to speak. 'I think we just need to know – are you staying together, or not? Are you getting married? So we can work out what to do going forward.'

They looked at each other, in indecision. 'We really need to talk some more,' said Esme.

I glanced at Olly, but he wasn't looking at me. 'Right,' I said. 'We can give you some space. I'll call Jacob and tell him he's leading this morning's brainstorming sessions with Amber.'

'Texting Amber now,' said Olly.

I bit my lip. I was being less than chill about this. *No, don't text Amber, she might lure you away from me.* I gave myself a little shake. 'Who's got the picture?'

Ajax named one of the tabloid newspapers. I frowned. 'How do you know about it? Why didn't they come through me or Olly?'

'I've partied with the editor in the past,' said Ajax. 'He wanted to give me a heads up.'

Or he wanted to enjoy making you squirm, I thought.

'Can you make it go away?' The way he was repeating the phrase showed the depth of his anxiety.

I shook my head. 'Not entirely. But we could negotiate it to something else. Maybe you give a no holds barred exclusive interview, talking about your complex relationship with Esme and your regret at things you've done. Is it already on the record that you're bi?'

He shook his head.

'Well, you can explain that, too. Esme can either totally

understand about this encounter and support you and be happy to marry you or you can split on good terms, whatever you decide.'

'Right.' Ajax looked dazed.

'Darlings.' Esme stood up. 'We trust both of you implicitly. Give us a few minutes. Ajax and I will message you when we've decided.'

'I'll see you outside,' I said to Olly, who was already walking towards the door. He nodded. I turned to Esme. 'Can I have a quick word?' Ajax went back to their bedroom without a word, as Olly left. Esme turned towards me with an indrawn breath. 'Lizzy, I didn't mean to lie to you – it didn't even feel like a lie—'

'I don't care about that,' I said bluntly. 'I want to know who said there was something going on between me and Olly.'

'Oh.' She looked surprised by that. 'It was your sweet little PA. What's her name?'

'Sasha,' I said, trying not to grit my teeth at the fall in my chest. Sweet Sasha, who I'd spent time mentoring, who had been my team player, who in some way I couldn't fathom, had become hostile to me. Whispering gossip into the ears of Esme and Ajax. 'Thank you.'

'She actually said it to me a couple of weeks ago,' said Esme. 'I just dismissed it but when I saw you two the other day, well, I thought I caught a frisson.'

'Great,' I said, trying to control my tone.

'Just for the record,' she said, turning, and I caught the

scent of her expensive perfume. 'If you were, I wouldn't blame you.'

'Thanks for your input,' I said frostily.

CHAPTER THIRTY-SIX

Olly was leaning against a wall texting furiously when I came out of the hotel. I stood next to him, searching for Jacob's number in my contacts. 'You okay?'

'Fine,' he said, eyes fixed on his phone.

I hit Call on my phone and Jacob picked up in two rings. I told him that there had been a hitch in proceedings which I would explain later, and said he and Amber would be leading the brainstorming sessions that morning.

'What?' Jacob groaned. 'Really?'

'JFDI, sweetheart,' I said. 'I'll make it up to you somehow.'

'Venice sucks,' he said, and put the phone down.

I stared at the phone for a long minute then smiled at Olly, who had finished his texting. 'Don't you love the smell of crisis in the morning?'

He smiled back, but half-heartedly. We walked together, quietly, along the street, dodging tourists.

'Shall we start again?' I said. 'Are you okay?'

He opened his mouth, and I could see he was about to brush me off again.

I put my hand out, not allowing him to break eye contact. 'What's wrong?'

We stepped to the side of the street in tandem.

'I'm just not sure how to be with you,' he said softly. 'Wanting to cool it? That was pretty quick. And I don't want to get caught up in a rollercoaster situation where we keep misreading each other. Look.' He put his hands in his pockets, straightened his shoulders. 'I get it, if you want to step back, I'm not going to force anything.'

I stared at him, unable to frame the right words.

He took in my doubtful expression. 'Message received.' He gave me a strained half-smile. 'No worries.'

I swallowed hard. It had been difficult enough telling him I didn't see him as casual. Saying more was downright petrifying. But what was more scary? The idea of losing him entirely before we'd even begun. I looked into his eyes. I had five seconds to decide it. To decide to break my cardinal rule. No work relationships. No mixing business with pleasure. But then again, I'd already broken it.

'I was scared,' I said.

His eyes fixed on my face. I had his attention.

I ploughed on. 'I've worked hard to get where I am. Mixing personal and professional hasn't worked for me.' I felt my lip curl. *Jack Dillane*. 'And let's be honest, if things went bad between us, you'd be the local stud, I'd be slut-shamed.

And even without that' – my voice faltered – 'my instinct is always to pull back first. To test, if you like. But I don't want this to end. When I say this, I mean us . . .'

'I know what you meant.' His voice was hoarse, his eyes darkening and brightening at the same time. I pressed my body against his, raised my lips to his. We kissed tenderly. 'So you want this?' he said. 'For the avoidance of doubt.'

I nodded. 'But if we go for it,' I said, 'don't fucking hurt me.'

I saw the words ricochet through him. 'I'd do anything other than that.'

Our phones chimed in tandem. We let go of each other; Olly glanced at his. 'The verdict's in,' he said.

The butler showed me and Olly into the lounge area of the suite. Ajax had forwarded the message from the newspaper editor to our emails, and we opened it on our phones: a three-line missive which said they planned to run the story the following day unless, dot dot dot. The picture was also attached and I gazed at it gloomily. I'd hoped it might be blurrier than I remembered, but this was no magic eye image; Ajax's identity was clearer than clear, and it had been taken in broad daylight. It wasn't as if he could claim he'd got drunk at the masked ball or something similar.

I was looking at it when the bedroom door opened and Esme and Ajax emerged. They stood together in front of us.

'We can't go ahead with the wedding,' said Esme. 'That's our decision.'

'I'm sorry to hear that,' said Olly, formally. I nodded in agreement.

Unexpectedly, Ajax burst into tears.

We all stood there, awkwardly, in the silence.

'Okay,' I said, when Ajax had finished sobbing. 'I'm going to suggest something.'

Everyone looked at me expectantly; I gestured for them to sit down.

'Your statement only has to be short. Give just enough information – or non-information – for everyone to wonder what has happened, but we can make it clear it's amicable. Meanwhile, one of us should get on the phone and negotiate with the editor, an exclusive interview with Ajax on our return, which we can prep for in detail.'

Ajax put his head in his hands. I glanced at Olly, and he nodded. 'I can call the editor,' he said. 'I know him, and Ajax is my guy after all.'

I made a deferential head tilt. 'Absolutely. I'll do the statement draft.' When I looked at him my expression probably said *and then can we go back to bed please,* because I saw him swallow hard and suppress a smile.

Esme was rubbing Ajax's back. He really did seem inconsolable, his serenity completely gone.

'Let's all take a breath,' I said. 'Try to relax, Ajax. We have enough to do the statement.'

Olly slipped away to call the editor. Esme persuaded Ajax

to go and lie down, got on the hotel phone and booked a massage for him that afternoon. Then she sat quietly near me, sipping a coffee.

'Is he all right?' I said, as I tapped away, quietly typing out a noncommittal statement and reading it in my mind again and again. 'Does he need a doctor? A therapist?'

She gave a cheerful exhalation. 'He'll see both when we get home. He's just shocked that someone found out what he was doing. It's that invasion of privacy. Plus, I think there was about five percent of him that thought we might actually get married. He'll be fine, though, once he's cried it out. He's like a little rubber ball. Bounces right back.'

I glanced at her. She was dressed in leopard print trousers and a cream silk blouse, barefoot, her hair loose and wavy, her signature red lips and purposefully smudged eyeliner just so. As she gazed out of the floor-to-ceiling windows, out at the lagoon, she looked almost meditative.

'You seem . . . calm,' I ventured.

She gave a quiet little laugh. 'I know I don't say it, Lizzy, but I do always expect things to go wrong. I . . . want it, even. Chaos fuels art. I've been drawing all morning; I've got ideas stacking up in my brain. It's normal, boring, everyday life that really gets to me.'

'I see.' I carried on typing. Decided not to tell her that I really loved boring, normal life. A quiet day, that would be good. A walk in the park with the sun on my back. A slow breakfast. Preferably – I practically whispered it to myself – with Olly there, making me laugh. But then Esme and Ajax were used to having money and autonomy now, so literally any kind of day was available to them. Experiences could be bought; so could people. No wonder the ordinary lost its appeal. Everything lost its appeal, if it was all there for the taking, minimal effort required.

'Someone needs to get on the phones and cancel the investors' meeting,' I said. 'I can ask Sasha to start making calls?'

'Oh,' said Esme airily, 'don't do that.'

'I'm sorry?'

'I'll be fine to speak tomorrow.' She nodded, smiling cheerily. 'It's going to be a splash, isn't it? It'll be great for Chroma. What's the saying? There's no such thing as bad publicity? Also, the hotel has set everything up, including the most amazing flower displays. No need to waste them.'

I sat very still. Since when did she care about wasting flowers? 'Maybe you want to speak to Ajax about that?'

'No.' Her smile was impermeable.

'And if I advise against it?'

'Then I respectfully ignore your advice.'

'Right,' I said.

Later on, I was going to go back to my hotel room, try to do a shoulder stand, maybe even a plank, and then I was going to lie in corpse position until things clarified for me.

CHAPTER THIRTY-SEVEN

Olly and I decided to walk to the venue where the brainstorming was taking place. We'd agreed to synchronise announcing about Esme and Ajax, so that the employees in Venice didn't message the UK team anything they didn't know, and we'd updated Jacob and Amber via messaging. Walking took longer, allowing us both to clear our heads and put in calls to the two colleagues who would announce to the London staff. Olly had been negotiating hard with the newspaper editor, who'd finally agreed our terms; I'd been crafting the statement and trying to process the idea that Esme might be a sociopath.

'Who's going to announce it to the Venice team?' Olly said, as we walked. 'You or me?'

'Flip a coin,' I said.

'Flip a coin? I've only got my card. It's not 2010.'

'Fine.' I dug around in my bag and found my coin purse. 'Let's just say I'm more prepared than you. Heads or tails?'

He winked. 'Tails, lass.'

'How can you make tails seem filthy?'

'It's a gift.'

I smiled and flipped the coin. As we looked down onto the cobbles in the hazy light, a tourist brushed past me and Olly put his hand to my waist, gently pulling me close. There was something so protective about the gesture, it took all of my self-control not to melt into him.

'Keep touching me like that and you'll get in trouble,' I murmured.

'That's the plan,' he said, pulling me towards a doorway, his hand cradling the back of my head as he leant to kiss me.

The taste of his mouth, the slow rhythm of his kiss, pulled me under, like a swimmer caught in a riptide. It wasn't Olly in trouble. It was me. As he kissed me everything around me faded and there was just us; his touch, which I was blooming under. I felt dizzy, unbuttoned, ready for anything. I couldn't tell if it was just lust or infatuation, but frankly, I didn't care who was there, I would have been with him right there and right then, and as for being professional, I was over it.

I had never felt like this before.

It was – yet again – our phones, our bloody phones, that broke the moment: the buzz in my back pocket, and the sound of his ringing. He answered and I heard him begin a chat with Amber; mine was a message, shortly followed by another. Then another.

UNKNOWN NUMBER: Hey Lizzy. I'm enjoying Venice. Just like old times.
It's Jack, just in case you were wondering.
This is my new number.
And I wouldn't block it, if I were you x

I tried to ignore the violent thud of my heart in my chest. I'd thought I was going out of my mind when I saw someone who looked like Jack Dillane in the streets of Venice. I'd never been the fanciful type, but if you were going to be fanciful – or unhinged – anywhere, then surely Venice was the place? And yet, I hadn't been imagining anything. He wasn't a figment of my imagination, and right now, I wished he was. *Remember, you're not afraid of anyone,* I reminded myself. And yet, the element of threat in his words seeped into me. I heard Olly finish his call.

'You okay?' he said. 'That was Amber. She and Jacob are about to start the afternoon session. I told them we're ten minutes away. What was the result of the coin toss?'

'Tails,' I said. 'Which means you're telling the kids what's happened.'

'I thought it meant I could *choose* whether I told them or not.'

'Whatever.' I shoved my phone in my pocket and wrapped my arms around his waist, giving him a squeeze and breathing in the scent of his skin.

'This new touchy-feely you is delightful,' he said, putting his arms around me.

I smiled up at him and let go. 'I suppose we'd better cool off, as we're heading into an allegedly professional arena.' I glimpsed his phone lock screen, a picture of his niece and nephew laughing and looking adorable. There was so much about his life that I didn't know. And there was a ton of things he didn't know about mine, either.

'Thank goodness you're here,' said Jacob, taking me aside as we arrived. 'Everyone's just back from lunch. I didn't have the strength to start another session. Are they really splitting up?'

I nodded, taking the cup of coffee he was offering me.

'My prayers are answered then,' he said. 'The idea of stitching EKArts and Resilience Needs into a combined whole was giving me nightmares. Is there any chance I can get home tonight? Sleep in my own bed with my own husband?'

'Nope, sorry,' I said. 'Esme wants to give a speech tomorrow.'

He groaned and raked his hand through his hair. 'Surely I'm not needed for that?'

I could sense his exhaustion. 'Let's talk later. Is everyone together in the usual room?'

He nodded.

I watched Olly tell the group about the split, as I checked emails on my phone. He said it with admirable simplicity: Esme and Ajax were no longer together, the split was amicable, the Chroma project would still be going ahead and the rest of EKArts and Resilience Needs in the UK were being told the same thing right now. 'No drama,' he said, at one point. But I was watching the faces of the team, their mouths open; I saw people nudge each other, the glances, the bitten lips. When Olly finished speaking the room erupted into an excited babble. If anything, they were even more frenzied than when Esme and Ajax had got together.

I thought of Ajax, crying in the hotel room. I thought of Esme, the woman I'd considered to be a vulnerable artist, who was currently behaving like a cool-eyed publicity hound. I had witnessed her suffering in the past, and I felt I had known a woman whose artistic brilliance proceeded directly from her sensitivity, but now I had no idea who she really was.

'Guys,' I shouted. Gratifyingly, the noise died down at once. 'Remember you've all signed confidentiality agreements.' I looked around the room, taking in their faces. 'Keep this information within the companies until the press statement has been released. Also, can we all please remember that Ajax and Esme are people? People with real lives, and real feelings. Let's just get the job done and get back to London. Do *not* speak to journalists, that's down to Olly and me.'

I listened; the babble was slightly less intense. Some of Olly's team were approaching him to ask questions. As I stood there, Sasha came bouncing over.

'Well,' she said, laughing. 'I am *shook*. What a day! So glad I came here. Wouldn't have missed this drama for the world.' She gave a little double clap.

I tried to suppress my irritation. 'Being callous over the break-up of someone's relationship isn't a good look, Sasha,' I said. 'And, while we're at it, nor is spreading gossip about me. As my assistant, you're meant to have my back, not be sticking knives in it.' Seeing her smile fade, I felt slightly guilty about going so hard at this, but I needed her to understand it wasn't okay. Plus, when she'd been dropping leaden hints about me and Olly, we hadn't even been doing anything, apart from swapping sarcastic ripostes and some accidental perfect kisses.

Sasha's eyes were wide. 'What— what do you mean?' she said, in a small voice.

'Esme said you told her there was something going on between me and Olly,' I said. She opened her mouth and I held up my hand. 'Speculating about other people's private lives is something we all do, I get it. But why would you start rumours about me within the business? Why would you go to the *head* of that business?'

She looked worried, and about fifteen different thoughts were flitting across my mind as I looked at her. Sasha was young. She hadn't seen sexism at its worst, and I knew if I told her the range of remarks and physical gestures I'd been subject to in my twenties, she would be shocked. There had been such a sea-change in the way our professional world worked. At her age I was busy pretending to shrug it off when a man got too close, opened his legs in front of me or tried to look down my top. I was sure Sasha didn't understand how much sex had once been used as a weapon in the workplace, but I also knew that what she had done – whispering rumours into Esme's ear – was not an innocent thing. It was calculated. And it wasn't something the Sasha I thought I knew would have done.

As I looked at her, she gave a little shake and recovered her composure. 'Chill out, Lizzy-Lou,' she said. 'It was just a joke.'

Lizzy-Lou.

Hearing that name made my stomach drop, my shoulders tighten. As I processed it, I saw the falter in Sasha's expression as she gazed at me. And I felt it: the clicking of pieces falling into place.

Someone had manipulated her.

Someone who meant more to her than her career.

'Who's your boyfriend, Sasha?' I said.

All the colour drained from her face, and for a second, I thought she was going to faint. I glanced to my left, towards the door. 'Let's go and sit in the other room, shall we?' I said.

She nodded, and followed me into the ante room Olly and I had worked in a few days before, the silk covered armchairs facing the water. To buy myself some time, and to regain my composure, I pulled one of the chairs a little way from the others. Sasha perched on one and I sat down opposite her.

'Do you need a glass of water?' I said.

She shook her head.

I sat down. 'Is your boyfriend Jack Dillane?' I said.

She looked at me as though I had occult powers, and nodded. 'How did you know?'

I suppressed the instinct to swear under my breath. I had hoped, wished, it not to be true.

'There's only one person who's ever called me Lizzy-Lou,' I said, swallowing hard. 'And it makes sense of a few things.' Booking the hotel I'd stayed in with Jack; her high gloss appearance, tailored to his taste; her simmering, developing resentment towards me.

'We met at the press conference,' she said. 'We get on really well. But he talks about you all the time.' The bitterness that crossed her face marred her youthful prettiness.

'That's just the way he operates,' I said, suppressing a sigh or a scream, I didn't know which; my body was struggling to keep up with my brain. 'When I was with him, he did the same thing. It's a way of making you feel off balance, like you have to work hard to keep him. I suppose, him talking about me all the time pissed you off, and you thought you might get a bit of your own back, so you shit-talked me to Esme?'

'No, it wasn't like that,' she said.

I pressed my forefinger into the centre of my brow. 'I bet he told you we had a wonderful time in Venice.'

She swallowed hard, nodded.

'So you booked the same hotel? Thought you'd observe me and my feelings?'

She didn't nod but it was clear she had. 'He suggested it,' she said, almost whispering.

I felt the coldness of real anger in my body, sat up a little straighter. 'And what's the next move in your master plan?'

'There is no master plan!' she cried. 'He's just – obsessed with you, that's all. We're not established enough yet; in time he'll see how good we are together. And I was glad when I saw that you and Olly were sparking off each other.'

I narrowed my eyes at her.

'What? It's clear he worships you.'

I looked at her, unable to find any words for her, or for the depth of tiredness I felt.

'I didn't lie,' she said, in a small voice. 'I just didn't tell you. I'm sorry, Lizzy.'

I waved away the apology. 'What's Jack doing in Venice?'

'I don't know what you mean.'

'Stop lying.'

Her voice was rising in pitch. 'He came out a couple of days ago. It was really romantic, he said he wanted to surprise me.'

'Do *not* tell him anything about what has happened today.' *No*, I thought. *She has access to my inbox. She could see everything.* 'Have you told him much? About the company, or what's happening here?'

Her spine straightened a little, and I saw her barely masked defiance appear, her irritation at me. I was glad to finally see it: I was getting to the truth, at last. 'He's my partner. I don't think you've got the right to tell me not to speak to my partner.'

I shook my head. 'Do you not have the sense you were born with?'

'And you're not allowed to insult me,' she said, her mouth

in a thin line. What had happened to this girl? The Jack worm had eaten into her brain, it seemed. It was likely he had been coaching her; I could almost hear his tone in the things she was saying. He would have been whispering into her ear, encouraging her to push back against me, saying that I didn't have her best interests at heart. It was what he did: reframing your world so that you started to see other people differently, so that you doubted everyone except him. I'd only told him a few details about my family, but I remembered how subtly he had tried to suggest Alex and my father were burdens, burdens that other people wouldn't feel obliged to care for; that it was practically a restriction of my human rights to take my dad's daily calls. Luckily I'd hopped on a Zoom to Sara straight after that conversation ('What a bellend,' she said, 'sounds like a total psycho to me.'). With Sasha, Jack had picked an easier target: early twenties, ambitious but insecure. He was eroding her faith in the people around her: first it was me, then it would be her friends and the people she loved.

'Sasha,' I said, carefully. 'Please believe me. I know Jack. I know how charming, witty and persuasive he is. I also know that he is not a good guy. He can be manipulative, he can be controlling. And I think he might be using you.'

'So typical of you,' she said, shaking her head and looking above my eyeline. 'Why would he want me, when he's been with the amazing Elizabeth Brinks? That's what you really mean, isn't it?'

'That's not what I'm saying,' I said, trying to ride out the sting of her words. 'You're a brilliant young woman. You deserve more than him.'

She was still shaking her head.

'I've always tried to be supportive of you, and your career,' I said, labouring on. 'But this is a big betrayal, Sasha.'

She gave me an unpleasant smile. 'You insulted me earlier. I can report you to HR for speaking to me like that,' she said.

Enough, I thought. There was no salvaging this situation – certainly not here and now. I felt, with relief, my inner ice queen power up, the retreat of all emotion. I focused my unblinking gaze on her face, saw her self-righteous expression falter. Then I smiled, too.

'Go ahead,' I said.

She paused, uncertain. 'Lizzy—'

I stood up, brushed myself down. 'I have a meeting to get to. I'll deal with this later. In the meantime, go and pack. Everyone will be shipping out soon. I'll take care of my own emails, I don't require anything from you.'

She said nothing more and I walked out of the room and across the lobby, a metallic taste in my mouth, feeling outwardly calm but knowing everything was teeming underneath, packed tight, a tinderbox. I saw someone in my peripheral vision: Olly, approaching me. He fell in step alongside me. 'What's happening?'

I glanced at him, held his gaze, tried to convey my trust in him in that single look. 'Tell you later. I've got something to do.'

*

Out on the street, I glanced at my message conversation with the Unknown Number, checking for a new reply.

JACK: Hey baby.

LIZZY: What do you want?

JACK: It's time to talk.

LIZZY: You bet it is. Ice cream?

I knew he'd never rest until he'd tortured me a bit – *I may as well get some ice cream out of it*, I told myself. He agreed, naming a gelateria nearby, signing off with two kisses. *Two kisses*. It made me want to gag.

Turn him into a joke, my mind said. *There's no need to be afraid of him*. But that was the thing: there was still a very small part of me that *was* frightened of him. My brief relationship with Jack had turned into a power game, with him having the upper hand. I'd got out of it, but there was still that flicker of fear I felt at the idea of being in his company. I stood there for a moment, breathing the Venetian breeze, rolling my shoulders as though I was preparing for a run, or a fight. *Fight or flight*. But there was no point in running.

CHAPTER THIRTY-EIGHT

The gelateria Jack chose did cocktails as well as ice cream, and was positioned on the waterside, a quaint, narrow shop with a blue and white striped awning and a handful of tables and chairs outside. Even in the cold light of late winter, it was busy, and there was a throng of tourists holding up their ice creams and attempting to photograph them with the landscape of Venice behind. It was Instagram-a-go-go here.

Jack was late. I knew he would be. I ordered a gianduiotto with an Aperol spritz and sat down in a wicker chair at a metal table, just for once ignoring the buzzing of my phone. The ice cream came out in a hurricane glass, with a long spoon, and its smooth, creamy, rich deliciousness was so good that I almost groaned out loud with joy at the momentary reprieve it gave me.

'Hey, princess.' Ugh and double ugh. The douche of the hour had arrived. 'Ice cream at sunset, how romantic,' he said, pulling his chair up a little too close. I shifted mine away and carried on eating my ice cream. When I finally looked at him, he was sitting, his chin cupped in his hand, smiling at me.

'You need to order,' I said.

Still smiling, but with an undercurrent of annoyance in his eyes, he went in, returning with a large serving of pale green ice cream. 'Mint choc chip?' I said sarcastically.

'Pistachio,' he said, with a look that added *you pleb*.

We ate together in silence for a minute or two, our spoons clinking against the glasses, surrounded by the sound of happy voices talking in different languages, buffeted by the sweep of cold, canal-scented breeze. Anyone looking at us would have thought we were contented in each other's company, not two people who were facing off like cats getting ready to pounce.

'You've upset my girlfriend,' he said, eventually. I had wondered what his opening shot would be.

I finished my ice cream (slightly too quickly: I had a touch of brain freeze) and let the spoon rest in the glass. 'I think you're the one who's doing most of the upsetting,' I said.

'You say tom*ay*to, I say tom*ah*to,' he said. He tried to hold my gaze. 'You and I are just explosive, I guess.'

'Oh, come *on*,' I said. 'Damp squib, more like. Look, I just wanted to say to you: give Sasha a break, okay? I don't know exactly why you're messing with her but don't break her heart. And don't fuck her over so completely she can never get a job in this industry again.'

He savoured a mouthful of pistachio ice cream. 'Jealous, are you? She can take care of herself.'

He looked completely unbothered by the idea that his actions might damage Sasha. Looking at him closely, everything about him seemed contrived: the shadow of stubble across his face; his precisely styled black hair, sprayed rock solid; his perfect white t-shirt and jacket. Contrived, and hard-edged, without any sensitivity. Sure, Jack could be witty, but his wasn't the clean-cut cheerfulness of Olly, whose coolness was hard won and tested under combat rather than in the world of gossip and hearsay. In comparison, how had I ever found Jack even glancingly attractive?

'She's just a kid,' I said. 'I'm asking you leave an impressionable young woman alone. Don't do a number on her.'

I saw the look in his eyes. I saw that he was, indeed, narcissistic enough to believe I was jealous. 'Oh, believe me,' he said, lifting a perfectly shaped eyebrow, 'she's actually quite the adult in many ways.'

I felt myself wince in repulsion. 'You really are a scumbag,' I said, despite the fact I didn't want to show how annoyed I was. It was too late anyway: his eyes were fixed on my face, picking up every micro-expression. I toyed with my cocktail.

'That's no way to talk to me,' he said. 'I'm hurt. I might have to retaliate.'

I pretended to stifle a yawn. 'How would you do that?'

'I could publish some stuff.'

'Would anyone see it? I heard your clickthrough count was down.'

'Not after today, baby girl.'

I wished I had more ice cream to eat. 'I guess Sasha's been talking to you about things at EKArts.'

I hated the glint in his eye. 'More than talking. I've got pictures.'

No. I felt a sickening fall in my chest. Sasha had access to my inbox as well as my diary, and she must have seen the image of Ajax when he'd emailed it to me and Olly.

I decided I was now officially sick of this trip. The cheerful, chattering voices, the glittering water, the bone-chilling winter cold were all swappable, in a heartbeat, for my pyjamas, my cat, and a vat of tea. 'I guess it's fine if you want to breach copyright, use images you haven't paid for, the big guns will be out for you.'

He gave a belly laugh. 'Copyright? That's all you've got? That's a new one, Lizzy, I've got to give it to you. I think it'll be worth it to see Ajax and Esme exposed as the hypocrites they are.'

'Coming from the top hypocrite himself,' I said, thinking *pictures, plural?* there was only one. 'It's not a great shot, but it's worth a lot to the person that took it . . .'

'I've got more than one, baby. Esme's been caught on camera, too.'

'Esme?' I frowned, tilted my head, glanced around us, as though people might be listening.

That's when I saw him. Olly. Standing, as though he had just come into the street and caught sight of me. As our eyes met, I raised my hand, but he just stared, his expression set and grim. Then he turned and walked away, so swiftly that he had disappeared in a moment into the back streets of Venice.

'I've got to go,' I said, standing up.

'I really hope we haven't annoyed your boyfriend,' said Jack.

He was pathetic, and any fear I'd felt dissolved in that moment, swept away by the intensity of my dislike for him. I calculated what would be the single thing I could do that would annoy him the most. Then I picked up the Aperol spritz and dumped the orange drink over the top of his head. The word he called me was satisfyingly dark enough for me to know I'd hit my mark.

'Takes one to know one,' I said, and set off at a jog to catch Olly.

CHAPTER THIRTY-NINE

It was hard to run in Venice. So many people. So many cobbles. And I wasn't wearing trainers, but my pointy-toed boots, which looked smart but were pretty brutal on my feet. They slowed me down, so it felt like a miracle when I saw Olly, ahead of me, his dark head bobbing as he strode down the street in double quick time. 'Olly,' I called, ignoring people looking at me. 'Olly!'

He turned and saw me, his expression darkening. As I advanced towards him, he put his hands out to stop me getting near him. It was a simple gesture, but I felt like I'd been slapped.

'Don't,' he said.

I stopped in my tracks.

'I— I wondered why you'd rushed out,' he said. His voice was rough, but I heard the hesitation in his words, and it made my heart squeeze, made me want to reach out to him.

When I did, he took another step back. 'I guess it turns out that thing you had with Jack wasn't as dead as you said it was. Thought you'd give it another try, is that right?'

'What?' My mind was racing. 'Where has this come from? And how did you know where I was?'

'Where you both were, you mean.' His expression was brittle. 'Your PA came to me. Said she was worried about you, that you were in a state over an ex-partner. That you might be indiscreet, feed him information, because you were desperate to get back with him.'

I gave a croak of disbelieving laughter, but Olly did not smile back.

Someone snapped at us in Italian. I pulled him to the side of the street. Another stucco wall, pale pink, this one; a lantern above us that looked as though it was at least two hundred years old. Bad stuff happening in this beautiful place, again.

'And you believed her?' I said.

'I didn't. Until I saw you.'

I shook my head. 'She's playing games. She's trying to manipulate things.' I saw the incomprehension on his face, realising I hadn't shared my disquiet over Sasha. 'Also, you know me. I would never go against what I'd agreed. Never feed someone information behind your back. This is *me*, Olly.'

'I'm not sure I know the real you, Lizzy. I asked you where you were going and you could have told me. You were hiding it – that points pretty clearly to guilt.'

His words turned my blood to ice. But even worse was the way he was looking at me, as though he had entirely disconnected his emotions. Sniper stare. Mixed in with my hurt was that flicker of fear from the past, a legacy of Jack: he'd always wanted to know where I was, what I was doing, usually so he could criticise it. Criticise me.

'I don't have to tell you everything,' I said, coldly.

'I guess I have my answer about the pictures, then,' he said.

The ice in me transformed into fire. 'What the hell does that mean?'

He swiped open his mobile phone and handed it to me.

'This was posted ten minutes ago,' he said.

It was the Skirmish gossip site edited by Jack, and the sight of it made me short of breath. Under the headline 'Secrets and Lies' was the line 'Kinky Sex Games of Cheating Millionaires.' There was the Ajax picture. Then a picture of Esme, in her masked ball outfit, dancing with, er, Neil: a grainy mobile phone shot obviously captured by Sasha. The caption referenced 'indiscreet games in their Venetian sex dungeon with multiple partners.' It was at one hundred thousand views. Instinctively, I refreshed the page. One hundred and five thousand views.

I felt sick. I looked up at Olly's face, at the wall he had put up behind his dark eyes. 'You think *I* knew about this?'

He blinked, and I saw a flicker of doubt. 'You're one of four people in Venice who had access to that picture of Ajax. If all of this is concocted, then what were you doing with

Jack? Sitting there, laughing, having sunset cocktails at the edge of the canal?'

'I was freezing my bloody tits off,' I hissed. 'And it was *him* laughing, not me. I'm not the person who's obsessed with Jack – Sasha is. They're together, and it must have been her who gave him those pictures. He messaged me today and wanted to see me. I thought I could make the situation better in some way. Damage limitation.' I gave a hollow laugh. 'That man singlehandedly torched eight months of my life, and you think, what? I want to jump back into bed with him? I can't believe you think that about me.'

'So how did she get the picture?' he said.

'God, you still don't believe me, do you? She has access to my inbox.'

He stood there, his brow furrowed, considering my words. But for me the conversation was already over. I was sick and tired, the core of me retreating into nuclear winter. *How could he have thought that?* It struck me, hard, that in Olly I thought I had found someone who knew me instinctively on a deeper level. Who somehow had absorbed and understood all the different bits of my life, and still liked me. That he was someone who would always think the best of me. For him to doubt me was devastating. It was easier to be angry; to step back from a situation which had made me much too vulnerable. Mixing the personal and professional was always a terrible idea. My bad for forgetting that.

'Think what you like,' I said, hearing the ice in my voice.

'Okay,' he said at the same moment. 'I get it.'

'Oh, I've convinced you, have I?' I said, dredging sarcasm up from the emptiness I felt. 'Because you were one step away from calling it in to Ajax, weren't you? Were you looking forward to getting me fired?'

He stared at me; he couldn't deny it.

'I trusted you, Olly. Why couldn't you trust me?'

'I'm sorry,' Olly said abruptly. 'I went off the deep end. Everything was pointing that way. Plus, I was jealous—'

It was my turn to put out my hand to stop him. 'I don't want to know your reasons for wanting to throw me under the bus. It's clear we don't know each other at all. This was all a big mistake, so let's consider it over as of now. Great nice guy act, by the way. You even had me fooled.'

Without looking at his face, I turned and marched in the opposite direction. I heard him call my name, but I kept going. I walked and walked until I was streets away, and I knew he wasn't following me.

As I walked, I looked through my phone and dialled a UK number. When it was answered in two rings I exhaled with sheer relief.

'Lennox?'

'Hey, Lizzy. I heard the news.' Lennox was the head of our internal IT systems. He was also one of the most practical people I'd ever met, and had never got on board with the idea of the Chroma app. For a moment I blinked, wondering which news he was talking about. There was so much.

'Sad they're not staying together,' he said.

'Yes, absolutely,' I said, thinking, oh, *that* news. 'Listen, I need you to block a member of staff's access to the EKArts system. All drives, and emails.'

'Right.' I could hear the hesitation in his voice. 'Whatever you say. You'll put this in writing?'

'As soon as I get back to my hotel room. But you need to lock them out immediately.'

'Understood.' I offered a prayer of thanks for his cool efficiency, even if I was closing the stable door after the horse had bolted. I could hear him typing. 'What's the name, please?'

I took a breath, looked out at the sweet glassy blue of the Venetian sky. I was shivering against the cold.

'Sasha Robinson,' I said.

It was only when I got to my hotel room that I finally allowed myself a moment. Changed into my pyjamas, emailed Esme about what had happened, looked at pictures of Pebble on the phone, sent by the luxury cattery she was staying in (another line on my spreadsheet). I even put a coat on over my pyjamas and went to reception to see how I could order in some cakes and hot chocolate. The receptionist frowned and nodded gently. As I turned away, I heard her say in Italian, 'This lady is very sad'.

This lady *was* very sad. But it was only sitting in the bath later, my tension unlocked by the warm water, that I allowed myself the space to cry.

CHAPTER FORTY

Money buys you an in to all the best places, and it also provides an out, too. That night, Ajax decided it was time to get out of Dodge, and by the morning he and his closest staff had gone, including Olly.

I knew this because Olly had messaged me. Several times. Progressively later and later, but I could not bring myself to reply.

OLLY: I'm sorry.

OLLY: Lizzy, I'm so sorry.

OLLY: I just went into emergency mode.

OLLY: Please, will you speak to me? Tell me I've been an asshole and let me apologise.

At midnight, woken from an exhausted doze, still feeling empty, cold and hurt, I sent him one line.

LIZZY: If you send me one more message I will block you.

He left me in peace after that. Early that morning, I received an email to say that the belongings of Resilience Needs staff who had moved to The Hexagon were already being removed to their offices in Clerkenwell. Chroma would be a collaborative venture, but there would be a brief hiatus before the project was taken forward. There was no intention for the two companies to be merged.

Everyone else started trickling home, depending on availability of flights, even though our office manager was claiming she was going to 'rip a new one' for anyone who tried to change their tickets at great expense. The collective hangover from the trip – colds, embarrassment, disintegrating marriages back at home – was going to be a big one.

To give me some strength, and in lieu of buying more cakes, I Zoomed Sara in Australia. She had just finished applying a mud mask when she appeared in front of me, her hair wrapped in a towel turban.

When I told her about Sasha, she claimed to be attempting to raise her eyebrows. 'I guess with this girl there's no such thing as hoes before bros,' she said.

'Is that even a thing?' said Dex in the background.

'Yes,' Sara and I said simultaneously.

'Rah to the sisterhood,' he said, and went to watch some sports re-runs on the television.

I smiled, but the smile faded as I thought about the situation. 'I thought we were tight, Sasha and me,' I said. 'I mentored her, I did my best to be a supportive manager. Before Jack turned up, she told me a lot of what was going on in her life, said she wanted to learn from me, be inspired by me. I thought we trusted each other. What did I do that meant she didn't see things that way?'

'Don't even think about blaming yourself for this,' said Sara.

'But—'

'Uh-uh.'

'But—'

'*Nope*. I mean it.' She sighed. 'I've known people like Sasha before. I'm not being funny, Lizzy, but most people have a work persona. I know we're supposed to bring our *whole selves* to work but most sane people know that's bullshit. If she flattered you, then showed you her vulnerability – which it sounds like she did – she was essentially inviting you to care for her a bit, take her under your wing. And you obliged. That doesn't mean she gave a monkey's about you. I'm sorry.'

I nodded. I knew she was speaking the truth. But it didn't ease the sting that I'd been essentially *taken in* by Sasha. I prided myself on having good judgement about character: I thought I'd been getting the real, unvarnished person. With Jack Dillane, I'd always known he was a dodgy one; his wickedness had even been part of his charm to start with. I'd ignored all the red flags going up, even when they were waving madly, deciding (wrongly) it was a risk worth taking. But with Sasha, not even a bit of me thought she was anything other than she presented herself to be, and the fact she now thought of me as 'the enemy' had blindsided me.

'It sounds like she's in competition with you,' said Sara, picking up a glass of rosé. 'That's the patriarchy. Make women hate each other and compete with each other for resources.'

'Why are *we* friends then?' I said. 'When we met, we worked in the same place.'

'That café was hardly a cutthroat environment, but we would always have been friends,' she said, 'and that is because we are both exceptional human beings who have the emotional and intellectual breadth and depth to rise above prevailing cultural norms.'

'I'm so glad we cleared this up,' I said.

'Hon, my mask is dry, I have to wash it off in a min, anything else to tell me?' she said.

'I've been having sex with Olly,' I offered.

She all but spat out the mouthful of wine she'd just taken. 'And this is *second* on the agenda? Below your regular issue fake ingénue girl?' she screeched.

'I wasn't going to tell you. I just wanted to see rosé explode out of your mouth,' I said.

'And?' she said.

'It was amazing. Then I told him not to message me again,'

I said. 'Please note, this is a slightly abridged version of what has happened.'

'Elizabeth the first, you are one sexy badass,' she said. 'My mask is properly cracking now, can I call you back in a min for the deets?'

'I promise, those were the highlights,' I said. 'I should probably go to bed now. So is it okay if we catch up when I'm back in His Majesty's United Kingdom?'

She rolled her eyes. 'All right then, you fucking tease. But make it soon. I love you, Lizzy boo.'

I winced at the memory of Sasha calling me Lizzy-Lou.

'Love you, too, Sara boo.'

'It's been taken down,' I said, watching Esme as she looked out at the lagoon, a commuter boat passing, crammed full of suited workers, just another day. 'The Skirmish article.'

Esme and Ajax's lawyers had proved the worth of their eye-watering hourly rate by briskly filing charges of defamation and by representing the photographer who'd taken the shot of Ajax in a copyright claim. That hadn't stopped the rumours from spreading, of course, because by that time the article had been seen and shared over seven hundred thousand times, with every Tom, Dick and Harry taking screen shots of the pictures, which were appearing everywhere. The legal team were doing whack-a-mole every time a picture popped up (I guessed an intern was stationed to watch the alerts every time it was republished), so perhaps in six months the whole story would have mutated into vague rumour.

The good news was, Jack had had to publish an apology about the sex dungeon claims, and the newspaper who'd originally been due to run the story was still happy to have a no-holds-barred interview with Ajax. I'd been informed of this in a crisp group email from Olly, which had been signed 'Best, Olly'. I suppose, considering I'd stonewalled him, I was lucky he didn't sign it 'Regards'.

I'd considered messaging Jack and asking him if he had managed to get the Aperol out of his white jacket, but instead I blocked his new number. If he wanted to get in touch, the least he could do was buy a new SIM card. I felt sure he wouldn't go to that trouble.

As I greeted her that morning, Esme didn't seem that bothered by the claims. She was pleased she looked good in Sasha's grainy photo. 'And I'm quite flattered that they think I've got a sex dungeon.' She was now quietly occupying the suite that she and Ajax had shared ('I can starfish in the bed,' she said), and after a couple of facials and some steaming, she looked as fresh as a daisy. Sketches were piling up around her as her creativity released itself, and she'd been in touch with Chiara to discuss a possible exhibition of new work. She'd even had a make-up artist in to give her a newer, softer look: no smudged lined eyes or red lipstick, she was all bronze and gold neutrals. Ironically for a millionaire, she did indeed look a million dollars.

I stood near her, laptop in hand. She stood at the window, sipping an espresso (having just finished boiled water with a squeeze of lemon, obviously).

'Take a look in that box,' she said, gesturing towards one of the marble side tables.

I knew what it was, of course: it had the distinctive red leather and gold tooled decoration of a Cartier box. I put my laptop down, picked up the box, popped its catch, and gazed at the biggest yellow stone I'd ever seen, set on a platinum band. It was lavish. The stone was literally the colour of sunshine, but there was something jarring about it, too: the cool metal, the almost too-bright stone. I turned it around in the light, and it glittered.

'It's a coloured diamond,' she said.

'I never doubted it,' I said.

She winked at me. 'Look at the card.'

'It's obviously private.'

'Go *on*, Lizzy.'

I opened the folded piece of cream card. Written in perfect calligraphy were the words:

Ez. Like diamonds we were formed under pressure. My love for you is as permanent and as bright as this diamond. I love you forever. Ajax.

I looked back up at Esme.

'He arranged for it to be sent before' – she waved her hand in the air vaguely – 'everything. And he didn't bother to cancel it. Anyway, looks like he'll love me forever.' She smiled, misty-eyed.

I had no way of accurately reading this situation. 'Do

you think there's any chance you might get back together?' I hazarded.

'Not really,' she said, slowly. 'Also, there's someone else I've been kind of seeing casually. I think that might have more legs.'

I shut the box with a snap and put it back, suppressing my shocked reaction. Somehow, I managed not to raise my eyebrows. I took a sip of my own coffee rather miserably. She sounded bored, as though she was exchanging a set of trousers in a shop, or getting rid of last season's handbag. 'I hope this new relationship is very much under wraps,' I said flatly. 'The optics wouldn't be good if it came out now.'

'He's the soul of discretion,' she said, then whispered, '*Billionaire*. Anderson, who invited us to the ball.'

There was really nothing I could think of to say. So I sighed.

'Anyway.' She brightened up. 'I'll always love Ajax, too. Maybe I'll get this diamond cut in two? Have something made for him? An ear stud? He does look fab with a diamond stud in one ear.'

I thought, privately, perhaps they could just have a conversation rather than *cleaving a diamond*. 'Whatever you think,' I said. 'Shall we prep for this afternoon?'

She shrugged. 'Fine.'

The meeting for possible investors was still going ahead, with Ajax's agreement, although as Olly's 'best' email to us all had put it:

He would be grateful if personal matters are not

mentioned. These will be dealt with in the upcoming interview.

'Can I just say, before we begin, I do think this is madness,' I said. 'We're already taking a break on the app development, and it's not as if the details are nailed down. We could just cancel the meeting.' As we'd tempted a bunch of people to attend because we were putting them up in fancy hotels, it would have been perfectly legitimate to call it off. And it certainly would have been prudent given that *personal matters* were now off the agenda. Also, if I caught a flight in the next couple of hours I could be on the sofa with Pebble by nightfall.

'Fuck's sake, Lizzy,' said Esme gently. 'Give it a rest? I'm doing it.'

I put my hands up in surrender and opened the laptop.

CHAPTER FORTY-ONE

The signs were all there from the outset that we were going into a nightmare. The room where we were holding the meeting for potential investors had that same neutrally coloured decor with gilded details, and highly perfumed air as the hotel suite we'd done the press conference in.

By horrific coincidence, there were even some lilies, reminiscent of the monster lilies that had streaked my outfit with pollen in London. This time, however, I was wearing black, so, while I sneered at them, I wasn't as worried that they'd take me down.

Lilies. Jollies to Venice. Love-logoed merchandise. To think sustainability had been one of the headlines in my notebook at the beginning of the year.

I shook off my feeling of doom, filing annoyance where I could access it later. I'd been receiving messages from Katrina, one of our receptionists who'd stepped in to cover

Sasha's role. It had been thought prudent to use an internal person rather than a temp, considering all of the *very* confidential stuff that was happening. Sasha had flown home and been granted a month's sabbatical with minimal fuss considering that HR had bigger fish to fry. We would have to sort out our issues when she was back. Katrina was cheerful and efficient, and she messaged me now to say Esme's speech would be livestreamed to EKArts and Resilience Needs; the technical set-up was complete. I thanked her and, as the room started filling up, I went to see how Esme was.

Walking past security and into the room which had been commandeered as a dressing room, I found the make-up chair empty, Esme's assistant looking wan alongside the make-up artist who was ready to refresh her appearance.

'Where is she?' I said.

Wide-eyed, the assistant pointed at the closed door to her left.

I went to the door, knocked, and opened it before she could call for me to stop. I stood in the doorway, and swallowed hard, feeling a wave of dread rise up in me.

Esme was sitting on a large button backed sofa, her head in her hands, her normally expansive posture imploded so that she suddenly looked tiny, despite her beautiful clothes and the long silk scarf, trailing on the floor. The sight of her distressed reminded me of how she had been when I first knew her. How, gradually, I – we – had pieced her back together; had made EKArts what it was. How much I'd given to that process. Sorting other people's problems was an instinct, so bone-deep I had never questioned it. I just couldn't solve my own.

'Esme,' I said, as calmly as possible. 'Are you okay? The meeting is due to start in twenty minutes.' I walked slowly over and sat down beside her.

'Just a touch of stage fright,' she said softly. 'You know what it's like.' She looked up at me, and my first emotion was relief. She wasn't crying, and there was no tell-tale smell of alcohol (as a young artist, she'd been well known for self-medicating with vodka before big appearances, all part of her wild child image). I felt myself soften in sympathy. I sometimes forgot that although she loved being in the public eye, there were aspects of it which would always be alien to her, leaving her feeling exposed. Speaking in front of finance people was one of those things; the nonchalance she had shown earlier was an act of bravado, a defence.

'You've got this,' I said, comfortingly. 'These people are all here because they're intrigued by the idea of Chroma. You've already sparked their interest. That's half the battle.'

To my alarm, her eyes suddenly filled with tears. 'It's not the whole battle, though, is it? This was meant to be me, and Ajax, together. What if they ask me something technical?' She put her hand on mine. 'I don't know if I can do it without him. And I . . . miss him.'

Cannot compute, my brain told me. Trying to align her sadness with the cool front she'd shown earlier. Trying to calculate what she wanted, what she needed. It was 1pm in London – if I put a call in to her therapist, perhaps she could speak to her this afternoon, but certainly not before the meeting, which was *very soon*.

'We'll have time to sort everything out when we get back to London,' I said calmly, mechanically. 'But for now, do you want to cancel this speech? We can do that, but we should do it now.'

'No! No. Chroma needs this. I'll do it, Lizzy, I promise. Just get Ajax on the phone. I need to speak to him. To clear my head.' She wiped her face with her hands. 'I'll go and get my make-up done, but I need to speak to him before I go out.'

I watched her stride across the room and pull the door open, heard the soothing voices of the team outside as they greeted her.

For some reason, I felt like crying, too. Which was not how I usually rolled until Venice. I got my phone out, pulled up the contact I thought I'd never use again.

>   **LIZZY:** It's me. Can you help me please?

He saw it immediately; when I saw he was typing I sat back down on the sofa, trying not to tremble.

>   **OLLY:** What do you need?

>   **LIZZY:** I've got Esme here and she's melting down.
>   She needs to speak to Ajax.

OLLY: ... typing.

I pressed my lips together.

OLLY: Hold tight. Let me see what I can do.

I sat still. Tried not to drum my feet on the floor. The door opened and Esme's assistant stuck her head round, a questioning look on her face.

'Just waiting to hear,' I said. She nodded and went again. My phone buzzed.

OLLY: Hi, Lizzy. Ajax is at home at the moment, but I've spoken to him and he'll call her now.

LIZZY: Can you tell him to call my phone? I'll hand it to her.

OLLY: No problem.

I walked into the next room, where Esme's face had been made up in record time by a Michelangelo of a make-up artist called Tania. 'He's about to call me.'

The phone started buzzing; I put it into Esme's manicured hand. As she answered it her face softened, and she sprang up and went into the next room, closing the door behind her.

'Would you like me to do your make-up, too?' asked Tania softly. 'Esme said you might also be speaking.'

'No, thanks,' I said, 'I'm not speaking.' I sat down on a chair nearby and looked at my phone. No more messages from Olly.

> **LIZZY:** She's talking to him now. Thank you, I appreciate it.
>
> **OLLY:** You're welcome.

He showed as 'online' for a single moment more, then he was gone.

We sat there for a hair-raising five minutes which felt more like fifty. It was now ten minutes before the meeting was due to start.

Finally, the door opened, and Esme emerged. I was relieved to see she hadn't cried away Tania's work, and she looked blissfully calm. I stood up, pocketing my phone.

'Everything okay?'

Esme nodded and smiled. 'Absolutely. Back on track.'

I felt a surge of relief. This was why I admired Esme. Yes, she was sensitive, raw, mercurial, but she was also strong. Capable of delivering when you needed her to. I'd seen it a hundred times.

'Great,' I said, smiling. 'We've got ten minutes, so let's just briefly refresh the points to cover. I've put notes out on the lectern, but it's good to get them in your head, too.'

She came to me, placed her hands on my shoulders. 'Lizzy.'

'Yes?'

'Ajax agrees that you need to go out there, rather than me. You tell them about Chroma. I'm really not in the space to face all the potential investors out there. And I don't think we should cancel the event, not now that everyone is here.'

I felt the ground slope away beneath my feet. 'What? No, Esme. They want to see you, not me.'

For a moment, I thought I'd reached her. I'd always been able to speak the truth to her; she had always been able to hear it.

Until now. 'I don't think that's relevant,' she said, and I could almost see it: her shining armour unfurling itself, that blissful, titanium-plated serenity protecting her from anything that didn't fit with her point of view. She glanced at her assistant. 'Jay, can you order me a water taxi? I'd like to go and rest at the hotel. I know you'll do it wonderfully, Lizzy.' She kissed me on the cheek, and I stood, frozen, trying to recalibrate my thoughts, with a sinking feeling as I did so. A rich person's plaything. Senior Director; convenient servant.

When I looked up, Esme had already gone, ushered out on a fragrant breeze with her assistant and security. Tania stood beside me, and she offered me a hesitant, empathetic smile.

'Can I take you up on the offer of make-up now?' I said.

She gave me a double thumbs up.

CHAPTER FORTY-TWO

Afterwards, I would remember the upturned faces, some of them nonplussed, some of them annoyed. The exact sound everyone made when I announced that both Ajax and Esme were 'indisposed': half groan, half comprising the sound of a bunch of people muttering 'what the fuck?' to each other.

The lens of the camera, filming the meeting, to be live-streamed to the offices in London. Later intended to be used for content.

I did my best ice queen impression for the first five minutes, because I knew I needed to keep their attention and, preferably, their respect. Cold-eyed, unblinking, stance upright and inflexible, softened by the occasional smile. If I could have co-opted some snakes for hair I would have done. But the whole point was, I shouldn't have been the story. I played a short demo film for Chroma which had been cobbled together back in the UK and sent over that morning. It was slickly done, but there was no hiding that it was a bunch of stock material which included crashing waves and sunrises. The phrase 'Art is Love' vibrated on screen; I saw the colours from the film on the faces of the front row. One man looked at another and mimed a 'cut' gesture across his throat. The other sniggered.

Film over, I read through the spiel about Chroma and said I wouldn't be commenting on Esme and Ajax's personal lives, but that they would be working on this project together. That we were hopeful everyone here would want to be part of this story at its inception and that we would be reaching out to each of them individually about whether they would like to invest.

Finally, taking a big breath, I opened the floor to questions, still staying poker-faced. The first hand raised was one of Ajax's contacts. He was smiling.

'Considering Ajax posted five minutes ago on socials, telling any haters to go and eff themselves, isn't it a bit rich to expect people to take his advice on love and positivity?'

I felt the colour drain from my face. And I knew they would see it, too.

'Noted,' I said. 'Thank you.'

The next person I asked to speak was well-known to me, a contact of Esme's from the art world, who had a diverse portfolio.

'More of a comment than a question,' he said.

'Okay,' I said, attempting a smile.

'This is an absolute fucking shambles,' he said. 'So I won't be investing.'

And so it went.

Afterwards, I found the quietest corner of the smallest, darkest café I could find, and ordered coffee with biscotti.

> **OLLY:** I saw the meeting. What a bear pit. I can only apologise for Ajax's post.

> **LIZZY:** Has it been deleted now?

> **OLLY:** Yes. I would have got to it sooner, but I was at home with my family, took a day off to see them. Bad timing.

I blinked back tears. I hadn't even thought of that, I was so wrapped up with Esme and her difficulties.

> **LIZZY:** I'm sorry this debacle interrupted family time.

> **OLLY:** It's fine. Over and out.

I nodded to no one in particular. Wrapped in my coat, my laptop bag dumped at my feet, I dipped the first biscotti into the coffee and then took a bite. Its deliciousness barely touched my misery. My phone vibrated on the table.

DAD: Morning love. Just spoke to Natasha, my account manager here. The service charge is going up. She needs to have a chat with you. Thanks

Natasha the account manager could do one, I decided, practically *feeling* my blood pressure rise.

LIZZY: Hi, Dad, she already has my phone number and she shouldn't be bothering you. I am in Venice, I will call her tomorrow.

DAD: Could you let me know when you've done it? X

The kiss at the end meant he was really worrying.

I swore under my breath. I was doing that a lot recently. It was only a matter of time before I started swearing out loud when alone, then a slippery slope to me being one of those wild, ranty people that stand in the middle of the pavement shouting while other people carefully avoid them.

Tears came to my eyes for the hundredth time. Was I going to have a nervous breakdown in Venice? I finished the biscotti and coffee, paid, and went out to walk back to my hotel. I could feel the phone vibrating in my pocket with message after message. There would be work queries, and I was sure the Comms team were dealing with fallout from the Skirmish article. There would probably be a furious, sarcastic missive from Jacob asking if the lilies had been gold plated and was Esme planning on taking a cruise ship home from Venice. There would be HR asking to set aside time in the diary to resolve the Sasha issue, and whether I had kept a log of what had happened. There would be Dad worrying.

Everything urgent, everyone anxious, nervous, annoyed, and looking to me.

Back at the hotel I packed my masked ball outfit back in its wrapping: it was due to be collected from reception. Borrowed, not bought. Luckily, I hadn't spilt punch over it.

I packed my suitcase, decided to leave for the airport sooner rather than later. I couldn't stand rushing. As I waited for the boat, I answered some of the emails — those that just needed a simple response.

I watched the light on the water as the boat zipped its way to the airport. I still loved Venice. I hadn't seen a single piece of art, visited a church or seen the Murano glass. But I'd been bathed in this beautiful light, I'd felt joy alongside my sadness, and although I knew I would be glad to get home, I felt suddenly wistful leaving it behind. I remembered Olly saying 'let's come back', and that was impossible, because we were over. That gave me the kind of lovesick feeling I last had when I was a teenager.

My phone buzzed. It was Jacob. I prepared myself for a stream of annoyance.

> **JACOB:** Are you okay? I can't believe Esme sent you into that. When you're back let me buy you lunch, darling.

His kindness unlocked my emotion in a way his anger never would have done. I wiped away a tear, puffing out a breath in an attempt to hold things in, typing 'Thank you x' and stuffing my phone back in my pocket.

In this Venetian light, I was ready to look at hard truths. I'd been skating over reality for years. Giving the best part of me to my work. And that had been fine, absolutely fine, but time was ticking on. Work was not loving me back. The life I had built didn't feel like a real life, a full life. At work, I was great – or had been great; at home, I was hanging on. The brief moment of joy that I had felt in Venice with Olly had reminded me of what happiness looked like. We might have crashed and burned before we'd even got off the runway, but he'd shown me a different way that was possible. He had been my wake-up call.

The driver asked me if I had enjoyed my stay. I managed to say yes, smiled, thanked him, tipped him.

After I'd checked in at the airport, I opened Dad's thread.

> **DAD:** When are you back from Venice Lizzy?

> **DAD:** I'm worried about things.

I absorbed his stress, felt it in the centre of my body, the punch of failure.

> **LIZZY:** Hi Dad. Messaging isn't the best way to sort these things. Let's have a cup of tea when I get back.

The moment I sent it, I felt afraid that he would be upset by it. So I opened another message.

> **LIZZY:** Take care Dad. Love you loads xx

> **DAD:** Okay x

Okay was fine. Okay was normal. *He's fine*, I told myself. *Stop worrying.* My daily mantra when it came to Dad and Alex. Listlessly, I checked my emails again, flipping between work demands and a couple of professional networking sites where I looked at job adverts.

One certainty had emerged from my tired mind. I needed to change. Somehow, tiny degree by tiny degree, my life had become untenable. I was the archetypal frog in a pan of cold water, sitting there as the water heated to boiling point. It was time to leap out. But how?

They were calling my flight when my phone buzzed again.

> **OLLY:** Hi.

It took me milliseconds to reply.

LIZZY: Hey.

OLLY: Can we reconnect when you get back? I really don't want to be on bad terms. It's been great working with you.

Great working with you. The jolt I felt was harder than the one Dad's message had given me. *Reconnect?* Like we'd had a minor disagreement in a meeting, or he'd accidentally broken my favourite work mug. But I took it like a pro, standing stock still in the middle of the airport, my phone in my hand. Looking like any other person, reading a work message. So what if I felt . . . desolate. Bereft.

My tired mind flicked through a thousand options like the departure boards above me. And the answer it gave was . . . I'd been right. Right the first time we'd kissed, when I'd said we shouldn't get involved. Work relationships like ours were messy things, muddying the waters, risking reputations and professional fallout. Olly and I had been reckless. And if he'd recovered his sensible head, then I should, too.

The flight call went out again, spurring me to make a decision. I typed a response and sent it without even re-reading it. Because I didn't want to send it. But it was the best thing to do.

LIZZY: Thanks, but there's no need to reconnect. This was a mad situation and it sent us both a bit mad, too. No hard feelings here. All the very best.

I put my phone on airplane mode, and set off for my departure gate.

CHAPTER FORTY-THREE

The luxury cattery delivered Pebble back to my flat two hours after I'd got home. My second load of washing was in, and I was drinking my third cup of tea, dressed in comfy leggings and an enormous fisherman's knit jumper I'd bought in a local charity shop the winter before. I'd opened a window to let the traffic fumes in, or 'air the room'. London was still cold, but there was a certain brightness to the air which indicated spring might be on its way, eventually. I'd got used to Venice's Renaissance colour and light, but there was something about the familiarity of London's pale sunshine that caught happily at my heart.

Carefully delivered in a sustainable cardboard cat carrier, which, the courier perkily told me, I could re-purpose as a cat enrichment activity, Pebble looked out at me, almost definitely furious and completely oblivious to the three-figure sum I'd paid out for her care during the Venice trip, solely because she'd scared our neighbour so much with her disappearing antics a few weeks before. I made a mental note not to tell Dad that I'd paid so much for her care: I could just imagine the words *but she's just a cat* writ large across his features.

I let Pebble out and she disappeared under my bed while I made my fourth cup of tea and called Natasha, Dad's Account Manager, to assure her that I could pay Dad's increasing service charge. I even managed not to click my tongue when she told me the amount, or to enquire whether they were putting gold leaf in the desserts, or even to snarkily slip in something like *still doesn't include any utilities then?*

Natasha liked talking and was in the process of using eighty-five words when ten would do. Just as I thought my sanity was finally slipping from me, Pebble reappeared and climbed into my lap, where she proceeded to 'make biscuits', kneading me lovingly with her paws and purring. My angry little cat had somehow decided to demonstrate her (grudging) love for me.

I listened to Natasha's voice, as Pebble kneaded, my slow blink echoing hers in a declaration of love. When I finally managed to hang up the phone, I leaned forward and kissed Pebble on the head.

She glared at me, leapt off my lap, and skittered under the bed.

'I'm going to get a dog in my next life,' I called to her. I lay down on the sofa, watching the play of light on the ceiling as my breathing steadied. I was home, and relieved to be home, but a sense of homesickness still had its claws in me. Perhaps because I was homesick for a person, rather than a place.

The next day, 8am, and I was walking into The Hexagon, curly hair just about in check, wearing a denim jumpsuit (not black!) and white and yellow Adidas sneakers, coffee in hand and gliding like I'd never had a professional worry in my life. Whatever choppy waters were waiting for me, I was ready.

Katrina was at Sasha's desk, cheery and organised but also clearly a little nervous. I smiled warmly at her and saw her relax. 'Thanks so much for holding the fort,' I said. 'Do we need to have a catch-up?'

'That would be good,' she said. 'I've mainly sent holding messages for enquiries when Becky and Jana couldn't deal with them.'

'Thank you,' I said. 'Let's speak at eleven.'

She left and I turned on my computer, watching email after email download, one per second. I'd answered a load the day before, sitting on the sofa, but of course they had freshly replenished themselves overnight.

I opened the top email (usually not my policy, I always start at the bottom normally) but this one was from Esme and was titled, mysteriously, 'Conversation', so I went to it first.

> Sweet Lizzy,
> We need to converse about your role with us, going forward. In all honesty, you did a less than stellar job promoting Chroma to the VIPs. Of course, your five

percent is anyone else's one hundred percent, you are my first class high achieving warrior, Lizzy. And yet. I have noticed a certain cynicism in you of late. I understand why you are cynical, I really do. A woman doesn't achieve all that you have in this stormy warry world without growing a thick skin. But Chroma does not need cynicism: it is anti-cynicism. Ajax and I intend to start work on it again soon, and with open hearts.

Lizzy, you have always been my warrior. Can I co-opt you to fight on the side of Good, of Chroma?

Let's chat when you get the chance.

E xx

I stared at the words on the screen, my mind blank with the kind of anger that is so all-encompassing it clearly comes from feelings that have been long buried. 'What the actual . . .' I muttered to myself. There were at least fifteen things wrong with this email, but the main issue was the sheer injustice of it. I was being blamed for the chaos of the investors' meeting, when Esme and Ajax had just left their precious project high and dry? Their defenceless baby Chroma in the hands of a 'cynical' warrior? Also vom, it sounded as though she had joined a cult.

It was definitely the most cringey email I'd ever received at work, and I felt something give in me. Something that had been in the process of breaking for weeks, possibly months.

I was still shaking my head when there was a gentle tap on the door: Katrina popped her head round nervously. 'Ellie in

HR would like to see you,' she said. 'I'm sorry, I told her you were free, should I have checked with you before I said that?'

'No, it's fine,' I said. 'I'll pop up now.' *Any excuse to get away from this email,* I thought to myself.

As an experience in itself, I always liked visiting Ellie, our HR manager, unless some shit was going down. She had a lovely office, complete with a range of teas and coffees, a grey linen-covered button-backed sofa and a box of tissues on the nearby coffee table, just like a therapist. It was also one of the offices with smoked glass, so people couldn't be seen weeping or shouting.

When I knocked on the door, she opened it just a crack, then stepped out and shut it behind her. 'There's someone here who wants to apologise to you,' she said. 'It's Sasha.'

I felt my heart fall in my chest. Realised that, in that split second, I had hoped it would be Olly. That I was looking for him everywhere.

'Are you okay to speak to her?' said Ellie. 'There's no obligation to.'

'It's fine,' I said.

She nodded, and turned back, holding the door open for me.

Sasha was sitting in the middle of the grey sofa, and she was crying.

'Right,' I said, looking at her, aware that Ellie was watching my reaction.

She looked like the Sasha I remembered: gone were the

stilettos, thick make-up and smooth hair (it was good to see her fresh-skinned face), as were the figure-hugging dresses and manicured nails.

'Sasha asked if she could speak to you,' Ellie said, looking intensely uncomfortable, 'if you're okay with that, Lizzy? I'm going to stay in the room, of course.'

I nodded. 'Hey, Sasha,' I said, as she went into a fresh volley of sobs. 'How are you?' I took a step towards her, and found myself folding my arms across my chest, not wanting to sit next to her. Whatever warmth had been between us was totally gone.

She shook her head, catching her breath. 'I'm so sorry, Lizzy. I know I let you down. I know I betrayed your trust. I wanted to— to— apologise, in person. I wanted you to know that I can't believe what I did.'

The silence hung in the air a moment too long.

'Right,' I said. 'Thank you for the apology.'

'I've told Ellie everything,' she said, her breath juddering. 'It's in writing. I violated the confidentiality agreement. I gave the pictures to Jack.'

I nodded, not knowing what to do, what to say.

'He dumped me.' She was crying again, so bitterly I could hardly bear to look at her poor face. 'He said I was just a stupid little girl.'

I flashed back to Venice, nearly three years before. Me and Jack on the edge of the lagoon, arguing about me taking a call from home. 'You think you're all grown up,' he'd said, 'but at the end of the day you're just Daddy's little girl, aren't you?'

That's when it had hit me: he wasn't just a bit wicked. He was plain nasty.

'He said that to me, too,' I said, glancing at Ellie, who looked back sympathetically. 'You'd think the dumbass would get some new lines.'

'He said it to *you*?' Sasha looked astonished.

'Yes.'

Ellie cleared her throat, and we looked at her. 'Thank you, Lizzy. Obviously, in light of what Sasha has admitted to, we will be going through a formal disciplinary procedure.'

I nodded, and Sasha did, too. She was starting to calm down, shocked out of the onslaught of pure emotion. She took another tissue and started to dab at her face. 'Would you ever work with me again?' she said, plaintively. 'I really did appreciate all of your guidance. You are amazing, Lizzy.'

I tried for a smile; I think I got halfway there. 'Let's just see what happens,' I said. 'But thank you for speaking to me, and for telling the truth. It's the right thing to do.'

She caught her breath. 'I can't believe I was so unprofessional,' she said. 'I shouldn't have let everything get so personal.'

That, I had sympathy with. 'Business always gets personal, whether we want it to or not,' I said. 'Because we're people. Not machines. But I take your point.'

'I'm going to get Jamie to walk you out, Sasha,' Ellie said. *Walk you out*, such a sweet way of saying that Sasha wasn't allowed to speak to anyone, to go to her desk, have access to the company's systems. Sasha nodded and stood as Ellie dialled an extension and spoke to Security. We stood, looking at each other; for a moment I thought she was going to ask for a hug, and I was relieved when she didn't. Despite her apology, things had fundamentally changed between us, and if she was asking for affection from me, I wasn't sure I could give it.

I tried to smile again, and managed it this time, because I saw her smile back in answer, as though we were doing a muted call and response. 'All the best, Sash,' I said.

The door opened, Sasha nodded, and went with Jamie.

When it closed behind them, Ellie gave a little huff of relief. 'Sorry if that blindsided you,' she said. 'I just didn't want to tell Katrina, when I called to get you. Didn't want her to feel strange or for the rumour mill to get started.'

'Nice try, but I predict everyone knows by now,' I said, with a rueful smile. 'And it's good that I'm here, because I need to discuss one more thing with you.'

'What's that?' she said, checking her calendar. 'I've got five minutes before my next Venice-related HR issue to deal with. What on earth went down out there – no, don't tell me. Is five minutes long enough?'

'It is,' I said. 'It's my resignation. I was going to email, but as I'm here, I may as well do it now.' I took out my phone, opened my email, typed a few lines and pressed Send. I smiled at the aghast look on her face. 'Do you need to call Jamie? Have me escorted out?'

It was EKArts policy for senior members of staff who resigned to go on 'gardening leave' the moment they handed their resignation in. A clean break, with no access to ongoing plans or – more importantly – financial systems. Ellie postponed the meeting she'd been due to have and came with me herself, carrying a cup of coffee and watching as I put my out of office on and shut down the computer, then handed her my work phone. The wide-eyed, mouth-open expressions of the team in the main office were something to behold.

'Bye, guys,' I called to them, my coat looped over my arm, thermal cup refilled with fresh coffee. 'I've just resigned. It's been great working with you all.' I gave them my best, brightest smile. Inclined my head towards Ellie, then walked towards the lift with her. As I walked, I tried to take it all in, so I could keep it in my memory, this place I had spent so much time in, whiling away some of the best and worst hours of my life. Hours when perhaps I could have been building a life – although it wasn't worth worrying about that now. It was both exactly like every other place I'd worked in, and also different: its own special micro-climate. I breathed in the particular scent of the place, the lavender cleaning fluid used by cleaners in the early morning, combined with that semi-industrial office smell – carpets and ink – and the aroma of late breakfasts: croissants, breakfast sandwiches, coffee and tea. The sound of the lift chime as it opened; the quality of the light inside, artificial and faintly jarring. In the mirrored lift, as I chatted to Ellie, I saw the shadows beneath my eyes, looked up at the real light as I exited, this glass, faceted building, bright like a diamond but somehow not healthy, in a way. Half artificial light, half greenhouse light, too bright, no happy medium.

I made to shake Ellie's hand, but she embraced me, lifting her coffee cup as she looped an arm around my shoulders and squeezed. 'I'll miss you,' she said. 'Coffee sometime?'

'Absolutely,' I said, 'I'd like that.' *If we ever get time*, I thought. *Unlikely.* I smiled at the security staff, exchanged a few words, and handed in my badge.

I suppose I could have gone for a tea somewhere, maybe taken a walk in the park, or (justifiably) gone to the pub for a celebratory (or compensatory) drink. Instead, I went home, rattling my way on the northern line to Oval. As I sat there, dazed, I could identify no emotions other than relief, amazement that I'd finally left EKArts, and quite a large dollop of uncertainty. The memory of Esme's email still stung: a bruise I couldn't help pressing. I'd love to think leaving would have caused a crater-like impact on the company, made her think a little, but I had the creeping feeling that it wouldn't have mattered at all. Right now, she was shrugging it off, nonplussed, perhaps a little perturbed, but with her eyes pinned on the future, looking for new people and new opportunities.

All of my obligations had evaporated, and the realisation was so dizzying and puzzling, that I almost missed my stop. At Oval, I stood there on the empty mid-morning platform, putting my coat on, and thought of all the urgency of those emails, now hitting the brick wall of my out-of-office reply. The late nights, the YouTube scripts, the spreadsheets with their ever-evolving formulae, the long meetings where, occasionally, someone would hit the table with their fist, or trade passive aggressive comments. All of this had very suddenly departed from my life. There was a hole where the main business of my life had been.

Wilting, I walked home from the tube, my steps becoming slower and slower. By the time I reached home I could admit to myself that I was completely exhausted. Opening the door, surprising Pebble in the act of sharpening her claws against the sofa arm, I took off my coat, dropped my bag, curled up on the sofa and fell asleep. When I woke briefly, stripes of sunlight on my face from the open blinds, I found Pebble had curled into the back of my legs.

CHAPTER FORTY-FOUR

The next few days were a bit of a blur. Ironically, after months of longing for a break, I found it hard to adjust to the non-urgency of my days, and after the second day of rising at ten and eating at strange times, I re-imposed routine, and started polishing my CV. I would be drawing on my small nest egg of savings to live, which made me jittery, but this was counterbalanced by the relief I felt at not being in The Hexagon, the sudden absence of a weight that I hadn't even known I was carrying. When a friend offered me some consulting work to tide me over, starting in two weeks, my job hunt became less frantic and more strategic. I wanted different. I wanted work-life balance.

In all, Pebble and I felt as though things were looking up. I had conversations with friends, some on the phone, some via messaging, and the main people in my life knew apart from Dad and Alex. I was due to visit them at the weekend so I would tell them then; with Dad's tendency to panic I knew a real-life chat would definitely be better.

True, I was still very much discombobulated and lacking in energy; and also true, I hadn't been cooking healthily, relying on takeaways and the kind of food that was so highly processed it basically just tasted of salt and sugar combined. But when I established my new early-rising routine I also established the process of putting make-up on and wearing clean clothes, so I was at least in the land of the living when someone knocked on my door one afternoon at the point I'd been about to start watching a glossy property show, dressed in leggings, furry ankle boots and a teal lambswool jumper which had a high neck and was extra snuggly.

Frowning, and wondering who had buzzed the visitor into the building, I went to the door and opened it on the chain, then reared back at the sight of the person standing there. 'Jacob?!'

His poreless, perfect face loomed at the door crack. 'Fuck. So this really *is* where you live. I had just presumed, you know, another place with the same name.'

I shut the door and leaned against it. Imagined Sara clapping her hands with delight: finally, a man from Finance at my door.

'Lizzy?' Jacob's muffled voice sounded woeful. 'That wasn't my best opener, I admit. Can I speak to you, please?'

'How did you get my address?' I bellowed. It was all well and good letting Olly come over when I'd been worried out of my mind about Pebble, but letting Jacob, world-of-interiors, into my lousy little flat? *Nah. Noooo. Nope.*

'Duh,' said Jacob, through the keyhole. 'I looked on the EKArts database, obviously. You going to report me for a GDPR breach?'

'Might do,' I snipped. Did I fancy ringing up EKArts and saying there'd been a data breach? Not really.

'I come in peace.' I heard tension in his clipped voice. 'Can you please open the door? There's an old man staring at me.'

I took the chain off and opened the door. Bill was standing on the landing, gimlet eyes fixed on Jacob, in lofty defiance. 'Is this man bothering you, Liz?'

Jacob mouthed *Liz?* at me.

'It's fine, Bill,' I said. 'Thank you for checking.' I looked back at Jacob. 'Wait here.'

I shut the door again and looked around the flat, stifling the enormous sigh that was rising in my chest. Mercifully, I'd cleared away the takeaway boxes and run the hoover around earlier. My only issue was my paranoia that the flat smelt of cat and biryani. I walked across the room, opened the window, turned the plug-in air freshener on, plumped the cushions on the sofa, then went back to the door.

'Okay,' I said. 'You can come in. Although I'm afraid it's not a tastefully restored townhouse in Kensington.'

'I married money, Lizzy,' said Jacob. 'I don't come from it. I know what a normal flat looks like.'

'Oh, for God's sake, come in, before I change my mind,' I grumped.

'*Thank* you,' he said, with exaggerated politeness. I turned away as he walked in, not wanting to see him look around and take it all in, and also trying not to visualise his own stunning kitchen extension which he'd once shown me a photo of. No bifold doors and marble floors here, mate. When I glanced back, he'd already taken off his coat and folded it neatly, placing it over the back of the sofa.

'Coffee?' I asked gloomily.

'Is it proper coffee?'

'I make it in a cafetière.'

'Then, yes.'

I made the coffee, deciding not to make excuses about the flat: he could think what he liked. Jacob carefully sat down on the sofa and looked around.

'What a beautiful cat,' he said, in the voice of someone making an effort, as Pebble shot past his outstretched hand.

'Don't tell her that,' I said, putting the coffee down in front of him and sitting next to him on the sofa. 'She hates compliments. Makes her sink her claws into people.'

He gave a wintery smile. 'I do miss your humour.'

'I'm sorry?' I said. 'You miss me? Don't let word get out.'

'I'll just deny it if it does,' he said, with a shrug.

We sipped our coffees in silence for a moment.

'So,' he said. 'Ask me how things are going at EKArts.'

'No,' I said, mercifully just about keeping a whine out of my voice. 'I don't care.'

'Fine.' He sighed. 'Ask me how Olly is.' He feigned my voice '"How is Olly, Jacob?"'

I pressed my lips together.

He glanced back at me. 'Pining. That's how he is.'

'Someone on Tinder broken his heart?' I said, in a brittle voice.

Jacob rolled his eyes. 'Mercy. Pining for you, you silly cow.'

I shook my head, concentrated on my coffee, trying to ignore the thud of my own pulse.

Jacob leaned forward, trying to catch my eye. 'What's wrong with you? That man is as fit as fuck and every time he looks at you it's like there are fireworks going off in his eyes. And now he's wandering around like a romantic poet searching for his muse. And the muse is you, Lizzy, much as it surprises me to admit it.'

'That's mean! Why do you care, anyway?'

His face wriggled. 'You saved me a lot of money over the years. Don't think I didn't appreciate you downgrading your travel.'

'Gee, thanks.'

He gave me a sidelong glance through narrowed eyes. 'I don't want you getting too full of yourself, but you were my favourite colleague, Lizzy. Unlike most people, you actually give a shit about the people around you. You try to make things better. And I like Olly, too. A lot. Nothing better than a bit of Scottish totty. Far nicer than that very *changeable* boss of his.' He raised his eyebrows.

'Look, don't think I'm not grateful for your concern.' I quailed at the darkling look he was directing at me. 'But you've got it wrong. We had a – thing, a spark. But he's not interested.'

'Has he not messaged you? Spoiler: I know he has.'

The idea of Olly confiding in Jacob made me blink with surprise. But Jacob was watching me earnestly.

'Yes, he has. But he was very formal. Asked if we could "reconnect" as he doesn't want there to be bad feelings between us. Trust me, there was nothing heartfelt about it. If anything, it felt as though he was just ironing out a professional wrinkle.'

He muttered something sweary under his breath, knocked back the last of his coffee, and placed the mug carefully on the coaster in front of him.

'Lizzy, I'm going to level with you. Oliver MacLeod is in love with you.'

I opened my mouth to interrupt him, but he held up an index finger to stop me.

'He is. In love. With you. And you're in love with him.'

'No, I'm not!' I said, indignant. But even to my ears, it sounded unconvincing.

'Well.' He took a breath. 'Perhaps Olly is overestimating things. He said Venice was special for you both.'

Venice. The memories of being with Olly in Venice seemed like something from another world. But they were scored into my mind: his touch, the white sheets, the scent of him. Had there been choirs singing as we were in the throes? That's how far the experience was up there as opposed to being part of the real world.

'Lizzy?'

When I looked back at him, his face had softened. 'And that's exactly the same expression he had on his face.'

'Do you want more coffee?' I picked up the mugs. When he shook his head, I took them to the kitchen area. 'My life is complicated,' I said, to the kitchen counter rather than to him. 'It's full of difficulties and obligations. It's messy.'

'Come back here.' Jacob patted the sofa, and I winced as I saw dust motes fly out. I traipsed back over and sat down.

'My very dear Lizzy.' He was deadly serious, which was alarming considering who I was speaking to, his blue eyes holding my gaze in complete solemnity. 'Everyone's life is complicated. Everyone's life is difficult. Don't push people away because you think you'll be too much.' He put his head back, inhaled loudly. 'Sweetheart, trust me when I say this man wants you. All of you. And he's a good guy. I like him. And I say that very rarely.'

'This indeed is true,' I said, nodding.

'Wouldn't it be nice,' he said, looking around him, something like sadness flitting across his face, 'to let your defences down? To' – he gave a little shrug – 'let the light in a bit?'

I regarded him in stunned silence.

'Jacob,' I said solemnly. 'Is this the secret of your success? Do you have a tattoo that reads "let the light in"?'

'Fuck you, bitch,' he said, and I squealed with laughter. 'I was going to hug you, but it would be wasted on you.'

He got up, gently removed his coat from the sofa and put

it on. 'That plug-in air freshener is heinous,' he said. 'I'm going to send you some melts.'

'Thank you,' I said, rising and standing opposite him. 'What will they smell like? Old Library mixed with leather and whisky on ice?'

'You should be so bloody lucky. You'll get bergamot and lemongrass and be grateful for it.'

'Thank you, my liege.'

He hugged me then, carefully, keeping his torso an inch away from me at all times. But the gesture was so unexpected, so not-Jacob, that tears sprang into my eyes.

'I appreciate you coming south of the river,' I said.

'I wish I could say it's been a pleasure,' he said, observing my pot plants.

'Will you tell Olly you've come?' I couldn't help it.

His eyes focused on mine. 'No.' A slight smile. 'You're on your own, kid.'

I nodded, walked with him to the door.

'Laters,' I said.

'Laters.' He produced a card, put it in my hand. 'My address and phone number. Do not lose it. Some people you want to keep.'

And just like that, he was gone.

CHAPTER FORTY-FIVE

That weekend, I took the train to see Dad and Alex. Since Jacob's visit, I'd started writing a message to Olly more or less a hundred times, and each time I had discarded the draft. Even typing 'Hey!' or 'How are you?' seemed awkward, loaded, both too formal and too casual considering everything that had happened between us. Ironically, considering how easily we had communicated in the past, firing off messages left, right and centre, I was now completely unable to find the right words or identify the right approach. I'd loved the unfiltered way we had spoken to each other, making each other laugh, but typing 'Hey Olly, are you in love with me?' which I wouldn't have thought twice about before (imagining him laughing his ass off when receiving it) now seemed ridiculously awkward.

That ship has sailed, I convinced myself.

As I sat, watching the London suburbs pass the train

window in a spring-lit blur, I acknowledged how strange it had felt, resigning from EKArts, without discussing it with him and making jokes about it. Somehow, Olly had become the person I'd vented to and laughed with, my everyday partner in crime. *I miss him*, I thought, the ache in my chest surprising me. It was all Jacob's fault, turning up on my doorstep with his perfect raised eyebrows and deep concern for the course of true love.

My thoughts went something like: I don't want Olly to be sad. I want to talk to Olly about being sad. I'm sad. I may just be a tiny little bit in love with him. A very tiny bit: in fact, it probably isn't love, it's infatuation. An infatuation that will evaporate like mist over the Venetian lagoon. Don't think about Venice, Lizzy. That bedroom in Venice. That feeling. Had I ever felt that. Much. Pleasure? No, no, I hadn't. That much pleasure, and that much emotional connection? Again, a definite no. Temporary madness, possibly I was drunk, high on ... tiredness? I was not in love with him. It was infatuation; worse, lust. By Christmas, I wouldn't even remember his name. I should think of him as a pin-up, an unattainable being like a pop star. Olly as a pop star (laughs). Olly hurting. No. *No*.

My phone pinged and I snatched it up. Dad, checking when I was going to arrive. I was due to have lunch at The Rowans, then we would visit Alex. He asked, 'Have you ordered Aubergine?' which I was puzzled about, until he wrote 'Sorry, autocorrect. Uber.'

As it happened, I hadn't. Instead, I took a local taxi,

driven by a man called Steve. Steve was very smiley, until the moment when another car cut him up and he turned into a steaming madman with a really inventive range of insults to hand. Steve put Jacob's wrath into the shade; he was, without a doubt, the angriest person I'd ever met. He didn't draw breath between shouting insults at other drivers until we pulled up at The Rowans and he turned to take my payment with an angelic smile. My hands were practically in cramp from how hard I'd been clinging to the seat.

'Have a really excellent day, love,' he said, as I tipped him.

I arrived to find Dad had already ordered my lunch for me, having been a bit anxious that we might be waiting for a while if an avalanche of lunch orders came in from fellow residents. Everyone here ate early, he explained. He'd chosen quiche with potatoes, green beans and carrots, and was hovering by a table for two, far from his usual eating spot. 'It's best if we eat on our own table,' he said. 'I normally sit on a six-place one, but everyone has their own place. I don't want to disturb things.' He gave me a wink. Breakfast wars were still a thing, apparently. One Sunday, pancakes had been made and there had practically been a riot.

We chatted about superficial things over lunch. I waited until we had coffee, and we were sitting in one of the communal reception rooms, the doors open onto the garden, before I felt I could broach my news.

'Dad?' I said, still hesitant.

He looked up, smiled, then a frown crossed his brow. 'Oh,

I'm sorry, Lizzy. I forgot to tell you – Alex doesn't want us to visit. Jenna says he's particularly cross today. He's thrown a few punches, I'm sorry to say. We can FaceTime him at three, if you want to say hello to him.'

'Right,' I said, feeling a pang of disappointment. I wasn't offended – offence didn't exist in Alex's world. He knew what he wanted, and sometimes it wasn't you.

'Anyway,' said Dad. 'What were you saying?'

I cleared my throat, trying to push through my awkwardness. I hadn't realised how hard this would be: how much my work had validated me, that unconsciously I was always demonstrating to my father how valuable I was, how hardworking. How much, even though I was past thirty, I wanted his approval. 'I just wanted to let you know I've left my job, Dad,' I said.

His mouth opened in an 'o' of surprise. 'Oh dear. Are you all right?'

'Yes. It was my choice.'

He sat back in his chair, looking bewildered.

'Don't panic,' I continued, valiantly. 'I've been putting money aside over the years for emergencies. Not that this is an emergency!' I was gabbling. 'But it's back-up. I'm just taking stock, and I'll get a new job soon. Also, I thought I might move this way? Flats are cheaper here. As you know, anywhere is cheaper than London. And I'd like to be closer to you both.' I knew my faux-bright tone must have sounded jarring.

My father nodded. 'Right,' he said quietly, taking a sip

from his coffee cup and putting it down on the table next to him.

'So you're okay with that?' I said, my voice as uncertain as that of a teenager. The teenager I always was, in some ways, around my dad.

He glanced up at me. 'You don't need my permission, love.'

'You're not worried?' I said.

He gave a little laugh. 'Do I need to be?' He hesitated, clasping his hands, eyes dipping to the floor. 'Will you be able to help us, still?'

I saw how much he hated asking. He was a proud man; I knew that he couldn't reconcile his self-image as a self-sufficient person with the administrative and financial help I gave him and Alex. How he tidied it away in his mind as something small, insignificant.

I had a role to play in this, too, and I played it perfectly, even now. 'Yes,' I said instinctively. 'I'll find a way.'

'Lizzy.' Dad's voice was gentle. 'I know I rely on you. Too much, sometimes. But I'm sure things will be fine. You've always worked everything out before.'

I felt a little fall in my chest. *Yes*, I thought. *I always have. I always will.* But now, just for a moment, I didn't want it to be true. I wanted to be taken care of. But Dad needed me. He needed me to protect him, never more so than now. There was a kind of innocence in his denial of the world, a bewilderment when a problem occurred. Yes, I'd been forced to be the practical one. But that was because I had it in me, just like Mum had. I was strong enough to deal with things. It was part blessing, part curse.

I watched him select a biscuit from a plate by his cup, his bright blue eyes taking in the details as he made the choice, and I felt a rush of love and protectiveness towards him. I knew the serious part of our conversation was over; he was ready to put it away, it was more than he could cope with. We were all just doing our best, after all. He offered me the plate and I took a Jaffa cake.

'Thanks,' I said, taking a bite. 'Is it a cake, or a biscuit? That's what I want to know.'

'A cake, obviously. Unlike this.' Dad showed me his own choice, a chocolate Hob Nob. 'Now, did I tell you about my excursion to the golf club the other day?'

CHAPTER FORTY-SIX

I arrived back home feeling strangely depleted, second guessing myself. Had I made the wrong decision, leaving my job? Had I been forced into making a catastrophic, expensive mistake by my sheer irritation at Esme? I was so lost in my thoughts as I came through the front door, I barely heard the sound of flat doors opening and feet on the upstairs landing.

'Hey, Lizzy!' Myra appeared, a strange expression on her face.

'Hey.' I smiled. 'Is everything—'

I saw Bill's head appear over the rail of the upper landing. 'Liz! Surpriiiiiise!' He let off a party popper. So did Myra. And, in a blur, I saw a figure racing down the stairs before me, leaping off the third stair and doing an impressive star jump.

'Sara?!' I screeched. 'Oh my God!'

We clung onto each other, my best friend and I, in a fierce, haven't-seen-you-in-five-years hug. When we came out of it, Sara held me back, examining me, smiling brightly. 'Your tan's worn off,' she said. 'And where the bloody hell have you been all day?'

'At Dad's,' I said. 'So has your Botox.'

'It broke down on the aeroplane.' She kissed me on the forehead. 'You look rough.'

'Is this what passes as affection, these days?' asked Bill, quaveringly.

'You absolutely did the right thing,' Sara said, sitting cross-legged on my sofa as she picked up a slice of stuffed crust Margarita pizza. 'This will be a new beginning for you. The only way is up.'

I sighed and contentedly bit into a slice. This is what I needed: Sara's certainty. She'd started bossing me around from the moment she entered the flat, and I loved it. Pebble apparently also loved it, because she had, insultingly, decided to curl up on Sara's lap and act like the world's most affectionate cat.

'Also, I'd forgotten how small this place is,' she said, looking around. 'Lizzy, it really is time for a change.'

My studio flat was four times the size of the suitcase Sara had brought with her, and her time in sunny, spacious Australia had made her see it through the opposite of rose-tinted glasses.

'Just tell me what to do,' I said, 'and I'll do it.'

She thought about it, inspecting her gel nails, perfectly

shiny and decorated with smiley faces. 'First, we're booking you another spray tan. Then we're going on a trip to a spa. And we are going to brainstorm the shit out of your career.'

'Have I ever told you I love you?' I said.

Sara stayed for a week before travelling on to her mum in Yorkshire, and we talked ourselves hoarse. She stayed at an Airbnb nearby, turning up every morning with fresh fruit salad for breakfast. She made me go running with her on grey London pavements, attended yoga classes alongside me (performing the perfect head stand), and bought me a new notebook, for evening discussions on work and life, so I could draw mind maps and envision my perfect new life. We talked about her life in Australia, her love for Dex, and her latent homesickness for English tea and sarcasm. We talked about how I could change things. In short, we talked as though she had never left, and as if we were excitable women in our twenties, just with some added experience and a touch of world-weariness.

As promised, she oversaw yet another spray tan and a night in a bouji spa place outside London, where we got head massages and sat in a sauna until we were both glowy skinned. By the time she left, waving at me from a train window at King's Cross, I felt like a new me – but also, really, like the old me. The Lizzy who had taken life by the horns, and thought anything was possible. In the safety of our late-night discussions, I'd started processing my experience at EKArts, understanding how it had dragged me down, and how I could prevent the same thing from happening in the future. It was far from straightforward, but somehow Sara had opened a door for me, just a crack, letting me see there was a real future for me, and that it could be bright and exciting.

As the train started to pull away, Sara raised her hands in a heart shape, and I did the same. Then I stood, watching the train snaking its way out of the station through shafts of light. I stayed until it was gone, then I headed out of King's Cross, out into London in the springtime, full of life and possibility.

My joyful emptiness, the stillness of my flat, with Pebble next to me, meant I could let my own thoughts in, noting ideas, writing lists and imagining what life could be. When Sara Zoomed me from her mum's, I was able to say to her that my mind had cleared and I definitively knew what I did not want to do.

'I don't want to work for a celebrity ever again,' I said.

'Yay! For you,' she said. 'Boo! For me, because no gossip. But I get it.'

'I don't want to work in the art world.'

She tilted her head. 'But you love the art world?'

'No,' I said. 'I love art. That's a different thing.'

'So, do you know where you do want to work?'

I took a deep breath, anticipating her alarmed expression. 'A garden,' I said.

Her eyes flickered for the briefest moment, then she smiled.

CHAPTER FORTY-SEVEN

It was a Tuesday evening three months after I'd left EKArts, and I'd just painted the fingernails of my right hand fuchsia pink and the fingernails of my left hand, pale grey. Pebble was asleep on the cat tower Sara had bought for her ('sorry, I know your flat is tiny, but Pebble *needs* this') and I was watching *Runaway Bride* for the twenty-seventh time, at a conservative guess. The part-time consulting work I'd been doing had bolstered my bank account. I was well rested, I was a regular at yoga classes, and I'd booked myself onto a ceramics course.

But to top everything off, and the reason I was smiling was ... I'd got a new job. A perfectly formed job, that had fallen into my lap like a ripe apple from a tree.

Sara said that her lists and pep talks had seeded the idea, leading to me manifesting the job of my dreams. I'm not into manifesting. What I had done was spotted a job ad, done extensive research, a visit to the place, a quick chat with their HR, and then the hottest application I could muster. Although, obviously, there was some serendipity involved, because the job I wanted came up. So . . . perhaps Sara could have that one.

In a couple of weeks, I was going to be the Head of Communications and Content for a charity that ran several botanical gardens. Not only were they doing important work botanically, they also had a strong emphasis on diversity and inclusion, including outreach for young people with disabilities. I'd opted to work at the site nearest to Dad and Alex, which was commutable from London but also opened the door to me moving out of the city. My office would be situated in the midst of one hundred acres of gardens and trees.

Every time I thought about my start date, I did a little hand clap of glee.

When my phone vibrated, I reached for it immediately. I saw the name on the screen and felt a spike of stress even before I entered the lock and opened the message.

> **ESME:** Hey, sweet Lizzy. I hope you're enjoying your freedom.
>
> . . . typing.

I stared at the phone, feeling dread seep through me. The same feeling you get when an ex contacts you out of the blue, and you want to run away, hide, or block them. The only person who might have trumped her in terms of displeasure was Jack Dillane.

> **ESME:** I've been meaning to get in touch because I want to say goodbye properly. Lunch? At The Teynham? Xx

I tossed the phone aside and carried on watching the film. Twenty minutes later it vibrated again.

> **ESME:** Go on, Lizzy. For old times' sake.

Twenty minutes after that.

> **ESME:** I'm going to keep asking, you know.

I batted my third-coat-of-varnish nails in the air and thought about her offer. An expensive meal. A last look at the person who had been my professional focus for the most intense years of my life. Closure.

Don't do it, screamed ninety percent of my brain.

You'll never get over it without one last look, whispered the other ten percent, softly and persuasively. I picked up my phone.

> **LIZZY:** You're on.

A week later I found myself at The Teynham, awaiting Esme at her usual table. It would have been a great flex to have turned up late, but I am constitutionally unable to be anything other than early. Plus, Esme was always late, so trying to be later than the late person ran the risk of losing the table. I arrived five minutes early and, with a flicker of rebellion, took the seat she normally sat in, facing outwards with a clear view of the room; a petty, but surprisingly satisfying, thing to do. As I waited, I adjusted the folded cuffs of my white cotton shirt (half tucked in to black jeans), put my hands to the cream-coloured fake pearl necklace, and caught a satisfying hit of my most expensive perfume. I wanted to look calm, perfectly chilled out, and elegant. I wanted to show her that leaving EKArts had transformed me, not diminished me. I felt transformed inside, but did it show on the outside? I inspected my pink and grey nails, annoyed with myself for even caring what she thought.

The truth was, I felt sick. Sitting on the tube, every cell in my body told me never to go near Esme ever again. I knew, on some level, that our relationship was irretrievably toxic; I'd been trying to do the best, most professional job I could, but I'd also put too much of myself into it. My not having a life had suited her down to the ground, with her midnight phone calls and early morning messaging chains about her insecurities, her bright, impractical ideas which required me to translate them into reality. Her rejection of my performance at the potential investors' meeting had been deeply unfair, but it had also been a betrayal of the more-than-just-professional bond we'd had. I'd simply replicated my family dynamic in my working life: I'd been

Esme's chief problem-solver, and I'd expected her loyalty in return.

In a way, I didn't blame her: she'd just been doing her thing. She was mercurial, sensation-seeking; it was like expecting loyalty from a butterfly. I was also responsible for allowing it to happen. But at the last, she hadn't even had the guts to cast me aside directly, pouring her passive aggressive feelings into an email instead. My jumping from EKArts had suited her as much as it suited me. After all, she and Ajax were always after what was shiny and new: apps, partners, directors.

Esme was almost exactly ten minutes late. When I caught sight of her it was like slipping back in time, back to our scores of confidential lunches: the grey, satin, draped dress she wore, the enormous eyes with their fake lashes, tousled hair, porcelain complexion. I knew she was totally indestructible, but still there was that vulnerability in her expression. I got up from the table as she approached. She held her arms out to me and instinctively, I took a step away, smiling as brightly as I could. 'It's good to see you,' I said.

There was no stopping her; she kissed the air a foot away from my face either side. Short of head-butting her or flouncing from the room, I couldn't prevent it, and those options seemed unnecessarily dramatic.

She looked sidelong at the waiter. 'Just bring us a selection of whatever's best. Thank you.'

'I'll have the blue cheese salad, please,' I said, catching his eye. 'And sparkling water.'

Esme said nothing, a faint smile playing over her features. She took in where I was sitting – her chair. 'I guess a different view will be refreshing,' she said.

'I thought it best not to sit with my back to the room,' I said. 'You never know when someone's going to stick a knife in your back, after all.'

She tutted gently under her breath. 'So sharp, Lizzy. Let's just have a lovely time. Like two old friends bidding each other *au revoir*.'

I preferred a hard goodbye to au revoir.

'Will you have some champagne, if I order some?' she said.

'Not for me,' I said, as agreeably as I could.

She tsked. 'Oh, come on, Lizzy. I'm trying to be nice. I'm trying to celebrate all of the great things we did together.'

She ordered it anyway, as I knew she would, and I let the waiter pour us both a glass. He was a young man, and his hands trembled as he lowered the bottle, his gaze flicking towards her face as though he couldn't stop himself from looking at her. Fame. Esme had that megawatt charisma; that artful, expensive, dishevelled look. She would always be a goddess of sorts. But you shouldn't get too close to goddesses; they were just as likely to brand you with misfortune as let you bask in their golden light. He put the bottle into its cooler with gentle hands and walked away; I saw him talk excitedly to a colleague.

'I've hired a friend of yours,' said Esme, breaking into my silent musings. She named Steph, someone I'd worked with in my last job. 'She's a brand maven, you know? So positive, so incredible.' I heard the barb in her words, the easily denied dig. *So positive, unlike you.*

I thought of sunny Steph being put through the mincer by Esme and felt sad for her that she hadn't checked with me before applying. 'Treat her well,' I said.

'You make it sound like working for me is a chore,' she said. 'I don't think it's too bad, all things considered.'

My face made an expression which she obviously didn't like, and I thought of Olly, months ago, telling me *we're going to have to work on your face.* The memory made me smile, and when I looked back at Esme, I saw she didn't like my smile either. That she was waiting, itching to say something.

'So why did you ask me here?' I said. 'There's clearly a reason. Let's not pretend it's because you like me.'

She paused, took me in. 'You're quite the hostile psychologist today,' she said. 'By the way, Ajax has got the most wonderful therapist. Does excellent inner child work. Why do *you* think I asked you here?'

I mulled the question for a moment, watching the bubbles rise in my champagne glass. 'I think you wanted to show me you're doing well. That I'm expendable. To give the impression of – what? – professional competence. I've seen behind the curtain, though, so you'd have to be very persuasive.'

She raised an eyebrow. 'And you're not impressed? I guess *we see what we look for.*' This was one of her mottos that she used when creating art; she had even stitched a textile banner once with the words embroidered on there, now worth six figures.

'Quite right,' I said, with a nod, turning the glass by its stem. 'And it goes both ways. You're never going to be able to look at me straight because I know what's behind your façade. And I'm never going to be able to look at you straight because ...'

'You know, Lizzy,' she interrupted. 'Many people have tried to shame me in the past, and I can tell you now, it's impossible.'

'I'm not trying to shame you. And you didn't let me finish. I'm never going to be able to look at you straight because you betrayed the trust between us.'

Her face showed precisely no emotion.

'I came here because I wanted you to understand that,' I continued. 'How much of myself I put into my work. How much I gave to EKArts. To you. Only for you to dismiss all of it – that last email. It was inexcusable, Esme. Do you see that?'

Even as I said the words, something clicked in me, a sudden realisation emerging into the light. She would never try to understand. Never bend. She sat back in her chair, folding her arms, a slight smirk on her face.

I waited a moment for her to answer, then realised she wasn't going to. 'Are the underlings rebelling, Esme?' I said. 'The lesser mortals asking for a moment of consideration?'

'So dramatic, darling,' she said, looking into the middle distance.

'And it's your loss, *darling*,' I said. 'Because I'm the best at what I do. Even if I forgot that, for a moment.'

'And I'm the best at what I do,' she said. 'I quote: "The most exciting artist of modern times".'

The quote was fifteen years old, journalistic exaggeration in one of those 'thirty under thirty' lists. But I let her have it. She *was* extraordinary. I nodded, raised my glass. 'Cheers to that.'

We both drank, ate a few mouthfuls, the atmosphere superficially calm but curdled beneath.

'For the record, I think you're going to regret not being part of the Chroma project,' she said, softly. 'We all have to change, reinvent ourselves, adapt.'

I tilted my head, looked her in the eye. 'For the record,' I said, 'my only mistake was not leaving sooner.'

Her mouth twitched slightly, the only sign she had heard me. 'I just think it's going to be huge,' she said.

Quietly, I put my knife and fork down. 'I've got to go,' I said. If I stayed, we would keep talking in circles. Our dynamic would never be fixed; we were locked into it forever.

'Where are you going to be working?' she said, watching me as I reached for my jacket, and put it on.

'A lovely little place called none of your business,' I said. 'No more calls, please, Esme.'

She laughed throatily. 'My dearest, darling Lizzy. Don't worry, I'll pick up the bill.'

'This one's on me,' I said, looping my bag handle over my shoulder. 'I got what I came for.'

For the first time, her fake smile faded. 'You're full of surprises.'

'I wish I could say the same about you, Esme.' I said. 'Good luck. Try not to break too many things, and too many people, this time around.'

As I left the restaurant, touching my debit card to the payment machine, I heard the clamour of her, rising from the table, changing her seat, the waiters rushing to rearrange her dishes and glasses, to make everything perfect for her again. The woman I'd met at that party a few years ago, the one who had told me how she had first made art, sitting on the floor, cross-legged, charcoal stick in hand, was long gone. Esme was someone else now. Perhaps she always had been.

CHAPTER FORTY-EIGHT

It was a month after I'd started my new job, and I was working in the office one afternoon, the window open to the sound of birdsong, answering a message from my estate agent, Amy. I'd been doing a mix of remote and in-office working – commuting to Hertfordshire for the purpose. Having put the flat on the market, Amy had carried out a viewing that day with some prospective buyers.

> **AMY:** Hi Lizzy! The viewing went great, waiting to hear their thoughts. Just one small thing! Is there any chance you could pop your cat away when I'm doing a sole viewing? She was clawing your poor sofa! And she flipped her food bowl, so the clients were slipping on the food! Also, she doesn't seem to like me very much, which is weird, because usually cats love me.

I snorted with laughter and felt immediately guilty. Poor, poor Amy. But the idea of imprisoning Pebble for the purpose of a ten-minute viewing wasn't really fair to my cat when I was out all day. I carefully composed an apologetic message.

> **LIZZY:** So, so sorry Amy. Pebble does seem to know when there's going to be a viewing and she does attempt to make as much mess as possible. I am working from home three days next week, let's try and schedule all the viewings for when I'm there, so I can keep things tidy and pop her into her carrier when you arrive.

'Night, Lizzy!' My assistant, Xavier, waved at me as he passed my office door. 'Thanks so much for letting me be part of the content planning meeting today.'

'It's no problem,' I said, smiling. 'Have a good evening.'

I looked down at my lap: my cheerful, fuchsia-coloured nails; my floral maxi-dress, a little experiment in not wearing black. In the last few weeks, I'd felt lighter than I had in years; noticed myself smiling for no reason. I took a sip of my raspberry tea and reopened the document I was working on.

My phone buzzed. My gaze flicked to it, thinking I'd see another message from Amy, but instead . . .

> **OLLY:** Lizzy Brinks. It's your opposite number here. Are you still out there?

My breath caught; I couldn't help the smile that unfurled itself across my face.

> **LIZZY:** Depends who's asking.
>
> **OLLY:** Sensible, very sensible. Let the right one in, etc.
>
> **LIZZY:** So what are you here for, Mr MacLeod?
>
> **OLLY:** I guess I couldn't stay away.
>
> ...

I counted my breaths, watching as he typed.

> **OLLY:** That might be the 250th message I've typed, only this one, I sent.
>
> ...
>
> **OLLY:** I wanted to see how you are.
> Correction: I want to see how you are. Present tense.
>
> **LIZZY:** What a coincidence, I thought about contacting you, too.

> **OLLY:** Don't flirt so hard, it's too much for me.

I laughed out loud.

> **OLLY:** Have you forgiven me for doubting you in Venice?

I typed the response without hesitation.

> **LIZZY:** Yes. It was a mad time. Have you forgiven me for threatening to block you?

> **OLLY:** There's nothing to forgive.

> **LIZZY:** Meet me.

> **OLLY:** Meet me.

> **LIZZY:** It seems our messages crossed each other.

> **OLLY:** We always were on the same wavelength.

I sat back in my chair, pressing my palms to my face, against the blush working its way across my cheeks.

We met at the ticket gate of a London garden on a day of sunshine and showers, Olly smiling at me as he watched me walking towards him. He was dressed in a white linen shirt and grey linen trousers, sunglasses set back on his head, almost like we'd planned to match our outfits, because I was wearing a white, collared halterneck jumpsuit with sandals, my hair roughly tied up, and just a touch of make-up. Two weekenders, come for a walk. When I saw him, I couldn't stop myself from smiling, my grin stretching ridiculously broad across my face. He looked gloriously relaxed, tanned from more access to sunshine, I presumed. Glory be, that *collarbone*.

I stopped a foot from him and smiled up at him, not sure what to say. Hoping that, when we spoke, the spell wouldn't be broken.

'Look at you,' he said, his voice soft, but the smile on his face plain and joyful for me to see. 'Out of mourning, bonnie lass. You're too beautiful.'

'Hi hi hi,' I said, trying to keep the nerves out of my voice, and failing. 'You look pretty good out of the suit, too. Look at us, all casual.'

He kissed me on the cheek and I felt a twinge of disappointment, because frankly at the sight of him, even from the end of the road, I'd wanted to run hard into his arms, but I could see the uncertainty in his face and knew it was very like him not to go steaming in there. We were just ex-colleagues, right?

'It's muddy in there,' he said, looking at my outfit. 'We should probably stick to the paths. No off-road wandering.'

I opened my cloth shoulder bag to reveal ankle-length wellies. 'I brought these as a precaution.'

'Nice.' The smile twinkled in his eyes. 'Are you an outdoorswoman now?'

I shook my head. 'All the gear, no idea.'

He laughed, and my heart stopped clean in my chest. I had known I wanted to see him. But the sound of his laugh really was the best sound in the world. Standing there, a metre from him, my feelings for him were so intense, like high definition after watching a black and white film.

'No need to pay,' I said, as we approached the turnstiles, and I saw him reaching for his wallet.

He looked at me, questioningly.

'I work here,' I said. 'Or rather, for the organisation as a whole.'

His gaze held mine in a way that made me feel dizzy. 'Elizabeth. Aren't you full of surprises?'

'Funny, that's what Esme said when I gently explained to her she was full of shit.'

Grinning, he shook his head. 'I have so many questions.'

Smiling too, I turned away, walking ahead to speak to the person staffing the ticket counter, and show them my work ID. I took some deep breaths as we walked into the gardens. *Hold back*, I told myself, but my heart was fit to burst. I cautioned myself, allowing my catastrophic inner voice free rein, saying things like, *He's probably here to tell you he's engaged to Amber! Maybe you'll be asked to be best woman at the wedding!* Anything to stop me from confessing that I missed him so much it physically hurt.

'Want to know if I've managed to keep a plant alive?' I

teased, keeping it light as he moved forward to walk alongside me.

'Mmmm, well, your herbs were a bit *do these dry bones live*,' he said. 'Have you?'

'Yes!' I shouted, and he laughed again, reaching for my hand. We locked fingers.

'There's another serendipitous reason why it's good we're meeting in a garden,' he said. 'I realised, after some consideration, the moment when I fell in love with you, and it involved flowers.'

I stopped dead, turned and stared at him, gobsmacked.

'When you ploughed through the lilies at that first press conference,' he said, looking anywhere but at my face. 'Obviously.'

'Obviously,' I said. 'Although, you said it was the kiss? Or the blush? Not that I'm being pernickety ...'

'Oh, that,' he said. 'No, that was when I fell in lust with you. Related, but different.'

He tugged at my hand and we continued walking, apparently jointly agreeing to ignore what he'd said, my heart thudding in my chest. We found a map, and decided just to meander. As we walked, I told him about my departure from EKArts. Finally, near a small lake, we stood and looked at the water together as more clouds gathered overhead.

'You should know,' said Olly, 'I'm on gardening leave, and have been for some time.'

I did a double take. 'Ajax fired you?'

He laughed. 'Easy, easy, obviously we're not calling it

that. Because there are no grounds. But it turns out the caviared scrote "didn't think I was sufficiently committed to Chroma". I left a month after you.'

I swallowed hard. 'Do you have another job lined up?'

'Of course. I'm working for better people. Less moneyed ones. I've finally learned my lesson.' He put on a cartoony voice. 'The moral of the story is, millionaires can't wuv you back.'

I belly laughed; so did he. And the feeling, of laughing *with* Olly, I can't tell you what an immense relief it was. Like arriving home after a long journey. 'I need to say,' I said, finally catching my breath, 'I have missed this so much.' When what I meant was, I've missed *you* so much.

He put his hands to my waist, gently pulling me towards him. 'You've got no idea,' he said. He pressed his mouth to my lips, then my neck, and I couldn't stop the sigh of joy that escaped me. When he spoke, it was without looking at me, his face nuzzling my hair. 'I was convinced you didn't want anything to do with me. I wanted to respect your decision. So I did everything I could to try and forget you.'

I reared back, comically. 'Not the dating apps?'

He shook his head. 'No. Not the fucking dating apps. Think box sets, gym sessions.' He leaned close, playfully whispered 'hypnotism', and I sniggered. 'Then, when Jacob finally told me, last week . . .'

'Oh Jacob,' I laughed. 'He came to see me ages ago!'

'He finally broke.' He held me back from him, held my gaze with his divine brown eyes. 'Thank God. And he said there might be some hope. I don't want to put pressure on you, beloved commitmentphobe,' he said roughly. 'But can we give it a go?'

'I mean, yes, totally,' I said, trying to sound anything other than desperate, and failing. 'Go, go, go.'

'Go, go, go,' he echoed, a smile stretching across his face, the quality of it making my heart ache with joy.

'You'd better be going to kiss me,' I said, 'otherwise I'm going to—'

I never got to say 'implode', because he very definitely kissed me, his mouth clashing with mine as we caught each other's rhythm, greedy for each other. A breathless, melting, altogether almost indecent kiss, which took me back to Venice but also pushed fast forward on all the impulses I had to climb into his lap and do more than kiss. I think a passerby may have wolf-whistled, but I didn't care. When we parted I mentally congratulated myself for still standing upright.

'Just checking,' he said, pushing my hair away from my eyes, fixing his own dark eyes on mine in a way that turned my body into a melting mess.

'Checking what?' I managed.

'That you have the most perfect kiss I've ever experienced,' he said.

'I think it's a combination of the both of us,' I said. 'So technically, *we* have the most perfect kiss.'

'I think it's down to you.'

I batted him on the arm, but the truth was I could hardly breathe with the happiness I felt. Luckily it started to rain, so

I gathered myself and we found a bench sheltered by trees, where we huddled together.

'Why didn't you want to meet when I messaged you first?' he said, as I nestled against him. 'Were you still angry with me?'

'No,' I said. 'We were still colleagues. It was messy. And I thought you had detached yourself from me, that you were trying to act professional. You used the word "reconnect" for goodness' sake.'

'Lizzy, in my world, "can we reconnect" is practically a marriage proposal,' he said.

My heart flipped and I ignored it. 'Can I get a translation app for "your world"?' I said. 'So something like "can I get you a cup of tea" means, "you have the most beautiful eyes I've ever seen".'

'And "would you like to borrow my umbrella" means "can I . . ."' He leant over and whispered something that made me choke with laughter and blush a deep crimson.

'We may need to get a room for that.'

He nodded, the smile fading a little. 'I'm sorry I got it wrong. I've missed you so much. I felt so strange without seeing you every day.'

'Me too.' I gave him my hand and he took it in both of his, carefully, gently.

The rain stopped, as suddenly as it had started.

'Okay, can I ask, what are you planning to do in the next few months?' he said. 'Apart from changing your phone number the moment you get home.'

'Sell my flat. Make Pebble furious by putting her in a cat carrier. Find a flat somewhere green and clean, near my family.'

I saw him take this in, digest it. 'Can you do me a favour?'

'Depends what it is,' I said cheerfully, when what I thought was *yes, absolutely anything*.

'Make it easy to get to from London,' he said, holding my gaze steadily, my heartbeat drumming in response to his softened gaze.

'I was already planning to,' I said. Trying to push back all my joyous imaginings, like: me getting up from my desk to see him arriving from London to spend an evening together, cooking together, drinking wine, laughing, going to bed.

'And maybe,' he said, 'your new place could be more comfortable for you. I see you in a cottage. Little garden, crammed with sweet peas and roses. Now that you have the gear. You know, sweet, fragrant.'

'Sounds great. But I'm on a budget, and that sounds expensive.'

'Well, maybe there's something we can do about that,' he said mildly. 'Just as a matter of convenience, we could – get that cottage together?'

I stared at him.

'Too much,' he said. 'Breathe, Lizzy. I take it back, if you want me to, but don't, if you don't want me to.'

I considered my poor, cautious, frozen little heart, which was now bursting with joy. 'I think we may need to sit down at the tearoom and discuss future plans,' I said.

'They do champagne, right?' he said. 'I definitely feel like celebrating.'

I laughed. 'I'm not sure they stretch to champagne.'

'Maybe we can raise a scone to each other, then.' His expression was bright. 'As long as I'm with you.'

Warmed by the look in his eyes, I looked up at the break in the clouds, the glimpse of blue sky and bright summer sunshine emerging after the rain. 'To the tearoom, then,' I said, my hand in his, my heart floating up to the sky like an untethered balloon.

'You're the boss, Lizzy Brinks,' he said.

ACKNOWLEDGEMENTS

I am hugely grateful to my editor Clare Hey for her enthusiasm and skill, and the team at Simon & Schuster UK who have worked so hard on this book, especially Sara-Jade Virtue and the Books and the City team. Grateful thanks to: Aneesha Angris, Lily Searstone, Laurie McShea, Isabelle Gray, Pip Watkins, Olivia Allen, Maddie Allen, Robyn Ware, Katie Sormaz, Rachel Bazan, Gail Hallet, Misha Manani and Molly Crawford. Thank you also to Amanda Rutter for copyediting, and Gillian Hamnett, for proofreading.

As always, my heartfelt thanks to my agents Jane Finigan and Daisy Parente at Lutyens & Rubinstein for their advice, support and integrity. Sincere thanks to Sarah Lutyens, Lily Evans, Anna Boyce, Prema Raj, and Tara Spinks at L&R. Much gratitude also to David Forrer at Inkwell Management.

Chris Mann discussed communications and the joys of

press conferences with me; and Deborah Roberts Schultz, former 'work spouse' extraordinaire, pointed me in the right direction to make fashion choices for both Olly and Lizzy. Most importantly, my sister Lisa talked me through the complexities of the current benefits and care system in relation to people with special needs. I am grateful to all of them.

Olly's tattoo is inspired by a Buddhist story which I read about in *Mindfulness for Worriers* by Padraig O'Morain.

I am grateful to the writing friends who have been there for me for over a decade: Melanie Backe Hansen, Sophie Hardach, Jason Hewitt, Kate Mayfield – our meetings are a rich source of inspiration and support. Antonia Hodgson, thank you for being an amazing writing colleague and friend.

Huge thanks to the many romance writers who have welcomed me to the fold, especially all of the lovely Instagram and S&S people – you know who you are! I am especially grateful to Laura Wood, who gave me my first ever blurb for *Wild About You* and combines huge talent as a writer with the most generous nature.

I hesitate to list the number of friends and acquaintances who have supported this book because I don't want to miss anyone out! Your support has been amazing and I am so grateful to you all. Special honours go to Amanda, Emily, Siân, Debs, Lucy, Ruth, Natalie (and Willow), Christine, Caitlin D, Barry and Fiona for fighting in the trenches with me. I am always grateful to the Bookworms, and to my pilates, clubbercise and dog-walking angels (especially Emma and Chris).

Badger, you can't read this but thank you for being such a gentle soul and for keeping me company at the writing desk.

To my family, as always, love and thanks: Mum and Dad for always believing in me; Lisa, Samuel and Harrison; Angela and family.

This book is dedicated with love to my husband Aelred, who is there for every sunrise and sunset. I'm so thankful for you, and for the life we've built together. I love you.

Finally, my heartfelt thanks to the readers of my books – all of you! I am so grateful for your support and for taking my characters to your hearts. The book community on Instagram has been so supportive, as have individual booksellers. I appreciate every kind comment, every book read, every post. Thank you so, so much.

Discover more from Sophie Loxton

Available now

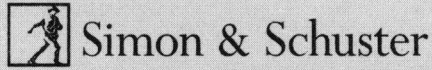